KILL JESUS

The Shocking Return of the Chosen One

L. Ron Gardner

VERNAL POINT
PUBLISHING

CONTENTS

Some time in the not-too-distant future ...

Part 1

The Quickening

TEN MINUTES BEFORE HIS POLITICAL science class was scheduled to begin, Jack Cohen sat in the lecture hall at State University in Washington, D.C., staring at the palms of his hands. A hole, about one-eighth of an inch wide and three-eighths of an inch deep, perforated the center of each of them. Not many things in life unsettled him, but this certainly did. He had no idea how these puncture-like wounds got there, let alone how to keep them from bleeding. Every few minutes a smidgen of blood would ooze from his hands, and he'd wipe it away with his handkerchief — only to have to do it again moments later.

The lecture hall at State U was cavernous, seating several hundred students, allowing Jack a semblance of anonymity. He looked up; no one seemed to notice his problem. No one seemed to notice him at all, except for the beautiful and bewitching raven-haired girl seated two rows in front of him. Every class he had made it a point to sit behind her, so that he could feast his eyes on the back of her perfect hourglass figure. Every class she seemed oblivious to his presence. Until now.

In a flash she rose from her seat and strode directly over to him. She wore black low-cut jeans and a red tank top that barely contained her ample bosom. Her midriff was bare, her stomach tan and taut. "You've been staring at me all quarter," she said. "If you think I'm hot, why haven't you asked me out?"

Jack laughed out loud, welcoming the respite from his wounded hands. The brazen behavior of this ballsy chick confirmed what he already knew: she was a total turn-on. Not only was she gorgeous, but she radiated energy — wild, dangerous sexual energy. But rather than engage in a flirty exchange, he stated his position: "Yes, I think you're hot, but I've got a girlfriend. Otherwise, I'd ask you out. What's your name?"

"Mary McDonald. And yours?" They shared a hearty laugh. She, along with everyone else in the lecture hall, already knew who Jack Cohen was — a three-time national high school wrestling champion, and a three-time all-state defensive back who scored 800s on his SATs and was valedictorian of his class. A brilliant scholar and gifted athlete, he could've gone to Oklahoma or Iowa on a wrestling scholarship, played Division 1 football, or easily been Phi Beta Kappa at Harvard or Princeton or MIT. What she didn't understand was why he was taking classes at State University.

"Tell me something, Jack. What are you even doing here?"

Jack chuckled. It wasn't the first time he'd been asked that question, and probably not the last. He told her that he chose to stay in D.C. because his father, girlfriend, and martial arts trainer all live there. "Besides," he said, "I like this town. It's got history, and one of my goals is to make my own history here. Our country is crumbling before our eyes — and if it can be salvaged, the leadership to save it will have to come from Washington."

"Wow! I love your ambition and idealism," Mary smiled, her blue eyes sparkling with admiration. "You could end up the first Jewish president. With the connections your dad has, it's possible. Is that your goal?"

"I'm not sure. I'm leaving all my options open at this point. Right now, I just want to concentrate on my studies, my job at the physics lab, and martial arts. I'm majoring in physics along with poly sci, and I just might devote my life to understanding the world via a Theory of Everything, rather than to trying to save it via a political solution. Cosmology fascinates me, so I could easily end up an astrophysicist. But I also want to be a professional fighter, and maybe a comedian."

"A comedian? C'mon, you're kidding."

"No, I'm not. Honestly, like most Jewish guys, I see the world from a different angle, and that enables me to creatively mock it. Also, I'm usually cool and detached and don't take life too seriously. I could be another Seinfeld."

Mary stepped closer to Jack. He could tell that she had Chloe on, the same perfume that his girlfriend, Polly, wore. But it smelled different on her — better even — and he knew that could be dangerous.

"How about your political idealism?" she asked. "You don't take that seriously?"

"I do and I don't, if you know what I mean." Her scent was becoming intoxicating. Time to change the subject. "How about you? If you're a poly sci major, too, you no doubt believe in the ideal of making the world a better place."

"Yeah, I'm a poly sci major," said Mary, "and I see true socialism as the answer. Capitalism is all about greed and materialism; it's anti-spiritual. And like you, I'm into the cosmos.

"In fact," she continued as she inched even closer, "I've checked out your natal chart with mine, and even though you're a Capricorn and I'm an Aries, the aspects between our charts are really good. If the cosmos says we're a good match, why fight it? A couple of dates with me and you'll forget all about your girlfriend."

Jack could feel his entire body twisting into a knot. As charged as he was sexually about Mary, everything else about her made him uneasy. Forget the fact that their political viewpoints were diametrically opposed; she honestly seemed to believe in that astrology crap. What a bimbo. Even if he were tempted to go out with her — and, God forbid, even got lucky — what on earth would they possibly talk about once the lights went back on?

Besides, Jack loved Polly and had a good thing going with her. They'd been together for three years and planned on getting married after he graduated. The last thing he wanted to do was screw that up.

"I was starting to think you were a bright girl, Mary, but now I'm beginning to wonder. First of all, read Carl Sagan, the late, great astrophysicist and cosmologist. He totally debunks astrology. Second, socialism doesn't work. It reduces productivity, and rather than freeing people, it enslaves them. And, third—"

"Modern capitalism isn't about individual entrepreneurs starting their own businesses," Mary interrupted. "It's about giant multinational corporations ruling the world. Without governments limiting them and redistributing wealth, we'd be living in a Brave New Monsanto World and eating nothing but genetically modified food.

"As for Sagan, I've read him and think he was a pompous, pontificating asshole who didn't know the first thing about astrology. He never studied it. He was a linear thinker who used only one side of his brain. Greater minds than his — Paracelsus, Copernicus, Kepler, Galileo, Tycho Brahe, and Isaac Newton — practiced astrology. In fact, when someone asked Newton how he could believe in astrology, he responded: 'I've studied it; you haven't.'

"And as for your girlfriend," Mary continued, "her name should be Pollyanna, not Polly. She's got her Sun, Mercury, and Venus in Libra, so she's sweet but superficial — and since Libra is an air sign, if anyone's an airhead, it's her, not me. I'd like to think that a super-profound guy like you would prefer an esoteric chick with chutzpah like me, rather than a Stepford babe like her."

Jack was stunned. Where did this girl come from? Not only was she hot and smart, she had clearly done her homework. Her take on Polly was especially spot on, though he didn't want to admit it.

What Jack didn't realize was that Mary had calculated her every response to push all his buttons.

He was about to reply when suddenly she noticed his hands. "My God, you're bleeding," she said. "What are you, a masochist?"

"No, no," said Jack sheepishly. "I have no idea what they are or how I got them. They just appeared right before you came over. If the bleeding doesn't stop by tomorrow, I'll see a doctor and get it checked out."

Mary drew herself closer, her fingers lightly caressing Jack's chin as she stared into his deep brown eyes. "You know, I work at a strip club," she whispered. "Guys always ask me to do sadistic stuff to them, like punch holes in their body." She paused, soaking in his trepidation. "I could be your personal dominant and do your piercing for you."

Jack laughed uncomfortably. Now he really didn't know what to make of this chick. Her eyes were cold and hollow, and yet so inviting.

"You don't really work at a strip club, do you?" he asked hesitantly.

"Yeah, I do," said Mary, relaxing her pose. "At Sodom and Gomorrah.

That's how I pay for my schooling. But I might be looking for another job soon, because the church down the street is trying to close us down. The fucking Bible bangers think we're a bad influence, probably because they're afraid we'll cause twelve-year-old boys to get boners just by walking by."

Jack's mouth dropped. "I don't understand. I thought you were a — I mean, you don't go home with the guys who frequent your club?"

"Of course not. I'm a good girl. You believe me, don't you?" She licked her lips playfully while casting her eyes on the visible bulge in his jeans.

"I'm not sure what to believe," replied Jack. "But if I were twenty-one, I'd definitely want to come by and check you out at your club."

"You don't have to be twenty-one. I'll get you in tonight," she cooed. "I'll even give you a free table dance that you'll never forget."

Jack was about to thank her for the invitation, when he felt a tap on his right shoulder. He turned around and found himself greeted by a tall, gangly boy who reminded him of Jughead from the Archies, only with flaming red hair.

"Hi, Jack, I'm Orson. Sorry for interrupting, but I wanted to make sure I talked to you today."

"Pleased to meet you," replied Jack, lowering his books to shield the boy from the sight of his enormous erection. "What's on your mind?"

"Jack, everybody knows you're a wunderkind, a genius — and that you have political connections and political aspirations. Consequently, I'd like to invite you to an Ayn Rand Objectivist discussion group tonight. Have you read *Atlas Shrugged*?"

"No, I haven't, but I was planning to read it and her other books this summer." Being a conservative, Jack was fully aware that much of modern conservative thinking stems from Rand's philosophy.

"You won't have to wait until summer," said Orson. "Professor Potts is going to announce that the school is being shut down due to lack of state funding. It's just like in *Atlas Shrugged*: the country is imploding because the government has killed the golden goose, private industry."

Jack nodded in agreement. He liked this Orson and his analysis of the government's role in the demise of the country. Moreover, he was excited about the discussion group — and knowing that Mary McDonald was listening right behind him, he was glad for an excuse to skip on her club that night. "I'd love to go," he said. "Thanks for the invite."

"Mind if I go, too?" Mary asked Orson. "I've read *Atlas Shrugged* and *Capitalism: The Unknown Ideal*, and I'd like to discuss some of my concerns with Objectivism."

Orson smiled warmly at her. "Of course, you're welcome. I'm glad to hear you've read Rand and want to discuss her philosophy." He asked for Mary's name as he pulled out two fliers from his backpack and handed them out. "Here are directions to the cult. I look forward to seeing you and Jack tonight."

"Cult?" That word got Jack's attention.

"Yeah," Orson replied. "We Randroids classify ourselves as a cult, as a parochial collective."

Jack and Mary broke into laughter. Nice to know that Jughead had a sense of humor.

A thought crossed Jack's mind. "Hey, Mary, don't you have to work tonight?"

"I'm calling in sick," she said, eyeing him intently. "This meeting is too important to miss, if you know what I mean."

Jack knew what she meant, and chuckled.

The three of them began exchanging small talk when suddenly the voice of Professor Peabody Potts boomed from the lecture hall podium: "Class, I have an announcement: Effective today, the rest of the school quarter is canceled. The state is deeply in debt, as you all know. Consequently, funding to keep the school open is unavailable; thus, by state order, we are immediately shutting down State U. Hopefully, the situation will be rectified this summer and the school will reopen as scheduled in September. Students will be notified regarding the situation."

The lecture hall buzzed with excitement. Everyone knew the state was broke, but few had suspected the university would be shut down without notice.

"Just as I predicted," said Orson. "We can discuss this situation at the meeting tonight. I'm sure Brother Bill, our rector, will have some insights regarding the shutdown."

"Brother Bill?" Jack asked.

"Yeah, we playfully call him that. He doesn't appreciate it, but he's a good sport and a cool guy. You'll dig him. He's smart as a whip, and makes Peabody seem like a pea brain by comparison."

Orson reached out to shake Jack's hand. That's when he noticed the bleeding. Before Jack could attempt an explanation, Mary pulled out two long, sharp knitting needles from her purse. "Jack's a masochist and I'm a sadist, and... well, you know."

Jack, for his part, felt another charge in his groin. As much as he liked Mary's quick thinking, though, he wasn't sure if he could trust her.

Meanwhile, poor Orson began to wonder whether he'd made a mistake in inviting Jack to the talk. Finally, Jack burst into laughter. "Orson, we're just pulling your leg. Honestly, I don't know how the holes got there, but tomorrow I'll see a doctor and try to find out what the problem is."

Orson stared at Jack, stared at Mary, and then stared again at Jack. "You two are a card," he said. "I'm sure we'll have fun tonight. See you at seven at Bill's apartment."

As Orson walked away, Mary affectionately put her hand on Jack's shoulder. "Jack, we can meet at Marty's Malt Shop at six and go to Bill's apartment from there. After the meeting, we'll go to my place, and I'll give you a very special massage. I'm also a certified massage therapist, you know."

Again Jack laughed. This chick was too much, a complete contrast to his conservative Polly. But as hard as his cock was throbbing, his head told him to keep it cool. "I'll meet you at the malt shop, but skip the massage," he said. "I know you're hot, and I love your energy and humor, but I've got a great relationship with my girlfriend and I want to keep it that way."

Mary pretended that she understood, but the pout on her face said otherwise. *Looks like this one will take a little longer to reel in*, she thought to herself.

*   *   *

Polly greeted Jack with a kiss as he entered the apartment. She had just come out of the shower. Her strawberry blond hair was tightly wrapped in a white towel, her lithe body clothed in a pink terrycloth robe. "How was school today?"

"Unsettling," he said. "First, the school year was canceled due to the lack of state funding. Then this happened."

Jack extended his hands, causing Polly to gag at the sight of his bleeding palms. "Jack, those holes are deep," she said. "You've got to see a doctor. I'm going to put some antibiotic gel on them so they don't get infected."

As Polly returned from the bathroom with the gel, Jack informed her about the Objectivist meeting that evening: "I'm going to an Ayn Rand discussion group tonight. You're welcome to come along."

"Oh, Jack, I tried reading *Atlas Shrugged* when I was in high school," she said as she took care of his hands. "Frankly, I found it terribly long and boring. The characters were a joke, completely unrealistic. The good guys, the capitalists, all had Hollywood looks and impeccable character, while the bad guys, the socialists, all were ugly scumbags."

"Polly, I don't care about Rand's talent as a writer — I'm interested in her political philosophy. It's a cornerstone of conservative thinking in America, and as a conservative, it's something I've got to familiarize myself with. Now that the school year has been canceled, I finally have the time to really study it."

"Jack, I know you're right, but you know that politics bores me," said Polly, wrapping his hands with gauze. "But I also know that politics is important for your future, so go have fun tonight."

"I will," said Jack as she leaned in for a kiss. As much as he adored Polly, it would have shocked him had she decided to come along. In fact, in a way he almost felt relieved when she said no — and that bothered him.

"I'm going to get dressed now," said Polly. Although Jack gazed at her admiringly as she made her way to the bedroom, he could not stop thinking about Mary McDonald. That bothered him, too.

• • •

Marty's Malt Shop was an institution in Washington, D.C., an honest to goodness burger joint, the way they used to be. Aside from offering Diet Coke and some vegetarian fare on the menu, about the only concession to modern times was that the jukebox now played hip-hop. The tables were clean, the booths spacious, and the décor blue and white, while the French fries were the best on the entire East Coast.

Mary was already waiting by the entrance when Jack pulled into the parking lot around ten minutes to six. He was dressed the same as he was that afternoon (except for a pair of black gloves), while Mary had changed into a blue jean miniskirt, no stockings, with black grunge boots, and a black low-cut top that exposed a goodly portion of her ample breasts.

Jack had barely turned off the ignition, and already he was getting hard. His attraction to this siren was becoming relentless, and he was afraid that temptation would get the best of him.

They seated themselves at a booth. "When we're done with the Objectivist meeting," said Mary, "I'm going to take you to meet Mother Mary."

"Mother Mary?" asked Jack.

"My spiritual guru," said Mary. "I had planned on introducing you tomorrow, when she has her weekly Satsang. But when I texted her before you got here — and told her that you were the famous Jack Cohen — and that your hands, for no conceivable reason, had mysterious Jesus-like holes in them — she told me to bring you over tonight."

Jack's head started throbbing. It almost always did whenever something seemed terribly wrong. "I don't think so," he said, shaking his head for emphasis.

"Oh, Jack, you really need to expand your mind," said Mary. "As Sir Arthur Eddington, the great early 20th-century astrophysicist said, 'Life is not only stranger than we think, it's stranger than we can think.' And he also said, 'Physical science is concerned with a world of shadows, just a fragment of ultimate reality.' So the material 'reality' that you buy into is, in platonic terms, just a reflection of a reflection. And you need to open up to the Higher Reality that includes and transcends these reflections, these shadows."

Jack still felt cause for alarm, and yet he couldn't help but find Mary amusing. "And your point is?"

Mary didn't answer. Instead she slid closer to him, draping her right arm around his shoulder while pulling the table closer so that it shielded his lap from view. "You need to loosen up, Jack," she said, running her fingers through his sandy brown hair. "You are sooooo conventional, a chip off the establishment block. If you had a modicum of free spirit in you — and some balls — you'd come over to my pad tomorrow and drop some acid with me."

She quickly glanced at the other booths in their section. No one was paying attention to them. Then she lowered her left hand onto his crotch and began massaging his tight, rigid cock. "We'll chow down on some pizza, and talk a little politics and philosophy," she whispered. "Then we'll do what your hormones are just aching to do right now — fuck my brains loose."

Jack looked at her, half aroused, and half deathly afraid that he would embarrass himself, not to mention his father, by ejaculating in a public place. Sensing his horror, Mary stared at him playfully for what seemed an eternity before finally sticking her tongue out at him. The two of them broke into laughter, while Jack was visibly relieved. Thank goodness she was only funning with him. At least, that's what he hoped.

A waitress came over to take their order. Mary asked for a veggie burger, a small salad, and a soy milkshake. Jack asked for a beef burger (emphasizing the word "beef"), medium rare, but without the bun, and a glass of water, no ice.

As the waitress turned and left, Jack couldn't help but notice how even their food orders showed just how different he and Mary were. "Mary, I've got to level with you," he said. "On the one hand, I'm infatuated with you, and I'm sure we could have fun for a while. But we are totally different people, with totally different points of view on virtually everything. I don't see how we could possibly develop a serious relationship."

Mary rolled her eyes and yawned. "Let me get this through your thick skull one more time, Jack: You are too uptight, too conventional, too married to the zeitgeist. I'm a super-hot chick. I have studs hitting on me every day, most of whom would give their right arm for a chance to fuck me — and I'm offering you my love for free. *You're the guy I want.* Just go with the flow and see what happens."

Jack attempted a reply, but stopped at the sight of the waitress arriving with their food. He was about to sink his teeth into his burger when Mary dropped another bombshell: "Oh, I forgot to tell you: Mother Mary is also a physics professor. She has a PhD from UC Berkeley and worked with my late father, also a physicist, for many years at Lawrence Livermore Lab. Perhaps that will raise her in your estimation and satisfy your snobbish, highbrow, secular-humanistic taste!" She took a lusty bite of her veggie burger and licked her lips suggestively.

Jack grinned sheepishly. Maybe he was wrong about Mary McDonald. Clearly she was a very bright girl, and if her spiritual guru was in fact a physics professor, then perhaps there was more to that mystical bullshit than meets the eye. "All right, I apologize. I'm looking forward to meeting Mother Mary tonight — I really am."

"All right, high five!" said Mary, extending her palm outward as Jack extended his. "You know, I'm really not trying to convert you, Jack. I just want you to have an open mind about spiritual reality. You're such a gifted and disciplined guy, I know you'll make a great yogi."

They finished their meal, Jack paid the bill and then offered to drive her to the Objectivist meeting. "No, no, I'll meet you there," she said. As they got up to leave, Mary clasped Jack's right hand and asked him about his wounds.

"Polly put some gel on them," he said. "I'm sure they'll be fine by tomorrow."

"Let me see," she said as she removed the glove. To her amazement, the bandage was completely red, with blood continuing to ooze through it. "Oh, Jack, it's as bad as it was earlier today — but I'm sure Mother Mary will have the answer. I can hardly wait to see what she says."

* * *

Mary and Jack arrived at the apartment within a minute of each other. The front door was partially open, and they peered inside. The living room was small and sparsely decorated: a couch, a coffee table, a dozen open folding chairs, no artwork on any of the walls. Perhaps Brother Bill was a monk-like intellectual, Jack thought, maybe a Zen aficionado. The living room extended into the kitchen, where a dozen men and a couple of women were all standing, happily chatting and helping themselves to refreshments on a nearby folding table.

As Jack knocked on the open door, a tall, balding, fiftyish-looking man came briskly from the kitchen. "I'm Bill," he said with a vigorous handshake. "Welcome to the Objectivist Forum."

Jack and Mary followed Bill into the kitchen, where Orson immediately recognized them. "I told you Jack Cohen was coming tonight. And he's wearing gloves because he knows we're pariahs, untouchables." Everybody laughed as they made their way into the living room to begin the discussion group.

"OK," said Bill. "Let's start with the shutdown of State U. Any comments?"

"Like I told Jack at school today, this is *Atlas Shrugged* coming true," Orson immediately responded. "Government on every level has bankrupted our country, and the closing of the university is just a symptom of the underlying problem. When they turned D.C. into a state, I predicted this would happen. We all need to drop out from the mainstream and form our own communities based on individual rights, individual property rights, and the free-trader principle. Universities should be privately owned enterprises, not state-run brainwashing institutions."

"State-run universities are a blessing for the economically disadvantaged," replied Mary. "Without government involvement, poor people wouldn't have a chance to move beyond blue-collar jobs. Universities would only perpetuate a rich, elite class, and class distinctions would be accentuated rather than dissolved. A state-run university benefits the 'common good' — and, unlike Rand, I do believe a true social common good can be identified."

"Spoken like a true liberal fascist," interjected Robert, a smartly attired gentleman with Wall Street written all over him. "I don't recognize your 'common good.' You and those of your ilk are the real elitists, using force — unconstitutional taxes — to steal my money and force me to contribute to state-run, left-wing, neo-Marxist universities that perpetuate the Mafia State."

He looked at Mary askance before continuing. "Judging from your attire, Miss, you can't be more than twenty-one. Orson says you're studying political science at State U; clearly you're brainwashed and naive. Political science is an oxymoron, as is economic science. Big Government pushes this crap to further its own power, its own agenda. When they start teaching Ayn Rand and Murray Rothbard at State U, then maybe I'll support it. But it should be *my choice*, not yours, if I want to support a particular university with *my* money."

"Please don't take any of this personally," said Bill to Mary. "You're obviously bright and well-spoken, and it's great to have someone here tonight to articulate the liberal position, even if you are a minority of one. If you feel you're being ganged up on, let me know and I'll call off the dogs."

"Thank you, Bill, but I'm not the least bit intimidated," said Mary with a laugh. "I've read Rand and Rothbard, and I'm familiar with the Objectivist and Libertarian positions, some of which I share. Besides, it's fun debating men who are old enough to be my father."

Then she cast her eyes on Robert. She was certain she'd seen him patronize the VIP Room at Sodom and Gomorrah, though probably under an assumed name. "By the way, sir, I'm twenty-three and a working gal, so I no longer qualify as a naive college student."

Robert smiled graciously, if not awkwardly, as if he suddenly recognized her, too.

"Well, Mary, at least you've read and considered the right-wing arguments," said Bill. "You've been brought to the water, so to speak, but no one can force you to drink. My hope is that you'll eventually grasp the primacy of individual rights and awaken to the fact that when your collectivist ideals are *forcefully* — and I emphasize 'forcefully' — enacted, constitutionally guaranteed individual rights are violated, and this amounts to fascism on top of neo-Marxism. The egalitarian State that you envision may seem to benefit some, but it does so at the expense of others. To rational right-wingers, it is the height of hubris and irrationality for left-wingers like you to force your wasteful and ill-conceived social-engineering projects on those of us who abhor them. These government projects and programs are not only unproductive and anathema to a free marketplace, they are also immoral, violating the sovereignty of individuals who are forced to pay for and participate in them."

"I hear you, Bill," said Mary. "But you're ignoring the social contract: the need for a humane society to compassionately uplift those who are less fortunate. Your neo-Darwinian ideals are liberating on one level, but fail to consider man in a larger, integral social context. We're all interconnected, but you just want to focus on the individual, not the whole. Thus, from my perspective, the right-wingers are the ones who are guilty of dropping full context."

"No, you do *not* hear me," said Bill disapprovingly. "All I can hope is that you eventually will."

Paul Goldman, a handsome, thirty-ish fellow wearing khakis and a green cardigan sweater, asked to change the subject. "I'm eager to ask Jack about his father and the Federal Reserve."

"Honestly, Paul, I really don't know much yet," said Jack, without waiting to hear the question. "Being just nineteen, I've been mostly occupied with school and sports this semester. But I am well aware of the criticism of the Fed, and I intend to study the matter in detail this summer, so I can talk about it intelligently." He waited a beat. "*Then* I'll confront my father."

"Fair enough," laughed Paul. "Perhaps we'll have a chance to speak again."

"Excuse me," said a disheveled middle-aged man in dungarees, "but I want to make sure that Jack reads the right stuff." Identifying himself as "Jim," he was a familiar caller to certain late-night radio talk shows. When he wasn't swearing that the Fed "was the biggest rip-off scam in history," he would spout off on some conspiracy theory or another before the host inevitably cut him off.

He recommended that Jack start with *The Case Against the Fed* by Murray Rothbard and *The Creature from Jekyll Island* by G. Edward Griffin. "Those two books are oldies, but goodies," said Jim. "Once you read them, Jack, you'll *hate* the Fed as much as I do, and you'll want to string your old man up along with his fuck-face boss, Greengold."

Jack measured his words carefully, knowing full well that every eye in the room was on him. "Jim, I seriously doubt that I would ever want to hang my dad — but if the Fed is as evil as you and others say it is, then I could see myself working to get rid of it. Maybe I'll bring my dad here to discuss the subject after I read the books you recommend."

"Dream on, kid," snarled Jim. "Your old man wouldn't show up here if we had a harem of hookers waiting for him. He's a pawn of the banksters, and he knows it — and he also knows that when we grilled his ass, he'd be squirming like a toad and looking for a loose floorboard to hide under, along with the rest of the cockroaches."

For a moment Jack was speechless. It was bad enough that this nut job was in his face. But the thought he might actually be right was too much. "Jim, I appreciate your passion, I really do. Let me do my homework first, then we can discuss remedies."

"Fuck my passion and fuck remedies," snapped Jim with the aggression of a pit bull. "The Fed has to go, *now*! This country is bankrupt and ready to default, and when you realize the Fed is the culprit, printing — really counterfeiting — endless 'greenbacks,' making the dollar virtually worthless, we need to take the bastards out — and that includes your old man!"

Bill, fearing the discussion might escalate into something nasty, opened the sliding glass doors to the patio and called for a ten-minute break. Jack waited for Jim to leave with the rest of the group before breathing a sigh of relief.

• • •

The first thing Jack noticed when he stepped onto the patio was the cigarette

Mary pulled from her purse. "And you call yourself a health nut," he scolded her. "You eat organic food, yet you pollute your body with cigarettes."

Mary took a deep drag then blew the smoke directly in his face. "Jack, you've been brainwashed," she replied, laughing as he recoiled from the air attack. "Smoking is good for you, believe it or not. In fact, the longest-lived people in the world are known to have been smokers."

Seeing that he was stupefied, she blew another stream of smoke in his face and laughed again. "And since you're dying to know how that could be possible, I'm going to tell you: They smoke pure organic tobacco — which is what I smoke. I have a machine at home that rolls them perfectly."

She took another drag. "Oh, occasionally, I'll smoke a commercial cigarette, but most of the time I smoke my own organic ones. Besides, I only smoke a half-dozen per day. I might be a bad girl, but I take good care of my body — *real* good care!"

Jack was about to reply when once again he found himself in the presence of Crazy Jim. Now that he had a good look at the man, something about him seemed familiar.

"Jack, I just want to congratulate you for taking my shit like a man. I got right in your face, but couldn't submit you." He extended his hand in friendship. "Jim Mulligan."

Suddenly a light bulb went on. "Jim Mulligan, the great mixed martial arts champion?"

"Yep, that's me. I'm amazed that you know who I am. It's been twenty years since I fought."

"I've got videos of your fights," said Jack with a hearty handshake. "In fact, I've adopted some of your moves. I'm going to be a professional fighter myself. I'd love to have you come by the gym and watch me work out. And I know that my coach would also enjoy it." He reached for his wallet and pulled out a card. "Here's my phone number."

Jim took the card and turned toward Mary. "You're a beautiful gal — beautiful inside and out. You've got balls and you're unpretentious. I hope Jack knows how lucky he is to have a prize like you. And once you outgrow the liberal bullshit, you'll be in a class by yourself."

"Thank you, Mr. Mulligan. That's very kind of you. Every girl loves a compliment. But I've got to tell you the painful truth: Jack doesn't want me as his girlfriend. He doesn't even want to have sex with me."

"Dude, are you fucking crazy?" yelled Mulligan. "I've been around hot bitches my entire life, and this chick takes the cake. If I wasn't married, I'd propose to her right now. You won't find another body/mind/soul combination like hers on the entire planet. What the fuck is wrong with you?"

Jack smiled, but not before shooting Mary a look that spoke daggers. "Jim, I love Mary, I really do. But what she didn't tell you is that we just met today — and that I already have a regular girlfriend, one that I plan to marry."

"Dude, I don't care if you're Jesus and Buddha rolled into one," said Jim with a friendly slap on the back. "You're nineteen, and your hormones are raging. Before you know it, Little Jack is gonna end up in her pussy. Don't bother fighting it. It's going to happen."

"See Jack?" said Mary as she slithered next to him, pointing her index finger back and forth between his penis and her pussy. "It's fate."

By now Paul Goldman had decided to join the conversation. "Looks like you're caught between a hurricane and a tornado, Jack. If you need emergency medical help, here's my card. I'm a doctor."

Jim laughed and playfully threw his arm around Paul's neck. "Hey, buddy, join in the fun. I love these kids. And believe it or not, Jack is a martial-artist wannabe. After I mess up his face teaching him my moves, you can fix it for him." Jim shot a wink at Jack. "Dude here is a facial plastic surgeon."

"I can see that," said Jack, examining Paul's business card. "Hopefully, I won't need his services for a long time."

"Anything you can do to improve my looks?" asked Mary, striking different poses.

"Not a thing, sweetie," said Paul. "You're a prototype, not a project. If all the women looked like you, I'd be out of business. I'd probably be a B.M., like Jim."

Jack looked quizzically at Paul. "What's a B.M.?"

"Bookmaker," said Paul. "Someone who takes bets on sporting events — football, basketball, baseball, boxing, even mixed martial arts. Bettors have to lay 11/10 — $110 to win a $100 — and the extra $10, or 10 percent, is his commission, which he collects if the bet loses."

"Isn't that illegal?"

"Of course, it's illegal, Jack," said Jim. "But when your old man and Alfred

Greengold flood the economy with trillions of dollars of greenbacks — literally creating them out of thin air, which amounts to counterfeiting — that's legal. If that doesn't tell you how fucked up this country is, nothing will.

"I hate to be the bearer of bad news," Jim continued, "but your old man is nothing more than a puppet of the banking cartel, a servile member of the U.S. Government Mafia, the biggest racket on the planet. He and Greengold electronically create money and give it away to their buds, their fellow banksters. And the taxpayers get struck with the bill. It's theft, plain and simple. Fact is, the Federal Reserve isn't even federal; it's a private, unaudited corporation, the banking cartel in drag, which systematically rips off the American people."

Jack's head was spinning. He loved his father dearly, but once again he suspected that everything Jim was saying was true. He wanted desperately to go home and confront his father — but only after he educated himself on the Federal Reserve.

To his credit, Jim Mulligan realized he had come down hard on Jack; after all, he was just a kid. "I'm sorry, Jack, I really am. I need to stop ragging on your dad. Enough's enough. You got the message, and it's up to you to do with it what you want."

"Thanks, Jim. It's tough for me to digest what you're saying, but I'm a truth seeker. And if my dad is culpable for screwing the country, then I have no choice but to deal with it."

Jack left that evening with a handful of books: the two on the Fed that Mulligan had recommended, plus another three from Brother Bill: *Capitalism: The Unknown Ideal, Introduction to Objectivist Epistemology*, and *Objectivism: The Philosophy of Ayn Rand*. "Once you read them, you'll be armed and dangerous, a philosophic force to be reckoned with," said Jim. "In fact, given you're a genius, it wouldn't surprise me if eventually you expand upon Objectivism and take it to a whole new level — and if you don't, I'll tighten my famous chokehold on you until you do!"

●　●　●

Later that evening, after the discussion group broke up, Jack followed Mary to Mother Mary's. As exhausted as he was from the day's events, he wished he could postpone the meeting for another day, when he would be sharper. But there's no time like the present, as the saying goes, and besides, he was curious about Mother Mary — what she would say about his hands... and what she could tell him about Mary.

Mother Mary lived in a large, elegant Victorian house with an intricate Zen garden in the front yard. Jack admired the artfully manicured topiary as he followed Mary inside. As they entered the main room, the temple, he sensed a unique presence, a heavy, yet peaceful silence that evoked feelings of reverence that he hadn't experienced in a long while.

Mother Mary was seated in a throne-like chair at the head of the room. She was slim, attractive, about forty years old and dressed in a white hooded robe that covered her entire body. Mary McDonald approached her, bowed down in reverence, then sat before her in the full lotus position. Mother Mary laid her hands on Mary's head, causing it to jerk violently up and down, then revolve from side to side. Occasionally she laid her hands on Mary's body in much the same way, also causing her to convulse. This went on for several minutes while Jack stood there, transfixed.

Finally Mother Mary ordered Mary to her feet. "Why don't you wait in the garden, my dear? I want to speak with Jack alone." Then she motioned for Jack to come closer as Mary McDonald left the room.

"I've been waiting for you, Jack, much longer than you think," she said with a knowing smile. "Have you ever seen an aura?"

"No, I haven't, Mother Mary."

"Well, I'm looking at yours right now, and I can tell you that I've never seen one like it."

That makes two of us, thought Jack. *I've never seen anything like you, either.*

"I've been around great gurus — enlightened spiritual masters — but none had an aura like yours, Jack," Mother Mary continued. "You are the Great One that the world has been waiting for. This world is a prison, and you are the One who is going to instigate a worldwide awakening. *The Matrix* was just a movie, but this is for real. You are the One."

"I don't understand," said Jack. "I'm smart and a good athlete, but I don't have any unique powers. I did experience a wonderful stillness and peace when I entered this temple, but I'm not particularly spiritual — and I'm certainly not a saint or a guru or capable of enlightening anybody. In fact, I'm hoping that *you* can enlighten me. Can you explain what you just did to Mary?"

"I transmitted *Shakti* to her," Mother Mary explained. "Shakti is the Hindu yogic term for the Holy Spirit. What you witnessed was a spiritual force that caused her head to jerk; those jerks, called *kriyas*, are spontaneous purifying movements. Because of my ability to awaken and transmit Shakti, the Holy Spirit, you might say that I'm like John the Baptist."

"And what would that make me — Jesus?" Jack meant that as a quip, but to his astonishment Mother Mary was dead serious.

"As a matter of fact, yes," she said. "I believe you *are*, or were, Jesus... Let me see your hands."

Jack removed the gloves and showed his hands to Mother Mary. "Jack, those are not man-made holes," she said upon examination. "They spontaneously appeared as a sign that your time is ripe. In fact, I believe it is significant that they appeared right before you met Mary. She was the connection that led you here — and I'm the connection that will lead you to your Destiny."

Mother Mary sensed his skepticism. "You don't have to believe me now, Jack — but I guarantee you *will* know this for sure very soon."

She stuck a super-slim cylindrical ruler down the holes of each hand. As she suspected, each hole was three-eighths of an inch deep, one-eighth of an inch wide. The three-to-one ratio removed any doubt from her mind: Jack Cohen *had* to be Jesus Christ — the prophesied One who, for the sake of humanity, would demystify the Trinity, the three-in-one God.

This is too fucking weird, thought Jack. *I'm an atheist; I don't even believe in God. How can I possibly save the world?*

Every instinct in his body told him to turn around and bolt. And yet, for some inexplicable reason, he wanted to hear more.

"I know this is hard for you to accept," Mother Mary said. "The world, the secular and religious establishment, will not accept you, either, or the Truth that you will bring as the Son of Man. You will figuratively, if not literally, be crucified again."

Then she pointed to his hands. "That explains the holes, and the blood from your wounds," she continued. "They are a harbinger of what is to come for you. My mission is to prepare you for your Mission. You cannot decline your Mission, Jack; Destiny declares that it must be carried out."

All Jack could do was shake his head. "I really don't know what to say — I'm interested in science and politics, not religion. In fact, I'm sure there is a scientific explanation for the energy you transmitted to Mary."

"Jack, I'm not asking you to believe or accept anything," Mother Mary smiled. "Just be open to what I'm saying. And I'm sure you're right: there must be a scientific explanation for the Shakti — and you're probably the One who will provide it."

Jack drew a deep breath, slowly exhaled, and took a seat on a nearby chair. "Are you going to give me the Shakti tonight, like you did with Mary?"

"No," said Mother Mary. "You should read some books first and get an intellectual grasp of the spiritual process. Besides, I want you in a more relaxed state when I initiate you. Right now you're in turmoil because of your hands, your new friend Mary, and the heavy Jesus trip I'm laying on you."

"Will the holes in my hands go away now?"

"I'm going to give you some yogic Ayurvedic ointment — you can get it from Mary when we're done. Fill the holes with it twice a day. The holes have served their purpose now; I predict they will heal and vanish within a few days. If they don't, let me know. Don't waste your time going to a doctor. A physician can't help you with this. Your problem is metaphysical, not physical."

"Mary said you're a physicist."

"I was, but I moved beyond physics to metaphysics many years ago. I will help you make the same transition."

Mother Mary then told Jack that she used to work with Mary's father, before the government "murdered him for knowing too much. He was always too outspoken."

"Like father, like daughter, I suppose," said Jack.

"Yes, I suppose that's true," said Mother Mary. "Mary doesn't know this, and I don't see the point in burdening her with it. Her mother died when she was young, so I kind of adopted her after her father's death. She was already sixteen and very independent, but I've always loved her and have always been there for her."

Jack asked Mother Mary whether he and Mary McDonald were astrologically compatible. "Aries and Capricorn is not a combination I usually recommend," she replied, "and your Mercuries square each other, meaning conflict in communication and ideas. But your Venus/Mars/Jupiter/Neptune inter-aspects are fantastic, so you will be each other's ideal lover. The magnetism is so overwhelming, uplifting, and other-worldly, it will be very difficult for you to resist each other."

Jack sat up and rubbed his hands. "I don't understand that girl at all," he said. "On the one hand, she is very spiritual. On the other, she works at a strip club, smokes, drinks, cusses, and does drugs. She's like Jekyll and Hyde."

"That's my Mary," laughed Mother Mary. "She's a wild tantric yogini. You'll never tame her, so don't even bother. Just try to survive her — and watch out for her cutting tools. She's a bit of a dominatrix and might want to experiment on you."

Jack stared at her blankly for the longest time. "You're putting me on now, aren't you?"

"No, I'm not. She uses pain to lead men to a spiritual realization — rich, powerful men — men who can control our future. Everything in the universe is energy, and Mary enables her clients to transmute the intense but contracted energy of physical pain into the free-flowing energy of erotic and spiritual bliss. That's tantra yoga."

That may be tantra yoga, but the "erotic" part alarmed Jack. What exactly did that mean? There are other ways to control people besides inflicting pain. Was Mary sleeping with any of her clients?

"No one is putting a gun to your head, Jack," continued Mother Mary. "If you're not moved to play with her, then don't. But my guess is that she was Mary Magdalene when you were Jesus, and I doubt that you can resist the karmic connection."

"Mary Magdalene?" said Jack quizzically. "Don't you mean Marquis De Sade?"

They shared a laugh, which was the desired response. But it wasn't long before Jack was worried again. Mary Magdalene, after all, was a whore. The implication was pretty clear.

Just as important, even if he did succumb to Mary McDonald, where did that leave Polly? "What do I tell my girlfriend?" he asked.

"Whatever you want," said Mother Mary. "Your life is going to be turned topsy-turvy anyway. The Jack you know now is going to be replaced with a Jack you can't even imagine. Once you're Spirit-baptized and then reborn as the One, you'll be the Avatar, and the rules that apply to ordinary men will no longer apply to you."

"*But I'm an atheist,*" Jack insisted. "How could this possibly be?"

"Jack, the only reason you're an atheist is because the only God you currently know about or can conceive of is either an anthropomorphic or cosmic one," Mother Mary replied. "But if you Google Bernard d'Espagnat — a renowned physicist who worked with de Broglie, Fermi, and Bohr — you'll see that he won the Templeton Prize for hypothesizing the existence of a hypercosmic god: an impersonal, unknowable God that exists outside of time and space.

"D'Espagnat based his hypothesis on experimental tests of Bell's theorem," she continued. "The word 'Avatar' means 'one who incarnates from without' — in other words, from outside time and space. Thus, although you were born in this domain, the Earth plane, you were sent from the Divine Domain, the Uncreated. And you were sent here to save humanity."

Jack still found all this talk of Jesus and reincarnation far-fetched, to say the least. Yet a part of him looked forward to becoming "Spirit-baptized" — and, being a scholar, he was curious enough about d'Espagnat to want to check him out.

Mother Mary got up and led Jack to a plastic container near a Buddha statue in the rear corner of the temple. She opened the lid and handed him several books: *Some Sayings of the Buddha According to the Pali Canon* by F.L. Woodward ("The best book on original Buddhism I've encountered," she said); *The Zen Teaching of Huang Po* by John Blofeld ("The best one on Zen Buddhism"); *Talks with Sri Ramana Maharshi* ("Must reading for every serious spiritual aspirant"); *First and Last Freedom* by J. Krishnamurti ("His finest work," she insisted, "a unique, psychologically oriented mystical text"); *The Cycle of Day and Night* by Namkhai Norbu, *The Golden Letters* by John Myrdin Reynolds, and *Teachings of Tibetan Yoga* by Garma C.C. Chang — all of which, she added, "are about Dzogchen and Mahamudra, the highest Tibetan Buddhist meditation teachings" — and *The Knee of Listening, The Method of the Siddhas*, and *Hridaya Rosary* by Adi Da Samraj, a controversial figure whose books "are among the most profound spiritual texts ever written."

Then she handed him copies of *The Philosophy of Sadhana* by Deba Brata SenSharma and *Pratyabhijnahrdayam* by Jaideva Singh. "These books are on Kashmir Shaivism," Mother Mary explained. "They are of particular relevance

22

because the *Shaktipat* yoga I teach is derived from Kashmir Shaivism. My Indian guru was a Kashmir Shaivite."

She rummaged through the container until she found "two must-read Indian classics," the *Bhagavad Gita* and the *Yoga Philosophy of Patanjali* by Swami Hariharananda Aranya. Finally, she gave him two books on Christian mysticism: *Meditations on the Tarot* by Valentin Tomberg, and *The Foundations of Mysticism* by Bernard McGinn. "These last two titles are particularly important for you to read, Jack, because as Jesus you will essentially be teaching Christian mysticism.

"Most of these books are real oldies, and some are out of print," she continued, wiping the dust from her hands. "But they're all classics. I suggest you read them twice — once before you're initiated, and again after you get the Shakti."

Jack packed each title carefully into his leather pouch. "Thank you, Mother Mary. I will treat these as if they were my own, and I will devote myself to studying them."

She touched his face and smiled. "I know you will. Given your intellect and discipline, I expect you to average more than a book a day. Therefore, I'll schedule our next meeting two weeks from tonight, at seven. Mary will tell you how to contact me — and if your hands don't heal, or if you have questions of any kind, don't hesitate to call."

Jack bowed before Mother Mary and thanked her again. As strange as this evening was, he knew this place was special and looked forward to his next meeting with his new teacher.

◦ ◦ ◦

Mary greeted Jack in the Zen garden by leaping into his arms and wrapping her legs around his waist. She clasped her hands tightly around his neck. Whatever lingering resistance he had melted in her scent, and as they kissed passionately she knew she had caught him at last.

"I know you're glad to see me," smiled Jack. "But don't you want to know how things went with Mother Mary?"

"I already know," said Mary, stroking his chin with her fingers. "She texted me before you came outside. She said you're Jesus, the Chosen One — and I believe her. But this time, instead of preaching moralistic religion to the masses, you'll enlighten them with the crazy wisdom of wild tantric teachings."

"I don't know about that," Jack chuckled. "But I do want the Shakti. I want to know what that energy is and how it can be applied. I also want to understand how it relates to the spiritual silence or presence I felt in the temple."

He shifted her body slightly, gliding his hands beneath her skirt. If this were Polly, she would have made him stop. But Mary McDonald was another girl, quite possibly from a whole other world.

"Tell me," said Jack as he kissed her lightly, "what do you feel when the Shakti makes your head jerk and your body shake?"

"Different things," said Mary. "Sometimes the Shakti is overwhelming and uncomfortable, and other times it's blissful. But it's always intense. And it's especially intense when I'm in the temple or meditating with Mother Mary."

"I can't believe the way you humbly bowed down to her. She's like your stepmother, yet you worship her."

"And I'll worship you when you become the Chosen One," she said, putting her tongue in his mouth. "I'll be your servant, your devotee."

"Why?" he asked between kisses.

"Because that will serve me," she said, "and better enable me to serve the world. You will be a perfect conduit to Infinity, Jack Cohen. By connecting to you, I can channel your Energy, your Shakti, and help bless the world."

She motioned for him to let her down. He complied. She slid behind him, thrusting her pelvis against his backside while draping her hands across his groin. "But until then, you will be my slave."

"You're absolutely crazy," Jack started to laugh. "How can I not love you?"

She spun him around. "Kiss me, slave." Again he complied. They held each other for the longest time and kissed in the moonlight.

Jack's body wanted to give in to pleasure, but his mind was elsewhere. As much as he wanted Mary McDonald, he could not help but wonder whether she was sleeping with any of her clients. Hell, Mother Mary all but said she did.

"What else do you do with the guys at your club?" he asked.

"What do you mean, what else?" Mary snapped. "Are you insinuating that I'm a bad girl?"

"Of course not," said Jack. "I just want to make sure that you aren't fucking any of those guys, that you're just doing your tantric work on them."

"I'm not fucking them," she insisted. But her tight face and shaken demeanor told Jack otherwise. She had lied to him before, and he suspected she was lying again.

"I don't want a whore for a girlfriend," he said.

Mary looked at him coldly. "I don't fuck my clients. I service their fantasies, and that is all."

She decided to change the subject. "This is the ointment Mother told you about," she said, pulling a clear unlabeled glass bottle from her purse. "Be sure to completely fill the holes with it until they disappear."

Then, realizing that she had unsettled Jack, Mary tried to ease the tension. "Jack, I know you're upset right now, and need to sort out your feelings regarding not only me but everything else you've experienced today. I sincerely apologize for making your life more difficult. My goal is to make you happy. Ayn Rand said that romantic love for a woman is about hero worship. And you are the hero I worship." With that she kissed him slowly and gently, and he passionately embraced her.

"Tell you what," she said. "I have to work at the club tomorrow night. Why don't you come by around ten-thirty. You can party with me and my girlfriends. We'll have a blast."

"I will," he said. As dangerous as Mary McDonald was, Jack was falling for her... and he knew it.

* * *

Sodom and Gomorrah was a relatively new gentlemen's club located on the outskirts of the Adams Morgan district, the hub of D.C. nightlife. Unlike Madam's Organ, the colorful blues bar known for its tit-shaped roof, not to mention the décolletage of the giant redhead whose caricature graces the side of the building, Sodom and Gomorrah was remarkably nondescript, at least on the outside. Housed on the ground level of a darkly lit brick building, it had no signage, no address, no indication whatsoever of what went on inside. Rumor had it that the owners preferred it that way, but no one really knew for sure.

Jack parked his SUV around the corner around 10:25 p.m. Behind the roped-off entranceway stood a half-dozen men, one of whom was his friend

Jud. Twenty years old, and gangly in a Crispin Glover kind of way, he and Jack had been off-and-on buds since grade school. A chemistry major with a depraved mind, Jud dressed like a punk rocker and fancied himself a ladies man, though in fact all of his sexual conquests existed entirely in his head. He was dying to find out what happened inside Sodom and Gomorrah, and when Jack invited him to meet him there that night, he jumped at the chance.

"I didn't think you'd show up, bro," said Jud. "This isn't exactly your scene."

"Not exactly yours, either," said Jack.

"Yeah, but you know me," said Jud. "When your friend said we could have all the free beers we want, I was in right away — and if one of her friends throws in a blowjob, even better!"

"Yeah," said Jack with a half-laugh that seemed more like a cough. "Even better." He tilted his head toward the front door. "Let's go."

Jack still had his reservations about this place. But being all of nineteen himself, there was only so much he could do to resist them. Besides, if he was going to understand Mary McDonald, he had to see her on her own turf — at least, that's what he kept telling himself. The truth was, he was no better than Jud, nor any of the other patrons inside. At least for tonight, he was just another carnal dickhead, submerged in a den of iniquity.

The massive bouncer looked like someone who could have played left tackle in the NFL. At six foot eight, he was seven inches taller than Jack; at 340 pounds, he was nearly twice his size. He wore a black sleeveless T-shirt that prominently displayed his huge biceps, and black Ben Davis pants. The first thing he noticed was that Jack and Jud were underage. "You must be Mary's boys," he said. "She said you'd be here around ten o'clock."

"That's us," said Jack. "You need our names?"

"I got your names, pal. What I need is a hundred bucks."

"A hundred bucks?" gulped Jack.

"Apiece."

"Mary told me we wouldn't have to pay to get in."

"Mary doesn't make the rules around here. She just thinks she does. Besides, I'm taking a big risk by letting guys like you and Screech inside."

Jack looked at the bouncer, looked at Jud, then again at the bouncer. He felt certain he was being ripped off, but said nothing of it. As much as he lusted after Mary McDonald, he wasn't sure that Sodom and Gomorrah was the kind of place where he wanted to be seen. Never mind the would-be Messiah nonsense; he had his father's reputation to think about. Better to get through the evening as inconspicuously as possible, without making a scene. He reached for his money clip, pulled out two C-notes, and handed them over.

The bouncer slipped the money inside his pocket and unroped the entranceway. "Have a good time, gentlemen."

The main room of Sodom and Gomorrah was loud, dark, and sticky. Jud made a crack about the DJ's choice of music, but Jack wasn't paying attention. He was too busy looking for Mary. At one point he counted fifteen girls, including an Asian chick giving a lap dance and two naked blondes pole-dancing on stage. But Mary was nowhere to be seen.

A waiter named Mason escorted them to a table next to the stage. Jud ordered a bottle of Budweiser, no glass. Mason was about to take Jack's order when suddenly he realized who Jack was. So much for being inconspicuous.

"Pleased to meet you," said Mason with an enthusiastic handshake. "I've got to tell you, I'm a huge freestyle wrestling fan, and you're the best high school wrestler I've ever seen. I saw you demolish Kinsler at the Under-18 Nationals, and a year later he's an NCAA champion. It should have been you."

"Thanks, man." Jack didn't like being recognized — not here anyway — but even he was not immune to flattery.

"Why did you quit?" asked Mason. "You could have been another Cael Sanderson."

"I haven't quit," said Jack. "I'm a better wrestler than ever. I'm constantly working on my moves, strength, and conditioning. But my goal is to be a mixed martial arts champion — in fact, I want to beat Sergei Putin. Not only do I want to beat him, I want to pulverize him. I want to grind him into dust. He's a sadistic bully, a piece of human garbage, and I want to give him a piece of his own medicine. I want to prove that nice guys can rule in MMA."

"That's a tall order," said Mason. "Putin is almost superhuman — Olympic gold medal in boxing, plus a world championship in wrestling. Nobody else has ever done that. No one has even come close to going the distance with him, plus he's only twenty-four, so he's just peaking now. The pundits say he's unbeatable, by far the greatest mixed martial artist ever."

"Yeah, but even Achilles had a weakness," said Jack, flashing the quiet confidence that only comes from winning. "I won't be ready to fight him for a couple years, but once I perfect my striking skills and chokeholds... we'll find out if he's invincible."

"Well, Jack, I can't tell you what a thrill it's been to talk to you tonight. Can I get you anything?"

"I'm good for now, thanks. But can you tell me where Mary McDonald is?"

Mason scanned the floor. He couldn't spot her, either. "She must be in the VIP room — she's the star of the bar, you know. Politicians come down from the Hill every night to see her. On a good night, she can pull in five grand without breaking a sweat."

Jack didn't like the sound of that, but sometimes the truth hurts.

Mason realized he'd said too much and made his way back to the bar. "I'll let her know you're here," he said.

* * *

Mary finally approached their table about twenty minutes later. She wore a black studded leather thong, clear stiletto platform heels, and heavy eyeliner. Her breasts were bare, her nipples hard. She sashayed past Jud, letting him have a good long look before planting herself on Jack's lap.

"Dude, you weren't kidding," Jud finally said. "She is fucking off the charts."

"Nice to meet you, too," Mary laughed. "You must be Jud. Jack said you constantly fantasize about strip clubs — and now you're here."

She got up and stood between the two boys, her arms akimbo, her legs spread wide apart. She leaned in toward Jud, cocked her eyebrows, and went into character. "Are you ready to donate to our sperm bank? Or are you just a pathetic voyeur?"

Jud sat there, completely at a loss for words. Jack told him that Mary was a handful, and now he understood why.

Mary pulled a cigarette out from Jud's shirt pocket and ordered him to light it. He did. She took a couple of deep drags, slid a finger across his chin, and blew a wall of smoke directly in his face. Again, Jud was tongue-tied, completely intimidated by her seductive, dominating presence.

"Just as I thought," she tittered.

Now that she'd rendered Jud submissive, Mary turned her attention to Jack. She slid to her knees and kissed him slowly before grasping his hands, turning his palms up so she could inspect them. To her amazement, the holes were completely gone. "My God, your hands — it's a miracle."

"Yeah, it is," said Jack. "About as much a miracle as someone like me ending up in here with a Persephone like you."

She stuck her tongue in his ear, teasing Jack with playful licks. Then she unzipped his pants and slowly pulled them all the way to the floor. To no surprise, Jack was already throbbing, but Mary was just getting started. She put her mouth around his cock and began to deep-throat him. As Jack groaned in ecstasy, she put a condom on her finger and stuck it up his asshole to make him even harder.

Mary was about to make him explode when she felt a tap on her shoulder. "I'm sorry to interrupt your lollipop, sweetie, but I need you upstairs *now*." It was Harley, the club manager, who always treated Mary like a daughter. He had the height and frame of Joe Pesci, and the weathered face of Harvey Keitel. "I have some VIPs who paid big bucks for the privilege of being abused by you. Destiny and Desiree will take care of your friends."

Reluctantly Mary removed herself from Jack and gave him a kiss goodbye. "Sorry, baby, but duty calls. I'll see you both later."

Destiny was a light-skinned African-American woman with small breasts and an athletic body. She wore a red bra and panties and black thigh-high boots, while her entire backside was covered with exotic tattoos. She laid a tray of various mixed drinks on the table then slung her arms around Jack. "Mary told me to show you a good time," she whispered into his ear. "It's going to be a pleasure to service a hunk like you." She massaged his neck and shoulders with one hand while stroking his cock with the other.

"You're like Superman," she said. "But I'm like Kryptonite." Jack wasn't sure what she meant by that, but at the moment he didn't care. He clutched Destiny by the nape of her head and pulled her even closer.

Desiree, in the meantime, greeted Jud by twerking in front of his face. When she turned around, he recognized her as the Asian chick they'd spotted when they first arrived at the club. She was twenty-two, a few weeks younger than Destiny, attractive and well-built. She wore a black G-string, red pasties, clear stilettos.

Jud gazed at her admiringly. At first he thought she was an eight, but her ass was definitely a ten.

Jack seldom drank, and when he did it was never more than a few beers. But tonight would be different. As much as he was enjoying Destiny's erotic massage, it still bothered him to think that Mary might be upstairs screwing those VIPs — or any of her other clients. His head was bursting with questions, but it was too loud to talk right now, and besides, from the way Destiny was groping him, conversation was the last thing on her mind. So as long as he was giving in to the ways of the flesh, he might as well get good and drunk. He could always question Mary tomorrow.

He picked up a tall glass with a brownish concoction that appeared to be a Long Island Iced Tea. He'd had one once before, at a frat party. He knew it was a drink that went down easily, even if it did pack a wallop.

Destiny smiled wickedly as he took his first sip. "I was hoping you'd choose that one, baby. I made it just for you."

Jack raised his glass, gave her a toast, and downed it all in one gulp. He had no way of knowing this, but he had played right into Destiny's hands. Before long he was slurring his words and becoming increasingly woozy.

She stood up, reached for his shirt collar and pulled him to his feet. Now that the Mickey had taken effect, the fun was about to begin. She put her arm around his shoulders and walked him into a private room — her private room, which she kept bare except for a massage table, a medicine cabinet, and a tattoo machine.

She put him on the table and stripped him of his clothes. Knowing what she had in store for him, she thought about using his belt as a restraint, but why bother: In his condition Jack Cohen wouldn't be moving a muscle for a good long time. Instead she gazed lustfully at his perfect form and proceeded to go down on him.

A few feet away, Jud and Desiree were getting it on in an adjacent VIP room. Unlike Jack, Jud had limited his drinking to beer, knowing what hard alcohol did to his libido. But he was visibly concerned when he noticed that Jack had problems walking, and thought about calling Mary. "Don't worry," said Desiree. "I'm sure he'll be fine." Then she sat Jud down, ordered him to drop his pants and planted herself on top of him.

Aroused as he was, Jud came almost immediately. But as he was still fully erect, Desiree continued to ride him hard until she was completely satisfied.

Meanwhile, Destiny squealed with delight; even though Jack was barely coherent, his cock was as hard as ever. Now it was time to give him something to remember her by. She got up, long enough to set up her tattoo machine. Then she continued to perform fellatio on Jack while stitching her name on his thigh.

By the time she had finished tattooing the Y, Destiny knew he was about to explode. She took her mouth off his cock and began jerking him vigorously, when suddenly the door flew open. In barged Mary McDonald, followed by a now-dressed Jud, his camera phone at the ready. As it happens, Mason had also seen Jack staggering to the VIP room and had her summoned downstairs. Once Mary heard the tattoo machine running, she suspected the worst and told Jud to call Harley.

Destiny shot Mary a glance before giving Jack one last jerk, then watched with glee as his sperm shot high in the air. By the time it landed, Mary had already grabbed Destiny by her hair, causing her to scream in pain. Then she slapped her face with such force that Destiny crumpled to the floor.

"You fucking cunt," said Mary. "How dare you do this to him."

Destiny was ready to fight back, but before she could land any blows, Harley the manager stood before her, with Mason at his side.

Harley had Mason restrain Destiny while he retrieved Jack's pants. His wallet had been picked clean. Noticing Destiny's purse in the corner, he picked it up and emptied it of cash, transferring half the bills to Jack's wallet. Then he fired Destiny on the spot.

"You got ten minutes to get the fuck out of here — and you better pray that Jack is OK. Because if he and his old man file charges, bitch, I'm coming after you!"

"This is bullshit," seethed Destiny, motioning toward Mary. "Bitch here gave me five hundred bucks to take care of her man. Said I could do whatever the fuck I want!"

"I don't give a shit," said Harley. "I want you gone, now!"

Destiny was not one to admit defeat easily, but she knew this battle was over. Mary could do no wrong in Harley's eyes, especially considering the amount of green she brought in every night. Besides, there were dozens of other clubs in town with VIP rooms. With a body like hers, Destiny knew that she would not be out of work for long.

What bothered her most as she gathered her belongings was the sight of Jud's camera phone. It was off right now, but for a moment she could have sworn that the record light was on when he and Mary entered the room.

Meanwhile Mary wept inconsolably as she held Jack in her arms. None of this would have happened if she hadn't brought him here.

"He'll be OK," said Mason. Having worked as a sports trainer before coming to the club, he was able to read Jack's vital signs. "He's breathing normally and his pulse is strong and even. Just take him home and put him to bed."

"Thank God," said Mary. Then she collected herself, reached for Jack's keys and told Jud to take his car home. "Call Polly and make up a story," she said. "Tell her that Jack fell asleep on your couch — tell her anything. I'm taking Jack home with me."

· · ·

Jack glanced around the room. His eyes were still heavy, and his head felt like he'd been pounded with a concrete slab. Judging from the pictures and knickknacks, he appeared to be in a bedroom — someone else's bedroom — and he had no idea how he got there.

He threw off the sheets. To his relief, he was fully clothed. He felt a weird sensation around his left thigh, but beyond that nothing appeared to have happened. At least, he hoped that was the case.

He got up, drawn in part by the scent of rice wafting in the air. Whoever had brought him here was cooking up something good.

He made his way into the kitchen. Mary stood by the oven, wearing a pink kimono robe. "Good morning," she smiled. "Glad to see you up again. How are you feeling?"

"Better, though a bit wobbly. How did I get here?"

She poured him a glass of water and told him what had happened, including the tattoo. "Jack, I cannot tell you how sorry I am. I won't even ask you to

32

forgive me."

"That's OK," he said. At the moment everything was still too surreal for him to make any judgments. He reached inside his pocket and pulled out his cell phone. "I should call Polly."

"I already took care of that," said Mary. "Jud told her that you had food poisoning so she wouldn't worry about you. He also took your car home. As soon as you feel better, I'll drive you there to get it."

He got up and ran his fingers through his hair as part of an effort to stretch. Suddenly every bone in his body ached.

"Come," said Mary, taking him by the hand. "Let me give you a massage."

She led him in to her living room, which she had patterned after Mother Mary's temple. The massage table was already set up. Jack could hear flute music playing softly in the background, while jasmine incense filled the air.

Mary helped him remove his shirt and pants before laying him on the table, face down. As she kneaded and stroked his back, Jack again drifted off to sleep, his mind filled with pleasant thoughts.

This was the side of Mary McDonald he wanted to know better. The soothing, gentle side. The part of her that made him to want to forget all his doubts.

· · ·

When he awoke he could hear Mary rummaging about in the kitchen. He sat up, got dressed, and made his way to the adjacent dining room. Mary had set up two places, while a brown rice casserole with tofu and veggies was ready to be served.

"You're just in time," she said with a kiss. She sat him down, said a silent prayer and invited him to dig in. He ate like he hadn't had a good meal in six weeks.

"You never cease to amaze me," said Jack. "You're a great cook, you give a great massage, and your house is awesome."

"Why, thank you, Jack," Mary beamed. "I appreciate your kind words — and once you get your strength back and can perform sexually, you'll find out I'm a great fuck, too!"

Jack laughed. He loved her sense of humor and knew that he would fuck her this afternoon. But now that his head was clear again, he had to confront her about her profession: "Mary, I know you're a call girl. I know you make thousands of dollars a night servicing rich clients, including bigwig politicians."

Mary sighed heavily. Might as well come clean and get this out of the way. "I'm sorry I lied to you, Jack. But if I had told you the truth up front, you would never have given me the time of day. Now that you know, you can decide if you still want to see me. I love being with you, Jack — I don't want anything from you, except to be with you."

"I love being with you, too, Mary. But how can you be my girlfriend and a hooker? I can just see myself dropping over and finding you in bed with a politician. And how much time will you have for me?"

Mary got up, clutched his hands, and knelt beside him. "Jack, I know you feel the chemistry between us. It's like we're magnetized to each other. We're meant to be together; it's karmic. Let's just go with the flow and see what happens. You can just think of me as your mistress, but instead of paying me thousands of dollars like my customers, you get me for free... and when I make love with you, it will be real love, not pretend."

Then she leaned in and kissed him, and Jack Cohen didn't resist. The woman, after all, had made a compelling argument.

"All right, we'll give it a shot and see what happens," he said. He had no idea how to explain this to Polly, but he could worry about that later.

There was, however, one thing he was dying to know: For all her worldliness, not to mention her clientele, Mary McDonald could have any man she wanted. Why on earth would she want a nineteen-year-old kid like him as her boyfriend?

Mary smiled as she clasped his hands. "Jack, there are more things in heaven and earth than are dreamt in your philosophy."

"Hamlet," said Jack.

"Very good," said Mary. "Now don't you see? It's not a matter of preference — it's a matter of love. I love everything about you... except maybe your politics. You're my soul mate; you match my animus, my unconscious inner male. Besides, you're in the process of becoming a mature man — and in a few weeks, when you realize that you are the One, you will become the prototypical Man, the Son of Man... and I will worship you."

Jack shook his head and laughed. "I don't know, Mary... I just hope you don't toss me out on my ass when you finally realize I'm just an ordinary guy. I mean, can you imagine Jesus with a hooker for a girlfriend? Even if I get the Shakti, I don't see how that will turn me into a saint. You've got the Shakti, but you're hardly a saint."

"I beg your pardon, young man, but I *am* a saint," Mary said with feigned indignation. "In fact, among Washington politicians I am known as The Saint. I donate generously to various charities, and I teach politicians tantra yoga. Just because an individual is into drugs, sex, and rock 'n' roll does not exclude them from sainthood."

She stood up and undid her robe just enough to show that she was nude underneath. "Jack, you are so parochial and conventional," she tittered. "But, trust me, I'll make sure you get over your Puritanism and inhibitions."

"Well, if sticking needles into politicians qualifies one as a saint, then I guess you're a saint," Jack chuckled. "That certainly gives a whole new meaning to *voodoo politics*."

They shared a laugh and playfully exchanged high fives. Then Mary grabbed one of his hands, turning the palm upward. "OK, Jack, if you're not Jesus, explain to me how you got the holes in your hands and how they miraculously vanished after you saw Mother Mary. Explain to me why there are no scars, no signs the holes were ever there."

Jack was speechless. He had no explanation, and she knew it. "Don't you see, Jack? There is only one possible answer: You were Jesus, and I was Mary Magdalene, a prostitute and your secret consort. We've been reincarnated here and now to continue your work of universal Redemption."

Jack sat there for the longest time, but still he had nothing. All he could do was shrug his shoulders.

"Atlas shrugged, and John Galt changed the world," said Mary. "Jack Cohen shrugged, and Jesus *will* likewise change the world."

They chuckled at the analogy, then she draped her arms around the back of his chair and straddled him. Her nipples were hardening; he stuck his arms inside her robe and clasped them gently around her waist. She continued to exalt him:

"Trust me, Jack: when you get baptized, it won't be like me or anyone else getting baptized. You were born with an already perfected subtle, or etheric-energy, body. You've already done all the spiritual work in your past incarnations. You are a perfect, unobstructed conductor of Divine Energy.

Mother Mary told me that your aura is that of an Avatar, a Buddha or Christ. When the Shakti, the Holy Spirit, hits you, there will be no resistance in your psycho-physical vehicle. You will, almost instantly, be fully En-Light-ened."

Jack was impressed. "That's a very cool description of the spiritual process, Mary. Maybe I'm missing something, but it sounds just like electricity — like you just plug into the Source and allow its Energy, or Spirit-current, to flow through you and en-Light-en you."

"You're right, Jack, electricity is a great metaphor for the spiritual process. Maybe your destiny is to fully explicate the relationship between electricity and spirituality. Mother Mary told me you were intrigued with the physics of spirituality. Maybe I'll just call you Electrical Jesus from now on. You were a carpenter before; now you're an electrician."

They laughed and kissed for a long time before Mary pointed to his thigh. "Not to kill the mood," she said, "but what do you plan to do with your tattoo?"

"I think I'll keep it," said Jack.

"Really?"

"Yeah."

"And how will you explain it to Polly?"

"Polly tends to believe what she wants to believe," said Jack. "I'll just tell her I did it on impulse, as a reminder to fulfill my destiny, whatever that might be." Then he shot her a shit-eating grin. "And besides, it *will* remind me of what my destiny might be if I allow another crazy bitch to seduce and drug me."

"And what would you tell her if you woke up one morning with *my* name on your leg?"

Jack laughed uncomfortably. He wasn't sure if Mary was serious, but he wouldn't put anything past her.

One thing he did know: his cock was hard and he was feeling like his old self again. He would have his way with Mary McDonald before this day was through.

. . .

Mary felt the bulge in Jack's pants, but wasn't ready to make love to him yet. "Soon," she said, teasing him with a kiss. "Very soon."

She got up, tied her robe and slipped on a pair of brown sandals. Then she took him by the hand and decided to show him some of the house.

A late afternoon breeze greeted them as they stepped out to the patio. After being cooped up inside all day, Jack welcomed the fresh air.

The first stop was her personal gym, located next to the patio. Jack's jaw dropped when she opened the door: All of the equipment was state of the art, better than he'd seen in most health clubs. "Wow," he said. "You must have sunk a fortune into this baby."

"About a hundred grand," she purred. "I paid for it by draining the vital fluid of a lot of dirt-bag politicians."

She led him to her swimming pool and adjoining Jacuzzi, just beyond the patio. She kicked off her shoes and dropped her robe. Jack knew she had a killer body, but as it glistened in the sun it seemed heaven-sent.

"I'm hot," she said, twitching her nose. "Let's go for a dip."

Knowing he just ate a big meal, Jack declined. "I think I'll watch."

"Suit yourself," she said as she dove into the pool. Jack was a good swimmer, but as he watched Mary motor effortlessly from one end of the 25-meter-long pool to the other, he doubted he could keep up with her.

"Wow," he said as she climbed out of the pool. "You swim like an Olympic champion."

"State champ," she corrected. "I won two high school state championships in the crawl and three in the breaststroke."

He toweled her off and helped her with her robe. After walking him around the grass tennis court, she showed him the putting green before finally leading him to the Jacuzzi. As she dropped her robe, she did a slow pirouette, allowing him to gaze admiringly on her nude, sculpted form.

She draped her arms around him. "You have too many clothes on," she cooed. She began to undress him, licking her tongue with anticipation as she admired his full-blown erection. She gave his penis a playful tug and drew him into the water. She clasped his body and kissed him intensely as they knelt to the Jacuzzi floor.

After a while Mary reached into a plastic box next to the Jacuzzi and pulled out a cigarette. She took a deep drag, holding it in her lungs for several seconds before blowing the smoke in Jack's face. It was marijuana. Though Jack was not one to do recreational drugs, he'd been to enough campus parties to know the smell of pot.

He refused when she offered him the joint. "Mary, I have a number of goals in life, and smoking dope won't help me achieve them."

"Au contraire," she replied mischievously. "One of your goals is to fuck me today. Unless you try the pot now, that isn't going to happen."

Jack didn't like the sound of that, but before he could say anything to resist, Mary dove her head into the water. She captured his penis with her mouth and had him hard in an instant. Every fiber of his body boiled as she expertly massaged his entire shaft, going deeper and deeper and deeper until he was in her power.

Finally she popped to the surface, his member now clutched in her hand. "What'll it be, Jack? Your principles... or me?"

By now Jack could barely breathe, inundated as he was with waves of bliss from Mary's deft sucking and stroking. Plaintively he nodded yes and took a hit off the joint. After all, he rationalized, smoking pot was no great sin — and besides, if he wanted to fuck Mary McDonald, what choice did he have?

Mary released his cock; she didn't want him to ejaculate yet, plus the sight of watching him become progressively more stoned was too much fun to resist. For his part, Jack also enjoyed this marijuana high. As they passed the joint back and forth, he wondered to himself, *What wasn't there to like about this?*

They finished the joint and began to play with each other's body. Mary grabbed Jack's hands and put them on her breasts. "Feel them," she said. "They're both real, no silicone — and for your information, I'm 38-24-36."

Soon the breathing turned hot and heavy. "Let's go back inside the house," she said.

Certain that the next step was her bedroom, Jack eagerly complied. To his surprise, however, she opened the door to a side room and quickly pulled him inside. "Welcome to my private chambers," she said.

Jack gasped audibly as his eyes took in the room. The walls were covered with whips, chains, saws, and knives, while various medieval and modern devices of torture were spread throughout. A fully adjustable table with restraints dominated the middle of the room.

Mary grabbed Jack by his scrotum and led him to the table. "Politicians pay me thousands of dollars to sadistically torture them," she said with glazing eyes. "But guess what, Jack? You will get my full, unremorseful fury, absolutely free."

Jack started to laugh. *Surely, this was an act*, he thought — or, considering that he was completely stoned, perhaps he was hallucinating. But the force he felt when she slapped his face quickly told him otherwise.

"On your back," she said, pointing to the table. "Now."

Mesmerized, Jack did as he was told. "I'll let you make love to me," Mary McDonald said. "But first I'm going to remind you who's in full control."

She spread his arms and legs apart and quickly strapped him down. "Mary, what are you doing?" he said.

"Don't worry, Jack, I won't hurt you," she said tauntingly. "You believe me, don't you?" Then she gave the restraints a sudden jerk, laughing almost hysterically as she secured his arms even tighter.

"Are you ready for one of my special Sessions from Hell?" she said, her hands on her hips. "What'll it be, Jack — are you man enough for the rack and my other instruments of unbearable pain? I can even erect a cross and allow you to re-experience what you went through as Jesus. It would be our own little 'Passion Play.'"

Jack felt his penis stiffen, even as he stared in horror. Though he had never entertained masochistic fantasies before, the fact that she was about to torture him had somehow made him excited — and that disturbed him most of all.

Knowing he had no other choice, he decided to play along. "OK, Mary, what do you plan to do with me?"

She reached for a black leather bag on a nearby table and pulled out a syringe. "This is filled with mefloquine, a neuropsychiatric drug used as a tool of torture," she said diabolically. "The U.S. military uses it to interrogate prisoners of war, to extract information and confessions from them. Now that you're completely helpless, I'm going to inject it into your balls. The drug will totally disorient you, cause you to hallucinate, and enable me to completely control your mind as well as your body."

She leaned over the table, clutched his throat with her free hand, and stared coldly into his anxious eyes. "Once the mefloquine takes effect, I'm going to torture you in myriad ways that will provide you with incomprehensible pain — and me with indescribable pleasure. Then, when I am finished toying with you, I will use my tattoo gun and mark every inch of your body. That way, the entire world will know that you are my slave, my property."

Jack felt his mouth go dry. Mother Mary had warned him that Mary might try something like this — and though he desperately hoped that this was just a game, the cold, domineering sneer on his captor's face made it clear that she was serious.

She pointed the syringe straight in the air and gave it a tiny squeeze. Her nipples hardened and her body writhed as drops of mefloquine landed on Jack's chest. "One more thing," she said, a finger on his cock. "Unless you submit to me now — unless you allow me to torture you and make you my slave — you'll never get inside me. Our relationship will be over... and you'll end up with nothing!"

She slowly circled the table before taunting him one last time. "So what'll it be, Jack?"

Jack closed his eyes. His chest was heaving, his cock was throbbing, his entire body was on fire. Mary McDonald was a hellcat, even more than he had imagined. But as aroused as she had made him, he did not like being strapped down, let alone the thought of submitting to her merciless torture.

"Mary, why are you doing this?" he pleaded, tears forming in his eyes. "Why are you forcing me to make this kind of decision? You said you worship me as a hero figure — now you say that the only way I can be with you, is to let you humiliate and torture me. I cannot comprehend why you're doing this to me, but it is absolutely sick!"

Jack had barely finished speaking when suddenly everything went black. If Mary said anything, he couldn't hear it; if she was administering the drug, he couldn't feel it. All he knew was that his head was spinning, while his body felt cold and clammy.

* * *

He awoke to find his limbs free, his clothes back on, and his head resting on Mary's lap. They were no longer in her dungeon, but sitting on her living room couch. She had put on white leggings and a pink silk blouse, half buttoned. She smiled warmly as she caressed his face and planted her lips against his.

Considering what she had just done to him, Jack didn't know what to think, but in that moment he decided to trust her. "How long was I out?" he finally asked.

"Not long," she said. "It was all an act, Jack. I never intended to hurt you."

"Well, you could've fooled me," he said with a sigh of relief.

He sat up and examined his wrists. Other than a slight trace of red from the restraints, he felt no bruises, his head was clear, and he did not appear to be in any pain. "So tell me, Mary, why did you do it?"

"Believe it or not, Mother Mary told me to do it. She said it would be a good experience for you, that it would bring your unconscious, deeply suppressed sexual desires to the surface and force you to confront them."

Jack shook his head. If Mother Mary was in fact behind this, that didn't surprise him at all.

"Tell me, Jack," said Mary. "Did the possibility of being drugged, tortured, and tattooed in any way excite you?" She already knew the answer, but wanted to hear it from his lips.

"Yes," Jack laughed self-consciously. "I will confess, I was as sexually excited as I've ever been. You had me on a string, mesmerized by your wicked sexual power and presence. Between you and your torture chamber, I was sweating bullets. And being stoned only intensified the experience."

"Well, I have news for you — one of these days, you're really going to have to let me strap you down and do my thing on you. Mother Mary told me that because you were crucified as Jesus, you probably have a deep, repressed desire to be tortured — and the only way to exorcise that demon is to subject yourself to someone like me."

Mary glanced downward and couldn't help but notice that Jack was again stiff as a board. "The truth is as plain as your hard-on," she tittered. "Deep down, you really do want to be strapped down — but you're chicken. You're afraid of me, afraid of what I might do to you. You don't trust me, do you?"

Once again Jack felt as though he had entered some super-erotic Twilight Zone. On the one hand, as vulnerable as he was in the dungeon, Mary could have easily drugged him and had her way with him, as Destiny had tried to do at the club... but she didn't. That told him he could trust her: What more evidence did he need? On the other hand, Mary had nailed his mental state to a tee; now she wanted his body.

"You're right, Mary, I am afraid of what you might do to me," Jack admitted. "I don't want to end up permanently damaged, stuck with embarrassing tattoos, or addicted to whatever dangerous drug you might inject me with. You excite me to no end, but I'm not willing to submit to you."

She sat facing him at a perpendicular angle, her knee brushing against his thigh. She undid another button from her blouse to reveal a pink satin bra. "Oh, Jack, Jack, Jack," she said, shaking her head. "After all we've been through so far, don't tell me you want to stay in the closet."

"What's that supposed to mean?"

"You're like the art critic who admires a Hieronymus Bosch painting, but is afraid to enter the landscape when given a chance," Mary explained. "Or it's like I'm Alice in Wonderland, and as much as you love reading my story, when given the opportunity to go through the looking glass, you demur because you'd rather stay in your safe, contracted, boring and conventional world. In other words, you're just a fan, not a participant.

"But I'm not concerned," she continued, tapping his groin. "I'm just starting to work on you — and once I get my tentacles deep inside you, you will submit to me, and my world will become yours."

Once again Jack was awestruck. Mary was as sharp as she was sexy. "OK, I'll give you that," he said. "Now let me ask you this: The politicians who submit to you surely don't risk being physically damaged or stuck with embarrassing tattoos. And yet you want to treat me differently, even more severely. Why?"

"Jack, if you want to pay me five thousand dollars per session and become my client, then I will treat you like I do the politicians," she said wryly. "But I'm not interested in turning scumbag politicians into my personal property. You, however, are totally different because I love you and want you to be mine, totally mine — and I want the world to know it."

She draped his left hand across her thigh. "A politician will get what he pays for, but you will get what I want," she continued. "I cannot offer you any guarantees, except that the danger is real. You *will* be playing with fire. My goal is to drive you so crazy, you will *want* to jump directly into that fire."

Jack could feel a truth stirring inside him. He couldn't put his finger on it, but something told him that he could trust her. "All right, let me ask you this," he said. "If this is all about owning me, is that why you went off on Destiny —

not because she tattooed me, but because she dared to violate *your* property... meaning, me?"

"Oooh, very good, Jack," she said. "I think you're finally beginning to understand how this game works."

* * *

Mary was famished; scaring the crap out of Jack Cohen had given her quite an appetite. She led him into the kitchen, pulled out a half-empty quart of Haagen-Dazs Chocolate Chip Cookie Dough from the freezer, and reached for two bowls. "None for me," said Jack. "I don't eat junk like this. Normally I stick to protein and vegetables."

"Oh, Jack, you're such a drip," Mary said, rolling her eyes. "Don't bore me with what you *normally* do; it's not very exciting. You normally don't get drugged, sucked off, and tattooed in a strip club. You normally don't smoke pot in a hot tub with a naked vixen, or allow yourself to be tied up and humiliated by a dominatrix."

She opened the container and put a spoonful of ice cream in his mouth. "I suggest that when Polly asks you what you did while you were gone, tell her that you were a very bad boy, that you broke your diet and indulged in some Haagen-Dazs. If she has an iota of gumption, she'll take you out to the woodshed and whip your ass 'til it's black and blue!" Then she playfully tapped his bottom.

Jack laughed as he took the spoon, dug into the container and fed Mary a bite himself. "As long as you brought it up," he said, "I'm going to tell Polly the truth about everything — she's been my loyal sweetheart for five years, so that's the least I owe her. It will be up to her to decide what she wants to do, but at least she'll have all the facts."

"Bravo," said Mary, lightly clapping her hands. "I applaud you for doing the right thing. Not only am I more than willing to discuss the situation with her, I'll even share you with her — provided she doesn't mind having you bruised, battered, and burned." She laughed at her own cleverness.

They continued feeding each other from the container until there was no more. Jack had to admit the ice cream tasted good, even if it made him feel as bloated as the bouncer at Sodom and Gomorrah. Which reminded him...

"What's the name of the huge, 'roided-up dude who works the front door at your club?"

"You mean Bart?"

"Yeah. He charged Jud and me two hundred bucks to get in."

"That prick," scowled Mary. "I gave him two hundred dollars myself and told him everything was covered."

"That's what I thought," said Jack.

"Well, don't worry about it," said Mary. "I've got some cash in my purse. I'll reimburse you right now."

"That won't be necessary," Jack insisted. "I'll go to the club myself and ask for my money back."

"Jack, don't be crazy."

"I'll be polite," Jack insisted. "Then if I have to, I'll use a little *persuasion*."

"But, he's twice your size — he could hurt you!"

He put his hands on her shoulders and told her to relax. "Remember, Mary, I'm a professional-level mixed martial artist. My trainer, Patsy, tells me I can beat 90 percent of the pros in my weight division right now. I know I can handle him." Then he draped his arms around her waist and drew her closer to him. "Besides, to tell you the truth, I'm more afraid of you than your friend the bouncer. You're a very dangerous girl. If you ever strap me down again, I might be at a slight disadvantage against you."

"Not at all," said Mary, leaning in for a kiss. "In fact, I just called Jim, the bookmaker guy in the Objectivist group. He has the odds at exactly even if I drug you and strap you down."

"In that case," he said playfully, "why don't you take me upstairs and we can find out for ourselves? And when you lose... I'll *do what my hormones are just aching to do — fuck your brains loose*."

Mary squealed with delight, knowing he'd remembered her exact words from the malt shop two days before. "Then what are we waiting for?" she said, clasping his hands. "Let's get the show on the road!"

. . .

She led him upstairs, past her four extra bedrooms, and into her entertainment room, which sported a pool table, a ping pong table, several arcade games, and a high-end home-theater system. In the corner was a bar with a half-dozen barstools and a liquor cabinet.

Mary planted Jack on a stool then removed a pipe and a small gooey substance from the cabinet. "This is Nepalese hash," she explained as she put it in the pipe. "It's completely natural and not addictive, except perhaps psychologically for certain people, and it has more THC than pot, which didn't seem to buzz you all that much."

She ignited the pipe, took a deep hit and held the smoke in for several seconds before blowing it in his face. "Now it's your turn," she said giddily.

Jack took the pipe and smiled. He had assumed that this strange thing called hash was far more potent and dangerous than marijuana, so he appreciated that Mary had allayed his fears. He took a big hit, held the smoke in as long as he could, then let it go.

"Jack, I'm surprised I was able to get you to try pot *and* hash today," said Mary. "I really thought you were too conventional and uptight to experiment with recreational drugs."

"Don't underestimate your powers of persuasion," he replied after taking another hit. "I'm sitting here looking at the hottest, sexiest babe I've ever seen, and it's tough to resist your forbidden fruit — even if I am Jesus."

"Thank you, Jack, but I think you misspoke," she said, snuggling next to him. "You should have said, 'don't *overestimate* your powers of persuasion.' If my powers were as great as you think they are, you'd still be in the dungeon!"

"You've already got me on the highway to hell," Jack said playfully. "The way I'm going, the next stop might be your dungeon — only this time for real."

They laughed, they kissed, they laughed again. Before long Jack noticed how heavy his body felt; clearly this stuff *was* stronger than pot. But at the same time it relaxed him, making him feel euphoric and capable of profound insights — a realization that pleased Mary. "You're lucky, Jack, in that you seem to function almost normally on weed and hash," she said. "I'm the same way. Unlike most people, I get a lot done when I'm high — I get all kinds of revelations under the influence of drugs. I even meditate great when I'm high, even though Mother Mary says that foreign substances are retarding my spiritual evolution. But my rebuttal is that grass and hash are natural, not foreign, substances."

"Mary, Mary, quite contrary," Jack sang out. Then he paused for effect before finishing his thought: "Hey, that rhymes!"

They giggled uncontrollably before clasping each other like lovers. Jack reached under her blouse, undid her bra, and pressed her even closer. "Like you said in the kitchen," he softly whispered, "let's get the show on the road."

.   .   .

She took him by the hand and led him to her bedroom, where she pulled out a pipe and some hash from her nightstand. After they each took a few hits, she put on her favorite CD, a compilation of psychedelic music from Pink Floyd, King Crimson, the Scorpions, and the Jefferson Airplane. Then she fast-forwarded the disc to "Comfortably Numb," which was not only her favorite song in the mix, but one of the greatest rock songs of all time.

The music blasted from the sound system, overwhelming Jack at first with its depth, intricacy, and intensity. Like everything else about Mary McDonald, her choice of music was carefully planned to trigger just the right reaction.

They began slow dancing. "This music is surrealistic, phantasmagorical, quasi-mystical," she explained. "It's ideal for hash smokers and acid heads. If you're looking for metaphysical verticality in music, you can't beat this genre."

"Um-hmh," said Jack. Buzzed as he was at the moment, everything sounded fantastic. But as he listened more intently, he could understand why millions of people loved this song, even if they weren't stoned.

She slithered around him, wrapping his arms around her waist while grinding him with her ass. Then she did a slow strip tease, bending over to remove her leggings before doing away with her blouse.

"Now it's your turn," she said as she began to undress him. Jack swooned with pleasure as she touched his body in all the right places. It wasn't long before she had him lying supine on her bed.

"My God, you're unreal," he said, fixing his eyes on her perfect figure. "But I love you for your mind as well as your body. With your brains, you should be a professor."

"But I'm already a professor," she said as she continued to massage his front side. "Didn't I show you my sheepskin?"

Jack cocked an eyebrow. He didn't recall seeing a PhD sheepskin.

"It's in the dungeon, Jackie Poo. It's a PhD in sexology that I obtained online." She reached for the leather accessory bag on the side of the bed. "Just think," she continued. "You're about to receive a deep sex lesson from a very prominent professor of sexology — me!"

Jack let out a hearty chuckle... and then the nickel dropped. *"Jackie Poo?"*

Mary pulled out a humongous black dildo from her bag and waved it menacingly in front of him. "Because you're such a tight ass," she said coyly, "I am going to shove this deep up your *poo* hole and relieve you of your terrible malady. Hence, *Jackie Poo*."

Once again Jack was distressed. As aroused as he was, he wasn't sure he wanted that thing crammed up his ass. He was visibly relieved, at least for the moment, when she put it back in the bag.

Then she pulled out a bottle of oil and began to lubricate him. She was almost ready to have him, but there was just one more thing. "Have you ever read *Siddhartha*, Jack?"

"No," he stirred.

"You really should," she said softly. "It's a wonderful spiritual novel about a gifted spiritual seeker on his way to Nirvana who gets sidetracked by Kamala, a beautiful courtesan who instructs him in the art of physical love. Kamala always has something new to teach Siddhartha, and he spends years enraptured with her until he finally resumes his quest for Nirvana."

She rubbed more oil on her hands and slowly greased his shaft, causing him to moan with pleasure. "I am like Kamala," she finally said. "I will always have something new to teach you. But I don't want your first lesson to be Dildo 101... I want it to be Lovemaking 101."

She spread her legs slightly apart and gently slid him inside. "In other words, Jack, today we will make love like true lovers do," she said, pressing her body against his. "And because we are true lovers, this lesson will be easy."

Time stopped as they danced in passion, their bodies assuming various positions until Mary achieved orgasm. Deep down it pleased Jack to know that, in the ultimate game of control, it was she who came first. Still rigid, and still firmly inside her, he thrust himself with all his being and finally collapsed in ecstasy. Then they cuddled together as lovers do, before drifting off to sleep.

◦ ◦ ◦

By the time he awoke, it was dark outside. He checked his watch: 8:30 p.m. It had been a long, eventful day: some of it crazy and disconcerting, some of it intense and exciting. The only thing he knew for sure was that he wasn't ready to leave.

He reached over and nuzzled Mary on the back on her neck. She stirred slightly, but was still sound asleep. Quietly he slipped out of bed, not wishing to disturb her.

She found him in her study about twenty minutes later. He had stumbled onto it on his way back from the kitchen for a glass of water. The myriad of books on psychology, philosophy, spirituality, politics, and science that lined the bookshelves, not to mention the Mensa certificate and diploma from MIT, reminded him that he was in the presence of a serious scholar.

She noticed him gazing at the only item on her maple oak desk: a single framed photograph. "Those are my late parents," she said. "They were both professors, my father in physics and my mother in chemistry. I got a degree in chemistry from MIT, but decided to return to Washington and State U to study political science, my true passion."

She sat up on the desk, facing him as he stared through her diaphanous negligee. "You might think I'm just a self-centered, hedonistic whore, Jack," she said as she lit a cigarette. "But I'm passionately devoted to making the world a better, more humane place."

Jack assured her that he believed her. After all, it made perfect sense. Mary McDonald may have been a prostitute, a sadist, and a drug addict, but she was also a left-wing liberal.

He started perusing her library while Mary eyed him like a hawk. It wasn't long before he noticed that some of the shelves were conspicuously empty. "That's odd," said Jack. "Most people run out of space. Looks like you ran out of books."

"Oh, I have others," she replied nervously. "They're in the closet."

"Really?" said Jack. "Are they on the same subjects?"

Suddenly Mary's heart started racing. If only she'd left well enough alone. "Why do you ask?" she said, almost defensively.

A-ha, thought Jack. *Miss Uninhibited appears to have something to hide.*

He took a few steps toward the closet and noticed the key in the door. "Let me guess: they all deal with taboo subjects, and you don't want your visitors to see them."

"Jack, please... you really wouldn't be interested. Let's go upstairs." She sounded frantic and almost weak — a far cry from the Mary he knew, the one who thrived on control.

She lunged after him, hoping desperately to stop him... but it was too late. Jack unlocked the door to discover boxes and boxes of books on mind control, domination, sadism, torture, torture drugs, and head shrinking. He even found a number of titles on human dissection and cannibalism.

"Wow," he finally said in amazement. "And you said *I* have issues."

He turned around, eager to give Mary a taste of her own medicine, when he noticed her lying on the floor in the fetal position, sobbing profusely. It was one of those moments that every man in a relationship faces from time to time, when his woman becomes completely irrational and he doesn't know what to do.

He knelt down beside her, wrapped her in his arms, and gently stroked her hair. He held her that way for the longest time before asking if she was all right.

She sat up, nodded her head and wiped away her tears. In that moment she looked as intimidating as a Raggedy Ann doll.

"You must think I'm a psychopath," she finally said, clutching his hands. "I'm not, Jack; you have to believe me. I have never killed, eaten, or dissected a human being — I simply have a morbid fascination with those subjects. I need to read books on mind control, domination, and torture, because that's what I do for a living. But I only do those things on clients who want me to."

"And on boyfriends like me who don't." It was a gentle quip, one that Jack had hoped would elicit a smile. It not only achieved the desired effect, but made her laugh as well.

"What can I say, Jack? I enjoy my work... I'd be lying if I said I didn't. And between you and me, I especially get off whenever I torture a politician. But like I told you before, I also use my work as a form of spiritual catharsis: Intense physical and psychic pain can be a doorway to spiritual awakening."

Jack still wasn't sure how to respond. Her answers were plausible — they always were — but Mary had lied to him before. But at the moment he felt sorry for her, and he decided that what she needed most was the comfort of a friend. He drew her close beside him and gently caressed her head.

Perhaps it was emotion stirring inside her, or the sudden realization that she was as vulnerable now as she'd ever been in her life. For whatever reason, Mary McDonald decided to give in to the moment — and right now she wanted Jack to take her more than anything in the world. She slowly lifted him to his feet and led him back to her bedroom.

· · ·

Jack left Mary's around midnight. She dropped him off at Jud's apartment complex, where he picked up his car and drove across town to the one-bedroom unit that he shared with Polly. By the time he pulled into the garage, it was nearly 1:00 a.m. If he was lucky, she'd be asleep. Though he believed that the truth is always the right thing, he did not look forward to telling Polly about Mary and hoped it could wait until morning.

No such luck. Polly was waiting for him as he opened the front door. She sat on the couch in her bathrobe and slippers, her arms folded, the television playing in the background. She muted the set immediately. Now that Jack was finally home, she wanted some answers now.

"Where on earth have you been?" she said. "Why haven't you called?"

He sat down, took a deep breath, and told her everything — as in everything. The tattoo, the dungeon, everything. It was a lot for anyone to absorb, especially a girl like Polly. She covered her face with her hands and began sobbing uncontrollably.

It wasn't long before Jack began crying himself. He loved Polly dearly and felt terrible about the pain he was causing her. "Honey, believe me, I still love you," he said as he rubbed her shoulders. "I wasn't looking to meet another girl, but Mary seduced me... and I couldn't resist her. She's a professional enchantress, and she had her sights set on me. But she knows I'm not going to marry her — and she doesn't care if I stay with you. In fact, she's very liberal. She even wants to meet you."

Polly sat up on the couch, dried her eyes and gazed submissively at Jack. She told him that she loved him very much and never wanted to lose him. Then, to his utter amazement, she said: "If I have to share you with this Mary McDonald, I will. Maybe it will just turn out to be a short-term infatuation. More than anything, I want you to be happy. And if that means an affair with Mary, then so be it."

Jack expected all kinds of reactions from Polly. That was not one of them. Relieved as he was, it freaked him out, at least a little, that she accepted Mary so easily.

He put his arms around her and they kissed for the longest time. "I don't deserve you," he finally said. "What a loving, giving sweetheart you are."

For her part, Polly was looking on the bright side: Maybe Mary wasn't interested in stealing Jack from her — and maybe she might learn a few tricks from this siren. She certainly wanted to meet her. Her biggest concern was making sure Mary wouldn't completely corrupt him. After all, Jack's eyes were bloodshot, which told Polly he was still stoned. She could only hope that Mary wouldn't ruin his life by getting him addicted to harder drugs.

"Honey, this Mary sounds unbelievably exciting but terribly dangerous," said Polly. "Aren't you afraid she might seriously hurt or even kill you?"

"Of course I'm afraid, because I know the danger is real," Jack nodded. "But that's part of the excitement she embodies — and for whatever reason, I find it a turn on."

"Jack, I can't even begin to comprehend why you would want to risk life and limb for some cheap thrills," she said, shaking her head. "But you know me; I love you completely and I want you to be happy. If this is what you want to do, I will support you."

Jack gazed at her affectionately. "Honey, I love you, too."

Again they kissed and caressed. She was about to suggest that they go to bed when she noticed that his hands were cured. "Jack, it's a miracle: the holes have disappeared without a trace."

He told her about meeting Mother Mary and the treatment with the Ayurvedic ointment. He also mentioned her remarkable assertion that he was Jesus Christ reincarnated.

"Mother Mary said that just by knowing I was Jesus, the holes would disappear," Jack continued. "As incredible as it sounds, Polly, that's exactly what happened. I'm supposed to see her again in two weeks. She's going to baptize me with the Holy Spirit, and supposedly, I'll reawaken as the Chosen Son of God — but I'm not holding my breath. I mean, can you imagine Jesus with a dominatrix mistress?"

"No," said Polly. "But it does seem like a miracle that the holes are completely gone."

"Yeah, it does," Jack agreed. "And it is true that Mother Mary can transmit spiritual energy. I saw her do it to Mary with my own two eyes. So even though it's next to impossible that I'm Jesus, I am excited about getting initiated and investigating spiritual life."

Mother Mary also sounded like someone that Polly should meet. "Do you think she would initiate me?" she asked.

"I don't see why not," said Jack.

"Good, because I would also like to get involved in spiritual life, especially now that it's important to you," said Polly. "I never said anything before because I knew you were an atheist. But now that you're going to study under a guru, I also want to participate."

"I'll check with Mother Mary to make sure it's OK, but I'm sure she'll be happy to initiate you. You're welcome to read the spiritual books she loaned me. I plan to read at least one a day, starting tomorrow."

With that they kissed again and made their way to the bedroom. They undid the bed and were about to turn off the lights when Polly remembered the phone message. "Oh, my God, I almost forgot: Patsy called and said he has three sparring sessions set up for you with Sergei Putin!"

"Putin?" said Jack. "What's he doing in Washington?"

"Some important Russian politicians and lobbyists are in town this week on business, and they're feting him because he's a national hero," she said. "Patsy says Putin needs to stay sharp for his match against Andujar next month, so he made some calls and arranged for you to spar with him. The first one is scheduled for tomorrow."

"All right!" exclaimed Jack as he bear-hugged Polly and lifted her high in the air. He was ecstatic and could hardly contain himself. This was like a dream come true, a chance to measure himself against the greatest mixed martial artist of all time, the man they called "the GOAT."

He asked Polly to join him in the kitchen while he made some lemon balm herbal tea, a beverage particularly known for inducing sleep. The session with Putin would represent the ultimate test of Jack's fighting ability, and he wanted to make sure he was well-rested.

● ● ●

Patsy McMullen had trained mixed martial artists for nearly twenty years, but he had never worked with a talent the equal of Jack Cohen. Jack was not only a great wrestler, but a punishing striker with the ability to rain blows on his opponents from all angles. Although Jack had yet to fight professionally, and had only trained in mixed martial arts for less than a year, Patsy knew he had the potential to be a world champion. With Sergei Putin in town to spar, Jack would be able to test himself against the current champ.

Patsy greeted Jack at the gym and made sure he was good to go. "This is basically a grappling session, so the risk of getting hurt is minimal," he said. "The worst thing that could happen today is that Putin makes mincemeat of you on the mat. We can live with that. Just make sure you're 100 percent for the striking session."

Jack gave him a thumbs-up and asked for the scouting report.

"He's probably the strongest guy you've ever wrestled," said Patsy. "I just read that he benches 515."

Jack was unconcerned. "I didn't tell you this, but I benched 475 two weeks ago."

"That's awesome," said Patsy, "but that isn't 515. The first thing Putin will do is test your strength. He'll try to wrap you in a bear hug and throw you. If he feels he can overpower a guy, that's his favored plan of attack. Then, once he's got the guy on the ground, he punches him silly."

"Putin might be a little stronger in the bench," said Jack, "but unless he can do twenty-seven pull-ups, there's no way he can match my pulling power. Besides, in two to three years, I'll pass him in the bench, and then he'll have to deal with an opponent even stronger than himself. I'm more concerned about his single-leg takedown than his bear hug. He's the quickest 200-pound wrestler I've ever seen. Experiencing that quickness face to face will be a lot different than watching it on my laptop."

All Patsy could do was smile. "If there's one thing I admire about you, kid, it's your confidence."

"Does Putin know anything about me?"

"Only that you're a promising nineteen-year-old mixed-martial-artist wannabe. You're off his and everyone else's radar because you haven't fought professionally. But that's going to change after the sparring sessions."

"Damn straight," said Jack.

He made his way to the locker room to change into his gear. Once he made Putin sweat this afternoon, *everyone* in the MMA grapevine would know the name Jack Cohen.

* * *

Sergei Putin walked into the gym, changed into his fight gear, and grudgingly shook hands with Jack. He had no desire to exchange even cursory pleasantries. His only interest was in the business at hand: getting a workout and dominating his opponent in the process.

Proceeding to their respective corners, Jack and Putin eyed each other across the cage, each noting that the chiseled body of the other was almost identical in size and shape to his own. Knowing that Putin liked to initiate grappling action with his signature single-leg takedown, Jack decided to strike first by preempting Putin's move with his own single-leg takedown.

Patsy rang the bell, signaling the start of the first round. The two fighters immediately clinched, and as they did, Jack pulled Putin's head slightly to one side, creating an opening to his right leg. In a flash he swooped down to secure the leg, and before Putin could sprawl into a neutral position, Jack tripped him to the ground. In a twinkling he had accomplished what no other MMA fighter had come close to doing: take down the great Sergei Putin.

Alas, his triumph was short-lived. Putin immediately freed himself by ripping Jack's hand off his waist, and again the two fighters clinched. Jack attempted another single-leg takedown, but this time Putin was ready: He sprawled into a neutral position, whipped around behind Jack, and took him down — but Jack was not down for long, either. Locking his arm over Putin's arm (which was around his waist), he rolled him onto his back. Though Putin turned to his stomach, Jack had the reversal, riding the Russian until the bell sounded, ending the round.

Putin's mien was cold and impassive as he rose to his feet. He had underestimated the strength and abilities of his challenger; he would not let that happen again.

He bear-hugged Jack as the second round began and attempted to body slam him, but Jack sunk down and prevented the throw. Putin then dropped down, secured a single leg, and took him down. Jack responded by rolling the champion onto his back, but when he attempted to move onto him, Putin, unleashing a Brazilian Jiu-Jitsu move, wrapped his legs around his neck and under his arm, locking him into a triangle chokehold. Unable to move or breathe, Jack had no choice but to tap out.

They grappled for a few more rounds. Though Jack kept things close, Putin again was able to submit him, this time with a guillotine chokehold.

When the final bell rang, Jack extended his hand to Putin, but the Russian champ refused it, choosing instead to head straight for the locker room. Now that he realized Jack was a threat to his crown, he had no interest in acknowledging him in any way. His only thought was to get back to the hotel and find out who this kid was.

Patsy was put off by Putin's lack of sportsmanship, but Jack took it in stride. No MMA fighter had ever challenged the Olympic gold medalist before, but he showed that he could beat him in a straight wrestling match. Once Jack got some training in Brazilian Jiu-Jitsu, it wouldn't be long before he'd be able to use the champion's chokeholds against him.

*   *   *

A few hours later, Jack, still high on adrenaline, arrived back at his apartment. He made himself a health shake, pulled out one of Mother Mary's books, and began his study of spirituality. Now that school had been canceled, he could devote his full attention to spiritual and political philosophy. He looked forward to comparing and contrasting the teachings of the spiritual mystics with Ayn Rand's atheistic Objectivism, and he wondered if he would be able to reconcile the differences between them.

Before he knew it, it was 8:15 p.m. Polly would be home soon, and he wanted to take her out and celebrate. But first he had a score to settle at Sodom and Gomorrah.

He arrived at the club about twenty minutes later. He knew it would be almost empty at this hour, the perfect time to confront Bart sans interference. The big man was sitting on a chair in front of the doorway entrance, reading the sports section.

"Hey, buddy," Jack began, "remember me from the other night?"

"Yeah, I remember you," said Bart. "You're one of Mary's friends. You were the pussy who got carried out of the bar unconscious."

Jack didn't like being called a pussy, but he decided to let that slide. "And you were the guy who charged me two hundred bucks to get in."

"What about it?"

"Mary told me that she had already paid you. I'd like my money back."

Bart stood up to his full height, his chest out, his fists clenched and ready. "Well, I'd like you to get the fuck out of here before I bitch-slap you silly."

Jack coolly stood his ground, waiting for Bart to make his move — which he did, ten seconds later, when he tried to strike Jack with the back of his hand. But Jack avoided getting hit by quickly moving out of range.

Then, having already calculated his next move, Jack baited the big man. "You know, the problem with big, slow oafs like you is that you couldn't hit the broad side of a barn if it was standing in front of you."

Naturally, Bart was pissed. It was bad enough that he'd swung and missed. Now the little twerp thinks he's a comedian. He lunged after Jack with full rage.

Jack stepped to the side of the charging giant and leapt up, wrapping his right arm around his neck and securing it with his left. Then he rotated his body behind Bart and exerted pressure on his windpipe, cutting off his oxygen supply. In a matter of seconds, Bart went limp, and Jack guided his body to the concrete. Then he pulled out Bart's wallet, removed two Benjamins, and made a quick phone call to Sodom and Gomorrah. "This is the Washington Police Department. We want you to know that your bouncer is fast asleep on the concrete in front of your establishment."

Jack was pleased with himself; this was a perfect sequel to his sparring session. Still in stitches, he called Polly. He had told her he'd be seeing Bart that night, and like Mary McDonald, she was worried. But he immediately allayed her concerns.

"Polly, I just leveled the mountain, and I got my money back, too," he said. "I'll pick you up in a few minutes — and put on your sexiest dress. We're gonna boogie tonight!"

●　●　●

Jack spent the next day, Tuesday, preparing for his striking session with Putin. He also wanted to get a little reading in, but first he would call Mary. They had tentative plans for Wednesday night, and he wanted to make sure they were still on.

"Oh, Jack, I'm so glad you called," she said. "I miss you like crazy, but we'll have to wait until Sunday for our next get-together. The club just called, and they've booked me as an all-day, all-night escort the rest of the week. You'll never guess who my client is — Sergei Putin!"

Jack's heart immediately sank. "You're kidding," he said.

"No," she laughed. "Isn't that wild? His Russian politician friends are paying me fifteen thousand dollars a day to keep him entertained. The gig starts tomorrow — and you'll love this: I'll be accompanying him to his sparring session in the afternoon. I bet you'd love to see that."

Jack knew that life can be cruel, but this was something else: His beloved Mary would be fucking and entertaining his hated rival! A slew of negative emotions flooded his being, but somehow he suppressed them.

He took a deep breath and said, "Mary, I *will* be seeing that. The guy he'll be sparring with is me!"

"Oh, my God, Jack — that's insane. What a coincidence."

"Yeah, it is," said Jack. "But I'm glad I found out about it now. If you'd just shown up with him tomorrow, I think I'd have fallen over in shock."

"Well, I'll make sure I behave myself, so he doesn't know that you're my boyfriend." Then, Mary being Mary, she couldn't resist twisting the knife. "So tell me, Jack, does the fact that Putin will be fucking me make you terribly jealous and upset, and make you want me even more?"

"Of course, it does," snapped Jack. "You can't imagine the emotions I'm feeling right now."

"Oh, yes, I can," she said lasciviously, "and from my perspective they are all positive. Those extreme emotions will cause your body to produce extra sperm — which means I'll get a double shot when I see you on Sunday!"

Jack could only suffer. He knew she had him by the balls and was squeezing them for her own enjoyment. "What can I say? You own me and you know it. I'll be donating every last drop of my love to you on Sunday."

Mary began to finger herself. The fact that she was controlling the relationship had made her wet with delight. "I don't own you yet, Jackie Poo, but it's only a matter of time," she purred. "And when I do... well, you know what that means."

Jack did, all too well. Aware that she wanted him in her dungeon, he wouldn't put it past Mary if she actually wanted Putin to torture him in the ring tomorrow, so that she could finish the job on Sunday.

Then, to his surprise, she became sensitive to his feelings. "Look, Jack, I know you must be hurting now. But you know I love you to no end, and you know I'll be rooting for you tomorrow with every fiber of my being — I just won't be able to show it. But I will show it to you in *every* way when I see you on Sunday." Then she shot him a smooch.

"Thanks," he said. "I appreciate that. In the meantime, do me a favor: wear something sexy and provocative. That will inspire my glands to produce even more sperm cells before Sunday." They both laughed, and Jack, now feeling a little better, returned to his reading.

● ● ●

The first thing Jack did upon arriving at the gym Wednesday morning was inform Patsy that Putin's backers had hired Mary and that she'd be accompanying the champ at the sparring session. Patsy got a kick out of that. He'd been around the fight game a long time, but this was a new one for him.

A short while later Putin arrived, with Mary at his side. She wore a black bustier, matching leather pants, and black boots. When Putin headed to the locker room to change into his sparring gear, Mary took advantage of the opportunity to say hello to Jack. "He thinks I'm wearing this for him," she said as she embraced him. "But I really put it on for you."

She stole a kiss, and then another, before throwing caution to the wind. She clutched Jack tightly and tongued him deeply. So much for behaving herself.

Meanwhile Patsy McMullen stood there, mesmerized. He had heard many things about this bombshell. Now that he'd seen her in the flesh, he understood how Jack had been seduced.

Unfortunately for Jack, had Mary not caused such a distraction, Patsy could have warned them to pull away from each other before Putin came back. But distracted he was, and pull away they didn't. By the time the Russian champ emerged from the locker room, it was too late.

"What is this?" he scowled. "She is my escort and you are making love with her!"

Jack turned red with embarrassment. He knew the damage had already been done; all he could do was tell Putin the truth. "Sergei, I apologize. Mary is a professional escort who was hired for you, but she also happens to be my girlfriend. It is just a coincidence that she ended up here today. Obviously this was a mistake for us. It will not happen again."

Mary, for her part, was also contrite, but Putin would have none of it. His only thought was to punish them both — but that would have to wait until

Friday. Then, he would destroy Jack in their full-contact session, and make sure Mary experienced his wrath. Until that time, however, he was content to play possum, going half-speed today to give Jack a false sense of confidence.

"Let's get on with the session," he said, his voice devoid of emotion.

. . .

Jack arrived home around 1:00 p.m. Though he felt the striking session went well, he suspected that Putin had been holding back. Not that he blamed him; he would've done the same thing in his shoes. His biggest concern was whether he could handle and respond to Putin's lethal punching combinations and power when the bell rang for real on Friday.

He decided to call Jim Mulligan. He'd read *Capitalism: The Unknown Ideal* and *The Case Against the Fed*, and expected to be done with *The Creature from Jekyll Island* by Friday. More importantly, he hoped that the former MMA great might provide some guidance on Brazilian Jiu-Jitsu that could help him against Putin. "Jim, I've got to tell you that I love these books and will be confronting my father this weekend."

"Booyah!" Jim howled. "I'm sure he won't have an intelligent response, because there is none from the Fed perspective. He'll just feed you some bullshit and hope you buy it. When you don't, you'll see your dad for what he is."

"I'm afraid you're right," Jack frowned, "and it pains me deeply to know that my father is just a front man for the banking cartel."

"Life's a bitch, buddy. Wait 'til you become prominent and start exposing the Mafia Government — then you'll find out what real pain is. Those cocksuckers won't tolerate a charismatic young genius like you exposing their multi-trillion dollar scam."

Jack rolled his eyes. "Now you're just blowing smoke up my ass. What makes you think a crazy, young motherfucker like me is going to be the Man who blows the lid off the Gangsta Government?"

"Kid, I told you you're the nuts," laughed Jim. "That ad lib proves you've got the right stuff. I just want to tag along for the ride, 'cause it's gonna to be a wild one."

Jack filled him in about the Putin match and the latest development with Mary. "Kid, your life is stranger than fiction," said Mulligan. "Your new girlfriend is a high-class hooker employed by the greatest mixed martial artist ever, and now he wants to destroy you because he caught you two smooching on his dime."

"So you're saying I have no chance on Friday?"

"That's exactly what I'm saying," said Jim. "Unless you're the Second Coming, you're gonna be road kill. It's a boy versus a man."

"But I held my own when we sparred," Jack protested.

"Look, son, you're a phenomenal athlete. I saw your matches at the Nationals, and with your mind and athleticism you're probably the only guy on the planet with a legitimate shot at beating Putin — but you still have a lot to learn. What you saw today was hardly vintage Putin. What you're going to get Friday is a whole different animal... and now that you've made it personal for him, he'll really be out for blood."

Jack's head started throbbing. Now he needed Mulligan's help more than ever. "The match is at one o'clock. Do you think you can be there?"

"Tell you what," said Jim. "I'll not only be there, I'll get there a couple hours early so we can work on some moves."

. . .

Sure enough, Jim Mulligan arrived at the gym Friday at exactly 11:00 a.m. Patsy was thrilled to meet the legendary fighter. "Jim, you're the final piece to the finished product," he said heartily. "Jack's a terror on the mat and an outstanding striker, and once he adds the Jiu-Jitsu joint-locks and chokeholds that are your specialty, he'll be a real threat to Putin."

Jim motioned for Jack to join them on the mat. He knew Jack was a rare talent, but even he was amazed at how quickly the kid picked up on his instruction. Once Jack was shown how to do a joint-lock or chokehold, he immediately was able to incorporate it into a series of moves that would potentially lead to a submission.

The lesson continued until about 12:30 p.m., when Putin arrived with Mary. She wore a slinky red cocktail dress and a pair of three-inch wedges. She'd spent most of the past forty-eight hours doting on the champion, indulging his every whim, sexual and otherwise, in the hopes that would appease him (and make him forget what he saw on Wednesday). She thought she'd seen everything in her line of work — but there was a side to Putin that made even her skin crawl. If only she could warn Jack.

Jim introduced himself and said that he would referee. "That's fine," said Putin, again not bothering with pleasantries. "I want this to be an all-out sparring session, like a real match. But unlike a regular match, if there is a knockout or a submission, the victim, if able, can resume fighting after a break of not more than five minutes. Once one of us has three stoppages, the fight is over."

Then he turned to Jack and asked if he agreed. Jack nodded his approval.

"Fine," said Putin. Then he smirked as he added, "Of course, the referee should stop the fight once one of us is defenseless."

"Of course," said Mulligan. He knew he would have to be extra quick to protect Jack from the malevolent Russian.

* * *

The two fighters met and clinched at the center of the ring at the start of the first round. Knowing that Putin expected him to shoot for a takedown, Jack decided to surprise him with a strike attack. He pulled out of the clinch and quickly unleashed an uppercut that caught the Russian flush on his chin, staggering him. He dropped down, wrapped his arms around Putin's thighs, and barreled him onto his back. Then, with Putin's face exposed, Jack began pummeling it with a series of punches.

Seeing that the champion was in danger of being damaged, Jim stopped the match in accordance with the ground rules and called for a five-minute break. The dazed Putin struggled to his feet and applied an ice pack to his head.

Jack strode back to his corner, stoic yet euphoric. Once again he had managed to floor the great Putin. He glanced at Mary, standing alone in the far corner of the room. She badly wanted to smile at him, but knew that would be unwise. Deep down, however, she was ecstatic.

The bell rang for round two. The two fighters cautiously approached each other. After exchanging tentative, exploratory jabs, Putin hammered Jack with a right cross, then a left hook that sent him to the canvas. With Jack on his knees, defenseless, Putin moved in to finish him off — only to have Mulligan stop him. The match would resume in five minutes.

This time Jack staggered to his corner, where Patsy greeted him with an ice pack. Because Putin didn't have a trainer in his corner, Patsy refrained from dispensing any advice to him. It was a sense of fair play that Jack appreciated, even if Putin didn't. Besides, Jack was content to formulate his own plan of attack before round three.

When the bell rang, Jack went for a ground attack. The two clinched, jockeying for favorable leverage to initiate a takedown attempt. Obliging Jack's desire to wrestle, Putin shot for a leg first. Jack sprawled, and when he did, he pushed down on Putin's head, which afforded him a split-second opening to whip behind him for a takedown. Jack then tied up Putin with a leg ride, which provided him the necessary leverage to roll him onto his back.

Then he pounded the champ with head punches, which Putin fended off with his arms. Then Jack made a rookie mistake: He reared back to get extra power into a punch — only to find himself in a scissor hold, with Putin's legs around his neck. Now prone and in the defensive position, Jack attempted to stand up, but Putin tripped him with his arms. Unable to breathe, Jack was forced to tap out, ending the third round.

Jack shook his head in disgust as he headed to his corner. This was the third time Putin had submitted him with a chokehold. Quickly he went over the various moves Jim had taught him before the match; there had to be an answer.

Then, suddenly, it came to him. Putin had a habit of exposing his head whenever he tried a takedown. The next time the champ dropped down (for a takedown), instead of pushing down on his head as he had done in previous rounds, Jack would attempt to secure it in a guillotine chokehold.

Putin began the round by jabbing and moving, only to be stunned momentarily when Jack countered with a vicious right cross. Changing tactics, Putin charged at Jack, hoping to drive him to the mat with a double-leg takedown. Only this time, when Putin wrapped his arms around his thighs, Jack slipped his right arm around Putin's neck — which, predictably, the champion had exposed on the outside of Jack's right thigh. As Putin drove him to the mat, Jack secured his hold on the Russian's neck by gripping his right wrist with his left hand, thereby locking the chokehold. As Jack fell to the mat, back first with Putin on top of him, he crossed his legs around Putin's waist, driving his hips lower, thereby intensifying the pressure on his neck. Putin had no choice but to tap out.

Once again, Jack appeared stoic, but inside he was floating on air. He had just used Putin's signature chokehold to submit him; now he was just one round away from victory. He contemplated his options for round five and decided to test his physical strength by bulldogging Putin from the clinch. He had used this move successfully to pin numerous other opponents, but none of those wrestlers had anywhere near the strength of the Russian.

Putin, meanwhile, was furious. It was bad enough that Jack had humiliated him two days ago. Now he had done it again, this time with his own favorite chokehold. It was time to make this upstart pay.

He began round five by striking first, with a flying arm bar. In a flash he had a hold of Jack's left arm and had shot his own legs into the air, strategically positioning his right leg over Jack's neck and his left leg over his torso. By pushing with his legs, he now had leverage that enabled him to force Jack to the mat, with the arm bar still intact. Then he sat on the mat and pulled on Jack's arm, exerting pressure on his elbow.

Jack knew that unless he submitted now, he risked having his arm broken or severely damaged. As much as he hated to lose, especially to this savage brute, he knew there was no other option. Quickly, and demonstratively, he tapped out.

Only Putin wouldn't let go of his arm. Instead, he gave it a quick hard pull, resulting in a sickening pop that could be heard across the room.

"You piece of vermin," snarled Jim Mulligan as he pulled Putin off Jack. "That was uncalled for."

Putin said nothing, but the self-satisfied smirk on his face said everything. Jim glared at the champion in anger. He knew that the Russian was evil and sadistic, but experiencing it in person was another matter.

"Get the fuck out of here," he said.

Putin looked at Jim smugly before heading toward the locker room.

He returned a few minutes later, still pleased at the thought of Jack Cohen writhing in pain. But his smirk turned into a scowl when he saw Mary McDonald comforting his rival. As far as he was concerned, she was still on the clock, and her behavior was unacceptable. Hiding his wrath behind a cool exterior, he strode to the mat, snapped his fingers and beckoned for Mary to stand.

Mary was visibly shaken, her emotions a complete jumble. She was not one to jump for anyone; if she belonged to any man, it was Jack, not Putin — and it was Jack who needed her now. But she was under contract, and $15,000 a day was too rich for her to pass up. Quietly she grabbed her purse and followed Putin out the door.

They sat together in silence inside the limousine. There was no need for conversation, certainly not for Putin. A single thought filled his mind on the ride back to the hotel: *One down, one to go.*

* * *

Meanwhile, an hour later, Jim and Patsy were sitting with Jack outside the emergency room of a nearby hospital. Jack had already had X-rays taken; they were awaiting the results.

Several minutes later, Jack learned, to his great relief, that nothing had been broken. "My guess is that you have a partially torn ligament, which hopefully won't require surgery," the doctor reported. "I want you to ice the elbow and keep it elevated, then come back and see me tomorrow. We'll do an incision to determine the extent of the damage. The nurse will give you a prescription for a painkiller."

With that, Jack shared the good news with Patsy and Jim, and the three men headed back to the gym. "Buddy, I again want to congratulate you on your performance today," said Jim. "You were awesome. I can hardly wait until your arm is OK and we can start working on the Brazilian stuff."

"Me, too," said Jack. "I'm going to go bananas not being able to train. I'm just glad there's an Objectivist meeting tonight to take my mind off what happened today."

Jim smiled and shook his head. "Under the circumstances, buddy, I can't imagine you going."

"Oh, I'll be there," said Jack. "I'd just be sitting around anyway. I can always bring an ice pack."

"Cool," said Jim. "My twin brother, John, is visiting from Las Vegas. He'll be there. Dude is a trip. I know you think I'm pretty crazy, but this guy's off the charts."

* * *

Jim Mulligan introduced Jack to his twin, John, a few minutes before the Objectivist meeting at Brother Bill's was scheduled to start. The attendees were enjoying light snacks in the kitchen, and Jim led John and Jack into the

living room, where they could converse privately. Jack, who had a protecti\
wrap on his elbow, shook John's hand with his good arm. He was amazed a\
how much John looked and sounded like his brother. Jim's hair was longe\
and a bit more unruly, but beyond that he couldn't tell them apart.

"Yeah, we're like two peas in a pod," said John. "Except that he's an Objectivist, and I'm not; he's an atheist, and I'm not; he follows sports, and I don't, et cetera, et cetera. But we're both into the liberty movement and agree that the movement will never be successful without a brilliant, charismatic hero-type like you to champion it.

"Look at the Democratic Party, for example: Kennedy, Clinton, Obama, Martin, and now Mogambo. You're in that GQ mold — but unlike those Marxist-fascist idiots, you actually understand true liberty, and will champion it, as defined in and by the U.S. Constitution."

"Well, I know I'll get at least two votes," Jack quipped. "But, seriously, now that I'm studying the Objectivist and libertarian literature, I know that I want to devote my life to the cause of true freedom and liberty. And I'm excited about the possibility of becoming an MMA champ, and maybe an action movie star like Schwarzenegger or Bruce Lee, and then parlaying that into a political career. But that'll take a few years, so I hardly see myself as a realistic choice to champion the movement in the near or intermediate future — and at the rate things are falling apart, by the time I'm ready to make my mark in the political arena, it might be too late.

"Besides, I'm only nineteen. Even if I were to become an MMA champ and a movie star, what good would that do me today? After all, I'm just a kid. Who's gonna bother listening to me? At my age my legal options are limited. I'm barely old enough to vote."

John gazed at Jack with intense scrutiny. "Unlike my self-contracted brother," he said, pointing playfully at Jim, "I am very spiritual — and I've got to tell you, you're a very special being. I'm not talking about your physical or intellectual ability; I'm talking about your spiritual energy. I don't know if you meditate, but your aura and presence are incredible."

Jack was silent for several moments before he decided to tell John about Mother Mary and his hands. "Ordinarily, I'd dismiss what she said, except for two things: First, she's a physics professor, not some flaky fortune teller, and second, the holes in my hands disappeared like magic when I applied the

special Ayurvedic ointment she prepared for me. I don't believe in miracles, because that violates the law of causality, but I can't explain the spontaneous appearance and disappearance of the holes.

"By the way, I love that term 'self-contraction,'" Jack continued. "Did you get it from reading Adi Da's teachings?"

John was floored. "Unreal," he said. "If there's such a thing as an Avatar — if there's anyone who can champion a new Enlightenment, politically and spiritually — it's you, my friend."

Jim laughed mockingly, then quietly took his brother aside. "Before you go overboard, let me give you some facts. Our friend Jack isn't some Jesus figure; he's got a fucking ho for a girlfriend. If he's devoting himself to anything, it's becoming the baddest ass on the planet. He's what I used to be — a whoremonger/hurtmonger — which is cool by me, but no one's going to accept him as the new Jesus or Buddha. You've got to separate the religious crap from any political reformation."

"Bro, you're *almost* hopeless," sighed John. "I say 'almost' because once Jack realizes Who or What he truly is, you're going to be worshipping him."

"Hell, I already worship him," snapped Jim. "To me, he's a young, real-life John Galt with the potential to turn Objectivism into the law of the land, so to speak."

"Yes, but I meant worshipping him spiritually, entering into a sacred relationship with him so you can receive his Blessing Power, his En-Light-ening Grace."

"I know damn fucking well what you meant, John — I was just jerking your chain. But I ain't getting down on my knees for nobody, including Jack Cohen. I'll burn in hell for eternity before I worship any human being or imaginary Deity."

John laughed. He would save his brother some other day, but right now he wanted to talk to the kid. "Here's how I see it, Jack: You're going to awaken not long after you begin your spiritual *sadhana*, and within a short time after that, you'll be clear on your Dharma and your spiritual and political missions. It won't matter that you're not 'pure' in the conventional sense, because you can push the tantric ideal. That way you'll kill two birds with one stone: You'll free America from its puritanical bullshit (so no one can call you a hypocrite for banging one ho after another), plus you can market yourself as the 'saint'

or 'good guy' of MMA, in that you're doing a public service by kicking the asses of tatted-up dregs, like my brother here."

Jim gave his brother the finger. John smiled and did the same.

For his part, Jack appreciated the playful banter, but he wanted assurance that the truth about Mary stay between the three of them. "First of all I'm not a whoremonger — I had no idea Mary was an escort until I became involved with her, and I hope you'll keep that to yourself, as your brother, Jim, has promised. More to the point, I have no interest in sleeping with endless women. I love the two girlfriends I have now, and I don't want or need any more women in my life.

"Second, I'm no 'hurtmonger,' either. I'll compete in MMA because I love the sport and the competition, but I don't want to hurt anyone, except maybe Sergei Putin. Nor do I have any plans for 'marketing myself' or creating any kind of public image; I'm only interested in being myself. If the public can't deal with the real me, then screw them."

John shook Jack's hand with utmost respect. "All I can say is that you're way smarter than us. You're the Man. Just do your own thing, and we'll jump on your bandwagon."

"Yeah, Jack," cracked Jim, "you're way smarter than us, particularly my brother. Rand despised neologisms, and John here has new ones for me every time we're together. 'Self-contraction'? Gimme a fuckin' break; no wonder you couldn't cut it as an Objectivist."

"Jim, my boy, 'self-contraction' is a term coined by the late guru Adi Da," said John with a knowing smile. "It means the ego, the separate-self sensation caused by the avoidance of relationship to the Deity, whose very existence you deny. Instead you worship the ego, which is just a knot, a clenched fist in the midst of Infinity, caused by your ever-grasping 'rational' mind. But, you being a card-carrying Randroid, I expect you to disparage any apropos anti-ego term as a superfluous neologism."

Knowing that Mother Mary was a devotee of Adi Da's Daism, Jack was eager to get together with John to discuss spirituality. He suggested dinner Sunday night at Garibaldi's, one of his favorite haunts.

"Sounds good," said John. "Here's my business card, in case you need to call me."

Jack took the card and noticed that it said MAGICIAN. When he asked the obvious question ("Do you work in one of the Vegas casinos?"), the brothers Mulligan howled with laughter.

"What am I missing?" asked Jack.

"Booyah," said Jim, "my brother is a magician because he makes people *disappear*. From a left-wing perspective, he's a population control specialist. From a right-wing, or Darwinian, perspective, he's a professional herd thinner. Capiche?"

Jack paused for a moment. *If he does for a living what I think he does for a living, then my life is stranger than fiction.* "So you're saying that John is a professional hit man *and* a cannibal, who sometimes eats the guys he offs."

"You got that right, buddy." Then he shot John a look of mock contempt as he added, "And you have the nerve to call *me* unspiritual."

Jim thought that was funny as hell, but John could see that Jack was disturbed. For a moment, he regretted letting Jack in on his secret, though he suspected the truth would have come out anyway. He put his arm around the boy's shoulder. "Hey, I know what I do sounds ugly, brutal, and inhumane — but you don't know the whole story, the full context. I'll fill you in on Sunday."

Jack noticed that Brother Bill was about to call the meeting to order. "Let's grab a seat," he said. Whatever explanation John had for him, it had to be a doozy.

● ● ●

Bill began the meeting by introducing the two new attendees: John Mulligan, and a woman named Margaret. A recent transplant to the D.C. area, Margaret wore her hair in a bun, while her rimless glasses and librarian's demeanor made it seem like she had no sense of humor.

"Let's start by seeing if Jack did his homework," said Bill. "You were given three books to read: *Capitalism: The Unknown ideal*, *Introduction to Objectivist Epistemology*, and Leonard Peikoff's *Objectivism: The Philosophy of Ayn Rand*. Were you able to absorb and thoroughly understand the material in these books? If so, what are your thoughts?"

"Yes, I have, and I'm completely clear on Rand's philosophy," Jack said without hesitation.

"Oh, come on!" snapped Margaret. "There is no way anyone could completely absorb and understand Rand's philosophy in a week. I understand you're very bright, Mr. Cohen, but where is your humility?"

"Humility is not an Objectivist virtue," said Paul, the plastic surgeon. "If you've studied Rand, you should know that."

"Besides," added John, "the spiritual master Adi Da has a great definition of humility."

"And what would that be?" asked Margaret, peering through her glasses.

"Humility," replied John, "is a small penis."

Even Margaret got a laugh out of that one.

In the meantime Orson, mindful that Margaret was new in town, took advantage of the opportunity to fill her in on Jack's background: how he'd skipped two grades in school, never got less than an A in high school or college, and received many national awards for his academic and athletic achievements. "Ma'am, Jack really is a genius," he said. "Google his name, and you'll find endless articles about his almost endless achievements. If anyone can master Rand's philosophy in a week, it's him. "

"That's a very impressive litany," said Margaret. "But I want to see how much he really knows about Objectivism. If indeed he is a genius, he should have some profound insights to offer us on Rand's philosophy."

Knowing that all ears were on him, Jack cleared his throat and began to speak: "First, I want to say that I love Ayn Rand's philosophy and that I've never read anything like it before. I've taken several philosophy classes at State U, so I'm familiar with the writings of most of the big-name Western philosophers. But none of these men was able to create an integral, real-world philosophical system like Rand's. Rand is a system builder par excellence, and though her system, or hierarchy, is flawed in some respects, it provides a brilliant, quasi-comprehensive framework for understanding and interacting with reality.

"Before I discuss the flaws I perceive in Rand's philosophy, I want to talk about the positive ways her philosophy has enlightened me. First off, the five-branch schema she uses to frame her philosophical system — metaphysics, epistemology, ethics, politics, esthetics — is exemplary; if I ever create my own philosophical system, I'll include the same branches. Second, Rand's Objectivist epistemology, regardless of its flaws, is outstanding and has already provided me with numerous insights. And I'm sure in the future it will provide me with many more. Rand's identification of existence, identity, and consciousness as the fundamental philosophic axioms is, in my opinion, monumental. Prior to reading Rand, I had never thought of using axioms as the base of my philosophical thinking, but now, thanks to her, I'm even applying these three axioms to my understanding and investigation of esoteric spiritual life. Perhaps the most intriguing aspect of Rand's philosophy is her theory of concept-formation. No doubt there are glitches in her theory — and I plan on reading the books that focus on them — but this doesn't alter the fact that her theory is an ingenious one, which has enabled me to better understand how man forms concepts, acquires knowledge, and validates that knowledge."

He paused, took a sip of water, and proceeded to discuss Rand's ethics and politics. "I already knew about Rand's apotheosis of selfishness before I read her books," he said. "Now that I've read them, though, I have a deeper, more nuanced understanding of the ethics of rational egoism and the pseudo-ethics of its antipode, altruism. But Rand's equation of egoism with morality has implications beyond ethics, because once it is understood that egoism is the only rational morality, then it naturally follows that capitalism — egoism extended to the marketplace via the trader principle — is the only rational and moral socio-economic system. This direct connection between morality and capitalism was a revelation to me, and though I was already an advocate of laissez-faire capitalism, Rand provided me with what I lacked: the logical moral basis for my politics. Prior to reading Rand, I thought of capitalism as just an economic system... but thanks to her, I now understand it as essentially a social system of voluntary exchange between two or more parties.

"The last branch of Rand's hierarchy is esthetics," Jack continued. "To be honest, prior to reading Rand I really hadn't given art much thought from a philosophical perspective. I didn't even have a clear definition of art in my head. But Rand's concise definition of art — 'the selective re-creation of reality according to one's metaphysical value-judgments' — crystallized my thinking about the nature of artistic creativity."

He concluded his comments by praising Rand for her succinct and illuminating definitions, all of which enabled him to clearly grasp the essential meaning of such key concepts as capitalism, art, fascism, and collectivism. "Prior to reading Rand, my definitions of many important political terms were vague and nebulous — and I'm a political science major!" he said selfdepreciatively. "But now, thanks to Rand, I've become clear on the essential meaning of all the 'isms' — and when I discuss politics, I now have an objective, clearly defined basis for my considerations. I also appreciate the way Rand frames certain political 'isms' as clear-cut poles. For example, she presents the fundamental political choices as individualism versus statism, and capitalism versus socialism. Although Rand wasn't a Hegelian dialectical thinker, my philosophic approach will be to make use of these antipodes to arrive at a creative synthesis.

"Oh, yes, one final thing," he added. "I was enlightened by Rand's emphasis on the American system as a constitutional republic, for it made me realize that America is firstly a constitutional republic and only secondarily a democracy. In a constitutional republic, the majority, via the democratic process, cannot vote away the inviolable, constitutionally guaranteed individual rights of its citizens. But because Americans have been brainwashed to believe in the primacy of democracy (majority rule) over the rights of the individual, we see these rights consistently voted away.

"After I read Rand, I realized that Washington politicians, including Republicans, almost always refer to America as a democracy, and almost never as a republic. America forever seeks to 'make the world safe for democracy,' but has no interest in promoting the ideals of a republic. After grasping Rand's take on the totalitarian nature of democracy, I came across a pithy description of the democratic process on the web: 'Democracy is two wolves and a sheep deciding on what to have for dinner.'"

He glanced across the room to see if there were questions or comments. To no surprise, Margaret's hand immediately went up. "Ask away, ma'am," he smiled engagingly. "I promise I'll do my *humble* best to answer."

"I just want to apologize for doubting you," she replied. "That was a superb presentation for a nineteen-year-old who has only been studying Rand for a week. My only question is, When are you changing your name to John Galt?"

With that the entire group broke into laughter.

"I appreciate that, Margaret, but you've only heard the good about Objectivism," said Jack. "You might change your tune after you hear the bad. Unfortunately, there's no way I could ever be an Objectivist, because a card-carrying Objectivist has to accept Rand's philosophy in toto — and I could never do that."

"Then I suppose the real question," said Brother Bill, injecting himself into the conversation, "is whether Objectivism is really a closed system, as Rand and her protégé, Leonard Peikoff, see it, or an open-ended philosophy that can evolve beyond its founder's doctrine."

"Yes, you could put it like that," said Jack.

"Then let me answer it for you," said Bill. "The Ayn Rand Institute (ARI), the main, quasi-official Objectivist organization that Leonard Peikoff founded, is, understandably, adamant about protecting the integrity of Rand's philosophy. Consequently, they are rather parochial, contra any revision of her philosophy. But another prominent Objectivist organization, the Atlas Society, argues that for Objectivism to evolve, it must be an open-ended philosophy. Anyone interested in this debate should read David Kelley's book *The Contested Legacy of Ayn Rand: Truth and Toleration in Objectivism*. I personally side with Kelley, but have no problem with ARI's orthodox stance.

"I keep my Objectivist group small and informal because, like you, I don't embrace Rand's philosophy in toto," Bill continued. "As you've seen for yourself, Jack, I welcome intelligent criticism and reasoned dissent at my meetings. In fact, a couple of the regulars here are anarcho-capitalists, and they'd probably be shown the door at an orthodox Objectivist group. Although I don't subscribe to anarcho-capitalism and other aspects of libertarianism, I don't mind these individuals spicing up our meetings with their provocative anti-statist arguments."

Again, Jack paused for questions and comments; this time there were no takers. That being the case, he presented his assessment of the flip side of Rand's philosophy. Beginning with Rand's metaphysics, he told the group that he found the author guilty of concept-stealing relative to the term "metaphysics."

"*Meta* means beyond, so metaphysics refers to that which is beyond the physical," Jack explained. "But Rand delimits the metaphysical, reducing it to manifest existence — the physical. She *assumes* that there is nothing beyond manifestation, though she has no explanation for how existence came to exist. Hers and Peikoff's anti-Deity arguments pertain only to a creator-God, not to an acausal Being, or transcendental Existent, outside time and space. In fact, some physicists who specialize in quantum mechanics, including the renowned theoretical physicist Bernard d' Espagnat, postulate the existence of a hypercosmic God outside the physical universe.

"Secondly, Rand and Peikoff don't even consider the arguments and claims of the greatest spiritual gurus relative to this Being. These gurus aren't interested in convincing us that such a God exists; they are interested in providing us with a method, or yoga, for realizing it ourselves. In other words, the proof of the existence of such a Being becomes self-evident to a yogi, a spiritual mystic who can unite his being with the transcendental Being, the unmanifest Existent."

Jack then pointed out how his involvement with Bill's group and Objectivism happened to coincide with his newfound interest in yoga philosophy, thanks to his meeting with Mother Mary. "It's hard to imagine, but I met both Bill and Mother Mary within hours of each other, on the same night, one week ago today," he said. "Although I've just begun to attempt to integrate (or perhaps I should say reconcile) Objectivism with yoga and esoteric spiritual philosophy, I feel like I'm already well on my way — and once I start practicing yoga next week, when my guru initiates me, I should be able to 'seal the deal' and put it all together."

At that moment Jack noticed that his cell phone had been vibrating. Being all of nineteen years old, he was tempted to pick it up and at least find out who was calling. But this discussion was far too absorbing to interrupt. Whoever was trying to reach him would simply have to wait.

"You know, it's funny," Jack continued. "If someone had asked me about my religion a week ago, I'd have said I was an atheist. But now, after having read ten great esoteric spiritual texts since Saturday, I'm convinced there is a divine Being, or absolute Existence, that underlies and transcends relative existence. But the spiritual masters I'm reading couldn't care less if you believe in this divine Being, or Consciousness-Power; their only interest is in having you yogically, or ontically, *realize* your essential oneness with It."

He was about to move on to Rand's epistemology when again Brother Bill interceded. "I can see right now, Jack, that we need to delimit your critique of Objectivism to one branch of Rand's philosophy at a time," he began. "Your commentary on metaphysics has raised a number of questions. Let me ask the first one: You describe this divine Being as acausal, as a non-creator God. If this is the case, how do you explain creation? In other words, how did a dynamic space-time manifestation, the universe, arise from, or within, this static, spaceless, timeless, unmanifest Existent?"

"No one can definitively answer that question," Jack replied without hesitation. "Even the great spiritual masters, those who dwell in the unmanifest Absolute, are reduced to cosmological speculation relative to creation. Kashmir Shaivism's model of universal manifestation — which postulates that the divine Existent (God, or Siva), simply willed creation for His own sport, rolling the universe out as a 'dance' — makes the most sense to me. (Science, of course, would relate this to the Big Bang.) As such, the universe, or manifest existence, is a derivative of God (the unmanifest Existent), who does not interfere with His emanation. God is the Immeasurable (Existent), and the universe is what has been measured out from Him. According to Shaivism's paradigm, the universe was not created ex nihilo, but rather out of God's essence (or 'Substance'), which is Consciousness Itself."

"Yes, but consciousness without content, an object to be aware of, is a contradiction in terms," replied Brother Bill. "Rand herself makes that clear. So what is God conscious of?"

"God (or Siva) is Self-Existing, Self-Radiant Self-Awareness," Jack immediately responded. "He is aware of Himself via his own Spirit (or Shakti, or Light-energy, or reflective Radiance). Hence, his Self-Awareness is dyadic, or intradeical, in nature, rather than dualistic. As Rand says, 'spiritual' means pertaining to consciousness.

"But Rand's definition of spiritual is somewhat vague. More precisely, spiritual means the *energy* of consciousness. In other words, every state of consciousness has a corresponding energy. The energy that corresponds with God's 'State' of Consciousness is pure (or uncreated) Light-energy (or absolute vibratory Intensity). This Light-energy (or Spirit-force, or Vibration) 'crystallized' into stepped-down, progressively denser forms of energy and matter in the process of creation — and this is what physics studies. But true metaphysics, not Rand's idea of metaphysics, is the study of divine Consciousness and its uncreated Light-energy."

"Jack, I've got it hand it to you," said Brother Bill in amazement. "That is a fascinating and sophisticated theory of creation — the fact that I think it's complete hogwash is beside the point. What astounds me most is how much you've mastered Objectivism and Eastern philosophy in only one week's time. If I didn't know better, I'd swear you were already a professor."

"Hear, hear!" exclaimed John Mulligan. "This kid is not from this world.

I've been deeply involved in Eastern spirituality for years, and I can tell you for a fact, he is not just brilliant, he is the Avatar. His energy field is off the charts, and he hasn't even started meditating. Because you're all Randroids, self-contracted atheists, you can't even begin to comprehend his true status."

That silenced the room for a moment. No one was sure how to respond to John's outrageous declaration.

"Please excuse my pathetic brother and his mystical hokum," said Jim, breaking the tension. "It's too late to save him from his kooky ideas, but hopefully we can save Jack and get him off this tangent." Then he turned his attention to Bill. "I don't know how you can say that Jack has mastered Objectivism. If he had, he wouldn't be buying into the idea of a floating abstraction like God. As most of you know, since God cannot be proven, any talk about a divine Being, whether inside or outside the universe, must be classified as the arbitrary — which Rand says is worse than the false. So unless we straighten Jack out now, he'll end up as one of those libertarian anarcho-capitalist whack job deists, like my brother."

"Oh, but I think Jack presents us with a unique opportunity," countered Bill. "I don't want to censor him and simply dismiss his arguments without considering them rationally first. If we really want to convince him of the folly of mysticism, we must do so through intelligent debate — and besides, it's not as though we're dealing with some dumbass Bible thumper off the street. Jack is a super-profound young man who is going to present highly esoteric spiritual arguments. I don't know about the rest of you, but I look forward to this challenge... and knowing Jack as I've come to know him, I imagine he, too, looks forward to considering the atheist arguments of the group."

Jack found this all amusing; after all, it had only been a week since he himself was an atheist. "The *theory* is secondary to me," he said. "What matters is the *practice*. I have zero interest in any kind of blind belief. All I'm doing at this point is regurgitating the stuff I've read. But I can't believe that all the great yogis and mystics throughout history were just making up their experiences and manufacturing their insights relative to spiritual life."

Again Jack's cell phone began to vibrate. Again he chose to ignore it.

"All mystical or spiritual experiences are based on emotions, subjective feelings," said Raymond, a long-time attendee of Bill's group who made his living as an attorney. "These emotions or feelings reflect one's metaphysical value-judgments. There is no objective tangible God or great divine Object that one can point to. Hence, all 'spiritual' experiences pertain to an imaginary, subjective God, and all such experiences are therefore irrational, with no basis in objective reality.

"When Ayn Rand met William F. Buckley for the first time, she said, 'You are too intelligent to believe in God.' And I say that to you, Mr. Cohen."

"Albert Einstein and Isaac Newton believed in God," Jack replied. "I guess they also were too 'intelligent.' To minds like Einstein, Newton, Thoreau, and Emerson, the cosmos, the intelligible, harmoniously ordered universe, reflects the craftsmanship of an Absolute Mind, a Divine Intelligence. How could mind evolve from matter? Unless there was teleological Intelligence, a divine spark, embedded in matter, it's next to impossible.

"As a matter of fact, counselor, contrary to what you say, Divine (or Holy) Communion is *not* irrational, but rather *trans-rational*. The continuum is pre-rational, rational, trans-rational. But to worshippers of the rational mind such as yourself, acknowledgement of the existence of a Higher Power is tantamount to apostasy. Divine (or mystical) Communion is not, as you assert, based on subjective emotions or feelings — it is, in fact, trans-psychological, devoid of emotive associations. What an 'initiated' (or Spirit-baptized) mystic experiences is the Spirit Itself, the *objective* Light-energetic and Bliss-inducing dimension of God, or Ultimate Reality. When Divine Communion morphs into Divine Union and the mystic realizes his transpersonal *identity* as inseparable from the Deity, then his experience is perfectly 'Subjective' (transcending the subject-object dichotomy). The now Self-realized mystic (or yogi) abides in, and *as*, the Divine, and as a 'God-man,' his permanent 'State' (really non-state, or *Being-ness*) is that of Self-Existing, Self-Radiant, Self-Awareness."

John Mulligan gave Jack a standing ovation. "Fucking A! It's impossible to say it any better. Now all Jack has to do is to realize that State, and all you Rand-worshipping atheists will be groveling at his feet to get a taste of his Bliss-bestowing Shakti."

Jim could only shake his head. "This is just a temporary phase; he'll be an atheist again by this time next week," he said. "You've been meditating for twenty years, John, and you're the exact same asshole you've always been. But Jack's too smart to waste twenty years, let alone twenty days, meditating on a Deity that doesn't exist. He may talk the talk right now, but he won't be walking the walk."

Others began to grumble aloud, but Bill quickly restored order. "I don't see the social value of your esoteric mysticism," he said to Jack. "Since the God-man's state is only Self-evident to the God-man himself, it's hard to sell mysticism to the masses who can't grasp, let alone practice, what you're preaching.

"Moreover, what has this mysticism ever produced on a practical level? What great discoveries or inventions can be attributed to these 'sages'? I don't doubt that mystics tap into some form of bio-energy that quiets their minds and enables them to experience bliss — but that hardly equates to 'God-realization.' If these mystics and yogis were truly God-realized and in a constant state of 'super-consciousness,' you'd think that we'd see dramatic positive evidence of this on this 'gross plane' of worldly existence... but we don't. Instead, we see moralistic, mass-murdering religions created in their names. How many millions of people have died as a result of the Christianity that stemmed from Jesus and the Islam that followed Mohammed?

"That being said, for the sake of rational discourse I encourage you to give mysticism a try," Bill continued. "I'm sure everybody here will be interested in seeing where that takes you."

"I'm not blind to what you're saying about mysticism, Brother Bill, and I agree that the only way to find out for myself is to give it a shot," said Jack. "But in defense of the great sages, such as the Buddha and Ramana Maharshi, it's absolutely clear to me that they were Self-realized masters who radiated unshakeable peace and helped enlighten others.

"But you're right about the negative social consequences of religion — and if I do become Enlightened, my mission will be to remedy this by instigating a new Age of Enlightenment. I would combine aspects of Objectivism and libertarian politics with true spirituality that the masses can understand and practice."

With that Brother Bill called for a quick recess, which Jack took advantage of to check the messages on his cell phone. There were several texts, and one frantic voicemail, all from Mary McDonald: *Jack... help me... please.*

Her voice was as frightened as any he'd ever heard. Knowing she'd been alone with Putin — and knowing first-hand how vengeful Putin was — Jack could only fear the worst. He made his excuses to the rest of the group and raced across town to her side.

. . .

Jack called Mary the moment he was in his car. She was on her way home from the hospital; Sergei Putin had beaten her up. "Are you all right?" he asked.

"Yeah," she said. "My face is black and blue and swollen, but they told me that nothing is broken. I'm just a little sore right now, and more than a little shaken. Can you come over right away? I really need you."

"Of course, I will, honey. I'll be there as soon as I can."

Hate and anger raced through Jack's mind as he ended the call — hate for Putin, anger at himself. If only he had picked up the phone earlier. Then maybe, just maybe, he could have reached Mary in time and saved her from any harm.

As for Putin, he could not wait to get his hands on that son of a bitch again. He imagined himself in the Octagon, pounding the bastard's face into a bloody pulp before decapitating him with one last monstrous blow.

The sight of a headless Putin amused Jack, but also disturbed him. Perhaps Mary had influenced him more than he realized. Or perhaps he was thinking sadistic thoughts simply because she was on his mind. He wondered if these malicious reveries were the harbinger of a new Jack Cohen, or just a temporary aberration.

Regardless, he made a decision right then that would change the course of his life: He would drop out of school and concentrate full time on his training. Once his arm healed, he could build his body even faster, and take down that monster even sooner.

. . .

Traffic was light that night, and Jack was at Mary's house in less than ten minutes. By the time he arrived, her car was already in the driveway. When she opened the door, he winced at the sight of her, but she didn't seem to notice or care. "Oh, Jack, I'm so glad to see you," she beamed.

"I am, too," he said. They kissed, they embraced, they kissed again. Then he examined the damage to her face. Her nose had been bloodied, while the bruises around her cheekbones and upper body were noticeable. Putin had struck her just enough times to leave a message without causing any real injury. It was the kind of beating that people in the movies call a "professional job."

78

"Tell me what happened," said Jack.

"It was all very sudden," she began. "Out of the blue he began to slap me around. I didn't do anything to provoke it."

"He knows you and I are together," said Jack. "That's provocation enough. What else did he do?"

"He shoved me around a lot — I remember that," she continued. "Then when he realized I was trying to reach you, he really went insane. He gave me a bloody nose and then started paddling me. That was weird. He kept slapping my butt with his hand until I started to bleed. I took a Vicodin a while ago, but it's still red and swollen back there. I bolted from his hotel room as quickly as I could and headed straight for the hospital."

"Have you called the police?"

"Baby, you know I can't do that — that would expose me as a prostitute and mean the end of my business. Besides, if his Russian backers were to find out, they'd make sure I had an 'accident' and permanently disappeared."

That thought made Mary even more depressed. She decided to change the subject. "How's your arm? Is it broken?"

"Nah, it's fine," said Jack. "Doctor says it's probably just a partially torn ligament. It could have been a lot worse."

"Yeah, for both of us," said Mary. Then she began fretting about her looks. "I hate to be so self-conscious. I feel so ugly in front of you. Can you still love me like this?"

Jack couldn't help but chuckle. Mary McDonald was many things, but self-conscious was not one of them.

"I'll love you no matter how you look," he said with affection. "You are living proof that beauty is more than skin deep." Then he pulled her closer to him, firmly but gently, so as not to bruise her further. "As a matter of fact, you look hot to me right now, and I'm not putting you on." Then he took her in his arms and kissed her deeply.

That brightened Mary's spirits considerably, to the point where she began feeling naughty. She slipped her hand down the front of his pants and slid it across his cock, giggling playfully while massaging it ever so slowly. "Oooh," she said teasingly. "It's so stiff, I'm afraid I'm going to break it."

"Better you than Putin," said Jack, moaning happily.

She continued stroking him until he was about to spasm. Then she removed her hand from his pants, led him upstairs and told him to take her to bed.

• • •

When Jack awoke the next morning, Mary was busy in the kitchen. "You're just in time," she said, adjusting the ties of her robe. "I'm about to make you a double shot of organic espresso. I ordered freshly roasted beans from the Barista Coffee Company in Carmel and had them flown here overnight."

That sounded inviting, but Jack was even more captivated by the smell wafting in the air. "Did you make brownies?" he asked.

"I did," she said. "Organic chocolate brownies. My own recipe."

She bent over and removed a plate of hot, gooey, fudgy squares from the oven. "They'll be ready to eat in a minute."

Taking in the aroma, Jack recognized another scent, and it wasn't baked chocolate. "Your own recipe?" he said with a shit-eating grin. "Would that include... marijuana?"

Mary threw her hands on her hips in mock exasperation. "Oh, Jack, you're just too sharp for me — I tried to sneak it by you, but you caught me red-handed. What on earth are you going to do?" She smiled impishly and awaited his response.

"Well, you know if I was in training, I couldn't touch this stuff," he said. "But now that I'm out of commission for a while, I can do whatever I want!" Then he picked up a brownie and popped it in his mouth.

"Yum-mie!" exclaimed Mary as she sidled next to him. They scarfed down the brownies in record time, even as they fondled each other.

After a while he asked her about Putin. "I've been told that he's cleaner than me, a real health nut. Did he get stoned with you?"

Mary threw back her head and began laughing hysterically. It was against her business ethics to disclose information about her clients, but in light of what Putin did to her, she was happy to make an exception. "That dude is a serious doper," she said. "He loves doing amyl nitrate, 'poppers,' to increase the intensity of his orgasms. And he's on HGH and steroids — in fact, I'm amazed you fought him almost even, given the PEDs he was on. Take him off the drugs, and you'd kick his ass for sure."

"Wow," said Jack. "That certainly explains his fits of rage, with me and with you."

"Yeah," said Mary as she lit a cigarette. "I don't know if they have drug testing in MMA, but if they do, he's probably beating it with state-of-the-art masking agents provided by the top Russian chemists. He even had me inject steroids in his ass at the same time he did the poppers. He's a very kinky guy."

"Unreal," said Jack. "Absolutely unreal. So how was he up until the time he beat you? Was he a nice guy or an asshole?"

"A complete asshole," said Mary. "He never even pretended to be nice. He knew you're my boyfriend, and hurting me was another way of hurting you."

"I hear you on that," Jack nodded. "Did he say anything about me?"

"Oh, yeah, baby. He said you were the toughest opponent he'd ever faced, and that once you got more experience, you'd be a real threat to his crown." She took a deep drag from her cigarette and blew out perfectly formed smoke rings. "He also said he wants to kill you when you fight him for the title, and that he'll have a 'real surprise' for you when you get in the Octagon with him. I don't know what that means. Are you afraid?"

This time Jack laughed hysterically. "He's the one who should be afraid, because I'm going to dismantle him." Then he told Mary of his vision of the fight and his decision to drop out of school.

"I'm going to be an absolute beast by the time we meet again," he said with quiet confidence. "He can shoot all the 'roids up his ass he wants, and I'll still grind him into dust. He threw down the gauntlet with what he did to you and me. Now he's going to pay."

"Bravo, my man," Mary applauded. "Bravo! I want to be there to watch him get hammered. And right before you knock off his *cabeza*, I want you to say, 'This one's for Mary.'" Then she leaned in and gave him a big wet kiss.

Jack made himself another espresso as he discussed his future plans. "Tomorrow I'm going to meet with my dad and confront him on the Fed," he said. "After reading the books Jim Mulligan gave me and researching the subject, I'm now convinced that the Fed is the biggest scam in history, and I can't imagine what my dad can say that will make me believe otherwise.

"I look at our crumbling economy — schools and businesses closing, the unemployment rate soaring, the dollar tanking, and the disparity between the rich and poor greater than ever — and it couldn't be clearer to me that all of this stems from the long-time machinations of the Fed, now coming home to roost... I'm thinking of issuing my dad an ultimatum tomorrow: either he quits the Fed and publicly denounces them, or I will disown him as my father."

Knowing Mary to be a radical in every sense of the word, he figured she'd agree with him. When she shook her head vehemently, he could not have been more surprised. "Jack, you can't disown your father — he's the only family you have left," she reprimanded him. "I wish I still had a parent. You can criticize him and make suggestions, but you can't dump him!"

"I appreciate your concern, but if you read those books yourself, I believe you'd think differently," Jack replied. "My father is no different than a Mafia boss. If your father was a Mafia boss, would you be loyal to him?"

Mary thought for a moment and saw Jack's point. But cutting off ties with one's father, especially one as wealthy as Jeremiah Cohen, had other ramifications. "Jack, I love that you're headstrong, but you need to think this out," she said. "You're nineteen years old. Your father is worth thirty million dollars. How are you going to support yourself if you walk away from that?"

"I don't need or want his money, if that's what you're implying," he countered. "Now that I'm quitting school, I'll start my professional career as a martial artist and support myself. And, besides, Mary, if I need to borrow some money for a while, I know plenty of people who would be willing to help me out."

"You can count me among them," she smiled sweetly. "If you ever needed money, I wouldn't loan it to you, I'd just give it to you... no strings attached." Then, realizing what she'd just said, she broke into a mischievous grin. "Well, maybe no strings, but I would have to strap you down once in a while!"

They laughed as she kissed his cheek and drew her arms around him. Realizing that Jack was tense — and not wanting to kill the buzz they were enjoying from ingesting all that cannibas — she took him into the living room and laid him on the massage table. She took off his pants and shirt and dug her fingers into him, soothing the muscles of his back, legs and arms with her skillful touch.

After a while he asked for a glass of orange juice. She brought it to him right away and he drank it in one gulp. Then he turned over, resting on his back with his hands clasped behind his head. He was still deeply stoned, and loving it. "This is more intense than smoking it," he said. "I'm totally shit-faced and can't wipe the grin off my face."

"That grin will disappear as soon as you pass out from the sedative I put in your orange juice," Mary giggled impishly. "Then I'll transport you to the dungeon and lock you down!"

Once again Jack found himself between arousal and apprehension. He believed that she was just fucking with him, but with Mary McDonald one could never be sure. As much as he enjoyed her dominatrix persona, he couldn't help but fear what she might do to him in one of her wild and crazy states. He decided to call Polly and let her know where he was.

Polly answered on the first ring. When he didn't come home the previous night, she suspected he was at Mary's, but it was still a relief to hear from him. He filled her in on all the details of Friday before Mary snatched his phone. "Polly, I really appreciate your letting me share Jack with you," she said. "I'd really like to meet you. Why don't you and Jack come over on Tuesday? We can swim in my pool, relax in my Jacuzzi, and maybe do some LSD. We'll have a really good time."

Polly wasn't sure about the LSD part, but she wasn't about to pass up a chance to meet the mysterious Mary. "I think that sounds like fun," she said. "I can't wait to meet you, too."

Mary handed back the phone so Jack could say goodbye. Then she turned him over, removed his shorts and began to knead his back. "Oh, yes, we're gonna have a good time, Jackie Poo," she rhapsodized. "We'll drop acid and do a ménage a trois. Polly will no longer be Pollyanna after I teach her some of the tricks of my trade. I'll turn her into a bad girl like me, and then you won't have one dangerous bitch to deal with... you'll have two."

Still heavily stoned, Jack chuckled at the thought — but only for a moment. Suddenly his head exploded, and he immediately knew why: Mary was shoving a dildo up his ass. The extreme pressure caused him to grimace in pain. When he tried to resist, she clamped her hand over the back of his head and securely held him in place.

"Relax, baby," she commanded him. "The pain will turn into pleasure when I turn you onto your side and suck you."

Her eyes turned white. Clearly she was enjoying this. "Once you explode, I'm going to give you a double enema," she continued. "Then you will finally, *fully* understand that your ass is mine — all mine!"

Reluctantly he did her bidding and rolled onto his side. Mary massaged his balls and dildoed his ass while deep-throating his cock. Unable to resist the intense, multi-pronged stimulation, he quickly came in her mouth.

She swirled his cream around her lips and tongue before swallowing it in an exaggerated gulp. "Mmm mmm good, mmm mmm good, Jackie Poo's 'soup' is mmm mmm good," she sang. Then they laughed with delight as she freed him from the vibrator.

Now that she owned Jack's ass, Mary McDonald decided to kick it — at least, figuratively speaking. She paraded him into her game room and racked the pool table. Playing with intense focus, she almost ran the table, leaving just two balls.

"You're lucky I left you with two balls tonight, Jackie Poo," she said as her nostrils flared. "The next time we meet, I'll cut them both off and turn you into my eunuch slave."

They playfully exchanged high fives, and Jack knocked in the two remaining balls. While he racked the table for the next game, Mary humored him with a little joke: "An American couple went to a bullfight in Spain. After the bullfight, they headed to an exclusive restaurant next to the bull ring and ordered the house special: meat balls. The meal was so exquisite, the couple returned to the restaurant the following night and ordered it again. When they finished dining, the waiter asked them how their meal was. The husband replied, 'Not so good. Last night, the meat balls were big and juicy, but tonight they were small and tough.' The waiter smiled. 'Señor, the bull, he does not always lose.'"

Jack let out a loud guffaw as he proceeded to break the rack. Two balls found a pocket, and once again he ran the table.

Mary McDonald was impressed. She had made herself a small fortune luring clients into the billiards room and suckering them into wagers. No man had ever defeated her at her table... until now. "I had no idea you were that good, Jack," she cooed. "I think I may have met my match."

"I wouldn't say you've met your match," said Jack. "More like you've met your master."

He asked if she was up for a friendly wager. "You got it, buster!" she said with determination. "Best of five games. If I win, you owe me both your balls. If you win, you walk out of here with your gonads intact."

They laughed, they kissed, and then they shook hands. The game was on, but not for long, as Jack ran the table three games in a row.

All Mary could do was shake her head and bow to his greatness. "Jack, you're a pro-level player," she said. "How did you get so fucking good?"

"Practice," he said. "I grew up with a table. I played for hours every day and won all kinds of junior tournaments. But then I got bored with the game and started concentrating on wrestling."

Then he put down his pool cue and clutched her in his arms. "But I can still put the *ball in the hole* with the best of them," he said with a wink. "And if we go to your bedroom now, I'll prove it."

Mary playfully slapped at his balls before hurrying him upstairs. The first thing he noticed was the large wooden paddle on her bed. Before he had a chance to ask, she picked it up and explained its function.

"You've been a bad boy, Jackie Poo," she cooed. "Here I've been a gracious hostess, and you didn't even have the courtesy to let me win a single game of pool. If that isn't the epitome of rudeness, I don't know what is."

She playfully tapped her open hand with the paddle before continuing. "Consequently, I am going to spank you until your ass is black and blue," she said seductively. "It is often said that a great pool player is the sign of a misspent childhood. Clearly, you did not receive the proper discipline and punishment that a child needs. Now I'm going to remedy that."

She slid her fingertips along the edge of the paddle. "You managed to pass Dildo 101," she said. "If you can pass Pooper Paddle 101, you will be sufficiently psychologically healed to move on to Double Enema 101."

Jack kept a straight face for as long as he could before finally breaking into laughter. This girl was way too much.

He spun her around and removed her robe, exposing her black and blue derriere. "Very impressive, Dr. McDonald. I can see that you practice what you preach. No wonder you're so well adjusted."

Playfully she slapped his face before melting into his arms. They rolled onto the bed, made love for hours, and fell asleep in each other's arms.

● ● ●

Sunday morning Jack awoke at the crack of dawn. Being indoors all day had made him a little stir-crazy. Quietly he dressed himself and went for a walk while Mary remained asleep.

He decided to explore the canyon adjacent to her property. Hiking down the steep path, he tripped over a rock and tumbled headfirst into the thick bushes to the side of the trail. Fortunately, he was not hurt; the dense shrubbery cushioned his fall. But as he collected himself, he couldn't but notice the grisly object at the base of the thicket — a human skeleton, minus the skull, that appeared to have been picked clean! Fueled with morbid curiosity, he combed the immediate area for more human remains, but found none. He carefully gathered the bones in his arms and headed back to Mary's.

He found her on her patio, smoking a cigarette. She wore a white oversized shirt that covered her bruises and thigh-high snakeskin boots that spoke dominatrix. Her heart raced the moment she realized what he was carrying. *This is not good*, she thought. *This is not good at all.*

"Honey, look what I found in the canyon," said Jack with excitement.

She took an extra deep drag and averted his gaze as he showed her the headless skeleton. "My goodness," she said, collecting herself. "That must be the remains of an Indian. The Iroquois used to inhabit this area... or so I've been told."

She went inside to get some tools and a large trash bag. Then she helped him put the remains into the bag and brought them into the house. "One of my clients is a paleontology professor," she volunteered. "He'll be able to date the skeleton and determine if it's an Iroquois."

"I don't know, Mary. Maybe we should call the police. It could be a missing person or a murder victim."

Mary's face never changed expression, but inside her heart was still racing. "I told you I don't want to deal with the police because of my profession," she said as she lit another cigarette. "The last thing I want is any publicity, or anyone snooping into my business. Professor Patterson can handle this."

She hoped that Jack would get the hint about snooping, but wasn't sure that he did. That could be a problem.

On the other hand, if Jack were to persist, that would give her all the ammunition she needed to put him in the dungeon. *That wouldn't be such a bad thing*, thought Mary. *We'll have to ride this out.*

Putting aside her thoughts about the dungeon, she led him into the kitchen for breakfast. "Honey, I'm going to treat you to organic fruit and organic granola with raw goat's milk."

"Raw goat's milk?" said Jack, raising his eyebrows.

"Yes. It's delicious. Very sweet and flavorful."

The queasy look on Jack's face made it clear that he wasn't convinced. "You got any regular milk?" he asked.

"Try it once, Jack," she said. "Trust me, you'll never go back to cow's milk again."

Jack still wasn't sure about that, so he began with a small bite. Then he took another, and then another, before devouring the rest of the cereal.

In the meantime Mary perched herself on the counter, watching him intently. "I told you it was good," she said. "Will you ever doubt me again?"

She sat with her right knee up, her left leg dangling. By now she had unbuttoned her shirt, revealing a camouflage bra and a black cotton thong. She crushed out her cigarette and immediately lit another.

That's odd, thought Jack. As well as he had gotten to know Mary McDonald, he had never seen her chain-smoking before. By his count that was the third cigarette in a row since he'd come back with the skeleton. It bothered her that he had discovered those remains, and he was dying to find out why.

"Jack, you didn't answer my question."

His instincts told him it would be unwise to ask her about the skeleton, so he shifted gears. "Honey, I've got to be honest with you, just like you always are with me," he smiled. "When you didn't provide me with my Paddle Pooper 101 lesson last night like you promised, I began to have some doubts about you — not serious doubts, mind you, but little cracks of uncertainty."

She stepped off the counter, leaned toward him and blew a wall of smoke at his face. "Jackie Poo, I am very disappointed in you. The course is *Pooper Paddle 101*, not Paddle Pooper 101! Another grievous mistake like that, buster, and you'll find yourself in my reform school, and subject to extreme and unusual punishment."

She planted a foot on his chair, the tip of her boot pointing dangerously close to his groin. She continued to address him sternly. "Believe me, you don't want to go there."

Jack looked at the boot, looked up to Mary, then looked down again at the boot. Only this time he was staring at his clearly aroused phallus — and so was Mary McDonald. Before he knew it she had his pants down to his ankles and was on his lap, straddling him, her hands clutching the back of his chair, pinning their bodies close together. On her command he kept his arms at his side as she lowered herself onto his cock. Then she began to ride him, alternating slow shallow thrusts with deep intense ones until they both collapsed.

By now it was well past 11:00 a.m. Jack had a lunch date with his father at 12:30 p.m. There wasn't time to go home and change, but if he showered quickly he could still make it. Except for a slight bit of trail dust, his sweatsuit was clean and presentable.

Mary lit another cigarette and walked him to his car. Before they reached it, she snapped her fingers. "Oh, by the way, Jack, I forgot to tell you: Bart the bouncer was fired. They found him sleeping on the job — literally, fast asleep at his post, on the sidewalk in front of the club. I just found out yesterday."

Jack threw his head back and cackled almost deliriously. That's when he told her about his little visit to the club the previous Monday night.

"Fantastic," said Mary, still hee-hawing at his story as she kissed him goodbye. "He was such a prick anyway. Good riddance!"

* * *

Jack merged onto the turnpike, put his phone on speaker and checked in with Polly. He apologized for not calling earlier and told her about the human skeleton.

"Well, I hope the remains aren't one of Mary's domination victims," she joked.

Funny you should say that, Jack thought to himself. *I was thinking the same thing.* But that would trigger a long conversation, and he didn't have time for that now. So instead he told Polly their theory. "We think it's an Iroquois Indian. It's very unlikely that it's a recent death, because the bones were bare. We're going to have a paleontologist check it out." Then he promised her that he'd fill her in when he got home that afternoon.

Several things bothered Jack as he signaled for his exit. For one, there was the matter of the missing skull. He could have dismissed that as just an oddity, were it not for all of those books in Mary's study on the subject of head shrinking. Given her fetish, it wouldn't surprise him if she had hidden the head somewhere in the house.

Then he thought about Mary's odd behavior this morning after he discovered the skeleton. Clearly his discovery had unnerved her. Finally, he contemplated the remains themselves — they were in remarkably pristine condition, with relatively little decomposition. If they were as old as Mary suggested, they should have been a lot more brittle after exposure to the elements. Assuming the corpse was recent, she could have scraped the bones clean and stuck them deep in the bushes where no one was likely to find them.

What bothered Jack the most, though, was that he didn't take the skeleton with him. Something told him that this was no Indian, and that he should have called the police.

* * *

Jeremiah Cohen was a handsome, firmly built man in his late forties, with a salt-and-pepper mane that made him appear at least a decade older. The physical resemblance between father and son was striking, as were their sartorial tastes. He wore a lavender-colored golf shirt, tan khakis, loafers with brown socks. Jeremiah Cohen liked Sundays, if only because it was the one day of the week where he didn't have to wear a tie. But Sundays also afforded him the opportunity to stay in touch with his son. It had been weeks since they'd last seen each other, but as Jeremiah put it, "Deciding if the country needs another round of quantitative easing is an all-consuming matter."

They shook hands and embraced each other in the lobby of the Daily Grill. "I heard about your performance Friday against Putin," said Jeremiah. "Congratulations. I would have gone myself, but you know I hate violence and I'm no fan of fighting."

"I guess news travels fast in your circle," said Jack.

"News travels fast everywhere, son — especially in this town. I hear your arm's OK, too."

Jeremiah Cohen may have been well informed, but Jack was certain that what he was about to tell his father would catch him by surprise.

They went inside the restaurant. The hostess seated them, and they ordered drinks: Scotch and soda for Jeremiah, a glass of water, no ice, for Jack. Then they made their way to the buffet. Jack helped himself to some fruit, while his dad had the Eggs Benedict.

"So how have you been?" asked Jeremiah.

"To tell you the truth, the past couple of weeks have been crazy, and I'm still trying to make sense of it all," said Jack. "But you know I'm an excitement addict, and you know I like challenges. So rather than fight it, I'm approaching it like a surfer; I'm just going to ride the wave."

"That's my boy! With your brains, body, charisma, and courage, there is no limit to what you can achieve... if you don't self-destruct."

"Of course." Jack could feel a lecture coming on.

"I got an interesting phone call this morning," said Jeremiah. "I was told you visited Sodom and Gomorrah, and that you're now dating a girl from the club named Mary McDonald. Is that true?"

Jack wanted to know how his father found out, but in the end it didn't matter. "Yes, it is," he said. "What of it?"

Jeremiah motioned for another scotch, then looked Jack straight in the eye. "Son, Mary McDonald is bad news — I can't put it any plainer than that. She is a sadistic druggie who lives to destroy men — physically, mentally, *totally* destroy men. I've been told that she particularly likes to target politicians and turn them into her personal whipping boys. She enjoys drugging and torturing them; some have been permanently damaged."

"Dad, you're not telling me anything I don't already know."

"Really?" said Jeremiah as the server brought him his drink. "Then I suppose you know that she even brands her men like cattle, to assert her dominance."

For a moment Jack's heart stopped; he wasn't aware of that. Then again, as unsettling as that was to hear, it didn't completely surprise him. Assuming it was true, Mary branding her clients was not much different than Destiny and her tattoo machine — and besides, Mary would never do that. Not to him, anyway. At least, that's what he wanted to believe.

"Jack, you are wise beyond your years, but you are in over your head with her," Jeremiah continued. "Mary McDonald is a cunning, cruel bitch who will carve you up, spit you out, and revel in doing so. Has she got you into drugs?"

"Just marijuana and hash," Jack said quietly. "That's all we've done so far."

"'So far' is the operative phrase," replied his father. "If you 'stay the course' with her, she'll eventually inject you with heavy, dangerous, mind-altering drugs. Then she'll torture you to her heart's content."

Jack's mind spun at warp speed as he flashed back to that day in the dungeon. He didn't need his father to tell him she was dangerous; the syringe of mefloquine that she dangled before him was evidence enough. And yet he craved her — all of her, good and bad — in the worst possible way. It was as simple as that.

"Dad, I don't know what to say, except I'm in love with Mary, and she's in love with me. I'll admit she's a handful... but that's part of the allure. The chemistry between us is the big thing; I feel like I'm plugged into an electric socket when we're together."

"Yes, but if you stick your finger in an electric socket, you can get yourself killed."

Jeremiah did not say that to be funny, but Jack started laughing anyway. "Besides, Dad, you make it sound like Mary is ruthlessly victimizing these poor, defenseless Washington politicians... and I don't see it that way at all. These men, of their own free will, are paying her thousands of dollars for the privilege of letting her torture them. And besides, most politicians are scumbags, anyway — I'm certainly not going to lose any sleep if they end up destroyed."

Now it was Jeremiah's turn to chuckle. "You know, I've really got to hand it to you, Jack. Your oratorical skills are so outstanding, you can take a psychopath like Mary McDonald and make her sound almost noble. You should go into politics."

"Fuck you, Dad."

"I'm serious, son," said Jeremiah. "You're exactly what this country needs." He took another sip of scotch. "But I suppose you'd sing a different tune if you knew about her and Senator Shitzer."

"Ellsworth Shitzer — the corrupt bastard who disappeared? What's he got to do with Mary?"

Jack's father lowered his voice, to make sure they could not be heard. "There is no evidence linking the two of them, but I have it on good authority — very good authority — that he was one of her clients. My sources also tell me that he may have been killed... by her. As you know, his body has never been found."

All of a sudden Jack's head throbbed while a knot formed in his stomach. He wasn't about to tell his father about the skeleton he found that morning. Or the books he discovered in Mary's closet.

"Dad, I get it — you're concerned — and like I said, I know she's a handful. But I also know there's no girl on the planet like Mary, and I don't want to be without her."

"What about Polly? I thought you were going to marry her. That girl worships the ground you walk on. Does she know about any of this?"

"Polly knows all about Mary," said Jack. "She accepts the fact that I now have a mistress; Mary accepts that I'm still Polly's boyfriend and living with her. In fact, I'm going to introduce the two of them to each other in a couple days."

Jeremiah shook his head and ordered another drink. "I might have to rethink your future in politics," he said. "No one is going to buy you as an idealistic political reformer if you've got two girlfriends — especially if one of them is Mary McDonald, the most prominent call girl in Washington. I mean, use your fucking head, Jack: If I found out about your relationship with Mary, it won't be long before the media finds about it, and your political career will be over before it starts. Especially with the Internet. I just hope you're not stupid enough to let her have video on you."

Jack was beginning to lose patience. If there was one thing he hated most in life, it was being lectured. "So what would you suggest I do?" he asked.

"Go to Harvard," his father said without skipping a beat. "There is no guarantee that State U will reopen in September. You could transfer to Harvard for your senior year, get your degrees in physics and political science, get a Rhodes scholarship, and be on the fast path to the presidency. My buddies in the Bilderberg Group would groom you, and you could end up the first Jewish president before you turn forty. Not only that, Harvard gets you away from drugs, and keeps you away from Mary."

Jack took a deep breath. He knew that what he was about to say could sever their relationship forever, and he wanted to choose his words carefully. "Harvard is a breeding ground for fascist, neo-Marxist social engineers and elitist globalists," he began. "I have zero interest in going there, and you know how I feel about Mary. But I do have an interest in the Bilderberg Group... an interest in destroying their power and control!"

Jeremiah's right eye began to twitch, a nervous tic that usually happened whenever he was under stress. "You are young, naïve, and idealistic," he said with clenched teeth. "You have *no idea* how the world works. I just hope to God that this radical phase is temporary, and that in a few years' time, you'll look back at your present thinking and laugh."

"This is no phase," Jack coldly replied. "I *am* a revolutionary, and what you represent — the Federal Reserve — is what I'm interested in overthrowing."

He reached inside his leather pouch and pulled out his copies of *The Creature from Jekyll Island*, *The Case Against the Fed*, and *What Has Government Done to Our Money?* "Dad, I've done a lot of reading since State U shut down, including these books. I'd like to see if you can refute the arguments that each of these authors makes."

Jeremiah laughed uncomfortably. "I'm aware of these titles, and particularly the ones by Rothbard," he said, pointing to *What Has Government Done to Our Money?* and *The Case Against the Fed*. "What you don't understand, Jack, is how necessary the Fed is to maintain economic stability. Without the Fed, there would be extreme economic cycles, and the banking system would be tenuous."

"Bullshit," said Jack. "Economic 'science' is an oxymoron. Professional economists specialize in smoke and mirrors, and in formulae that have virtually zero predictive value. The Keynesian economics that you and Greengold subscribe to essentially amounts to expanding the money supply by printing more dollars. The proper term for this is *counterfeiting*. By printing more dollars, you effectively devalue the currency, weakening purchasing power. In short, the Fed is the biggest thief in the world, bilking the American public out of untold trillions of dollars. In addition, you have lowered interest rates to zero, which means people with money in the bank or on a fixed income get killed by inflation and are effectively forced to gamble in the stock market, which is propped up by your artificially low interest rates. The Fed wants the public to believe that they are championing the fight against inflation, but that is all propaganda — the reality, as Murray Rothbard points out in his books, is that the Fed is the sole culprit responsible for inflation, which is a hidden tax levied on the unsuspecting public.

"The Federal Reserve isn't even federal," the younger Cohen continued. "It's a private banking cartel that is accountable to no one. They are unaudited and have a monopoly over our money."

Jeremiah shifted uncomfortably in his seat, but beyond that he was speechless. Jack proceeded to read his father a few quotes:

> If the American People ever allow the banks to control the issuance of their currency, the banks and corporations that will grow up around them will deprive the people of all property until their children wake up homeless on the continent their fathers occupied. The issuing power of money should be taken from the bankers and restored to Congress and the people to whom it belongs. I sincerely believe the banking institutions having the issuing power of money are more dangerous to liberty than standing armies.
>
> THOMAS JEFFERSON,
> U.S. President

> The bold effort[s] the present (central) bank has made to control the government... are but premonitions of the fate that awaits the American people should they be deluded into a perpetuation of this institution or the establishment of another like it... You [the central bankers] are a den of vipers and thieves. I intend to rout you out, and by the grace of the Eternal God, will rout you out.
>
> ANDREW JACKSON,
> U.S. President

> Whoever controls the volume of money in our country is absolute master of all industry and commerce... when you realize that the entire system is very easily controlled, one way or another, by a few powerful men at the top, you will not have to be told how periods of inflation and deflation originate.
>
> JAMES GARFIELD,
> U.S. President

> The Federal Reserve Banks are one of the most corrupt institutions the world has ever seen. There is not a man within the sound of my voice who does not know that this nation is run by the international bankers. Every effort has

been made by the Federal Reserve Board to conceal its powers, but the truth is that the Federal Reserve System has usurped the government. It controls everything in Congress and it controls all our foreign relations. It makes and breaks governments at will.

THOMAS Mc FADDEN,
Chairman of the House Committee on Banking and Finance

Jeremiah's eye continued to twitch. "What is your point, Jack?"

"My point is that I intend to follow in the footsteps of Andrew Jackson and 'rout out' the den of vipers and thieves," Jack explained. "The concept behind the Federal Reserve was tried twice prior to 1913, and both times it failed. Too bad Jackson wasn't around in 1913 to derail the third attempt by the banking cartel. The banksters, thanks to their influence over Congress, were able to institutionalize the Federal Reserve System, and the rest is history — a sick history that has bankrupted our once great nation, putting us umpteen trillions of dollars in debt.

"The fractional-reserve banking system institutionalized by the Federal Reserve is, as Rothbard puts it, 'only a euphemism for fraud and embezzlement.' This system radically expanded the credit of banks, literally allowing them to play casino with their depositors' money — and when the banks lose, it's Joe Taxpayer that's stuck with the bill. According to Rothbard, the effect of this banking system is price inflation, inequitable redistribution of money, and ruinous cycles of boom and bust caused by counterfeit bank credit."

Jeremiah Cohen couldn't help but laugh. "You know, the problem with your argument is that you pin everything on the findings of Rothbard. You realize he was a professor of economics at UNLV. That doesn't exactly qualify him as a prominent academic."

"Typical elitist bullshit," said Jack. "Rothbard was way smarter than you and your entire Ivy League professor clique put together. My guess is that the only reason he ended up at UNLV is because the Keynesian-oriented econ departments at those schools didn't want a radical right-wing Austrian economist shitting on their party. I've just started his book *Man, Economy, and State*, and it's a quantum leap beyond any of the crap I've studied at State U, or that you've given me to read."

He wrapped up his comments by citing seven reasons for abolishing the Federal Reserve System, as stated by G. Edward Griffin in *The Creature from Jekyll Island*:

> It is incapable of accomplishing its stated objectives.
> It is a cartel operating against public interest.
> It is the supreme instrument of usury.
> It generates our most unfair tax.
> It encourages war.
> It destabilizes the economy.
> It is an instrument of totalitarianism.

Then Jack piled the books on top of each other and pushed them in the direction of his father. "Again, I ask you, can you refute these accusations?"

Disdainfully Jeremiah pushed the books aside. "I'm sorry, Jack, I'm a busy man," he said. "I don't have time for this nonsense. I have my beliefs about the Fed, and you have yours. I think it's best if we respect each other's views and leave it at that. I love you very much, and I don't want our relationship to become acrimonious over our differing viewpoints on the Fed."

All Jack could do was sigh in disgust. "That was not the answer I was looking for, Dad. So let me put it another way: You are the defacto chairman of the Fed. Greengold is the front man, but he basically defers to you on every decision; so you're really the man in control of the U.S. monetary system. If you want me to remain your son, here's what you *must* do:

"You *must* publicly, on major news networks, denounce the Federal Reserve as a counterfeiting machine, as a doomsday vehicle of ponzi economics that has reduced once great America to a pathetic nation of debt slaves. You *must* call for an end to the Fed and a return to sound money policies, including a return to the gold standard. Have I made myself clear?"

Jeremiah Cohen looked at his son as if the blood had been drained from his head. "Jack, you can't be serious. That would be political suicide for me, the end of my career in Washington. Everything I've worked for would be for naught." He motioned for the hostess to bring them their bill. "Ever since your mother passed, it's been just the two of us. Everything I have will be yours someday... You don't know what you're saying."

"Oh, yes, I do," said Jack. "You may be worth thirty million dollars, but it's tainted money, the product of insider information — and I don't want a penny of it. In fact, I don't even want my allowance from you anymore. I've got enough money in the bank to last me through the summer, and then I'll begin making a living as a fighter as soon as my arm is OK."

He stood up, leaving his father on the verge of tears. He pulled out a twenty and two fives from his money clip to cover his half of the bill and laid them on the table. Then he walked out of the restaurant. He didn't even say goodbye.

Jack Cohen hadn't even touched his food, but it was the best thirty dollars he had ever spent.

Part 2
The Awakening

GARIBALDI'S WAS ONE OF those places you can find in just about any urban neighborhood: an old-fashioned, family-style restaurant with red-checkered tablecloths, a boisterous staff, and food in generous portions. The parking lot was behind the kitchen, welcoming patrons with the aroma of fresh-baked bread. Jack's mouth was already watering as he pulled in just before 7:00 p.m. He hadn't eaten since breakfast, and he knew this meal would be far more pleasant than the one with his father earlier that afternoon.

John Mulligan was waiting inside in a booth near the rear of the restaurant. Both men ordered the prime rib special. John ordered chamomile tea, while Jack asked for a cup of hot water. "I'm impressed," said John. "Most people order cold water before a meal, without realizing that it puts out the digestive fire and causes the food in one's stomach to congeal. Too bad they don't teach that in schools instead of all the liberal propaganda."

Then he asked about Mary McDonald. Jack said that she was fine, aside from some bruises and discoloration. He was more eager to talk about the headless human skeleton that he discovered near her house. "Knowing that Mary is a sadistic dominatrix, my first thought was that it might be a victim of hers," he said. "My suspicion intensified when she became noticeably disturbed after my find. Then my dad told me that she may have killed Ellsworth Shitzer."

"If she offed Shitzer, she's done humanity a service," said John with a wide grin. "He was the ultimate hypocrite — clamping down on escort services while using them himself. Maybe she figured the douchebag deserved the death penalty for that."

"I agree he was a douchebag, but let's not jump to conclusions," Jack chuckled. "The operative word is 'may have.' Word on the Hill is that he was a client, but because there's no evidence linking them, she hasn't been investigated."

"Fair enough," said John. "So what do you think?"

"I'm very suspicious," Jack replied. "Especially because of the missing skull. Mary has books on head shrinking stashed away in her closet. My guess is that she beheaded him and kept his skull as a souvenir."

The morbid thought made both men laugh. "So what did you do with the skeleton?" asked John.

"Like an idiot, I left it with her," said Jack. He told him that she thought it might be the remains of an Iroquois Indian, and how she happened to have a paleontologist friend who would examine the find.

"What if it isn't an Indian?" asked John.

Jack shook his head. "Then I don't know what I'd do. If it was Shitzer, I wouldn't go to the police — that piece of shit deserves whatever came to him. But if it's someone else... I'd hate to be the one who provided the evidence that convicts Mary of murder."

"Now it's my turn to caution you, buddy: You're getting ahead of yourself," said John. "For all you know, she might have buried the skeleton as soon as you left, so there's no evidence to convict her."

Jack nodded at the possibility. He wouldn't put anything past Mary.

The waiter returned with their food and refreshed Jack's cup of water. Then, as he had promised the other night, John Mulligan revealed his background. "Here are the CliffsNotes: Navy Seal. Graduated from Harvard with a degree in economics. Started grad school at Princeton. Dropped out. Worked on Wall Street for a year. Joined the CIA."

"Let me guess," joked Jack. "Your specialty was assassinations."

"And now I'm a professional gambler and political revolutionary," John smiled. "Whenever I terminate members of the enemy — the anti-constitutional statists — I enjoy a meal of human meat, followed by a fine Cohiba and a shot of brandy."

He paused for a sip of tea. "I quit the CIA when it became morally reprehensible to me to kill people who did not deserve to be killed," he continued. "I subscribe to the libertarian credo, *do not initiate force.* Regarding my killing and eating the enemy, that happened a few months ago. We were stockpiling guns in the desert and were attacked. We responded in self-defense. Since that time, we've found a new hideout — but the government is looking for us."

Then he informed Jack of a Homeland Security program that also turned him against the U.S. government. "They are starting to pick out dissidents and imprison them in FEMA camps. These individuals are not charged with a crime, are not allowed to consult an attorney, and are not given a trial. They are simply detained indefinitely because they are deemed a 'threat to national security.'

"The Constitution has effectively been shredded by the Powers that Be, the fascist Mafia government," John Mulligan continued. "Consequently, war has unofficially been declared on patriots. The reality we now face was perfectly described by Thomas Jefferson: 'The tree of liberty must be refreshed from time to time with the blood of patriots and tyrants.'"

"Or as Che Guevara might've put it, we live in the heart of the beast," said Jack. "The question is, can we cut out that heart before the beast destroys us?"

"The problem with Che," chuckled John, "is that while he understood America is a fascist and imperialist nation, he didn't realize that the solution is not Marxism, but libertarianism."

He decided to lighten the conversation. "You know, from what you've told me about your girlfriend, she'd be perfect for our operation in Vegas. We could always use a good interrogation specialist."

"Mary would fit in perfectly, except for two things," Jack chuckled. "One, she's a left-wing liberal, and, two, you can't afford her. She averages thirty thousand bucks a week, and most of it is under the table."

Then he asked John if he ever worried about the dangers of his profession. "Oh, I fully expect to get caught and terminated by the government," John admitted. "But, hopefully, that day won't come until after the revolution has some wheels under it."

Jack extended his hand in comradeship. "Well, my mantra is the same as yours, brother: 'Give me liberty or give me death.' When they recently passed the comprehensive anti-gun law, that broke the camel's back for me. Luckily, now that I know you and Jim, I can channel my anti-government energy constructively."

"Brother Jack, you've got it backwards," said John. "The revolution is already under way, and we'll be channeling our anti-government activity through *you*. Without a charismatic hero, a national figure who galvanizes and educates the masses, the liberty movement has no chance. At the rate you read and process information, you'll be a walking encyclopedia on libertarianism in no time."

Jack appreciated the compliment and mentioned that he was currently reading *Human Action* and *Man, Economy and State*. "Any other books you can recommend?"

"Get *The Machinery of Freedom* by David Friedman," said John. "He explains how a stateless society could function and flourish. I would also check out 'The Story of Your Enslavement,' a YouTube video by Stefan Molyneux, and Murray Rothbard's essay 'The Anatomy of the State,' which you can find at lewrockwell.com. Both provide excellent counterarguments to people who are ignorant of libertarianism and unaware of the evil nature and criminal roots of statism."

The mention of Rothbard reminded Jack of how his father had ridiculed the economist's credentials. That prompted him to tell John about the ultimatum he'd given Jeremiah earlier in the day, and his decision to sever their relationship when his father chose the Fed over him.

"That's fucking unreal," said Mulligan. "Your dad is basically the guy who controls the world's money. With his connections, your road to political power and riches was paved out for you — and you told him to go fly a kite. You're my hero!"

Then he asked Jack if he'd read the *Bhagavad Gita*. "Yes," said Jack. "In fact I just finished it a few days ago. It actually inspired me to cut the ties with my father. When Krishna tells Arjuna that life is a battlefield, and sometimes the enemies you must confront are your own family members, I realized what I had to do."

Jack smiled wistfully. "Jesus also put Dharma above family," he continued.

"I may have lost my father today, but I also found a brother." The two men gazed warmly at each other and once again locked hands.

• • •

Jack spent most of Tuesday afternoon on the phone. First Mother Mary called to arrange a time for Jack's initiation; they settled on Friday evening, after the Objectivist meeting. Then John Mulligan called about getting together later in the week to discuss a project that could help finance their revolution. Finally, Professor Patterson, at the behest of Mary, called with the results of his examination of the headless skeleton. According to his findings, the remains were those of a male Iroquois Indian, somewhere between 250 and 300 years old.

Jack sighed in relief, but still one question remained: "How do you account for the missing skull? Is that common with Iroquois remains?"

"No, it's not," said the professor. "Nor can I tell you why the skull is absent; I can only tell you about what is present."

Jack thanked the professor for his time and ended the call. He was glad Mary was off the hook, and yet he was tinged with sadness. It had been two days since he'd seen his father. He knew there was no turning back — and yet a part of him silently wished that Jeremiah would have called, begging him to reconsider. But he didn't, and Jack resigned himself to the reality that he likely never would.

Jack hadn't told Polly that he had cut off ties with his father; he wanted to wait until he knew the break was final. Now that it was, he could no longer hide it from her. He would have to find the right time.

He poured himself a beer for courage. One brew led to another, and before he knew it Polly was home. She had the day off, and had spent most of it shopping. Knowing that Jack rarely drank, she couldn't help but wonder what had brought on this sudden imbibing. Jack was about to explain when the kitchen phone rang. Speak of the devil, it was Mary McDonald.

"Oh, Jackie Poo," she cooed, "I was thinking about you this very moment. Are you coming over tonight as planned?"

Jack put his hand on the receiver and told Polly that it was Mary. "Are you up for an evening at her place?"

"Absolutely," said Polly. "I am dying to meet this woman who has you wrapped around her little pinky."

Jack told Mary they'd be there at 7:00 p.m. "Fantastic," she whooped. "We'll drop acid and have a groovy, far-out time."

* * *

They arrived at her front door at the appointed time. Polly wore a blue paisley summer dress and white pumps. Jack wore jeans, a collared shirt, and sneakers. He was carrying his leather pouch.

Mary was all smiles as she greeted them. In the spirit of the evening's retro theme, she wore a sleeveless tie-dyed velvet dress and brown laced-up booties. Love beads adorned her freshly washed hair, while makeup disguised the bruises on her face. She greeted Polly with a warm hug and admired her wardrobe. "She's a sweetheart, Jack — cute, open, loving and sexy. I must say, you have excellent taste in women." The three of them laughed in unison.

"I could say the same for you," said Polly. "Especially the sexy part."

"Oh, you're not even seeing the real me," Mary beamed as she took Polly by the hand. "I'm still black and blue from Putin, but I'm glad you can see through the bruises."

"Hey, how about me?" said Jack with faux indignation.

"Jackie Poo has been a bad boy, so I'm ignoring him," Mary explained.

"Jackie Poo?" said Polly.

Mary crossed her pointer fingers and rubbed them in Jack's direction. "Oooh, naughty, naughty! You didn't tell her about your new sobriquet." Then she put her arms around Polly and playfully filled her in. "You see, Jack suffers from a tight ass, a constricted poo hole — and until we can loosen it up, he will be known as Jackie Poo."

Polly started giggling. "I can tell we're going to have lots of fun tonight."

"Trust me, my dear," said Mary. "We're going to have more fun than you can imagine."

* * *

The evening began with a guided tour of the house. Mary being Mary, she saved the dungeon for last. "What do you think?" she asked Polly.

Polly had heard about Mary's various "weapons of personal destruction," but even after seeing them with her own eyes, she couldn't quite believe it. "You don't really use all these things, do you?"

"Oh, of course, I use them," Mary said with annoyance. "I use *everything*. Nothing in here is for show. In fact, if you'll help me strap Jack down, I'll show you how some of them work."

Polly's face began to blanch. She wasn't sure if Mary was serious, and for that matter, neither was Jack. He knew it was a matter of time before Mary tried to embarrass him in front of Polly; he just didn't count on her doing it so soon. But he also knew that the best course of action was to play along, so he pretended to shake with fear. That made the girls laugh, which got him off the hook — at least for the time being.

Mary directed her guests to the kitchen and invited them to sit by the counter. She opened the refrigerator and pulled out a pitcher of a psychedelic elixir that she called Electric Kool-Aid. "Tonight we're going to turn on, tune in, and drop out," she said as she poured them each a glass. "The hermetic brew that we're about to imbibe is spiked with Clear Light, or windowpane lysergic acid diethylamide — that's LSD, Polly. One glass contains enough micrograms to propel each of us into the luminous void."

She handed a glass to Polly, who gazed at it cautiously. "I've done this drug dozens of times and am intimately familiar with its effects and side effects," Mary McDonald continued. "I'm well-suited to serve as your guide. We'll fly high tonight, for sure, but not high enough to catapult us 'over the cuckoo's nest' — though I'm sure that both of you believe I'm already there!"

With that they laughed and toasted each other. While the girls nursed their drinks, Jack finished his quickly and promptly asked for a refill. "I'm considerably bigger than both of you," he joked, "so it stands to reason that I should drink more in order to get the same effect."

At some point the conversation turned to books. Jack reached for his pouch and pulled out the titles by Rothbard and Griffin — the same ones that his father had refused to read two days before. He laid them out on the kitchen counter, while Mary retrieved a book of her own, *DemoCRIPS and ReBLOODicans: No More Gangs in Government* by Jesse Ventura. Then she hung her head as if in shame and made a heartfelt confession:

"I hate to admit I was wrong, but I've totally soured on the Democratic Party. Ventura's book was the final nail in the coffin — it crystallized what had been fermenting in my subconscious mind for quite a while. I can no longer rationalize allegiance to left-wing liberalism. I see it for what it is: fascism in drag."

Needless to say, Jack was ecstatic. "Now that you've seen the political light," he said, "I'm hoping your 'spiritual elixir' will enable me to see the Clear Light."

Mary McDonald giggled, pecked Jack on the cheek, then led him and Polly into her living room. She lit some incense and put on a psychedelic CD featuring songs from King Crimson, Deep Purple, the Grateful Dead, the Doors and other bands from the '60s and '70s. Though not the same acid rock CD that Jack had heard on the night he first slept with Mary, it did have some of the same tunes. As King Crimson's *21st Century Schizoid Man* blasted from the speakers, he couldn't help but think that the song perfectly described his present state of mind — torn between the old Jack and the new Jack being born.

Polly tilted her head to and fro as she silently grooved to the music. "Wow, the vibration in this room is utterly surrealistic — and yet I feel like I'm truly in touch with reality for the first time in my life," she said. "I can now see how amazingly unique you both are as human beings. I mean, Mary is so open, free, and wild, it's almost scary, while Jack is so powerful — so strong, present... and manly."

"Yes, Jack is very unique," said Mary, her hand draped across his thigh. "I've never met a man who's spent so much time with me without being strapped down and dominated."

He gazed into Mary's eyes. She looked more alluring and dangerous to him than ever. Sensing his excitement, Mary began to undress him, laughing giddily at his fully erect penis.

"All right," she said. "Let's all get naked!"

With that the women removed their clothes. Mary directed Polly to deep-throat Jack, while she began to French-kiss him. The more they caressed him, the harder and faster he breathed.

Knowing that he was on the verge of release, Mary signaled Polly to stop. "The night is young, Jack," she said. "I'm in charge of this party and I want it to be an integral one, not just an orgy of wild, erotic sex. I'll let you blow your load later. But first we're going to take advantage of this 'high time' and evolve all aspects of our being."

Now that his breathing had returned to normal, Jack began the discussion by revealing that he had effectively disowned his father. The news immediately saddened Polly. "Why didn't you tell me before?"

"I didn't want to burden you until I knew it was final."

"Jack, your idealism is out of this world," Mary said with admiration. "You gave up the super highway to riches and political power for the rocky and treacherous path of a revolutionary."

"She's right," said Polly. "That was very courageous." With that she and Mary kissed him.

Jack appreciated the praise and display of affection. "It will be interesting to see where the 'rocky and treacherous path' leads me," he said. "And speaking of paths, I heard from your friend the professor, Mary. He confirmed what you said all along, that the remains were those of an Iroquois Indian."

While Mary flashed a Mona Lisa smile, Polly confessed to fearing the worst. "I thought the skeleton was one of your domination victims. I want to apologize for ever thinking that."

Mary hugged Polly and planted a kiss on her cheek. "Don't give it another thought, sister — I forgive you." Then she glared accusingly at Jack. "Based on the *misinformation* you were given, your reaction is understandable."

She got up from the couch and, with her full weight, pushed down on Jack's head with both hands. "OK, buster, 'fess up: You also thought the skeleton was one of my clients... right?"

Jack tried to raise his head, but as Mary had leverage there was nothing he could do. She continued toying with him until she could no longer contain herself. Before long they both started laughing; she let go of his head and kissed him.

Polly loved the playful theatre. "Mary, you're more fun than a barrel of monkeys. I'm so glad that you're now my friend."

"I love you, too, Polly," Mary beamed. "Your sweet Libra energy is the perfect yin for my over-the-top Aries yang. You'll keep me sane and balanced — and just as important, you'll help me keep Jack in line. When I'm preoccupied and can't discipline him, I'll have you cram a dildo up his ass to straighten him out."

The three of them laughed raucously. Once they calmed down, Jack fell into a blissful, contemplative state. After a few minutes, he opened his eyes and said that he wanted to meditate. "I feel like all boundaries are dissolving and that we are all one in the Clear Light."

Mary McDonald was irked. Even when tripping the light fantastic, she had to be in control. "This is my party, and we'll reflect when I want to," she said. "Meditation is not scheduled until *after* we commune with Mother Nature. That means gazing at the cosmos while we soak in the Jacuzzi."

With that she led them out to the patio. As soon as they sat down in the tub, Mary baited Jack. "You ready to race me yet, or are you still chicken?"

She turned to Polly and explained. "I've offered Jack the opportunity of a lifetime, but he's not man enough to take advantage of it."

Polly shot her a quizzical look. "Meaning?"

Mary motioned toward the swimming pool. "My pool is 25 meters long. I want to race Jack two laps, 100 meters. If he wins, he gets to strap me down in my dungeon; if I win, I strap him down." She lit a cigarette from the nearby box and blew smoke in Jack's face. "If he can't beat a chain-smoking druggie like me, then I see no hope for him."

"I don't know if I should tell you this, Mary, but Jack is a very good swimmer," said Polly. "He was a lifeguard one summer, and I'm sure he would have made his high school swimming team if he had gone out for it."

"And I should tell you, Polly, that Miss Chain Smoker here was a three-time state champion swimmer," said Jack. Then he reached for Mary's hand. "OK, let's do it."

Mary laughed wickedly. "Get ready, buster. I swim my fastest on LSD; it's my performance-enhancing drug of choice."

They shook hands, climbed out of the Jacuzzi, and assumed their positions on the edge of the pool. Polly played referee. As it was past dusk, she switched on the patio lights so they could see her signal. She dropped her hand, and Jack and Mary hit the water. Hardly a hair's breadth separated them as they hit the wall at the 50-meter mark. The second half of the race was just as close as they accelerated toward the finish line.

For a moment it looked like Mary would win, as she inched ahead of Jack. But, with a mighty push in the last five meters, he edged her by a single stroke.

Once again Mary was peeved. She knew Jack was a phenomenal athlete, but never imagined that he could beat her. "I don't understand," she said, shaking her head as she toweled herself dry. "I could beat every guy on the boys' high school team, plus you've never been a competitive swimmer..."

"Oh, yes, I have," said Jack with a smile. "I swam competitively for about a year when I was ten."

That made Mary feel a little better, but as always she would have the last word. She motioned for Polly to grab Jack's cock, while she herself caressed his balls. They continued to fondle his genitals and playfully ogle him until he was fully aroused.

Then, just like that, Mary snapped her fingers and announced that play time was over. "Sorry, buster, but sex will have to wait," she tittered. "You'd better tell Little Jackie Poo that it's time for his nap." Then she snapped his ass with her towel and led them back into the living room.

She brought out Zen cushions and instructed her guests to sit on them cross-legged. Then she played another favorite CD, *Merlin's Magic Chakra Meditation Music*. The uplifting, ethereal music filled the room with heavenly vibrations.

"OK, people, now I'm going to teach you how to meditate," said Mary. "First, occupy your body. Feel yourself *as* the whole body, and be present as the whole body. To help you remain present, focus your attention on the empty space in front of you. Gaze into the empty space, the void, and feel your body pressing against it. To intensify your connection to the empty space, consciously breathe (or inhale and exhale) the air filling it. When you feel like you've locked in to the void, totally let go and let be. After a few minutes of utter self-emptiness, reconnect, or attempt to reconnect, to the void. Continue to alternate between focusing on the void and letting go."

She instructed them to hold their focus for approximately fifteen minutes. Then she took a mallet and banged it gently against a gong. That signaled the end of the meditation session.

Mary smiled sweetly at Polly. "Go ahead, my new Dharma sister. Tell me what you experienced."

"It was amazing," Polly bubbled. "I felt like I melted into the universe — and that the universe is love. But I couldn't stay in that state because my mind was going crazy... and it still is." She started giggling uncontrollably. The others quickly joined her.

"What about you?" Mary asked Jack when the laughter died down.

He shook his head, as if in denial. "I felt the same state of oneness and love that Polly did — but then, once the boundaries of separateness melted away, I began to have flashbacks... incredible flashbacks."

"What kind of flashbacks?" asked Mary.

"I remembered myself as Jesus carrying the cross and then being crucified," Jack continued. "I could feel the nails being driven into the same spots in my hands where I experienced the holes and spontaneous bleeding."

Instantly the three of them stared at Jack's palms. Without explanation a tiny amount of blood began to trickle out of each hand.

Jack could hardly believe his eyes. "The blood is oozing from the exact same places where the holes were before. But now there are no holes or marks, just blood."

Mary grabbed one of Jack's hands and licked the blood off the palm. She instructed Polly to do the same with the other. "It's another sign that your time is near," she explained. "It's holy blood — a precursor of the true Holy Blood, the Baptist Fire that will rage through you once Mother Mary baptizes you."

"That's three days away," Jack said, counting off three fingers. "I just spoke to her this afternoon."

Mary's body began to writhe. "I'm afraid your baptism will have to wait a little longer," she cooed. "I told Mother Mary that you need more preparatory work before you're ready."

"Preparatory work?" asked Jack.

"Yes," she replied, her lips wet with anticipation. "I let her know that I need to subject you to extreme torture and pain before you're ready to become Jesus again."

Even in his blissful state, Jack figured she was messing with him. He was about to muster a reply when suddenly he heard Polly sobbing.

"What's wrong, honey?" he asked.

"I think I'm freaking out," she said.

Mary put her arms around Polly and kissed her on the cheek. "Just relax and don't fight it," she said softly. "Your mind is going a million miles an hour. Acid is intense enough by itself, and when you add this unreal scene with Jack and me... well, it can be reality shattering."

She lifted Polly from her cushion and led her to the massage table. "Just relax, my Dharma sister," Mary instructed her. "I'm going to give you a massage and ground you."

Expertly she kneaded Polly's back, shoulders, legs, and thighs. It wasn't long before Polly regained her mental equilibrium and became talkative. "Mary, you called me your 'Dharma sister.' What does that mean?"

"It means we're sisters in the Way of Truth," Mary explained. "Dharma means Truth Teaching. Now that you've joined me in the search for spiritual Truth, I've adopted you as my spiritual sister. I don't have a sister, but you're such a sweet and loving being, I want you to be mine. Are you OK with that?"

Polly sat up and nodded. "Yes," she said. "I love being around you, and I'm honored to be your spiritual sister. But... I'm afraid of what you might do to Jack. You keep talking about torturing him — I don't know how to deal with that, and that's why I freaked out."

Mary sat beside Polly and gently stroked her hair. "Don't worry about Jack. He's a big boy and can take care of himself." Then she peered over her shoulder and pretended to glare at Jack. "Isn't that right, Jackie Poo?"

Jack stared into space and let out a slight laugh. "To tell you the truth, Mary, I don't know if I can take care of myself. I have intense energy rushing up my spine. My chakras are vibrating, and I'm trying to process this overwhelming experience. I don't know if this is the acid speaking, or what."

Mary smiled knowingly. "This is a good sign, Jack — you've awakened the lower Kundalini, the Serpent Power. Mother Mary will give you the higher Kundalini, Divine Power. Whereas the lower Kundalini rises up the spine, the higher Kundalini pours down the frontal line of the body."

She laid Polly back down to massage her while she continued to talk to Jack. "You're half way to becoming Jesus," she said dreamily. "Once I 'crucify' you, you'll be prepared to fully incarnate as him once Mother Mary gives you *Shaktipat,* Divine Power. The LSD is functioning as a catalyst in your Enlightenment process, and the next step in your Awakening will be your extreme dungeon session with me. Are you ready for our 'Passion Play'?"

Jack didn't hear a word she'd said. The Kundalini energy had suddenly subsided, and visions of Mary Magdalene had taken hold of his mind. He saw himself as Jesus casting demons out of a beautiful young woman dressed in a Biblical-era tunic. Then he saw himself, as Jesus, making love to her at night.

The resemblance between the young woman and Mary McDonald was uncanny; he was sure they were the same person. He closed his eyes to see if he could penetrate more deeply into the visions — but the second his eyes shut, an arm wrapped around his neck, and he felt himself being pulled to the floor.

The next thing he knew, he heard music playing, while Mary and Polly stood over him, pummeling his body. Jack came to his senses and started to laugh as the three of them rolled on the floor, hugging and kissing and expressing their mutual love and affection.

The music he heard was the song "Triad" by the Jefferson Airplane, from their *Crown of Creation* album. Jack took in the lyrics as they filled the room:

> You want to know how it will be
> Me and him or you and me
> You both stand there your long hair flowing
> Eyes alive your mind still growing
> Saying to me —"What can we do now that we both love you?"
> I love you two — I don't really see
> Why can't we go on as three

"Far fucking out!" Jack whooped. "Mary might end up killing me, but at least she liberated my ass before slicing and dicing it."

The three of them laughed, and their playful affection quickly morphed into wild, intense sex. The girls kept Jack on the precipice as they took turns sucking and fucking him, always stopping to switch positions just before he was ready to orgasm. This being Mary's party, she wanted to keep him pent up for as long as possible.

Jack laid on the mat, his eyes closed, his mind relaxed, his body at their disposal. For the first time in his life he realized that sex, from a universal perspective, was the ultimate fireworks show, a dazzling symmetry of light and explosives as they become one with the sky. His rocket was charged, and as the girls continued to arouse him he wondered what imagery would occupy his brain at the moment of ecstasy.

Finally, he could no longer contain himself. His shaft erupted, spraying the air with his semen. Mary and Polly laughed with delight and licked his member clean.

• • •

After a while Mary led them into the kitchen for refreshments. Jack's mind went into overdrive as he tried to make sense of his visions and Kundalini awakening: Were his experiences real, or merely a drug-induced illusion? If they were real, then clearly he had been Jesus, and Mary McDonald was Mary Magdalene.

Keenly aware of what he was thinking, Mary McDonald assured him that his journey into the Mystery was only beginning. "I can hardly wait to see how your journey progresses," she said lovingly. "You are on the brink of becoming the Avatar, and it will be exciting for me to be involved in your revolutionary Work."

She prepared a tray of fresh fruit: apple slices, grapes, melon balls, and pineapple. Mary and Polly drank iced tea, while Jack settled for a cup of hot water. He helped himself to a cluster of grapes when he remembered the plate of fruit that he'd left untouched two days earlier, when he had lunch with his father. It was the mention of Sodom and Gomorrah that day that made him lose his appetite.

"I forgot to tell you," he said to Mary. "When I met with my father, he knew that I had visited the club and that you were now my girlfriend. Any idea who tipped him off?"

"From what I heard, it was Bart," said Mary. "He really has it in for you, now that you cost him his job. My guess is that he found out who you were and put the word out on the street to spoil your reputation."

Then she smiled devilishly. "Did your father ask about me?"

"Yes, he did," said Jack. "He said you were bad news."

"Your father is a smart man," Mary smirked. "Maybe you should listen to him instead of tossing him out like a bag of trash. He wants to save your ass... while I want to enslave it."

"You might change your mind about my dad when I tell you what else he said." With that Jack confronted her about her alleged involvement with the disappearance of Ellsworth Shitzer.

"That is such bullshit," Mary said dismissively. Then, to make it clear that she did not wish to discuss this further, she turned her attention to Polly and asked if she wanted more tea.

"I'm fine," said Polly, extending her hand in friendship. "I don't care what they say about you, Mary — you're all right in my book."

Jack beamed with pride at Polly. He wasn't sure just how she'd take to Mary, but now her allegiance was clear. "Honey, I love you, and I can't tell you how much I appreciate you for embracing the open road. I am so happy to have you along on my journey into the Unknown." He kissed her deeply, and Mary soon joined them, as they pressed their bodies together as if to become one.

They decided to step outside for a moonlight swim. Once they began frolicking in the water, their bodies entwined and the three lovers again engaged in passionate sex.

When they finished they moved back to the hot tub. That was when Jack focused his attention on the shed next to the gym. He'd been to Mary's house twice before, but this was the first time he'd given the shed any thought. It was about the size of a one-car garage and had every appearance of an ordinary shed. Except for the huge padlock that dominated the entrance.

"What's inside there?" he asked.

"Oh, just equipment and supplies to service my pool," Mary said vacantly. "Nothing worth seeing... unless you get off on chlorine gas."

Jack laughed at her little joke, but didn't believe her. Most pool supplies aren't that valuable, and certainly not worth securing with an industrial-size padlock. There had to be something else inside — something important that Mary didn't want him, or anyone else, to know about. Whatever it was, he was determined to find out.

* * *

They adjourned to the living room, where Mary introduced her guests to the art of tantra yoga. "We're going to transform sexual energy into spiritual energy," she explained. "In other words, we'll have sex, but without orgasming. Once we're on the verge of cumming, we'll stop the sex and practice meditation. Our sublimated sexual energy will transmute into increased spiritual energy and powerful meditation. Any questions?"

"Yes," Polly giggled. "What happens if we slip up and cum?"

Mary slithered her body around Jack and gazed at him coldly. "It's a bad news/good news scenario. The bad news is that Jack loses his manhood; the good news is that we'll have fresh sausage for our early morning snack. Those blades in my dungeon aren't for show, you know."

The three of them laughed crazily and immediately began making love. Ever the director, Mary made sure they desisted at just the right moment and commenced the meditation. At once Jack fell into a deep state of Being. He felt as if he were effortlessly present as Presence itself, and that his Presence had no boundaries. As thoughts arose, he neither grasped nor rejected them, and they spontaneously dissolved. As he rested in this Presence of boundless, radiant Light, it was obvious to him that he was this Light, and that everything in the universe was simply a modification or permutation of it.

Meanwhile Polly found herself struggling. Unlike her earlier meditation session, when she experienced oneness and love, she spent most of this period mentally processing everything she'd experienced that evening. "I couldn't get beyond my thoughts," she explained at the end of the session. "I now see that meditation is a discipline that will take lots of hard work and have many ups and downs."

"Very astute observations, my sister," said Mary. "Meditation is hard for everyone... right, Jack?"

Jack, still in a state of ecstasy, could not disagree more. "I haven't done enough to say for sure," he said with a chuckle, "but the meditation I just 'did' was easy, because I did nothing but sit and *be*. My thought-forms spontaneously evaporated in the Clear Light, and I just basked in the radiance."

He could not have provided a clearer description. For at that moment Jack's entire form began to glow, as if he were a light bulb. Mary and Polly sat there agape. There was nothing they could say; they were bearing witness to a profound transformation, and knew it.

"Tell us, Jack," Mary finally said. "Are you just experiencing silent Presence, or is the Power from above pouring into you?"

"I feel immense pressure at my third-eye area," Jack replied. "It's as if the Power wants to pour into me, but is blocked. I assume that when Mother Mary initiates me, she will open that chakra and the divinization process will consummate itself."

"You assume right," said Mary. "She'll press on your third-eye area and open your *ajna* 'chakra door,' which will allow Divine Power, Light-energy from above, to irradiate your entire bodily-being. What's amazing is that even with your third eye closed, you're still receiving enough Light to make you glow."

Polly shook her head in amazement. "Mary, if we weren't on LSD, would we be able to see Jack shine?"

"Very unlikely," Mary replied. "I can see Mother Mary's aura when I'm on LSD, but not when I'm straight. I've done a lot of acid and been around a lot of so-called spiritual people while tripping — but aside from Mother Mary, Jack is the only person that I've seen glow."

She closed her eyes to savor the experience for a few extra moments. Then she had an inspiration. "As long as you're both still high, let's go back into the dungeon," she said with glee. "It is such a fucking trip when you're on acid."

She ushered them into her private chambers. She dimmed the lights and put on a CD of baroque music, playing it just loud enough for its haunting rhythm to reverberate throughout the room.

"Wow, this is so heavy and intense," said Polly. "I feel like I've just crossed the Bridge of Sighs and entered a netherworld."

Mary laughed as she reached for a book with the complete works of Hieronymus Bosch. While Polly gasped at the grotesque and surrealistic images, Jack contemplated the deep, dark energy of the medieval-like torture room.

"I still don't get it," said Polly. "How can you be a yogi and a sadist at the same time?"

"Simple," said Mary as she caressed her cheek. "You're a sweet, romantic Libra, and your dharma is one of harmony and balance. I'm cursed with nasty karma, with cruel, bizarre, and obsessive tendencies. If you knew astrology, or had an astrologer read my chart, you'd understand."

"So it's like having a split personality," said Polly.

"Not exactly, but close," said Mary. "Luckily I have a strong will, a spiritual orientation, and a positive outlet — namely, this dungeon and a slew of masochistic clients to help me keep it together."

"And what does Mother Mary say about your extreme tendencies?" asked Jack.

"Why don't you ask her?" said Mary.

"I already did," said Jack. "But I don't know if she was completely forthright with me."

Suddenly Mary felt very emotional. "Well, ask her again," she said. "She's my stepmother and spiritual teacher — and whatever personal words are exchanged between us, stay between us. I know that she warned you about me..." She hung her head and sobbed.

"I'm so glad to see you cry," said Polly, taking her by the hand. "I love your power and courage, but I'm also thrilled to see your soft, vulnerable side. It makes you more human and a little less of a... Super Bitch."

Jack joined the girls, and the three of them hugged tightly until Mary regained her composure.

By now they were well into the early morning hours. Mary invited them to watch some videos on the wall-sized screen in her game room. Given their heightened state of awareness, and eager to trigger a discussion, she suggested that they start with a YouTube video in which various experts debunk the findings of the U.S. government's *9/11 Commission Report*.

"You watch this and try to tell me it wasn't an inside job," Mary McDonald boiled. "I may not be a structural engineer, but even a moron can tell you that planted explosives brought down those buildings. WTC 7 was a controlled collapse if ever there was one. It wasn't hit by a plane, it just fell down.

"I started watching these videos a couple of days ago," she continued. "Between them and reading Jesse Ventura's books, it was a no-brainer for me to switch to libertarianism. The government investigation was totally bogus, and over a thousand structural engineers, architects, and professional airplane pilots signed a petition demanding a proper investigation — but that investigation never happened because the government is rotten to the core.

"Compounding the tragedy is that the mainstream media never pushed for one, either. Nor did they do any investigations of their own."

By the time the hour-long video ended, Jack was disgusted, too. "We study political science at a so-called institution of higher learning, and all they teach us is establishment bullshit and propaganda," he said. "Our professors are off-the-assembly-line idiots enmeshed in the Matrix. Why, for example, didn't 'Pea Brain' Potts ever broach the subjects of 9/11, Rand's Objectivism, or Rothbard's libertarianism?"

"You call him 'Pea Brain,' I call him 'Pea Hole,'" Mary chuckled. "Of course, his parents named him 'Pea Body.' If you went around life with a name like that, you'd be mentally and psychologically challenged, too."

By now it was 5:30 a.m., as evidenced by the sunlight shining through the game room window. As exhilarating as the evening had been, they were all beginning to crash. Jack and Polly quickly got dressed and made their way to the front door.

Jack kissed Mary and thanked her for another wonderful, crazy time. Now that she was a certified right-winger, he suggested that she come to the next Objectivist meeting on Friday night. "That ought to give 'em a rise in their shorts," he cracked.

"If not elsewhere in their pants," she smiled.

Then she embraced Polly and gave her a loving kiss. "You're my new best friend, the sweet little sister I never had. I love you." Then she whispered something that made Polly giggle, and bade them both goodnight.

Jack slowly and carefully pulled out of the driveway. Even though the streets were bare, he was still a little spaced out and didn't want to take any unnecessary chances.

"So what did she tell you?" he asked.

"Oh, nothing," said Polly. "Just that she wanted to go shopping together this week." She reached across and draped her hand right next to his cock. "She wants to buy me some skimpy outfits that will drive you wild!"

She raised her eyebrows as if in anticipation, and then started to laugh.

Jack thought that was funny, too, but in the back of his mind he wondered. While he was ecstatic that Polly had hit it off with Mary, he wasn't sure if he wanted her to become a mini version of his mistress.

* * *

The next thing Jack knew, it was almost 1:00 p.m. His legs felt like lead weights, and the baggy-eyed reflection he saw in the bathroom mirror was that of a man much older than nineteen. All he could do was shake his head. He had figured a drug as intoxicating as LSD would have negative side effects; now he knew for sure.

He stumbled his way to the kitchen. Polly was making lunch. She had the wisdom to call in sick from work; she felt as if her nerves had been singed. "I had a great time last night, Jack, and I definitely want to drop acid with Mary again. She is just so trippy and far out."

"Aren't you afraid of what she might do to us if her dark side gets the better of her?" he smiled.

"Not anymore," she said. "I don't believe she would ever hurt us. She just enjoys teasing you with her dominatrix persona... Jackie Poo!"

Jack took her in his arms, dipped her, and gave her a deep kiss. "So you're saying I should let her strap me down?"

"I wouldn't go that far," Polly said reflexively. That's tempting fate."

He sat down at the kitchen table while Polly made him something to eat. He opened the *Washington Post* to the Entertainment section. Immediately his eyes focused on a small article at the bottom of the page. A paleontologist named Paul Patterson was scheduled to appear that evening at the Mithras Bookstore in the South Beltway Mall. He would be discussing his new book, *Paleontology for Dummies.*

Hmmm... Patterson. That's the same guy Mary put me in touch with... The same guy I talked to yesterday, about the skeleton.

Perhaps it was just the burning curiosity he had about that mysterious shed near Mary's pool. But something told Jack it would be worth his while to attend that book signing that evening.

· · ·

After lunch, Jack decided to call Mother Mary. They discussed a new date for his initiation. He asked if he could bring along Polly.

"That will be fine," said Mother Mary. "Mary told me she's an open and loving soul who will take to spiritual life like a fish takes to water."

"Yeah, but thanks to Mary, she's also taking to drugs, wildness, and bitchdom," said Jack. "I know that change is part of life, but a part of me wishes that Polly remain sweet and innocent."

"I understand, Jack... but there are worse fates for a virile young man than to have two hot and sexy girlfriends. Am I right?"

"As always, Mother Mary." They shared a hearty laugh.

He told her of his plans to quit drugs once he was initiated and resumed his martial arts training. "I'm going to totally devote my life to becoming a world champion martial artist and an Enlightened spiritual master."

She told him that once he was initiated he no longer needed to devote himself to anything. "All your work was done in previous incarnations," she explained. "Once I open your third eye, you'll not only be fully awake spiritually, you'll also have full mastery of the *chi*. The *chi* will elevate your already world-class martial arts skills to a level that is quantum leaps beyond your competition."

"Meaning... I won't have any competition?"

"Exactly," said Mother Mary. "And when the time comes for you to face Putin, you will utterly destroy him... When I told Mary that, she almost had an orgasm."

Jack laughed as his mind flashed back to the thought of decapitating his rival in the Octagon. For a moment he considered sharing that with Mother Mary, but thought better of it. Besides, for all he knew, Mary McDonald had already told her.

Instead he decided to ask her another question. "Mary said that you postponed my initiation because you felt I needed to be strapped down and tortured before I could receive the Shakti. Did you really say that, or is that just Mary being Mary?"

For a moment Mother Mary fell silent. She was afraid that something like this would happen. "Jack, I warned you about Mary," she said. "I never told her to strap you down, and under no circumstances would I ever tell her to strap you down. I know you find her intoxicating, but she is like playing with fire. *You must be careful with her at all times.* Do you understand?"

Jack's head was beginning to throb. "Yes," he said solemnly. "I have no one but myself to blame if I end up in a box."

"Well, at least hold off your demise for another week or two," she chuckled. "My initiations are far more successful with live bodies than with dead ones..."

They shared a laugh, then Mother Mary informed him that she had second thoughts about Jack bringing Polly that evening. "I think you'll be more than capable of initiating her yourself, after I baptize you."

"If you think it's better that I come alone," said Jack, "then that is what I'll do."

They said goodbye, then Jack called John Mulligan. He told him that Mary had renounced her left-wing ideals and was joining the libertarian movement. "She'll be coming to the Objectivist group on Friday."

"My brother will like the sound of that," John cracked. "He has such a hard-on for her, he's contemplating paying for her services."

"Maybe I can get him a discount," Jack said wryly. "Many Christian mystics believe Mary Magdalene was a prostitute, but it would shock them to know that Jesus is a pimp in this incarnation." They shared a laugh and arranged to meet for dinner on Sunday night.

● ● ●

A few hours later, Jack drove out to the Mithras Bookstore. He arrived early, hoping that he could speak to Professor Patterson privately before his 7:00 p.m. book signing. He was in luck: A store employee directed him to the science section, where he found the paleontologist seated at a small table that was stacked with copies of *Paleontology for Dummies*. He was going over the notes for his talk.

Jack shook Patterson's hand and introduced himself. "We spoke yesterday over the phone. I want to thank you again for examining the skeleton I found."

Patterson looked at him with bewilderment. "I know you're Jack Cohen, and I'm pleased to meet you. You are no doubt one of the finest young men this city has ever produced. But I have no idea what you're talking about. I've never spoken to you before."

Now it was Jack's turn to be puzzled. Granted, some academics can be easily distracted; given his pending appearance that night, it was possible that Patterson's mind was elsewhere at the moment. But the professor seemed certain they hadn't talked before. Jack dismissed that as a possibility.

He picked up a copy of *Paleontology for Dummies* and looked for the author photo. It certainly looked like the gentleman standing in front of him. Something wasn't adding up.

"I know you're getting ready for your signing," Jack said. "May I ask you two questions?"

"As long as they're brief, yes."

"Do you know a Mary McDonald, and have you examined any local Iroquois Indian skeletons in the past forty-eight hours?"

Dr. Patterson shook his head. "I'm sorry, Jack. I wish I could help you, but I don't know any Mary McDonald, and I haven't looked at any Iroquois skeletons. As a matter of fact, there were no Iroquois Indians in Washington, D.C."

That sent a chill up Jack's spine. Now he knew that Mary had played him.

Whoever he'd spoken to yesterday, it wasn't Professor Patterson. Which made him all the more curious about what was inside that shed.

* * *

Two nights later, Jack met Mary at Brother Bill's apartment. Other than a quick phone call earlier in the day, in which he suggested that they get together at her place after the Objectivist meeting, he had not spoken to her since leaving her pad early Wednesday morning. He wasn't about to tell her of his meeting with the real Professor Patterson until after he had thoroughly searched her home for the skull — and that search would begin with that mysterious shed.

As always she was easy to spot. She wore a skintight, low-cut pale blue dress that exposed ample décolletage while drawing the other male attendees like flies. He kissed her affectionately, so as to remind the group that she belonged to him.

John Mulligan pulled him aside and winked. He'd never seen Mary McDonald before and, needless to say, he was impressed. "My bro and I see eye to eye about as often as a cat barks, but he's spot on this time: Your girlfriend is a drop-dead knockout, a man-killer extraordinaire."

Jack smiled uncomfortably. Now that he had reason to suspect her again in the disappearance of Ellsworth Shitzer, the choice of the word "man-killer" struck him as hauntingly apt.

He was about to attempt a reply when he was greeted by Brother Bill. "Good to see you again, Jack. I'm glad your girlfriend is OK and able to grace us with her liberal presence."

"I hate to disappoint you, Bill, but Mary is no longer a liberal. She's seen the light and has joined our team."

Ecstatic to hear that news, Bill called the meeting to order and invited Mary to tell the group about her political awakening.

She began by stating that she was a political science major and had read Rand and Rothbard long before her conversion. But because she "held out hope that the government, the State, could uplift the downtrodden masses, benignly rein in malignant corporatism, and curtail its own exploitative imperialism," she had continued to support left-wing Democrats up until a few days ago. The coup de grace for her was reading Jesse Ventura's classic

121

text, *DemoCRIPS and ReBLOODicans*, which crystallized what had been brewing in her mind for quite some time.

"I no longer have faith in the State," she said. "I now recognize it for what it is: a leviathan, neo-Orwellian, Mafia-like protection racket. I now see that liberalism — not classical liberalism, but progressivist liberalism — is fascist in nature, a legalized version of Al Capone on steroids. It enslaves the masses, making them weak and dependent; it partners up with rather than punishes malignant corporations; and in concert with the defense industry, it expands rather than contracts the U.S. war machine.

"Finally, the so-called liberals really aren't liberal. If they were, they'd legalize victimless 'crimes,' such as drugs, gambling, and prostitution. Ventura's book consummated my decision to change my allegiance. I realized that I could no longer, in good conscience, support left-wing progressivism, the ever-expanding, ever-more-repressive federal government."

With that the group broke into applause — everyone, that is, except for a longtime member named Joe. He was about Bill's age and, like most of the other men in the group, ogled Mary and thought of her constantly, even when he made love to his wife.

Noting that Mary's face still had black and blue marks, Joe told the group, with tongue in cheek, that he didn't buy her story. "My guess is that Jack here, Mr. Martial Artist Extraordinaire himself, slapped her around and knocked some sense into her until she saw the political light," he said, to uproarious laughter. "Not that I'm being critical, Jack. In fact, as soon as I get home I think I'll beat the shit out of my wife until she converts to Objectivism." That also broke everyone up.

Now that he was on a roll, Joe floated the idea of making Mary the new "Goddess of the Right," replacing Ayn Rand. "Here's the plan: We put her in a bikini, plaster her pictures and videos all over the Internet and, presto, every red-blooded male on the planet will want to become an Objectivist."

Mary rose from her chair, sashayed over to Joe, and gave him a high five. The crowd, as they say, went wild.

Somewhat embarrassed over the outpour, Brother Bill restored order by inviting Jack to discuss his findings on Rand's epistemology. Jack began by stating that, as fascinated as he was by Rand's epistemology, he also believed that she harbored beliefs that do not correspond with reality. "Rand claims that she has solved the problem of universals, which has plagued philosophers since antiquity. But I hardly find her argument convincing. In fact, though Rand is the master of definitions, she never exactly says what universals are, apart from vaguely conflating them with abstractions. Nor does she ever broach the subject of different categories of universals.

"In other words," Jack continued, "Rand's consideration of universals is superficial. According to Rand, only singular individual objects, such as an apple, exist in nature, and because the qualities of these objects, such as color, never exist apart from the object itself, any universal quality, or *qualitative* universal, such as redness, that can be attributed to the object itself is simply an *abstraction*, a mental construct that enables one to conceptually grasp the object. But many philosophers reject her claim, arguing that universals are *metaphysical* in nature, not epistemological — ergo, the redness of one apple is not exactly the same as another.

"But what if we were to consider a piece of uniform white paper that is cut into pieces that are exactly the same size — that is to say, identical pieces of paper. In this case, we have what is called a *specific*, as opposed to *qualitative*, universal. In my mind (and in the minds of many philosophers), the universal identicalness of these pieces of paper is metaphysical in nature, not epistemological. In other words, whether or not one recognizes the identicalness of these pieces of paper, their exact similarity is still a metaphysical reality."

Jack could tell from the sea of glazed eyes that he was beginning to lose his audience. "I suspect that many of you are not deeply into epistemology," he joked, "so I'll move on to a few other aspects of Rand's epistemology that I find problematic, such as her assertion that a child is born *tabula rasa*, as a 'blank slate' with no 'pre-programming' or any kind of innate talent. I find this line of reasoning both counterintuitive and unscientific.

"First of all, it couldn't be more obvious to me that individuals are born with particular natural intelligences — be they mental, physical, musical, artistic, or whatever. The 'gifted' child is not gifted because he worked hard and is 'self-made,' as Rand would claim; he is gifted because he is genetically endowed. My guess is that Rand's own psycho-epistemology — her own extreme anti-deterministic mindset — prevented her from seeing and acknowledging the blatant reality of natural talent. Moreover, it prevented her from taking the next, politically incorrect step: that certain races, on average, are inherently smarter than others.

"Culturally unbiased IQ tests prove the mental superiority of certain races. But because this is a touchy subject, the political and academic establishment has sidestepped this issue (and, perhaps, wisely so). And Objectivists, because of their myopic allegiance to Rand's philosophy, also ignore the scientific data on the subject.

"What most people observe directly — that talent or intelligence is much more a product of heredity than environment — is confirmed by scientific studies," Jack continued. "For example, identical twins separated at birth and raised in very different environments are apt to end up remarkably similar as adults. Not only do they tend to end up with similar IQs, jobs, and hobbies, they even tend to dress alike and often own the same breed of dogs. But because Rand was biased against genetic predetermination, she doesn't account for the overwhelming influence of genes relative to intelligence and learning ability.

"Rand's epistemology also fails to account for the fact that the way in which infants and young children learn is different than that of adults. For example, children up to the age of five, unlike older humans, quickly and easily learn multiple languages. It's almost as if they learn by an 'analog form of osmosis,' rather than by the Objectivist 'digital form of cognition' — the measurement-omission process that Rand expounds. But Rand doesn't address the fact that the hardwiring of a young child's brain (that is to say, their mechanism of learning) differs markedly from that of an adult. For her, one size, or one method, fits all. In my mind, that makes her guilty of the very thing that she preaches against: reductionism."

Jack went on to say that he was particularly fascinated by the one area of epistemology that Rand happened to reject: so-called "mystical knowledge," or knowledge that is gained by arational, non-sensory means. But he added that he would refrain from commenting on that subject until he obtained more first-hand mystical experience.

He opened the floor to questions. Paul, the plastic surgeon, wanted Jack's thoughts on Rand's measurement-omission theory. "Given the studies involving identical twins and the fact that infants and young children learn language differently than adults, do you patently reject her measurement-omission theory, or do you think it has some validity?"

"I think it is valid relative to rational, sense-based knowledge," answered Jack. "I applaud Rand for originating it, and it is a theory that I will continue to contemplate as I work on building my own philosophical system."

"I think Jack needs to contemplate Rand's viewpoint on universals more deeply," added Brother Bill. "The 'problem of universals' cannot be solved from any viewpoint other than Rand's Objectivist one. If you further contemplate Rand's assertion that there are only particulars, or discrete entities, in nature, I believe you'll realize that universals are simply abstractions that enable men to grasp reality."

Not sure if Brother Bill was right, Jack let the group know that he would further contemplate the subject and apprise them of his thinking at the next meeting.

Bill opened the forum to general discussion, which centered on the collapsing economy. Twenty minutes later, he called for a break. As the rest of the group shuffled out to the patio, Bill pulled Jack aside and suggested that they meet for lunch. Knowing that Jack's hobbies included computer programming, he wanted to discuss a joint effort regarding a potentially lucrative program that he was working on. They agreed to meet at noon on the following Wednesday.

Jack stepped outside and spotted Mary in deep discussion with the brothers Mulligan. "I just told Jim that I've finished reading *The Creature from Jekyll Island*," she said. "Now I understand what he'd been ranting about. If we could get every American to read that book, there'd be a revolution in this country for sure."

Then she urged Jack to tell the group the story of his confrontation with his dad. "All of us think it would prove enlightening," she added.

Jack agreed and, with Brother Bill's blessing, proceeded to do just that once the gathering resumed. He spoke for about fifteen minutes, and the group responded with a heartfelt ovation.

"So, tell us, Jack," said Brother Bill once the applause died down. "Now that you've renounced your father and everything he stands for, is there anything else you'd like to share with us tonight?"

"Yes," said Jack with a glint in his eye. "I now plan to devote my life to extirpating the Federal Reserve." Again the group clapped madly.

* * *

The rest of the meeting was devoted to discussing ways to educate the public about the evils of the Federal Reserve System. When the group broke up, Jack confirmed his Sunday dinner plans with John and Jim Mulligan, then headed for Mary's house. By the time he arrived she had changed into a black silk camisole with matching panties and heeled slippers. She led him straight to the bedroom, where she pulled out a hash pipe and a chunk of hash from her nightstand drawer and put on a heavy metal CD.

He took a hit from the pipe, slowly exhaled, and drew her body next to his. He kissed her affectionately and engaged her in a slow dance.

"Honey, I love this music," he said. "It's so intense, so ominous."

Mary McDonald chuckled. "Two weeks ago when I first met you, you weren't into dope and metal, and now you are. Trust me, before you know it, you'll be begging me to strap you down."

He slid his hands along her waist and thumbed the small of her back. "I wouldn't be so sure of that," he smiled. "This is just a temporary phase I'm going through. After I get initiated by Mother Mary and restart my martial arts training, I'm cutting out the drugs and becoming a saint."

"Oh, really?" she said, clutching his backside and thrusting his pelvis toward her. "I'll be the judge of that."

"No, I will," he said. "I talked to Mother Mary. She told me I don't have to get strapped down before she initiates me."

Mary didn't like the sound of that, though she happened to know it was true. But she also believed that she could still control Jack, so long as she kept him aroused.

"What else did she say about me?" she asked.

"That you're a dangerous girl," he said, "and that if I keep fooling with you, I'll end up dead."

She proceeded to grab his nose and pull on it. "Jackie Pinocchio, you are fucking fibbing. There is no way Mother Mary said that about me, and you know it." Then she tugged on his cock and rolled him onto the bed, where they passionately embraced and kissed.

Mary wanted him to take her, but Jack had something else in mind. Affectionately he looked into her eyes and came clean. "Mother Mary simply told me what I already know — that you're fire, and if I play with you I could get burned."

She took a hit of hash, blew the smoke right in his face, and laughed. "Then why do you play with me?"

"Because love is blind," he said sheepishly, "and I'm hopelessly in love with you."

She caressed his face with her fingertips and pressed her lips against his. "Every woman wants to be loved by her man," she said. "I am so happy that I have made you mine — *all mine*. And I love you to death, too."

With that they began to undress each other. As they did, Jack noticed the new tattoo that extended out from Mary's belly button: a black widow.

"Do you like it?" she asked coyly. "Or is it too domineering a statement?"

If Jack had been a little older and a bit wiser, he would have recognized the spider as an ominous sign of what was to come. But as bright as he was, being only nineteen, and by now deeply stoned, he didn't make the connection.

He kissed the spider, laughed wildly, and gave in to his carnal desires. After making passionate love, he and his mistress fell asleep in each other's arms.

* * *

Saturday morning Jack awoke at the crack of dawn. Noticing that Mary was sound asleep, he dressed himself quickly and retrieved the lock pick set from his travel bag. Some years before, one of his first after-school jobs was assisting the neighborhood locksmith. There, he learned that there was no such thing as a lock that could not be picked — even one as heavy as the deadbolt on that mysterious shed next to Mary's gym. Now, at last, he would find out what was inside.

Quietly he slipped out of the house and made his way to the shed. It didn't take long to undo the lock. He pulled the door open, turned on the light — and immediately gasped in shock. Before him, on a shelf overlooking a small desk in the corner of the room, sat a human skull; next to the skull sat a jar containing a man's penis. A plastic museum-type tag identified the skull as "Big Shit Head," while a second tag designated the penis as "Little Shit Head."

He picked up the jar and stared at the tiny prick floating in formaldehyde. He couldn't help but laugh. *If this belonged to Senator Shitzer, no wonder he was such an ass. With a dick that size, he probably suffered from "small man's disease."*

He checked the shed for other human artifacts and found none. Satisfied,

127

he locked the shed door and headed back to the house.

What he didn't know was that Mary McDonald was now wide awake, eyeing him like a cat. From her vantage point behind the living room curtains, she had seen everything. Now it was time to strap him down.

She hurried back to bed and pretended that she was asleep. She heard Jack as he reentered the house and made his way to the bedroom. He glanced at her briefly, then headed to the bathroom to shower. At that moment she got up and let out an exaggerated yawn, loud enough for him to hear.

"Good morning," he said, peering back into the bedroom. "I hope I didn't wake you."

"Oh, no," she said, admiring his naked form. "What would you like for breakfast?"

"I think I'll carb-binge this morning," he said, blowing her a kiss. "I'd like both waffles and French toast, and a couple glasses of raw goat's milk."

"Coming right up," she said as she threw on a robe. Once she heard the water running, she opened her nightstand drawer, pulled out a bottle of chloral hydrate, and slipped it into her pocket. Then she smiled diabolically as she made her way downstairs.

. . .

It didn't take long for the sedative to take effect. By the time Jack awoke, several hours had elapsed, during which time Mary had wheeled him into the dungeon and laid him spread-eagle onto her torture table. His arms and legs were locked in place, his mouth had been muzzled. His head still felt heavy from having been drugged, though he was able to move it around enough to observe his surroundings. To the right of him he saw images playing on a large high-definition screen in the back of the room. Given his disoriented condition, he couldn't tell for sure... but he thought he saw and heard the voice of Bette Davis.

To the left he saw a long stainless steel rod sticking out from what appeared to be a black metal grill. The grill was attached to a gas burner. He couldn't quite tell what was going on, but from the looks of things he saw that something was heating up. Next to the grill was a large book; hanging on the wall behind the grill was an assortment of various knives.

Jack looked up and closed his eyes. *This can't be happening.*

Then he recognized the now familiar aroma of organic tobacco. He opened his eyes and there she was, Mary McDonald, standing before him in full dominatrix regalia. She blew a plume of smoke in his face and let out a wicked laugh.

"For a while I thought you'd never wake up," she said. "Welcome to our Passion Play."

She slithered next to him. "I saw you come out of the shed this morning, Jackie Poo," she said coldly. "Now that you know what I did to Senator Shitzer, I have no choice but to eliminate you."

She paused and shook her head. He couldn't tell for sure, but he thought he saw tears forming in her eyes.

"It's a shame I have to do this," she continued. "I love you so much, and I really do want to see you become Jesus 2.0... If only you'd left it alone, Jack. Then you wouldn't have to die."

At that moment a surge of adrenalin ran through her, a feeling of omnipotence that was almost sexual in nature. She'd experienced this sensation many times before as a domme, but rarely as intensely as this. There were so many things she wanted to do to him, she could feel herself getting wet.

She pointed to the screen in the background. "That's one of my favorite movies — *The Dark Secrets of Harvest Home*, with Bette Davis. Have you ever seen it?"

Mary cackled at the muffled sound coming out of Jack's mouth. "Oh, that's right... how silly of me. You can't talk!"

She crushed out her cigarette and told him what happens to one of the characters in the movie. "A curious man finds out too much about a murderous feminist cult — sound familiar, Jackie Poo? The women blind the man, cut off his tongue, and keep him as a human pet."

She ran her fingers down his chest and draped them above his cock. "I could do that with you, Jack. I have a secret underground dungeon that nobody knows about — nobody alive, that is. I could keep you as my human pet, chained and perpetually drugged."

She massaged his groin sensuously until he became hard. "Your cum is so sweet and delicious," she giggled, "I'd harvest it as my health drink."

Mary reached for the book on the side table. Jack gasped; it was one of the volumes he'd seen hidden in the closet of her study: *The Mexican Drug Cartel*

Guide to Torture and Dismemberment. "While you were knocked out, I made use of the time by boning up on slicing and dicing techniques."

She laughed as she unbuckled his pants and pulled them down to his knees. Noticing his erection, she devilishly added, "Or should I say, boner-ing up."

She pulled a long, super-sharp knife off the wall and gently stuck the blade against his penis. Immediately it drew blood. She wiped the blood with a cloth and continued to brandish the knife. "This is my favorite weapon," she said matter-of-factly. "I used it to decapitate Shitzer. The first time I used it, I realized why the Mexican drug cartels and Islamic terrorists prefer this method of killing — it's so phallic... so sexy... so exciting."

Again she became aroused. She put down the knife, slid her fingers inside her black latex thong, and began to masturbate. The combination of thinking about what she was about to do to him, and knowing that she was prolonging his agony to the very last second, quickly made her orgasm.

She cleaned herself off, turned to the grill, and picked up the steel rod. She licked her lips and peered at him menacingly as she dangled it before him.

To Jack's horror, it was a branding iron with an image of a cross. His father had been right all along.

"You know, Jack, Mother Mary said that playing with me was like playing with fire," she taunted him. "Now you're going to get burned."

She pulled him to the edge of the table. Then she grabbed his right buttocks with her hand and squeezed it, causing him to flinch. "Ever since I learned that you were Jesus reincarnated, I have fantasized about branding a cross on your ass. Now I finally get to do it."

The iron was white hot, ready to do her bidding. She flashed it within a few millimeters of his eyes before driving it deep into his flesh.

Jack's muzzled scream filled the room, but only for a few moments. Then he was silent.

In the meantime Mary McDonald was in ecstasy as she admired his seared cheek. "Too bad you can't see it, Jackie Poo... it's beautiful," she said. "But we're just getting started. There will be plenty for you to see — until I take your eyes out!"

She pressed her thumbs against his eyes and again laughed hysterically. "But I'm not without a heart," she continued. "I'm going to leave you alone for a while before I proceed with your termination. Who knows, maybe you can find some final peace." Then she let out one last cackle before she left the room.

* * *

Jack braced himself for the inevitable when she returned a few minutes later. To his surprise, however, she freed his limbs, removed the muzzle, and gently caressed his face.

"The game is over," said Mary McDonald as she hung her head in disgrace. "I realize how much I love you, and I could never, ever kill you. You are Jesus 2.0, the God-man destined to save the world. I could never deprive humanity of your Saving Grace. Do with me what you will."

Jack stood to his feet and, to her surprise, smiled and warmly embraced her. "Don't worry, Mary, I've already forgiven you." He drew her close to him and kissed her.

She asked if he was going to turn her in to the police. He assured her that he wouldn't. "Ellsworth Shitzer was human vermin," he said. "The world is a better place without him."

She laughed in relief and let him in on one last secret: Shitzer was indeed a client, but his death was a freak accident. "He died from auto-erotic asphyxiation," she explained. "He was another kinky guy, and that happened to be one of his fetishes. He went out like a candle, and I couldn't revive him. Since no one knew he was here, I never reported it."

Mary couldn't tell if Jack was convinced. His face was expressionless, and she needed to know. "You believe me, don't you?"

He looked at her for the longest time before he started to laugh. "Have you ever given me any reason not to believe you?"

She sassily stuck out her tongue, then asked him what was on his mind when she left him alone. "To tell you the truth, not much," he said. "I was peacefully resigned to my fate, and to God's will. So I mostly thought about the philosophical 'problem of universals' — and then I had an epiphany. I realized that Rand and Bill are right: Universals are abstractions. The only things that exist in nature are particulars."

Mary couldn't believe it. "But you screamed when I branded you. That sounded like genuine suffering to me."

Jack shook his head and smiled. "I faked that, in the hope it would stop you from killing me... and for all I know, it did."

"You're a better man that I, Gunga Din," said Mary McDonald. "Or should I say, Jesus. I can only imagine what you'll be like after Mother Mary initiates you."

"I'm not Jesus yet, but I no longer feel pain like an ordinary human," said Jack. "Oh, it may have hurt a little, but my nervous system has changed radically just from the little meditation I've done."

Then, to her utter amazement, he said that he wanted her to brand the left side of his ass. "I think it will look so cool to have matching crosses on my buttocks. Then I will truly be the baddest ass on the planet, and no longer the pathetic tight ass you need to discipline."

So she did. He grimaced slightly, but didn't issue a sound. Mary administered antibiotic gel on both burns to prevent infection. Then she led him back into her bedroom, where they made love for hours.

When she awoke she found him gazing at the ceiling, as if he were lost in thought. "You know, Jack, in a matter of weeks you'll be world famous," she said as she snuggled beside him. "You'll have millions of followers who will hang on your every word. How will you handle the constant and intense scrutiny?"

"I have no idea," he said softly. "I'll be stepping on big toes with my messages, and the Big Boys will be looking to take me out. It's a question of how much I can accomplish before I'm silenced. I really expect a short, but hopefully spectacular, run. But it will be fun while it lasts."

Mary became somber. "Maybe we'll end up like Bonnie and Clyde, going out in a blaze of glory."

"Look at the bright side," he chuckled. "Your hot pin-up pictures will last for eternity. You'll cause more guys to jack off than Rita Hayworth, Marilyn Monroe, and Farrah Fawcett combined."

She playfully slapped him. "Jackie Poo, you are too much. Just too much." Then they clasped each other and affectionately kissed and embraced.

* * *

Sunday evening Jack met the brothers Mulligan for dinner at a downtown hof brau. As they sat down to eat, Jack filled them in on his ordeal in Mary's dungeon, and what had happened to Ellsworth Shitzer.

"I'm telling you," John Mulligan insisted, "that gal is gonna end up in charge of our torture and interrogation operation in Vegas. I doubt Shitzer was the first man she dismembered, and I doubt he'll be the last."

They laughed wildly before bringing Jack up to speed on their desert operation. "We're building an extensive underground network right now, focusing on accumulating weaponry," John explained. "Our arsenals will be state of the art — and unless the State wants a civil war, they'll let us secede from the nation and establish our own truly sovereign republic."

"How are you funding this?" asked Jack.

"Some well-to-do patrons are enabling us to buy up considerable chunks of land," said Jim. "But we'll need big bucks to build and solidify our base and operation. One of our ideas to generate money is to write a computer program that kicks butt in sports betting. We have twenty years of sports databases, just waiting to be decoded... and we think you're the perfect guy to develop the algorithm."

"What's the end game?" asked Jack.

"We want to make computer-generated lines on games that, on average, are closer to the final score than the betting lines," said Jim. "That's the whole enchilada."

"It sounds simple in theory," John added. "But it's a lot tougher in reality, because the betting lines are that good. Only a handful of players can consistently beat them in the long run."

"That's why I make a good living as a bookmaker," said Jim. "Plenty of computer whizzes have had their asses handed to them trying to beat the betting lines. If you succeed, Jack, you'll be among the select few. What do you say?"

"I'm game," said Jack without hesitation. "I can't guarantee I can beat the betting lines, but I'll give it a shot."

"Cool," said John. He checked his watch; he had just enough time to get to the airport and catch the red-eye back to Vegas. "You got any questions, talk to Jim. Meantime, we'll stay in touch."

●　●　●

Jack spent the next couple of days acquainting himself with the nuances of sports betting. By Wednesday afternoon, he was ready for a break, which arrived in the form of his scheduled lunch at the home of Brother Bill. The entrée was one of Bill's specialties: homemade Caribbean lasagna, a simple dish that became exotic, thanks to a subtle but exquisite blend of spices.

Jack complimented the chef, who in turn asked Jack if he'd changed his mind about Rand's position on universals.

"Yes, Brother Bill," he said. "The more I thought about it, the more I realized that only particulars exist, and that universals are simply protean abstractions that enable man to conceptually grasp and organize reality. I really appreciate your correction on this important philosophical matter."

Bill beamed at Jack with pride. "You are the perfect student, relentlessly devoted to truth — and yet, you're so precocious, you're ready right now to teach the entire world. You can become the John Galt that Objectivists have waited for."

"I beg to differ," said Jack. "John Galt was an atheist, and I'm a theist. I'll teach Objectivist epistemology and politics — but I don't agree with Rand's metaphysics, which I see as reductionist. From my perspective, Rand and Galt were guilty of what they preach against: Context-dropping."

Bill's smile promptly faded. That was not the response he'd anticipated. "Well, I succeeded in changing your mind about universals. Perhaps I can get you to do the same regarding spirituality."

"I'm afraid it's too late," said Jack. "I've already experienced the Numinous, and soon I expect to merge permanently with it. Tomorrow night I will be initiated by Mother Mary, Mary's guru, so that I can receive the Spirit without measure and thus reassume my True Nature as the One. By the time you see me again on Friday, I suspect you'll be the one who needs to reconsider spirituality."

Bill didn't like the sound of that, either. He decided to table that discussion and bring up the real reason why he had invited Jack for lunch. "I have a proposition for you," he explained. "It concerns the stock market."

Jack was intrigued. "I'm listening."

Bill explained that he'd spent the past eight years working on a computer program to beat the market. "It's a technical program, based on price and volume, but it's unique in that it mathematically identifies the cause of price/volume ratios, thereby enabling one to predict price movement."

"Sounds fascinating," said Jack. "What do you need me for?"

"I believe my program has virtually unlimited money-making potential," said Bill. "I need someone with genius-level computer programming skills who can help me integrate my findings into a functional algorithm that consistently works in multiple market environments."

Jack could feel his head spinning. Once again, his life seemed stranger than fiction. He told Bill that he had just met with the Mulligan brothers about working on a similar project concerning the sports betting market.

"Is there a conflict of interest?" asked Bill.

"Not at all," said Jack. "Your program sounds right up my alley, and it will be fun working on both at the same time. Who knows... maybe what I learn from one program, I can apply to the other."

"Then it's settled," said Bill with a smile. "Assuming you can come up with an algorithm that successfully integrates my findings, we can work out a percentage deal and sell the program for millions."

They shook hands on the deal and celebrated with a slice of Bill's homemade cheesecake.

. . .

Thursday began with a 10:00 a.m. phone call from Mother Mary. "Jack, I cannot tell you how excited I am as your initiation draws near. This will be an event of monumental cosmic significance. It will literally change the world."

"I couldn't agree more," said Jack. "My meditations and flashbacks to when I was Jesus have convinced me that I'm the Avatar."

He began to talk about what had happened on the previous Saturday, but Mother Mary already knew. "Mary McDonald tells me everything," she said. "I'm just glad she had the good sense to spare you."

"Maybe I can save her soul," said Jack. "I love her to no end."

"You didn't save her when she was Mary Magdalene," said Mother Mary. "Now you have a second chance."

They shared a laugh, then Mother Mary gave him final instructions. His baptism would take place at sunset that evening. "Be sure to fast for at least eight hours," she said. "Dress yourself in white, and bathe beforehand."

"Anything else?"

"Yes... whatever you do, stay out of dungeons!"

Again Jack laughed, and as he hung up the phone, he felt a glow radiating throughout his entire body. The time was nigh, and he could hardly wait.

· · ·

When he arrived at her house that evening, the front door was open. Mother Mary was in her temple, seated in a full lotus position. He reverently bowed down before her. She smiled, told him to relax his body, and laid her hands on his head. She pressed her fingers hard on his third-eye area, while resting her other hand on his crown.

Immediately Jack groaned in reaction to the immense pressure, but as instructed, he let go of his head and put his trust in her. Mother Mary removed her hands, and the moment she did, he felt his cranial bones begin to move. The shifting bones made a loud cracking noise, and he experienced instant relief as the pent-up pressure in his head morphed into a radiant force-current that poured into his Sacred Heart-center, two digits to the right of the center of his chest.

At that moment Jack knew exactly what to do. He directly communed with the down-pouring force-current, the Shakti, and merged his consciousness with it.

Suddenly, the force-current reversed direction, rushing up from his Heart-center to, through, and infinitely beyond his crown chakra — and as it did, Jack spontaneously realized Who he was: the Holy One Himself, temporarily appearing in the guise of Jack Cohen.

Jack knew that he had cut the Heart-knot and achieved what the Buddha called Nirvana, the Heart-release. He rested in the Blessing Power that, relative to his body, freely poured into and radiated out of his Heart-center. He recognized Himself as universal, timeless, spaceless Consciousness-Energy that had never been born and could never die. At that moment there was no longer any doubt: He was the Blessed One, the Avatar, and the ceaseless Blessing/Blissing Power he now experienced was his Self-Nature, the dynamic Self-Radiance of his Divine Self-Awareness.

Tears of joy streamed from Mother Mary's eyes as she watched him Awaken. When he looked at her, she bowed at him in reverence.

"Thank you so much," said Jack as he embraced her and kissed her cheek. "You have given me eternal Life. You will be my chief devotee, in charge of coordinating my missionary work. I could not ask for a more perfect lead disciple."

Mother Mary beheld the incarnate Blessed One and communed with his radiant Presence. "Jack, I am blessed and honored to serve you. Nothing could make me happier than to forever serve you and receive your Grace. From now on, my devotees will be your devotees, and my temple will be your temple."

Waves of Shakti poured from Jack as he gave her one last hug. She swooned in the Bliss-full emanation, and as he gazed upon her, he wondered if he would ever find another soul as pure and highly evolved as her.

* * *

He returned home, eager to initiate Polly. She stared into him as he entered the apartment, then fell to her knees as he Blessed her.

"Jack, you are En-Light-ened now and are consciously directing your Light-energy at me," she said. "I can feel your Love-Bliss, and I love it."

Delighted with her response, Jack put his hands on her head, causing her body to shake violently from the Shakti that he was transmitting to her. Polly had always been loyal to him; now that she was baptized, she was destined to remain his beloved consort. The knowledge of that greatly pleased him.

She fed him, and then he called Mary McDonald. "Honey, I'm En-Light-ened now. Mother Mary opened my *ajna* 'door,' and the Shakti poured down to my Heart-center and severed my Heart-knot. I am now *Siva-Shakti*, the Divine Being."

Jack couldn't see this, of course, but Mary was literally jumping for joy. She could hardly wait to be Blessed herself.

"No time like the present," said Jack.

With that he gave her the Shakti, right through the telephone. Mary felt the intensity of the Blessing, and beheld his Presence and Power. Then they arranged to meet the following night, before the next Objectivist meeting. He wanted her at his side when the group was confronted with his En-Light-ened Presence.

* * *

Friday evening Jack and Mary met at a bench not far from Brother Bill's apartment. They would have thirty minutes alone together before the meeting began at 7:00 p.m. They kissed deeply. Then, without saying a word, Mary fell to her knees and wept as she confessed her sins.

"Jack, I've been a bad girl, a terrible girl," she began. "It sickens me to know that I threatened to kill you — you, the Chosen One. I knew that you were destined to become the Avatar, and yet, for my own selfish enjoyment, I wanted to torture you anyway. Can you ever forgive me?"

"Mary, I've already forgiven you," he said as he gently stroked her head. "It was my destiny to meet you and experience your dark side. It was my choice to enter your world. Even when you locked me down and it seemed you were going to kill me, I knew what I was getting into. I do not blame you at all."

That lifted her spirits, and she smiled as he continued. "I am contemplating your karma as we speak. You are blessed with spiritual love and devotion, and cursed with deep, dark, diabolical predispositions. There is virtually nothing in between these two extremes. Until you fully Awaken, you will struggle mightily with your sadistic tendencies."

He gazed into her eyes intently. "Your salvation is Me. I am the Way to the Father, the Divine Being. Every time the urge to cause pain and injury arises, you must turn to Me and contemplate my Presence and Power. Through me, his incarnate Son, the Grace of the Father will save you. My Divine Shakti, the Holy Spirit, will Bless and En-Light-en you and outshine your afflictive tendencies.

"I know it is not possible for you to resort to Me in every moment," he continued, "but you must endeavor to do so. You are spiritually astute, so I'm not telling you anything you don't already know. Rather, I am re-emphasizing what you need to do."

She bowed her head in reverence, knowing that He was Right. "Thank you, Blessed One," she said. "Does this mean I must quit my work as a dominatrix?"

"No," said Jack. "Your clients want you to torture them. You're simply providing a service for men who are just as sick as you. But in a few weeks, my ministry will be pulling in millions. At that time, you can quit being a whore and instead become my beloved consort. You would join Polly as a personal *gopi* of mine, devoted to serving Me."

She stood up, threw her arms around Jack, and planted kisses all over his face. "Oh, Jack, I would love it! If you want, we could all live together in my house — you, me, and Polly. And I promise, I would get rid of my dungeon."

"Not so fast, cursed one," he laughed. "A wise leader uses everything at his disposal."

"I don't understand," she said.

He put his hands around her shoulders and gazed into her eyes. "You, sweet Mary, are uniquely gifted in inflicting pain. We may need you and your dungeon to help subdue our enemies."

The thought of that made her absolutely giddy. "Thy will be done," she said.

A broad smile crossed Jack's face as they strolled back to Bill's apartment. Mary, Polly and Mother Mary's acceptance of his En-Light-enment could not have been better. He suspected that the reaction of the Objectivists would be quite different.

* * *

The meeting had already commenced by the time Jack and Mary arrived. Brother Bill interrupted the proceedings and invited Jack to address the group regarding Rand and universals. Knowing how their Wednesday lunch had gone, Bill expected Jack to admit publicly that Rand was right.

To his surprise, Jack went in another direction, choosing instead to confess and elaborate upon his Awakening and describe his radical new insights:

"Yesterday my guru Spirit-baptized me and I awoke to my True Nature. Now that I have attained Self-realization, or Buddhahood, or Christ Consciousness, I have a fully En-Light-ened perspective: There are no separate objects in the universe. Every apparently separate thing, or existent, is simply the Divine Being, or Existent, appearing as a temporary modification or permutation of Itself. And I am that Divine Being, manifesting in the form of Jack Cohen. From the perspective of a deluded, apparently separate body-mind, Rand's perspective is correct; but from the perspective of a fully En-Light-ened One, there are no separate, self-existing objects; there is only the single Divine Subject, my Self, ceaselessly mutating into an infinity of transient forms."

A hush fell upon the room, not only because of what they'd heard, but also what they'd seen: For as Jack spoke his body glowed, radiating palpable energy that a Christian mystic might identify as the Holy Spirit. No one could deny what they had witnessed, even if they could not understand it. Even Jim

Mulligan, a dyed-in-the-wool atheist, couldn't help but acknowledge that he was mesmerized by Jack's loving force and presence.

At that point Mary McDonald informed the group that Jack was Jesus in his previous incarnation. "The deep holes that appeared in his hands, which he covered up with gloves at his first Objectivist meeting, were the harbinger of his Destiny," she said. "Now that he has awakened as Jesus 2.0, he will seek to save the world both spiritually and politically. I dare say we will be witnessing a phenomenon that hasn't been seen for more than two millennia."

Now that Jack had captivated the group, he led them outside to the apartment complex's swimming pool. Without saying a word, he walked atop the water, across the length of the pool, and back. Then he sat on the diving board, assumed the full lotus position, and asked if they had any questions.

"This is beyond unbelievable," said Brother Bill. "What we have just witnessed is literally impossible. I will have to reconsider everything I thought I knew."

Paul, the plastic surgeon, asked if it was possible to explain the Enlightenment process via Objectivist principles. "Absolutely," said Jack. "The spiritual practice that en-Light-ens a disciple is simply an amped-up version of Objectivism, so to speak. It is the conscious process of maintaining full *ontological* context, which awakens and intensifies the radiant Spirit-current, which en-Light-ens one.

"Rand says that consciousness, via the process of mental abstraction, is the faculty that identifies reality. Moreover, she says that logic — non-contradictory identification of reality — is the method for identifying reality. I think Rand is correct, but only on an *epistemological* level. If a disciple establishes and maintains a yogic — a direct, immediate *ontological* — connection with reality *prior to* retracting into mental abstraction, then the conscious force engendered by this connection translates into Spirit-power.

"Rand says that 'spirit' means 'pertaining to consciousness,'" Jack continued. "While that is also correct, she has no understanding of the relationship between Spirit-power and consciousness-force on an ontological, or yogic, level.

"Rand understood the principle of *logic*, which is mental — but not the principle of what I call *onto-logic*, which is spiritual, and which antecedes and supersedes cognition. *Onto-logic* is simply another term for yoga. Yoga is about

140

directly connecting to, and communing with, reality, prior to retracting into mental abstraction, which contracts one's field of consciousness and flow of Spirit-energy."

Paul criticized Jack for attacking man's conceptual faculty. "As deep as your message is, I'm afraid you're no different from any other mystic," he said. "It's as if you've painted cognition, mental abstraction, as the bogeyman that obstructs the spiritual process."

"I'm glad you brought up that," Jack smiled. "While it's true that thought must be suppressed to some extent in the earlier stages of meditation, once the yogi can rest in the Spirit-current, a radical recontextualization takes place. When that happens, conceptualization is no longer restrained — rather, it is subsumed and refined under the senior principle of spiritual Presence-Power.

"Obviously I'm still capable of complex abstraction. But in the case of an Enlightened One, thinking is naturally minimized, because 90 percent of thinking is just superfluous mental masturbation. Once the Spirit pours into you, it obstructs the arising of inessential thought-forms, which results in more focused and acute conceptualization."

The next question came from Orson, who along with Mary had first witnessed Jack's bloodied hands at State U. "Now that I understand the significance of the holes in your hands, I'd like to know if you can explain Christian spiritual truth in a Catholic context. I was brought up a Catholic, but later rejected the Church's teaching as nonsense."

"Truth be told, there is no better context than *true* Catholicism to explain spiritual Truth," Jack began. "As the 19th-century mystic and occultist Joséphin Péladin put it, 'The Eucharist is the whole of Christianity.' If you can understand and practice the *true*, mystical Eucharist, you will understand true spiritual life.

"At the Last Supper, the last meal he shared with his disciples, Jesus implicitly describes the spiritual discipline that leads to the Kingdom of Heaven, or Christ Consciousness. This discipline, the Eucharist, is the very essence of not only Christianity, but all great mystical (or yogic) traditions.

"The Eucharist is the sacrament, or act, of Holy, or Divine, Communion in its entirety — in other words, the holy, or spiritually holistic, act of connecting to the Divine Source, or Presence, and channeling, or receiving, its Grace, or Blessing Power, in the form of Light-energy. The word *Eucharist*, derived from Greek, means 'thankfulness,' within the context of communion. A true devotee of the Divine is always grateful for receiving God's Grace.

"Holy Communion is a synonym for *conscious* relationship, or at-one-ment, with God, *as Spirit*," Jack continued. "Therefore, the practice of Holy Communion is simply the discipline of conscious relationship, or at-one-ment, with the Holy Spirit. For a man to awaken as a Son who is one with the Father, he must permanently unite his consciousness (or soul) with Spirit-power, Divine Light-energy from above.

"But you can't be a true, or Spirit-connected, Christian unless you're baptized — and the baptism I'm talking about is by the Spirit itself. The Spirit, Holy 'Water' from above, literally pours down upon you, infilling your body-mind with intense, flowing Energy. This Energy, or Spirit-power, is your Saving Grace... but until you've been baptized, initiated by the Holy One, you can only be a believer, not a true disciple, or faith-full devotee, of the Lord.

"In short, you have to generate enough conscious force, or 'voltage,' in your communion practice to 'invoke the Deity,' to 'pull down' the Highest Power. In other words, your 'Plugged-in Presence' needs more 'push' to transpose into 'pulled,' or poured-down, power from above. You get this push by intensifying your concentration, by single-pointedly focusing your attention on the enactment of the Eucharist. Jesus emphasizes this in the Sermon on the Mount when he says, 'If thine eye [consciousness] be single, thy whole body will be filled with Light [from above].'

"When the Spirit 'touches' you, you must yield to its invasive pressure by relaxing your body and letting go of your mind," Jack continued. "Be as if dead: empty and effortless. This holding on to nothing in the face of Spirit's intrusion is the true meaning of 'poverty in the Spirit.' The pressure of the Spirit-current sensitizes you to your resistance, enabling you to palpably feel it. And when you feel it, the only intelligent response is to release it and let the Spirit-current move unimpeded through your body-mind, divinizing, or en-Light-ening, you."

"Are you saying that the essence of mystical Christianity is comprised of two complementary and opposite practices?" asked Paul. "One being presence, or communion, and the other being poverty, or self-emptying?"

"That's correct," said Jack. "The practices of presence and poverty constitute a dialectic, with presence, or relationship, as the *thesis*; absence, or inner emptiness, as the *antithesis*; and the descent of the Holy Spirit as the *synthesis*. In other words, the pressure of your conscious presence, or relational force, instigates your self-emptying (or surrendering), which 'produces,' or pulls down, the Spirit, which deifies you, transforming you into a Self-realized, or Christ-like, being.

"In engendering the descent of the Spirit, the two dialectical practices of presence (relationship) and poverty (absence) give birth to a third, synthesizing practice: the practice of *power*. The practice of presence is about *connecting*; the practice of poverty is about *surrendering*; and the practice of power, which integrates the practices of presence and poverty, is about *receiving*.

"The practice of receiving the Holy Spirit *synthesizes* the practices of presence and poverty by, in effect, *mediating* them. Thus, instead of full attention being focused on either the act of being present or the act of being self-empty, the act of receiving, or *conducting*, the Spirit-current involves the artful integration of both these gestures. It involves the *letting go* of psychical content while simultaneously *holding on* to the context of connectedness. In order to instigate the drawing-down of Divine Power, the Holy Spirit, the disciple must sometimes emphasize the 'pole of presence' (or relationship), and at other times the 'pole of poverty' (or self-emptying). But when the descent of Light-energy is intense, the disciple can dispense with the dialectical spiritual practices (of presence and absence) and effortlessly rest in the Bliss (or Blessing)-current from above."

The Objectivists murmured amongst each other. Clearly they had never heard Christianity expressed in such radical energetic terms.

One member of the group, a mechanical engineer, asked if any scientific principles could explain spirituality. "Call me wacky, but I believe Ohm's Law, which describes the functioning of an electrical circuit, parallels Eucharistic spirituality," replied Jack with a grin. "No one can prove or disprove that Ohm's Law applies to Spirit-conductivity. But, based on my own spiritual experiences, it is obvious to me that Ohm's Law, or some approximate variation of it, applies to Eucharistic spirituality. Consequently, even if Ohm's Law does not exactly hold true for the practice of Holy Spirit communion and conductivity, it still provides a nonpareil metaphor for understanding the mechanics of the Eucharist."

Jack motioned for Bill to get the blackboard from his apartment, then he began to explain Ohm's Law for the benefit of those unfamiliar with it. "Ohm's Law states that 'the strength or intensity of an unvarying electric current is directly proportional to the electromotive force and inversely proportional to the resistance in a circuit.' Ohm's Law — where V = voltage (electromotive force), I = amperage (intensity of current), and R = ohms (units of resistance) — can be summarized in three formulas:

$$V = IR \; ; \; I = \frac{V}{R} \; ; \; R = \frac{V}{I}$$

"Any form of the Ohm's Law equation can be derived from the other two via simple algebra," Jack continued. "Translating Ohm's Law into a Eucharistic formula is simple. All we have to do is to substitute communion, or connected consciousness (or consciousness-force), for voltage; spiritual energy (or intensity of the Spirit-current) for amperage; and ego-resistance (or degree of resistance to the Spirit-current) for ohms. Therefore, the Electrical Eucharistic formula — where C = communion, or connected consciousness (or consciousness-force); I = spiritual energy (or intensity of the Spirit-current); and R = ego-resistance (or degree of resistance to the Spirit-current) — can, like Ohm's Law, be summarized in three formulas:

$$C = IR \; ; \; I = \frac{C}{R} \; ; \; R = \frac{C}{I}$$

"As with Ohm's Law, any of these equations can also be derived from the other two via simple algebra." With that, Jack concluded his comments.

Once again the Objectivists were fascinated, though some admitted to finding the concepts too abstract to follow. This was particularly the case with those who had always struggled with math. So Jack broke it down even further:

"The Holy Spirit is the electric current (amperage); Holy Communion is the electromotive force (voltage); and ego-resistance is the resistance to the flow of the current (ohms). Ohm's Law applied to Eucharistic spirituality tells us that the intensity of the Holy Spirit-current is directly proportional to one's Holy Communal, or relational, force and inversely proportional to one's ego-resistance to the inflowing Holy Spirit-current.

"Once you've been baptized by the Holy Spirit, you'll be able to palpably and viscerally experience the seeming reality of Ohm's Law in Eucharistic spirituality. Then, and only then, will the Ohm's Law/Eucharist parallel make real sense to you."

Brother Bill called for a short recess, during which time they talked amongst each other while returning to the apartment. When the meeting resumed, Jack invited the entire group to his first scheduled Satsang at Mother Mary's temple, and informed them that he would, at that time, provide more detailed instructions on meditation. He then took questions for another hour before they adjourned for the evening.

As the attendees departed, Bill pulled Jack aside and said, "I guess this means you won't be able to work on my stock market program."

"Perish the thought," said Jack. "I agreed to work on your program, and whether I'm Jesus Christ 2.0 or just a deluded nineteen-year-old Avatar wannabe, I'm going to break your program down to the nth degree and get the answers you're seeking."

"I hope the same goes for us and our sports betting program," cracked Jim Mulligan, who was standing nearby.

"Absolutely," said Jack. "Not only will I be working on your program, too, but I'll even throw in a bonus."

"You're gonna let me have Mary for myself," Jim winked.

"Noooo," laughed Jack. "But once I start fighting professionally, I'm going to sandbag in all my MMA matches before I meet the Evil One — that way, we will ensure that Putin is a huge favorite. Then we'll bet everything we have on me at super underdog odds. It'll be a double killing: personal and financial. Plus think of the publicity that the fight will generate for my ministry... and the Revolution."

"Jesus 2.0 destroying the invincible Putin," said Jim. "Sounds fucking awesome to me!" On that note, he said goodbye and left.

Jack was also ready to leave. Before he did he made Brother Bill an offer he couldn't refuse. "I'd like you to be on my team," he said. "Mother Mary is going to manage my spiritual mission. I could use a good man like you to handle my political appearances. Think of it as an opportunity to make some coin before we get your stock market program in gear."

"You had me at 'good man like you,'" said Bill. "It would be an honor."

"Excellent," said Jack. "I'll ask Mother Mary to call you, and the two of you can coordinate my schedule."

He shook Bill's hand, then left with Mary McDonald, arm in arm. The two lovers would have their own private celebration at her palatial home.

. . .

As soon as they entered her bedroom, Mary pulled out a pipe and hash. "I wonder what this stuff is like from an En-Light-ened perspective," she said with a Cheshire Cat grin.

"As good as ever," laughed Jack after taking a toke. "But, just so you know, I'm only doing this tonight as an experiment. Beginning tomorrow, I will no longer do any drugs — and if you want to evolve spiritually, Mary, you'll have to do the same."

She nodded her head in mock agreement. "Blessed One, save me from temptation... but not yet!"

They laughed and continued taking hits on the pipe. It wasn't long before they were totally wasted.

Nor was it long before Mary was horny. She stripped down to her panties, unzipped his fly, and performed fellatio. Then she started to undress him, but Jack had another idea: "I want you to strap me down in the dungeon."

"You're fucking with me," she said.

"No, I'm not," he said. "I think it might be fun... We could make it part of my 'last temptation.' What do you say?"

Her eyes widened in anticipation. "That would be fun, but aren't you afraid of what would happen if my inner Hyde takes control? The last time I had you in my dungeon, I nearly killed you."

"Yes, but I'm Jesus 2.0. Nothing you can do can harm me."

"We'll see about that, buster!" she laughed as she paraded him to the dungeon.

Mary McDonald squealed with anticipation as she fastened him to the table. She had her Guru exactly where she wanted him, and her imagination raced with the possibilities.

What she didn't know was that, this time, Jack had *her* exactly where he wanted.

He allowed her to taunt him, as she had done before. He even let her threaten him with the knife, as she had done before. Then, once she felt he was completely powerless, he made his move. He said, "I'm going to disappear" — and, just like that, he vanished. Without his bodily form, the heavy locks that held his limbs in place fell to the table with a crash.

Mary stood there in utter shock for what seemed an eternity. She thought she'd seen everything, but this was unreal.

Suddenly she shrieked as she felt something biting her on the back of her neck. She turned around and, to her amazement, there was Jack, smiling playfully at her.

"Gotcha," he said. She fell to her knees in laughter.

They made love in the dungeon, then made their way back to the kitchen, where they enjoyed a late-night snack of ice cream and carrot cake. As decadent as that was, to Mary's astonishment Jack helped himself to another serving. "Jesus 2.0, how can you possibly beat Sergei Putin by engaging in marathon sex sessions, smoking dope, and gorging yourself on fattening food?"

"Oh, ye of little faith," Jack chided her. Then he took her by the hand, led her to her gym, and proceeded to bench-press 500 pounds for ten reps without breaking a sweat.

"My fucking God, you aren't even human anymore," she said in admiration. "Once you get in the Octagon with Putin, he won't know what hit him."

Then she noticed for the first time that his arm had completely healed. "It's a miracle," she said. "The Holy Spirit is pouring through you without measure, making you a God on earth."

She took him in her arms and kissed him before making an announcement of her own. "From this moment on, Jack, I will worship you in Truth and Spirit. I will be your slave; you will no longer be mine. And as further proof of my devotion, I will quit Sodom and Gomorrah and prostitution tomorrow."

Jack looked at her and smiled. It pleased him to know that she had taken the first step along the path of righteousness.

They strolled to the kitchen for shots of espresso. Then Mary had an inspiration: "You should display your *siddhis*, or powers, not only to the general public, but also to James 'The Great' Grande, the world-famous debunker of psychic phenomena. He offers ten million dollars to anyone who can, under laboratory conditions, demonstrate paranormal powers. Think of the publicity your ministry will receive if you can demonstrate your powers to him."

Jack, well aware of Grande, wasn't sure if that was a good idea. "Siddhis are a very iffy thing," he said. "The only reason I was able to walk on water tonight, or dematerialize in your dungeon, was because the cosmic conditions were right. It is much easier for a master to manifest siddhis in the exclusive company of his 'inner circle' of disciples. That's why Jesus walked on water only in the presence of his apostles. He never tried to do anything like that in front of the masses.

"Moreover, siddhis are hard to control, even for En-Light-ened spiritual masters. Do you have any idea why?"

"Probably due to Bell's Theorem," Mary hypothesized. "The non-locality of consciousness, the fact that consciousness is universal, outside of space and time, would make control of its power within space and time iffy. You, as a guru, perfectly coincide with Absolute Consciousness, but quantum reality dictates that absolute control of consciousness-power in space and time is somewhat a roll of the dice."

Jack could only gaze at her and smile. "Honey, I not only love you for your body, but also for your mind. Your answer was brilliant. In fact, I'm so turned on right now, I want to fuck your brains loose." With that they hurried back to her bedroom and made love well into the night.

Part 3

The Teaching

A CAPACITY CROWD, NUMBERING several hundred, packed Mother Mary's temple on the day of Jack's first Satsang. As he took the platform at the head of the room, Jack bowed to the congregation, assumed the full lotus position, and began his sermon:

"A week ago, in this very temple, thanks to the Grace of God and His agent Mother Mary, who owns this temple and invited you all here, I awoke as the Chosen One, Jesus Christ reborn as me, Jack Cohen. When the Holy Spirit, the *Maha Shakti*, cut my Sacred Heart-center knot, I awoke as the Christ Self, consubstantial with the Divine Being. I now, eternally, even while embodied, abide in the Divine Being (or Domain) — and this Divine abiding is Heaven (or Nirvana).

"I am not an ordinary guru; I am an Avatar, meaning One who incarnates from without. An Avatar descends into the world when conditions have become desperate, when darkness — meaning evil — obscures the Way to the Light, the Bright Domain of Heaven. I am a Heaven-born One, and I am here to show you the Way to Heaven, the Bright Domain.

"I have adopted the three pillars of Buddhism — the Buddha (Me), the Dharma (My Teaching), and the Sangha (Our Community) — as the

149

foundation of my new religion, which I call ISM, an acronym for Integral Spiritual Movement. The mission of ISM is to convert the world to our Movement, whose goal is to awaken humanity to Christian Heaven, which is the same 'Thing' as Buddhist Nirvana and Hindu Self-realization.

"I employ ISM as a double acronym," Jack continued. "Besides Integral Spiritual Movement, it also stands for Integral Social Movement, the sociopolitical movement I'm going to spearhead apart from Integral Spiritual Movement. Individuals will be free to participate in one or both movements. After our Satsang, free literature on both movements will be available at the table next to the door.

"Tonight, I will provide you with the Method for communing with the formless Holy One. However, since I am the embodiment of the Holy One, you can also just contemplate my physical form as a portal to the formless Spirit. God's Blessing Power pours through me without obstruction — by turning to Me, you, in effect, turn to God. This isn't something to be blindly believed; it's something to be directly experienced.

"My instructions tonight pertain to communing with formless Spirit, with the void serving as a doorway to God's Light-energy. But if you find yourself unable to understand or practice my Method of formless Divine Communion, then simply commune with my Divine physical form, which will serve as a conduit to the Formless One."

Jack raised his hands to the assembly and transmitted the Shakti. As he did, bodies swayed and heads jerked to and fro from the Energy. After a few minutes, he gave them instructions on meditation (or "communion") so that they could *consciously* "position" themselves to receive the Benediction, Blessing Power from above.

"You should experiment with my instructions and use the ones that best enable you to plug into the Divine Presence and pull down Divine Power," he began. "Although I will number the recommendations, be advised that they overlap and intertwine and do not have to be practiced in the order in which I present them:

1) Sit upright, but relaxed, on a chair, bench, or meditation cushion.

2) Establish what the Buddha called 'self-possession.' In other words,

feel yourself as the whole body, and then be consciously present as the whole body, the whole psycho-physical being. Randomly focusing your attention on your third-eye area and hands will enable you to coincide with your body, and thereby heal the body-mind split. When you consciously inhabit your whole body — and are wholly, or integrally, present to the whole (the totality of existence) — you are in proper position to receive and conduct the Holy Spirit, the Force-flow from above.

3) 'Gaze' into empty space. If you are 'self-possessed,' this 'gaze' will amount to being whole-bodily present to (or in direct relationship to) the void. As soon as you become aware that you have retracted from your 'position' of conscious connectedness to (or single-pointed focus on) the void, simply reassume, or attempt to reassume, your 'stance' of holistic at-one-ment. To this end, you can randomly use an enquiry (such as 'Avoiding relationship?') to instigate your resumption of communion with the void. When the void begins to 'shine,' it is experienced as Divine Presence. When the Power of the Presence pours down upon you, then 'emptiness' has morphed into Spirit, and your 'gaze into space' has transmuted into empowered Divine Communion.

4) Randomly focus your attention on your breath by being in direct relationship to your breathing cycle. When the breath 'comes alive' as *prana-shakti*, or palpable intensified life-energy, simply remain present to it. Your communion with the breath cycle will transmute into true, or infused, Divine Communion when the prana-shakti morphs into the Holy Spirit — the great Shakti poured down from above.

5) Totally relax your body (including your head) and utterly let go of your mind. Once you are able to connect to the Shakti, you will directly experience that letting go intensifies the force-flow (or pressure) of the Spirit-current. Be an empty cup, ready to be filled with Holy Water from above. When you experience the Benediction, the Divine downpour, remain motivelessly present to it. Your searchless beholding of the Shakti will enable you to spontaneously merge with it.

"These technical meditation instructions are all about facilitating communion, and then union, with the Divine," Jack continued. "It is up to you to test them out and determine how useful they are for your yoga practice. Truly speaking, no spiritual practice, in and of itself, is holy or sacred. The only 'Thing' holy or sacred is the Holy One Himself (including His Holy Spirit). Therefore, whatever practices bring you into communion with the Holy One are the ones you should employ.

"The practice of real (or divine) meditation is identical to the practice of real (or divine) Christianity, which is identical to the practice of real (or divine) yoga. Real (or divine) yoga is simply, *and only*, the practice of uniting one's individual soul (or consciousness) with universal Spirit (or Light-energy). When the two 'vines' of the Absolute (or Di-vine Being) — consciousness and Spirit — are permanently united in a yogi, then he awakens as En-Light-ened Consciousness (or Conscious Light). The Awakened yogi (now a Christ or Buddha) inheres in the Absolute, and his Spirit-full Soul is eternally one with the Divine Being (or 'Father'). This immutable 'State' (really a non-state) of Divine Union is called Enlightenment (or Self-realization) by Hindu yogis, Nirvana (or Buddhahood) by Buddhists, and Heaven (or Christ Consciousness) by Christian mystics."

The group sat in quiet contemplation for fifteen minutes. Again, heads jerked and bodies swayed from the force of the Shakti. Then, to the group's astonishment, Jack's body, still in a full lotus, rose from the platform and hovered in the air some five feet above the platform for a few minutes before descending slowly back in place. A great hush fell upon the room, then Jack broke the silence by opening the floor for questions. Thirty minutes later, he dismissed the congregation and invited them to his next scheduled Satsang.

As the attendees left, Jack engaged his inner circle of Mary, Mother Mary, Polly, Bill, and Jim. Knowing that they had just witnessed the beginning of a crusade that was about to change the world, they were teeming with enthusiasm. Mother Mary discussed plans to rent a larger auditorium for the next Satsang, as well as broadcasting it over the Internet. To take advantage of Jack's growing, built-in audience, Bill wanted him to deliver his political discourses immediately following his Satsangs. He also planned to schedule interviews and appearances for Jack with various right-wing political organizations.

Though Jack was pleased with the marketing plan, he made one thing clear: "Even though I'm spiritually Enlightened, I'm not infallible. Buddha and Jesus were wrong about some things, and even though, as Jesus 2.0, I might be an upgrade over previous Avatars, I'm still appearing in a human body-mind with limitations. You guys will serve as a sounding board for me and be free to make suggestions whenever you like."

He reflected further and displayed his otherworldly detachment. "I don't take any of this seriously," he said. "It's all just a game to me. I'm in this world, but not of it. I live outside time and space, in the Divine Domain — but I have to periodically remind myself that everyone else is enmeshed in Maya, and that my Work as the Chosen One is to Bless and En-light-en the masses, including you."

Then he gazed lovingly at his friends and directed them to focus on Him so that they could receive His Blessing Power.

* * *

Later that day, Jack dropped by the gym to visit Patsy. They hadn't seen each other since the day of his final sparring session with Putin.

"How's the left wing, kid?" asked Patsy. "I can hardly wait to restart your training."

"Believe it or not, the arm is fine, but I'm no longer going to train," said Jack.

To no surprise, Patsy couldn't understand why, so Jack led him to the weight room. There, he loaded 515 pounds on the bench press bar, and, just as he had done a few nights before in Mary McDonald's gym, snapped off ten easy reps. Then he slipped on training gloves, directed Patsy to the heavy bag, and proceeded to pelt it with bazooka-like shots, the last of which caused the bag to split open just as one of its support chains snapped.

Patsy could not believe his eyes. "A few weeks ago your max was 475 for a single rep," he said. "Now, after not working out for weeks, you're not only doing multiple reps with 515, but destroying a bag that's supposed to be unbreakable. That doesn't compute."

Jack put his arm around Patsy's shoulder and smiled. "I'm no longer completely human," he explained. "I'm a God-man now, an Avatar. A week ago, I Awakened; now the life-force and chi move through my body without obstruction."

All Patsy could do was shake his head. "I always knew you were a world-class athlete, Jack — now you're out of this world. Putin will never know what hit him."

Jack told Patsy about his plan to sandbag in his first few MMA matches, so as to make him a huge underdog in the title match with Putin. "Then we'll bet everything we have on me," he explained. "We'll rake in huge dough on top of the purse, which will be structured to heavily reward the winner. Putin will be dying to fight me, both for the mega payday and the chance to permanently damage me. But I'm going to pop his head wide open, just as I did with that bag. When I'm through with him, he'll be like Humpty Dumpty; no one will put him back together again."

"That's quite a scheme," said Patsy. "Let's just hope your powers don't mysteriously disappear before the fight — otherwise, you'll be chopped liver."

Jack assured him that was not likely to happen. "These powers are a natural extension of my Being-ness," he explained. "As soon as Divine Power began to flow unimpeded through my body-mind, these powers spontaneously manifested themselves. Because I'm irreversibly free and open, I don't see them disappearing."

Patsy took a deep breath, ran his fingers through his hair, and slowly exhaled. This was a lot for anyone to take in, and he was trying to process it all. "Are you saying you're not afraid of anything anymore?"

"No," said Jack. "But my fear isn't losing my powers before I fight Putin — it's losing my life."

Tears began to well in Patsy's eyes. He didn't understand that, either.

"I'll be saying some pretty outrageous things in my spiritual sermons and political talks," Jack explained. "I'll be pissing off a lot of people — some of whom will want to kill me. It's not that I'm afraid of dying... I just don't want it to happen until after the Putin fight. There are things I want to accomplish with my ministry, and there are things I want to do for my friends."

One such thing, he elaborated, was to provide for Patsy. "In the next day or two, I'll be taking out a couple of life insurance policies with you as the beneficiary. That way, should anything happen to me, you will be taken care of."

By now Patsy was no longer fighting back the tears. "Jack, I love you like a son. Please don't do or say anything stupid that could get yourself killed."

"I know," said Jack softly. "And I love you, too, as a brother and a father."

He closed his eyes and directed Shakti at Patsy. Instantly, the energy from Jack's hand put the veteran trainer at ease.

* * *

When he returned to the apartment, Jack kissed Polly and Blessed her with Shakti. By now he had decided that he wanted them to move in with Mary McDonald. Polly loved the idea. "That would be so much fun," she said. "We've been talking on the phone every day, and I know she is as devoted to you as I am. We will worship you together."

The sound of that pleased Jack, but there was one other thing Polly needed to know. "You better sit down for this," he advised. She did, and he went on to tell her about the day Mary drugged him, bound him, branded his ass with a hot iron, and then tried to kill him. He also let her know about Shitzer's death from sexual asphyxiation, which Mary insisted was accidental.

By now Polly's head was spinning; this was clearly upsetting news. But it also explained why Jack had insisted on keeping the lights off whenever they had sex the past couple of weeks. He didn't want her to see the branding marks.

"Why did you wait so long to tell me?" she asked.

"Because I didn't want to disturb you," he said, gently stroking her face. "And because I wasn't sure I wanted us to live with Mary. Now that I have decided, you deserve to know everything."

He laid his hands on her shoulders and brightened her with his Blessing Power. Now in a sprightly mood, Polly put her hands on her hips and did her best impression of Mary: "OK, buster, pull down your britches so I can assess the rear-end damage."

They laughed. He did. She was very impressed. "Wow, they look really cool," said Polly. "Someone looking at them who didn't know any better could easily mistake you for Jesus." They laughed again and kissed.

He asked her if she had any fear or reservations about moving in with Mary. She assured him she did not. "Now that she knows you are Jesus, her Savior, I can't believe that she would ever do anything like that to you again."

Then he picked up the phone, called Mary, and said that they'd be ready to move in by the weekend.

"This is like a dream come true for me," said Mary, "living with Jesus, my love and lover. I was Mary Magdalene, and I had to wait two thousand years to have you again. Now that I do, I want you with me as much as possible... And believe me, I will do everything I can to serve you and your mission."

. . .

Jack's second Satsang took place at a downtown auditorium. Several thousand attended in person; hundreds of thousands more participated via webcam. As in his first Satsang, Jack provided detailed instructions on contemplation and invited participants to commune with his incarnate physical form as a means to the formless Divine. He then directed his audience to meditate in silence, during which time he directed powerful Shakti not only across the auditorium, but also into cyberspace. Also as before, he astounded the crowd with a display of levitation, causing them to shout out with Spirit-intoxicated glee.

At the end of the meditation, he took questions from the audience, then invited those members of the congregation who happened to be handicapped to join him at the front of the auditorium. Ten people in wheelchairs soon emerged. He laid his hands on them and gave them Shakti. Miraculously, seven of the ten got up from their wheelchairs and began to walk again.

Though the crowd went wild, Jack insisted that he did not heal anyone; God did. If Jack did have such a capability, then all ten would have been cured of their affliction.

"All I can do is provide an open channel for Divine Energy, the Holy Spirit, the only true Healer," he explained. "The three who could not stand and walk after I touched them were not meant to do so at this time. Their karma dictates that, at least for now, they remain wheelchair-bound. Moreover, I cannot at will channel the specific Healing Power of the Divine. The cosmic energies must be in alignment for me to do so. I felt that rare universal consonance tonight, so I took advantage of it to help these people. The Divine Spirit-power I channel is constant, but not the specific Healing Power that accompanies it."

The husband of a woman who had just been healed thanked Jack for healing his wife. "I have suffered from sexual impotence for years," he said. "Nothing, including Viagra, has worked. Can you heal me?"

Jack smiled slyly. "Sir, I can heal the sick... but I cannot raise the dead."

The congregation roared with laughter.

After closing the Satsang with a Benediction, Jack urged the crowd to support his efforts as a mixed martial arts fighter. "I'll be making my professional debut Saturday night," he said. "My goal is to be world champion, and the man standing in my way is the current champ, Sergei Putin. I sparred with Sergei several weeks ago, and he maliciously, severely damaged my arm. Thanks to the Grace of God, it has healed quickly, and I am now ready to earn a title shot. If I succeed, I'll be able to parlay my crown into publicity for my ministry, which will enable me to save more souls." Again the crowd cheered in unison.

* * *

The next day, Jack relaxed on the couch with a classic text, *The Great Deformation: The Corruption of Capitalism in America* by David Stockman. He had just finished the first two chapters when his cell phone rang. To his delight, it was Jud Johnson. Jack was glad to hear from him; they hadn't spoken in weeks, since that night at Sodom and Gomorrah. For Jud, however, this was not a social call. "Dude, I just finished watching your webcast; and your act is impressive — very impressive. Especially that levitation trick. Now I understand why you spent a couple of high school summers studying magic."

"Thanks, but that was no act," said Jack. "I really did levitate, and I really did heal those people in wheelchairs."

"Whatever, man," said Jud flippantly. "Let me get to the point. L. Ron Hubbard said that the easiest way to make a million dollars is to start your own religion. I'm sure your Jesus 2.0 shtick will make you a mega mint. I just want to get in on some of the action — you know, make a little coin and bang some of your groupie chicks."

It saddened Jack to hear that, but he wasn't surprised. "Jud, I'm going to level with you. I can read your karma, and it's evil. Unless you repent and accept me as your Savior, you're headed for an unhappy ending. Before I was Jack, I was Jesus of Nazareth. If you allow me to Bless you, I can save you."

Jud rolled his eyes and laughed. "I've got you, buddy; you've got to maintain the act twenty-four hours a day, so it becomes second nature."

Jack silently transmitted Shakti to his friend, but he could feel the harsh resistance on the other end of the call. "Jud, I know you don't hear me right now, but soon enough you'll learn who I am."

"I hear you perfectly fine," said Jud bitterly. "It's bad enough you got that doper ho bitch Mary all to yourself. I just want you to spread the wealth, so I can become a millionaire, too. Delivering pizzas gets old, you know what I mean?"

Jack again beseeched his friend to reconsider his ways. By that point, however, Jud Johnson had heard enough. After hanging up on Jack, he called up the apps page of his camera phone, scrolled down to where it said Video, and opened up the file called S&G. Since he didn't get the answer he wanted from Jack, he would have to resort to Plan B.

. . .

By noon that Saturday, Jack and Polly had finished unloading the last of their boxes into Mary McDonald's home. Noticing that the move had exhausted Jack — and knowing that he had an important match later that night — Mary suggested that she and Polly invigorate him with a threesome. "The sexercise will get you good and loose for tonight," she said as she removed her top.

"You mean, good and *hard*," Polly cooed as she encased her hand around his cock. Before long, they were all in bed, their bodies entwined as one until they collapsed in ecstasy. Then they laid together for the rest of the afternoon, Mary cuddled under his left arm, Polly under his right.

At one point Mary asked why Jack hadn't delivered a political speech yet. "I thought the plan was to follow each spiritual sermon with a political one."

"That's still the plan," he said, "but I'm in no rush to start. As soon as I do, Big MoFoBro will begin targeting me."

"Big MoFoBro?" asked Polly. "Is that Ebonics or just urban slang?"

"That's Jackie Poo jargon," explained Mary, "because he grabbed it out of his ass. It's short for Big Mother-Fucking Brother." Then she made a comment about wanting to take a dildo "and shove it up the government's ass."

"Sounds like you're beginning to hate the government as much as Jim Mulligan," observed Jack.

"You would, too, if you learned what I learned yesterday," Mary replied with anger. She went on to explain that Mother Mary had informed her that the federal government was responsible for the death of her father.

"They had him doing human radiation experiments with plutonium that endangered both him and his subjects — and they lied to him about the nature of the experiments. He didn't know that he was exposing himself and others to deadly amounts of radiation."

Later Jack would learn that the impetus behind this painful truth was Brother Bill. Knowing that Mary had recently changed her political beliefs, and knowing how close she was to Mother Mary, Bill suggested that Mother Mary break the news about Mary's father. In his mind that would cement Mary's newfound allegiance to radical right-wing politics.

On that, Bill proved himself prescient. For as it happened, Mary had been reading up on the historical evils of our government, including such books as *Liberal Fascism, The Politically Incorrect Guide to American History*, and *Progressivism: A Primer on the Idea Destroying America*. "I've also been studying Austrian Economics and reading a lot of Murray Rothbard," she told Jack. "The only conclusion I can draw is that it's time for a revolution."

Jack nodded approvingly, then laid his hands on Mary. She began shaking violently, to the point where she fell on her side and writhed on the floor, like a snake, until Jack again touched her and made her still.

"How do you feel?" he asked.

"Like I've just gotten out of a washing machine," said Mary as she rose to her feet. "Kind of discombobulated, yet clean inside, if that makes any sense."

"Your aura looks better," Jack smiled. "You're a long way from being a pure soul, but at least a few of your demons have been exorcised."

Mary smirked. "Can you put them back inside of me if I get bored of being a good girl?" With that the three of them laughed, and Jack got ready to leave.

* * *

Jack's fight that night, against an unranked journeyman, was televised on ESPN. Though he ultimately won, he'd made it close, as per the master plan. He took advantage of a brief post-match interview to reiterate the nature of his cause: to fight and destroy Sergei Putin.

The next day, Sunday, he appeared before a convention hall filled with more than five thousand Buddhists of one persuasion or another. Mother Mary had booked him as a speaker at this annual gathering, and he was eager to expound his Dharma to the Buddhist community. He bowed to the assembly and began his sermon:

"Even though I call myself Jesus 2.0, I could just as easily claim I'm Maitreya, the foretold successor to Sakyamuni Buddha. I have attained the Heart-release, Nirvana, and I have incarnated on this Earth plane to help others attain the same exalted State. I have studied all the major Buddhist scriptures, and you'll see that I incorporate elements of them in my Dharma. But you'll also see that my Dharma is a refreshing new expression of the Way. In fact, it could be considered the fifth and final turning of the Wheel of Dharma — but it is up to you to determine if it merits that label.

"I call my Dharma 'ISM,' which is an acronym for Integral Spiritual Meditation. Meditation is the essence of Buddhism, so I'm sure you'll appreciate that my Dharma is all about meditation. Because I use electricity — specifically Ohm's Law — as a model for the spiritual meditation I teach, I call my model the Electrical Spiritual Paradigm, or ESP for short. And because I integrate ESP with Buddhist meditation, I call the Buddhism I teach Electrical Buddhism. Electrical Buddhism is the same Dharma as ISM, only with a Buddhist flavor."

Jack explained ISM and Ohm's Law to the audience, then used the mindfulness/meditation teachings of the Buddha to translate them into what he called Electrical Buddhism. "The Buddha taught the four ways of establishing mindfulness as the essential way to achieve Nirvana," he began. "These four ways involve contemplating, in turn, one's *body*, *feelings*, *thoughts*, and *ideas*. The 'structure' of each contemplation is identical: first establish concentrated focus (which equates to *voltage*), then let go and abide detached (which equates to *ohms* reduction). Implicit in these instructions is the understanding that the *synthesis* (*amperage*, the en-Light-ening Stream, or Flow), results from the integration or resolution of the *thesis* (right mindfulness) and the *antithesis* (utter detachment, or letting go).

"The *dialectical* electrical 'structure' of these instructions is clear. First there is the *thesis*: voltage (concentration, or consciousness-force); then there is the *antithesis*, ohms reduction (abiding detached, or letting go). The Buddha doesn't mention the *synthesis*, the Spirit, or 'Stream,' but it is implied, for without Light-energy there can be no En-Light-enment, no *Ananda*, or Nirvanic bliss. In fact, a common definition of Nirvana is the 'drying up of the *outflows*' (the psychical seed tendencies stored in the Heart-center that rise to the brain, 'crystallize' as thoughts, and contract one's mind into *samsara*, successive states of constricted consciousness). And it is the *inflow*, or descent, of Divine Blessing Power, the *Sambhogakaya*, or Nirvanic Bliss-current, that ends, or 'dries up,' the *outflows*. The Buddha is commonly referred to as the Blessed One because he unobstructedly channeled Divine Blessing Power; and you likewise can become a Blessed One if you learn how to channel, or receive, this Blessing Power.

"The difference between what the Buddha taught and what I teach is a matter of degree or fullness. Because my method of mindfulness, Plugged-in Presence, combines mindfulness (awareness, or presence) plus oneness (at-one-ment), it is fuller and more intense; hence I refer to it as mind-*full*-ness. In electrical terms, mind-*full*-ness generates more voltage, more conscious force, than mere mindfulness; hence it intensifies the en-Light-enment process.

"There have been four turnings of the Wheel in Buddhism: 1) *The Buddha's* original Dharma; 2) *Madhyamika's* emptiness Dharma; 3) *Yogacara's* Mind-only Dharma; and 4) *Vajrayana's* tantra Dharma. I contend that *Electrical Buddhism's* Plugged-in Presence Dharma is the fifth turning of the Wheel.

"Why is it the fifth turning of the Wheel? Because each turning after the Buddha's reflects one third of Ohm's Law, and the fifth turning, Electrical Buddhism, integrates those three, plus the Buddha's, into a unified whole. The first turning of the Wheel, by the Buddha himself, set the Wheel in motion; the second, by *Madhyamika*, emphasized emptiness (Poverty, or *Ohms*); the third, by *Yogacara*, accentuated Mind (Presence, or *Voltage*); and the fourth, by *Vajrayana*, focused on Energy (Power, or *Current*). The fifth turning not only unifies Buddhism, but also serves to integrate it with *true* Christianity. It does so because mind-full-ness, or Plugged-in Presence, is the same practice as Holy Communion, channeling the *Sambhogakaya*, or Clear-Light Energy, is tantamount to receiving the Holy Spirit, and Nirvana and Heaven are the same timeless State."

The assembly sat in awed silence; never before had they heard Dharma expressed on this level. Jack instructed them to remain silent and open and receive his Transmission. As he directed waves of Grace at the crowd, many among them began to shake or violently jerk from the Energy. Then, as was now his custom, he ended his talk with a display of levitation before leaving the stage to thunderous applause.

Backstage, he met with Mary, Polly and Mother Mary and learned that he had raised more than a million dollars in donations since his first talk. He smiled broadly and informed them of his plan to challenge Putin soon.

"I want to fight him within the month, before the government targets me," he explained. "Putin will agree to it because I'll seem like easy pickings and he'll pocket more than $100 million. What he doesn't realize is that after I scramble his brains, he won't know the difference between a dollar bill and a leaf of lettuce."

The four of them shared a laugh, then Mother Mary informed him of the latest developments. "I've received phone calls from several notable Las Vegas stage magicians who want you to perform your levitation as part of their act. But the most exciting opportunity is next Sunday — you'll be appearing at the ICC, the International Christian Convention, the annual gathering of Christian conservatives. This will be a real test to see if the Christian establishment accepts you as the Second Coming."

Jack was pleased to hear about the ICC, but had reservations about performing in Las Vegas. "Venues like the MGM and Bally's are not at all conducive for siddhis," he explained. "If I'm going to take that kind of chance, I want it to be in front of the Great Grande — that way, I can earn a cool ten million for our cause. Even though Grande's laboratory conditions also pose a risk, it's less than the one I'd face in Vegas. We can bet the prize money on me when I fight Putin."

With that he led them in a mini Satsang. Then Mother Mary let Jack know she would arrange a phone conference for him with Grande.

· · ·

The following Saturday, Jack stood before a convocation of Jewish rabbis who were intent on determining if he was the long-awaited Messiah. He spoke on the subject of holiness.

"What is holiness?" he began. "It's a word that we use loosely in speech, without really understanding it.

"Holiness is that which partakes of the Holy Spirit, the *Ruach Hakodesh*. The Holy Spirit is uncreated Light-energy. It is sacred because it is God's eternal Energy and man's only salvation. The Holy Spirit exists outside of time and space, yet it can be experienced by humans as a palpable, even visceral, Force-flow to those who have been 'anointed,' or 'initiated.' Because man is created in the image of God, we humans can receive and reflect God's Light-energy, His Spirit-power. We can behold the Splendor.

"The acme of Judaism is the mystical Kabbalah. Kabbalah means 'to receive,' and what a Jewish mystic receives when he connects to the Divine Presence, the *Shekinah*, is the Supernal Influx, the Holy Spirit. The Holy Spirit, the *Ruach Hakodesh*, is the action, or Energy, of the Presence, its En-Light-ening Power. In order to receive this Divine Blessing Power, one must connect to it; hence, the work of a Kabbalist, a true Jewish Holy man, is to 'plug into' this Divine Influx."

Jack directed the rabbis to focus their full attention on their hands and forehead, so as to integrate their consciousness with their body and become wholly at-one with the empty space in front of them. Once he saw that the holy men had self-nullifed, he "Blasted" them with Divine Elixir, filling their "empty cups" with Blessing and Blissing Power from above. At once their bodies began to shake, while many cried out in ecstasy.

"The word 'ecstasy' means to stand outside yourself," Jack explained. "That is what those of you who experienced the bliss of the Spirit-current just did. Instead of being curled up in a mental 'fist,' a self-contraction, you opened your consciousness to the Infinite, and received Grace, the Blessing/Blissing Power of the Holy One.

"Unless you want to be a wandering Jew, in self-imposed exile from the true Holy Land, what 'Is Real,' you will devote your life to connecting to and receiving this Grace, this Gift from Above — and as a true holy man, you will teach and inspire the members of your synagogue to do likewise."

Jack levitated for a few minutes then bowed to the convocation. The now enlightened rabbis stood in unison and showered him with applause. They *knew* he was the Prophesied One.

* * *

Later that night, he faced his second opponent, a journeyman named Owens, in a match that was also televised by ESPN. Again, the fight was close until the final round, when Jack knocked out Owens with a right uppercut to the jaw. Then he used his post-match interview to formally challenge Putin for the crown: "Somebody needs to road-grade the Mad Ruski, and that someone is me. I am God's Chosen Instrument, and one of my tasks is to rid the MMA of this Incarnation of Evil. He has maimed and mauled enough fighters. It's time for payback."

By the time Jack returned to the locker room, Putin's agent had already called. "He says that Sergei is 'mad as hell' and wants the fight as soon as possible," said Patsy. "We're meeting for lunch Monday."

• • •

The following evening, Jack took the stage at the annual International Christian Congregation, held at RFK Stadium. A sellout crowd of nearly 50,000 filled the seats, while thousands more sat around him on the field.

Unlike his appearances before other denominations, where he had been greeted like a rock star, Jack expected the conservative crowd to resist his message. As the sun set fast over the horizon, he wondered whether that was a sign that his own star might sink that day.

After a brief invocation, Jack began his sermon by saying that he would discuss three things: who he was, why he was here (in the world), and what his presence means for Christians today. "Much of what I will say is contrary to conventional Christianity," he began. "All I ask is that you keep an open mind to my story and my New Covenant.

"A few weeks ago, I awoke as a fully En-Light-ened being. But I didn't awaken as just a guru — I awoke as the re-Incarnation of Jesus Christ. In other words, I was Jesus in my previous life, and now, in the form of Jack Cohen, I have reappeared as him. I was an atheist until a few weeks ago, but the Holy Spirit, without measure, crashed down on me, re-Awakening me to my true Identity and ordained Mission. I spontaneously and distinctly remembered specific events such as the Sermon on the Mount and the Last Supper, and I knew, and know, Who I am. Moreover, I knew, and know, what my Mission in this life is: to save souls and save America from the Washington despots who have, in effect, 'privatized' her. Today I will limit my sermon to spirituality; tonight, in my international webcast, I will begin my political crusade. If you're interested in the future of America, be sure to tune in, because I'm about to shake this nation to its very foundation.

"Now, let's consider spirituality — specifically, Christian spirituality. In line with many mystics, I consider the Eucharist to be the essence of Christianity.

The *true* Eucharist, the sacrament of Holy Communion, is not a ritual; it is a discipline — the practice of literally, whole-bodily, communing with the Holy One via His Spirit. It is about *connecting* to the Holy Spirit and *receiving* its Blessing Power, or Light-energy, which literally, not figuratively, en-Light-ens, or 'saves,' you. The first time you receive the Holy Spirit — 'Holy Water' from on high — is called *baptism*, or *initiating* Grace; and as you continue to receive it in subsequent prayer or meditation sessions, it is referred to as *sanctifying* Grace. When you can perpetually rest in this Grace-current, your soul, or consciousness, has achieved Salvation, eternal rest in Heaven — the Divine Domain of unborn, ever-Blessing/Blissing Light-energy. In mystical terms, you have achieved Divine Union.

"To attain Divine Union, timeless rest in the Divine Domain, a Christian disciple takes three sacred vow — *obedience*, *poverty*, and *chastity*.

"*Obedience* is the moment-to-moment discipline of fixing your full attention on the Holy One, God. As soon as you notice that your attention has wandered, that you are no longer *at-one* with God, you need to *atone* for this sin by refocusing your attention on Him. The primal, or root, sin is to separate from God, and thereby 'fall' from Grace. Obedience is a synonym for at-one-ment, or communion, with God; therefore, when you practice Holy Communion, you uphold your vow of *obedience*.

"*Poverty* is a synonym for self-emptiness, or utter letting go. Whereas obedience is *presence* — being directly and immediately present to, or at-one, with God — emptiness is *absence* of self and mind. Being in direct communion with God generates a force, or pressure, and in order to release this pressure and allow it to flow (as Spirit-power), you must totally let go and release all resistance to its divinizing, or en-Light-ening, action. At the Last Supper, I made it clear to my apostles that a disciple must impoverish himself and become an 'empty cup,' a 'holy chalice,' in order to receive or conduct the Holy Spirit, Clear-Light Energy from on high.

"*Chastity*, the third sacred vow, pertains to living, or abiding, in the poured-down Spirit, the unborn, pure or 'virgin' Light-energy. Whenever you allow the Blessed Virgin to grace you with her Benediction, you *are* a pure, or chaste, soul. But the moment you retract from, or resist, the immaculate Clear-Light Energy, you *become* impure, a 'sinner.'

"The Three Sacred Vows can be viewed as a dialectic, with obedience (or *presence*) as the thesis, poverty (or *absence*) as the antithesis, and chastity (*Clear-Light Energy*) as the synthesis. The three sacred vows succinctly summarize what real spirituality, real mysticism, real Christianity, is all about. You practice Holy Communion (or radical *obedience*) by plugging into the Spirit and then emptying (or *impoverishing*) yourself, which allows God to Bless you (with His *chaste* Light-energy)."

At that point, Jack turned and faced the stadium scoreboard, which now displayed the URL for ISM. After inviting the crowd to visit his website for detailed instructions on the spiritual practices he'd just discussed, he made a few final points before leading them in prayer.

"I am not a Christian minister," Jack said. "I am Christ himself. I am sinless and perfect because I live in, and as, unborn, immaculate Light. I do not commune with the Spirit; I am Spirit Itself, temporarily appearing as a physical form. I am always already 'Saved,' and I have incarnated again in order to save you. Do not miss this opportunity to take advantage of my Presence and Power. It has been two millennia since I last appeared... and only God knows when I will again return to this Earth plane."

It was an audacious statement, to be sure — and as Jack had anticipated, it was not received kindly. For the first time in his ministry, he felt hatred, resistance, astonishment, and anger. In the eyes of the ICC, his statement was sheer blasphemy.

At that moment, darkness fell upon the sky, while the stadium lights took full effect. Jack knew that this meant nothing more than the passage of evening into night. But mindful of the tension in the air, he could not help but wonder if this was another bad omen.

"The spiritual discipline I have just described — communion with the abstract, formless Divine — is difficult for many people, especially beginners," he said, after clearing his throat. "If you find that you're unable to practice it, my recommendation to you is this: Turn to Me. Focus your full attention on my Blessed bodily form, which functions as a conduit to the Infinite. If you gaze upon Me, even pictures of Me, with single-pointed devotional intent, you will soon 'penetrate' through Me to the 'Other Side,' the formless, infinite Divine. And once you are 'locked in' to the Divine Presence, you will soon be baptized by its Power, the Holy Spirit.

"Some of you here tonight will be spontaneously baptized by, or in, the

Spirit in our prayer session. If you aren't baptized tonight, don't worry about it. If you devote yourself to the spiritual practice that I teach, in due course the Lord will initiate you via the descent of His Divine Power.

"Some of you may not be clear on the distinction between prayer and meditation. *True* prayer is the same thing as *real* meditation, which is simply the practice of Divine, or Holy, Communion. In *real* meditation, you psycho-physically 'position' yourself to receive the Benediction; in *true* prayer, you do the same. When you whole-bodily focus your full attention on the Lord and single-pointedly beseech him to Bless you with His Divine Power, or Light-energy, then your prayer is real meditation. But whether you call your spiritual practice 'prayer' or 'meditation,' once you receive the Benediction, Blessing Power from above, it becomes *infused contemplation*, and you simply gaze upon, or behold, the drawn-down Splendor."

He finished his comments and instructed the crowd to sit in meditative silence for fifteen minutes. Then, upon directing his powerful Blessing Power upon them, he felt their collective negative energy boomerang on him. His chest constricted and then his neck tightened, as if a noose had formed around it. For all intents and purposes, one had.

He tried to levitate, but could not move an inch. The crowd's resistance was that dense.

And yet, through it all, he managed to smile, if only to himself. He knew his Mission was destined to be an Ordeal. Tonight was only the beginning.

*   *   *

From RFK Stadium he was transported via limousine to Mother Mary's temple. There he would address some local yoga groups as part of a live webcast.

He entered the temple and made his way to the library room. He had made it a habit to visit the temple every day, and immerse himself in the rare, arcane texts that Mother Mary had collected. Besides scrutinizing the texts, he would also devote himself to Blessing the temple, saturating it with Divine Energy so as to transform it into a veritable hotbed for the Shakti.

By the time he finished reading, he was joined by Mother Mary. It had been less than an hour since he finished speaking before the ICC, and already she had been bombarded with thousands of hate emails from conservative Christians. "They think you're the Antichrist," she said. "They don't like the

Christian mysticism you preach, and they think you're the Devil, here to destroy fundamental Christianity and the mainstream Church."

Jack Cohen could only laugh. "Now I understand why many gurus are off the map and don't interact with the general public," he said. "But I'm the Avatar, so I've got to take the bad with the good. Fortunately, God blessed me with a remarkable physical vehicle, because He knew I'd need it."

"Well, at least you're back on your home turf," said Mother Mary. "The crowd you'll be addressing tonight at the temple are yogis who are open to your message."

"Yeah, but after I educate the world about *Siva-Shakti* tonight, and let them know that real yoga, real spirituality, is just Divine fucking — sticking the 'penis' of consciousness into the 'vagina' of Spirit — I'll be getting even more flak from the conventional Church. And after I follow my spiritual sermon with my political one, the State will also hate me. Come tomorrow, I'll be Public Enemy No. 1... I just hope my supporters outnumber my detractors."

Mother Mary chided him. "Well, at least the Buddhists and the rabbis appreciate you — and huge donations are pouring in. We'll have a mint to bet on your fight."

"No, we'll have a double mint," said Jack, smiling broadly. "Before my sermon tonight, put all the money into gold and silver vehicles — ETFs, futures, whatever you think is best. You trade the markets, so I'll leave it up to your judgment. In my political sermon tonight, I'm going to tell the world to take their money out of the bank and buy precious metals. The metals will start going crazy tomorrow, and we'll sell at a big profit before the Putin fight."

"Will do, Jack... By the way, I've scheduled CNN, Fox, and MSNBC interviews for you tomorrow. You'll be able to push the prices higher with just a few words. You're big news already, and you'll be humongous news come tomorrow."

"Yeah, everyone wants to know how I do my levitation 'trick.' But my real trick will be 'levitating' the metals markets to new highs."

Mother Mary decided to change the subject and catch up on Jack's personal life. She wanted to know how he and Polly enjoyed living with Mary McDonald.

He told her that life with Mary was hunky-dory and that he loved her house. "The layout is cool, and the living room reminds me of your temple."

"I'm glad you like it," Mother Mary beamed. "As it happens, I not only designed Mary's house... I own it."

"Really?" said Jack. "Mary gave me the impression that *she* owned the house."

"That doesn't surprise me at all," said Mother Mary. "She needed a place to stay when she returned to D.C. I was happy to make it available to her, and I'm honored to have her share it now with you, the World Teacher."

Then Mother Mary shared some personal news of her own: She had fallen in love with Brother Bill. "I thought I was through with men, but the chemistry between us is magnetic, similar to yours and Mary's," she said. "He's one of the smartest guys I've been around. Most importantly, he's seen the light and is now devoted to spiritual Truth and you."

Jack congratulated Mother Mary on her new relationship, then laid his hands on her head and Blessed her. It pleased him to know that his spiritual mother and chief political advisor were now more than friends.

．．．．

Mother Mary's temple was packed, wall to wall, while an estimated thirty million viewers tuned in to the live webcast. Jack greeted the yogis with a warm "Namaste," then laid the groundwork for the evening's sermon. While he normally kept politics out of his spiritual talks, on this occasion he felt moved to use the full moon's energy as a springboard to launch his "Jihad," his Divinely Ordained revolution.

"I am the World Teacher, the Chosen One," he began. "I am here to lead mankind from darkness to Light. But this metamorphosis will not come about without Holy Warfare.

"In the Hindu Yoga Bible, the *Bhagavad Gita* (which means 'Song of God'), Lord Krishna, an Avatar in the vein of Jesus and the Buddha, instructs Arjuna, an ardent but confused Truth-seeker, how to attain eternal peace and happiness in the midst of his hellish world of fratricidal warfare. Lord Krishna describes various types of yoga available to Arjuna (and other Truth-seekers), then points him to the highest yoga: Divine Yoga. And he summarizes this yoga thusly: 'Set your mind on Me and fight.'

"In other words, according to Krishna, the ultimate yoga — yoking oneself with God — is not just a passive resignation to the Supreme's Will, but a battle royale. Moreover, as life itself is warfare, Krishna informs Arjuna that a spiritual warrior must engage in this battle, with his mind unwaveringly focused on Him, the Divine Person.

"The *Bhagavad Gita* doesn't provide specifics about the practice of Divine Yoga... but I will," Jack continued. "Di-*vine* Yoga is simply, and only, the practice of uniting the 'vine' of your individual soul (or consciousness) with the 'vine' of universal Spirit (or Energy). Once this union is consummated, your divinized (or en-Light-ened) individual consciousness spontaneously realizes itself as timeless, universal Consciousness (or Awareness) and unborn, dynamic, Energy (or Power). The 'Me' of both Krishna and me is this timeless, universal Consciousness-Energy. Once you permanently unite your consciousness with Spirit, it will also be the 'Me' of you.

"Divine Communion is the spiritual practice that most directly leads to Divine Union. Consciously communing with, and receiving, Spirit-power (or Light-energy) eventually (in this, or a future, lifetime) results in Divine Union.

"Hence, Divine, or Holy, Communion is the yoga that I teach.

"The doorway to Spirit-power (or Light-energy) is the void. Simply, whole-bodily be in direct, immediate relationship to the empty space in front of you. Relationship = presence + oneness = plugged-in presence = maximal conscious force.

"When your conscious relationship to empty space is sufficiently locked in, sufficiently unobstructed and intense, then empty space 'dances,' and Spirit-power, Divine Shakti, is poured upon you. When you experience waves of Light-energy crashing down on you, simply remain in relationship to the radiant Influx and allow it to irradiate, or en-Light-en, you. Communion is simply sustained relationship, and it is these Grace-waves of Light-energy that enable you to sustain your Divine connection.

"In order to achieve a locked-in relationship to the void and then Spirit, you must 'fight.' As soon as you notice yourself retracted, or retracting, from the asana, or 'posture,' of relationship, attempt to reassume your connection. Spiritual warfare is this willful, repeated effort to 'position' yourself to receive Grace, the descent of Divine Power. This down-pouring of Grace will not happen without an intense counter-effort to your ego-centric tendency to retract from, or avoid, relationship to empty space and all that arises in it.

"The ego is not an entity; it is an activity, the activity of avoiding relationship — direct, immediate connectedness — to space, arising phenomena, and, ultimately, Divine Power itself. 'Fight' this ego-centric activity, this resistance, and do the spiritual 'work' I recommend: the practice of Divine Communion.

"If, like many beginners, you find yourself unable to practice communion with the formless Divine, then simply contemplate my physical form," Jack continued. "Simply be in direct, heart-felt relationship to my bodily-being. You can do this by gazing at photos of Me, or by watching live or taped videos of me on the Internet. My body is not an ordinary physical vehicle; its physics has been transformed by Light-energy. Therefore, when you behold Me in contemplation, you are not fixating on a gross material form — rather, you are beholding a Light-energy medium who is a doorway to the formless Other Side. At some point, you will 'pass through' my visible form to the invisible Spirit, which will cascade down upon you in waves of Grace. At that point it may seem as if I am a Divine Potentate bestowing Shakti upon you — but in reality, I am simply an unobstructed conduit to the Other Side. By consciously, openly entering my 'Field of Influence,' you have allowed yourself to receive the inflow of Holy Water that ceaselessly pours through Me.

"This discipline of focusing on the guru as a doorway to the Other Side is called 'Guru Yoga.' The same 'mechanics' that apply to formless Divine Communion apply to Guru Yoga; the only thing that has changed is the object of focus. Hence, if you practice Guru Yoga, as soon as you notice yourself retracted, or retracting, from direct, immediate relationship to Me, 'fight' to re-establish your connection."

After directing the crowd to visit his website for more details on the practice of formless Divine Communion, Jack shifted the focus of his sermon from spirituality to sociopolitics. "Krishna says in the *Bhagavad Gita* that as spiritual warriors we are obligated to fulfill our 'dharma,' our karmic duty in the world," he began. "This is so even in the face of fratricidal warfare — and the theme of dharma in the face of fratricidal warfare particularly pertains to me."

Jack then explained why he had disowned his father. "As the *Bhagavad Gita* preaches, we are obligated to engage in righteous warfare even when the enemy is family. In other words, rightful principles must be put ahead of wrongful people.

"My Dharma as Jesus 2.0 is to restore righteousness to the sociopolitical sphere. For this restoration to happen, the evil Federal Reserve must be abolished."

Jack then briefly described the history and nature of the Federal Reserve, and how his revolution could end its reign of fiscal tyranny. "By indiscriminately 'printing' (or electronically creating) money and putting it into circulation, the Federal Reserve increases the money supply, which causes inflation, a hidden tax that devalues the dollar. The only word for this is *stealing*. Counterfeiting is considered among the most serious of crimes by the government, but the Federal Reserve is itself the biggest counterfeiting racket the world has ever seen — and ever since it dumped the gold standard in 1971, it has been able to create fiat dollars out of thin air, with no restraining standard to rein in its out-of-control 'money manufacturing.'

"The 'Federal' Reserve isn't even federal; it's just the private banking cartel — the central banksters — controlling and manipulating the U.S. and world economy, and enriching themselves and the ruling elite in the process. The Federal Reserve, which was diabolically foisted upon the American public by a corrupt and complicit Congress in 1913, was the third attempt at central banking in the United States. The first two attempts failed, but the banksters managed to finagle their way into financial control of America a third time.

"That, in a nutshell, is why America is now $50 trillion in debt and on the verge of bankruptcy.

"Because the Federal Reserve, a private corporate entity, is not audited by the government, it can print money as it sees fit, distribute it to its banker buds, and even bankrupt the country in the process — all without being held accountable," Jack continued. "Congress has never held it accountable, because 90 percent of its members are too corrupt or stupid to care.

"In addition to being able to create money out of thin air, the Federal Reserve sets and controls interest rates. History shows that the Fed's irresponsible manipulation of these rates to 'stimulate the economy' has resulted in the creation and bursting of bubbles in the stock and housing markets. Because the Federal Reserve controls interest rates, it also, in effect, controls and manipulates the financial markets — which, contrary to mainstream propaganda, are anything but free. The right to control interest rates gives the Fed unbeatable inside information on market direction.

"As Jesus 1.0, I threw the thieving moneychangers out of the temple," Jack continued. "Now, as Jesus 2.0, I will attempt to do the same to the Federal Reserve. In his book *Secrets of the Temple: How the Federal Reserve Runs the Country*, author William Greider details the omnipotence of the Fed. After our revolution has eliminated the bastards, we can write a sequel — *Secrets of the Temple Exposed: How the Federal Reserve Was Run out of the Country* — and detail how the Fed was disempowered."

With that the yogis broke into applause, while many of them rose to their feet. As Jack acknowledged their support, he recommended that they read *The Creature from Jekyll Island* and *The Case Against the Fed*, as well as view the numerous educational videos on the Fed available on YouTube. Then he turned his attention to another 'f' word: fascism.

"Fascism is alive and well in America," he began. "With the passage of the National Defense Authorization Act (NDAA) in 2011, the government became able, on a whim, to indefinitely detain any U.S. citizen whom they consider a threat to 'national security.' They no longer had to prove a citizen guilty of a 'crime,' and citizens no longer had the right to an attorney or a trial. On top of the NDDA, President Obama, in 2012, signed the National Defense Resources Preparedness Executive Order (NDRP), which builds upon the NDAA and puts the government completely above the law, giving them unchallengeable control of virtually every aspect of American life whenever they deem it 'necessary.' With the passage of the NDAA and NDRP Acts on top of the already-in-place Patriot Act, signed into law by President Bush in 2001, America unofficially became a fascist state in 2012.

"And now, two decades later, President Mogambo is working to legally eliminate the U.S. Constitution and 'officially' transform America into a Marxist-fascist state. Bush called the U.S. Constitution 'just a piece of paper,' and Obama went a step further in trampling constitutional rights. Now, Mogambo is on the brink of eliminating the final barriers to an unobstructed totalitarian State.

"The term 'Marxism' is a no-no among Mogambo supporters because it, rightfully, has negative connotations. So they euphemistically refer to themselves as 'Progressives' and, disingenuously, disavow any allegiance to Karl Marx's *Communist Manifesto*. But anyone who knows anything about Marxism can clearly see that every policy decision the Mogambo people make, and every piece of legislation they push, reeks of Karl Marx. But what many do not understand, because it generally isn't taught in public schools or left-wing-infested universities, is that Marxism and fascism are two closely related variants of *totalitarian collectivism.* The State-run educational 'factories' teach that fascism is a 'right-wing' phenomenon, the polar opposite of 'left-wing' Marxism. In reality, fascism and Marxism are similar statist, or collectivist, ideologies."

To illustrate his point, Jack read the following excerpts from *The Ayn Rand Lexicon*:

> Fascism and communism are not two opposites, but two rival gangs fighting over the same territory... both are variants of statism, based on the collectivist principle that man is the righteous slave of the state.

> A statist system — whether of a communist, fascist, Nazi, socialist, or "welfare" type — is based on the government's unlimited power, which means: on the rule of brute force. The differences among statist systems are only a matter of time and degree; the principle is the same. Under statism, the government is not a policeman, but a legalized criminal that holds the power to use physical force in any manner and for any purpose it pleases against legally disarmed, defenseless victims.

> The difference between [socialism and fascism] is superficial and purely formal, but it is significant psychologically: it brings the authoritarian nature of the planned economy crudely into the open.

> The main characteristic of socialism (and of communism) is public ownership of the means of production, and, therefore, the abolition of private property. The right to property is the right of uses and disposal. Under fascism, men retain the semblance of pretense of private property, but the government

holds total power over its use of disposal.

The dictionary definition of *fascism* is "a government system with strong centralized power, permitting no opposition or criticism, controlling all affairs of the nation (industrial, commercial, etc.), emphasizing an aggressive nationalism..."

"Rand emphasizes that a *statist* system, which is what America has morphed into (after once being an *individualist* nation), is, like Caesar's Rome, based on 'unlimited power' and 'brute force,'" Jack continued. "This is the opposite of what I stood for as Jesus, the Prince of Peace, two millennia ago — and it is the opposite of what I stand for now as Jesus 2.0, Jack Cohen.

"As Jesus of Nazareth, I subscribed to the dictum *Do no harm*, which means *Do not initiate force against a person, or steal their property.* As Jesus 2.0, I subscribe to the same dictum. Again, not only is this the libertarian, *individualist* credo on which America was originally founded, it is directly, and irreconcilably, contrary to what President Mogambo, a Marxist-fascist, stands for and does. Yet, Mogambo, like Obama before him, has the audacity to claim that Jesus was a Democrat.

"Jesus believed in charity, in helping the poor. But when a corrupt Robin Hood-type government robs Peter to pay Paul by taking out a *huge* middleman's cut, that is legalized theft, not charity.

"Charity is *you* deciding whom you want to give your money to. Jesus never recommended the government as the answer to anything, least of all charity. Hence, Jesus was *not* a big-government Democrat — he was a libertarian."

A young woman stood up and said that she agreed with Jack, except for his assessment of Democrats. "The Democrats are the party of the common people," she said with utter sincerity. "We need them to protect us from the tyranny of Corporate America."

Jack resisted the urge to laugh. "Asking the Democrats to protect you from Corporate America is like asking the fox to guard the chicken coop. In reality, the Democrats, just like the non-libertarian Republicans, are fully in bed with Corporate America. The majority of Washington politicians have sold their souls to these special-interest groups, and their real goal is to do their bidding, not to protect the common man. This marriage between government and big business is called 'crony capitalism,' a genteel term for fascism. In short, the Republican Party represents *conservative fascism*, and the Democratic Party *liberal fascism*."

He recommended that the woman read *DemoCRIPS and ReBLOODicans* by Jesse Ventura. She thanked him and posed another question: "What is the most important political fact that Americans need to learn?"

"That the American system is *not* a democracy, it is a *constitutional republic*," Jack replied immediately. "'Democracy' means unlimited majority rule. An example of democracy is two wolves and a sheep voting on what they'll have for dinner. Democracy denies individual rights. Simply put, it is a form of totalitarianism, forced submission to the will of a group. Democracy is fine for certain functions, such as electing officials and representatives, but it must be a subordinate system, subsumed under the principles of constitutional republicanism.

"Even mainstream Republican politicians are allergic to the term 'republic,' because it threatens the statism they promote. That's why I refer to 'fascist' neoconservatives like McCock, Bhole, and Bush as Republi*crats*. These men, like Mogambo and the Democrats, are, or were, mere puppets of the New World Order gang, which has no interest in awakening the brainwashed masses to the *fundamental* principle of constitutional republicanism (meaning, the principle of *inviolable* individual rights that the State cannot abrogate). Hence, Bush, McCock, and Bhole, at the behest of the Powers that Be, devoted their presidencies to the imperialist mission of spreading statist, or *fascist*, democracy around the globe."

Jack concluded his sermon by issuing a call to action: "We need to end the Fed — and the only way we can do that is to take our money out of the banks and trade our Federal Reserve notes, our fiat-currency 'greenbacks,' for intrinsically valuable commodities — namely, gold and silver. We can bring down the 'house of cards,' the fraudulent Federal Reserve banking system, simply by lawfully withdrawing, or attempting to withdraw, *our* funds, which the banks are supposed to have, but might not, due to the fractional-reserve banking system (which improperly exempts them from warehousing laws and enables them to play casino with our money). We'll create a run on the banks and force them to prove that our deposits are available to us."

Then he challenged the yogis by using a bawdy metaphor to describe Divine Yoga. "In Hinduism and Buddhism, the term *Bhagavan* is used synonymously with that of 'Master' or 'Blessed One.' For example, in various written teachings of the great 20th century Hindu guru Sri Ramana Maharshi, he's often reverently addressed as 'Bhagavan,' and in canonical Buddhist scriptures such as the *Lankavatara Sutra*, the Buddha is referred to as 'the Bhagavan.' Etymologically, the term 'Bhagavan' means 'penis in the vagina.' In other words, a Self-realized Guru is one in whom the 'penis' of Consciousness is perfectly and permanently inserted in the 'vagina' of Spirit. And in tantric traditions, Self-realization, or En-Light-enment, is described as a perpetual cosmic orgasm, as the eternal union of the *lingam*, or male 'sexual organ' of Consciousness, with the *yoni*, or female 'sexual organ' of Energy.

"In other words, Divine Yoga is simply cosmic fucking," Jack continued. "As the 'male,' you stick your consciousness into (or consciously commune with) empty space, which 'dances' as Spirit once you're initiated. As the 'female,' you receive the Spirit, which 'comes down on you.'"

Once again the same young woman stood up and asked a question: "So are you saying, Bhagavan, that spiritually and politically we are all... um, getting fucked?"

Jack, along with the yogis in the temple, laughed. "Yes, everything I've said is about fucking and getting fucked. Spiritually, my message couldn't be simpler in theory: penetrate the Spirit and allow it to penetrate you.

"Politically, we, the citizens of the U.S., have been getting fucked by a neo-Marxist fascist government for more than a century. It's time to turn it around and start fucking them back. We'll begin by attacking their 'bread basket,' the banking system and the U.S. dollar.

"Now I want to make one thing clear: even though I am a warrior, I am a peaceful one. As I earlier stated, I subscribe to the libertarian dictum *Do not initiate force*. But when someone, such as the U.S. government, initiates unjust force against you or your property, then you have every right to respond in like to their aggression.

"In other words, we didn't start the 'fight,' but we aim to finish it. Moreover, withdrawing money from a bank is perfectly legal and non-violent — but if the banks can't give us our money, then they are the ones guilty of a forceful crime."

A young man with a prominent "Revolution Now" button pinned to his shirt asked if Jack had anything to say about the IRS.

"Yes," Jack smiled. "It stands for 'Infernal Rip-off Shit-fuckers.'"

Again the yogis roared with laughter, but Jack let them know he was serious. "The IRS is the American Gestapo, the Mafia collection agency for the Federal Reserve. They use force and intimidation to steal your money, label the theft 'taxes,' then use the ripped-off 'booty' to pay down the interest on the Federal Debt, the money owed to the criminal banksters."

Then he read an excerpt from The Freedom Articles, an excellent source of information available at freedom-articles.toolsforfreedom.com:

> Outrageous as it may be, there is not a single cent of all the income taxes collected from U.S. citizens that goes towards a single service or benefit the US Government provides. Want proof of this? The Grace Commission released a report in January 1984, under U.S. President Ronald Reagan, which stated that "100 percent of what is collected [in income taxes] is absorbed solely by interest on the Federal Debt and by Federal Government contributions to transfer payments. In other words, all individual income tax revenues are gone before one nickel is spent on the services taxpayers expect from government."

"Because we can only slay one 'dragon' at a time, we'll put the IRS on the backburner for now, and focus our initial revolutionary efforts on undermining the Federal Reserve," Jack continued. "But know that in my forthcoming political sermons, we'll revisit the IRS."

He wrapped up his comments with a brief quote from Thomas Paine: "It is the duty of the patriot to protect his country from its government.' I take Paine's enjoinder to heart, and I hope that you will do likewise and join me in my holy war against the State."

With that the crowd gave Jack a rousing ovation. Then, as he had done before in his previous Satsangs, he engaged the yogis, as well as his web audience, in silent communion before blasting them with the force of Shakti. Then he levitated his body, dematerializing in mid air, and reappearing on the stage a few moments later.

"What you just experienced en masse was a very unique and powerful descent of the Divine," Jack explained. "Many of you have now been baptized by, or initiated in, the Spirit. The great Jewish mystic Philo described this state of Divine ecstasy as 'sober intoxication.' My siddhis, my ability to levitate and dematerialize, are a demonstration of extreme bodily transformation by the Spirit. Even my cells have been divinized by the Divine, and this En-Light-enment of my whole body enables me to perform 'miracles,' feats of 'magic' that defy the known laws of physics. I am Blessed with these siddhis only because God deems them necessary for my Mission: my Avataric descent into, and regeneration of, this worldly plane of existence."

After taking questions and healing those with physical infirmities, Jack dismissed the congregation with a mandate: "You are my vanguard — yogis devoted to Truth on every level. Spread my Word and convert others to our revolution." Still high on Shakti, the yogis enthusiastically shouted his name as they filed out of the temple.

* * *

Jack had hoped to sleep in Monday morning. Besides his television interviews, he had a phone conference with James Grande scheduled for 10:00 a.m. and wanted to be at his sharpest. Polly and Mary, however, had other ideas. Lying on either side of him, they had gone an entire day without seeing him and their bodies were craving him now.

They peeled the covers off him and giggled at his morning wood. They planted kisses on his face and massaged him until he was fully erect. They rode him like a prize bull until he exploded, then took turns sucking him dry.

When they awoke an hour later, he told them both about the events of the previous day. Mary told him that she and Polly were worried. "We're afraid that the government or some Christian religious nut is going to assassinate you," she said. "We love you so much and don't want to lose you."

Jack was about to allay their fears when suddenly his phone rang. It was Patsy calling with an update on the Putin fight. "It's a done deal. You fight two weeks from Saturday. I got you a sweetheart deal: after the standard promoter's fee and percentage, it's a 90/10 split for the winner on the fight revenue."

"Fantastic," said Jack. "I figured Putin would agree since I'm a hot commodity now and look to be vulnerable."

Indeed, by now Jack Cohen was all over the news, with gold and silver prices soaring because of his sermon the previous night. The banks were about to open for the day, and every talking head on cable television expected a run on them.

Before he knew it, it was 9:30 a.m. He had just enough time to shower and dress before his teleconference with the Great Grande.

Grande's right-hand man was Conrad McGillicuddy, a career opportunist who had served as press secretary during Mogambo's first term in office. Along with a number of cabinet members, he left the White House after the President won reelection, though the two men remained in close contact. After weighing various offers as a television pundit, he accepted a lucrative position with the Grande Institute.

Jack had never met McGillicuddy, but he knew his reputation well enough to know that he was a shady character. When McGillicuddy answered Grande's phone, Jack decided to have some fun: "Hey, Conrad, how did you go from excuse maker for Mogambo to phone clerk for Grande? That seems like quite a comedown. Hopefully, you quit because you realized Mogambo is a fascist pig."

Predictably, McGillicuddy found Jack insolent and not the least bit funny. "If you're calling for the reason I think you're calling, I have bad news for you," he gloated. "We don't suffer fakes gladly. You may be able to fool the public with your levitation trick, but not us." He then said that Grande charges two thousand dollars for the privilege of being tested — a detail that Jack already knew.

Jack resisted the urge to retort and asked to be put through to Grande. After exchanging pleasantries, Grande commended him for his levitation and dematerialization performances. "You're the hottest act to come along in the magic biz since Uri Geller bent spoons back in the '70s," he said. "Perhaps you already know this, but some scientists at the prestigious Stanford Research Institute were convinced that Geller's demonstrations were genuine, when in fact he had tricked them with misdirection."

Then Grande laid down the gauntlet. "You won't be able to do that with me. I know every trick in the book, and our sophisticated testing techniques will expose you for the hoax that you are."

Jack expected nothing less. Even as a young kid he had always admired Grande for debunking those with alleged psychic powers. But Jack knew his siddhis were real, and he was ready for the challenge. Besides, the ten million dollars would add nicely to the pot to bet on the fight.

They scheduled the test for the following Monday morning. That gave Grande time to design his tests, while Jack saw it as an opportunity to practice some of Geller's tricks.

Jack checked his watch. His next appointment was a live televised interview with Judge Giordano of Fox News Channel; he had an hour to get to the studio. He focused his attention on the hands of his watch, willing them counterclockwise. To his delight, the hands began moving backwards at his command. "Uri Geller, eat your heart out," he laughed. Then he kissed the girls goodbye and headed out to the studio.

By now he had purchased a brand new Porsche Turbo. After all, he was just nineteen and a speed demon at heart; hence the car was an un-guilty pleasure he thoroughly enjoyed. As he pulled the high-tech coupe out of the driveway, he rested in the Bliss of his Self-nature and contemplated his Mission.

Jack knew he was courting disaster by directly confronting the Washington political establishment, but as Jesus 2.0, he didn't care. He was born for this work, and if that meant death before he turned twenty, so be it; for he was no longer the mortal Jack Cohen, but immortal Spirit. Besides, the way he saw it, God hadn't cursed him with an unwinnable battle — rather, He had blessed him with the most fun an excitement addict could possibly have.

Jack made sure that no cops were in sight, then hit the pedal. The needle on the speedometer climbed past 150 miles per hour, and as it did, he willed it back down to the speed limit and laughed wildly. The laws that governed other men no longer governed him.

* * *

The affable and astute Judge Giordano welcomed Jack to his show, *Liberty March*, then cut right to the chase: "You've created a monumental stir by claiming you're the reincarnation of Jesus, even referring to yourself as 'Jesus 2.0.' What makes you think you were, and are, Jesus?"

"I have vivid memories, and have had vivid dreams, of my previous life as Jesus of Nazareth," said Jack. "Also, deep nail-like holes spontaneously appeared and disappeared in my hands. Finally, just like Jesus, I am fully En-Light-ened, radiant and free, able to Bless disciples with the Holy Spirit."

"Very interesting," said Giordano. "You're also a mixed martial artist — in fact, it was just announced that you'll be challenging the legendary Sergei Putin in two weeks for the MMA light-heavyweight title. Oddsmakers have made you a 50-to-1 underdog, yet you've gone on record as saying that you will 'batter and bludgeon' the champ. If you're really Jesus, how do you reconcile such a vengeful attitude? Didn't Jesus say to love your enemies?"

Jack smiled broadly. He had anticipated this question and couldn't wait to give his answer. "It's very simple, Judge," he said. "I've changed my mind and decided the Old Testament had it right after all. But in the case of Putin, instead of an eye for an eye, it's going to be a head for an arm.

"God is not a forgiving pacifist, and neither am I. God kills every person, often times violently and painfully. In a single Tsunami wave, like the one in Asia a few decades ago, He'll wipe out half a million people. In the case of Putin, I'll only be wiping out one."

Giordano wasn't sure what to make of Jack, but this was damn good television, and he knew it. He asked Jack what he thought of Christian leaders who considered him the Antichrist.

"They've got it wrong," said Jack. "I'm not the Antichrist, I'm the Hyperchrist, taking Christianity to a whole new level. By teaching that true, or mystical, Christianity is essentially identical to true, or mystical, Hinduism, Buddhism, and Judaism, I am elevating Christianity from a parochial religion to a universal one. I was persecuted as Jesus 1.0 of Nazareth, and I don't expect anything different as Jesus 2.0 of Washington."

The topic shifted to politics. Giordano asked Jack about his relationship with his father, in light of his scathing comments about the Federal Reserve. Jack reiterated what he had said the previous night — that he had disowned his father.

Giordano was impressed. "Clearly, you're a young man with high ideals, placing the principles of honest money over that of family."

"My father has a net worth in excess of thirty million dollars," Jack replied. "How did he and all his bankster buds and politician friends get so rich? In addition to creating and redistributing money 'out of thin air,' the Federal Reserve sets interest rates, and anyone privy to an impending increase or decrease in the rates knows which way the financial markets are heading. This is tantamount to 'insider information.'

"In yet another way to enrich the banksters at the public's expense, the Federal Reserve instituted 'fractional-reserve banking,' the practice whereby a bank retains funds equal to only a fractional portion of its customers' deposits. This improperly exempts banks from warehousing laws and effectively allows them to 'play casino' with their customers' money. And if the big banks lose at their paper game of 'casino,' the government, at the behest of the Fed and at the expense of taxpayers, bails them out."

Giordano smiled in admiration. He never imagined that he and his fellow patriots would be blessed with a leader of Jack's magnetism. He asked how Jack planned to end the central banking system. Jack responded by imploring viewers to withdraw their money from the banks and invest in gold and silver.

The Judge then asked him to comment on the controversy over the IRS targeting ultra-conservative groups for audits. "I'm not surprised at all," said Jack, "because many of these groups, along with you and I, want to abolish the IRS along with the Fed. The IRS, like the Federal Reserve, is not really federal. It's a private debt-collection agency for the private Federal Reserve banking system. The IRS is a foreign corporation based in Puerto Rico, with its U.S. branch in Delaware. It is *not* a government agency; it is an organized crime syndicate, a money-laundering extortion racket that was established with one goal in mind: to steal our money through taxes and funnel it to the central banksters, the private banking cartel, a.k.a. the Federal Reserve. As Mayer Amschel Rothchild, the 'father' of privately owned central banking, put it: 'Give me control of a nation's money and I care not who makes her laws.' And the Federal Reserve/IRS combine gives the central banksters this all-subsuming control."

Judge Giordano smiled knowingly. "Why do you think the American public tolerates this 'theft on a grand scale'? Why don't they rebel and end the financial tyranny by calling for an end to the Fed and the IRS?"

"Because the public is brainwashed by public schools, left-wing universities, and the mainstream media," Jack replied. "Instead of being educated about the history and true nature of the Fed/IRS racket, the American people — or should I say, 'sheeple' — are programmed to believe that paying taxes is one's 'patriotic duty,' that each of us needs to pay our 'fair share.' In reality, a true patriot adamantly opposes income tax, which is unconstitutional (for as you have written, the Sixteenth Amendment, which supposedly 'constitutionalized' it, is a 'Great Fraud'). And every patriot knows that 'fair share' means the highest amount the government can extort from you."

"If income tax is unconstitutional, as you assert, then why have all the tax protestors gone to jail?" asked Giordano. "Certainly you're not advocating tax evasion."

"Judge, as you well know, the judiciary has sold the Constitution down the river. Hence, even though the tax code says income tax is 'voluntary,' the black robes — the paid-off puppets of the Mafia government — will throw your butt in the can, even if your arguments are supported by the Constitution."

Again, Giordano grinned. "So you're saying the federal judiciary is not the unbiased guardian of the clear guidelines of the Constitution?"

Jack let out a hearty laugh before resuming his attack on the Courts. "The federal judiciary has destroyed both the intent and the spirit of the Constitution. The Supreme Court, through one socialistic decision after another, has effectively declared individual rights subservient to statist dictates. The black robes, through their continual renderings of anti-constitutional judgments, have transformed sovereign citizens of America into slaves of the State. And the 'sheeple,' the brainwashed masses, pay no heed to the progressive erosion of liberty. Instead, they mindlessly obey, even pay homage to, their leaders, their slave masters."

"So you're saying the term 'leaders of the free world' is a misnomer?" asked the Judge with tongue in cheek. "What about President Mogambo and the men who preceded him? Do you see an ideological common denominator in them?"

"Absolutely," said Jack. "Almost every American president in the past half-century or so is a product of either Harvard or Yale. These schools are bastions of liberalism — really, neo-Marxism — and they produce elitist politicians whose goal is to conform both the U.S. and the world to the dictates of the Ruling Elite. These politicians, whether Democrats or Republicans, are hubris-filled 'social engineers' who believe they are uniquely endowed to inject 'progressive' socialist programs into the American 'bloodstream.' They are facile pragmatists who think they, like a master chef, can combine Marxism, capitalism, and corporatism into an integral brew, and then spread this concoction around the globe in the form of a 'New World Order.' The Ivy League 'church' has 'programmed' their brains, filling them with secular dogma that is socialist and statist in nature. The curricula at these elite academies have to be socialist and statist (or essentially neo-Marxist) in nature because these institutions of 'higher learning' are producing the 'leaders' of the 'free world,' and these leaders must lead via a program of 'progressive social engineering.'

"Why must they follow such a program? Because the New World Order Ruling Elite — the international banking cartel and the giant multinational corporations — say so. They insist on politicians who will partner up with them and help them create the Global Corporate State, a New World Order that reflects just the right combination of Marxism, capitalism, and fascism to meet their totalitarian needs.

"Since Ronald Reagan left office in 1989, Harvard and Yale have taken over the American presidency. Is this a coincidence? Hardly. The Global Elite, via their arm, the Bilderberg Group — a network of executives from the leading multinational corporations and top national politicians — has a special relationship with these schools, and they choose particular individuals from them in order to satisfy their agenda. In fact, my father wanted me to transfer to Harvard and have Bilberbergs tutor me, so I could become the first Jewish president. Baddad Mogambo is one of these chosen individuals, and the Bilderberg Group was instrumental in his election as president."

"So you're saying that not only the Democratic presidents since Reagan, but the Republicans, too, have been fascist, neo-Marxist Bilderberg 'products,' foisted upon the American public?"

"That's why they're called RINOs, Republicans in Name Only," said Jack. "They have no interest in preserving America as a constitutional republic. The word 'republic' is a no-no to them, and every other word coming out of their mouths is 'democracy,' a synonym for mob, or majority, rule. They worship and are controlled by the same Masters, the same Ruling Elite, as the Democrats."

Giordano took a quick glance at his notebook screen, which was out of the frame of the television camera. As he had anticipated, the show's email and social media accounts were flooded with responses. Regardless of whether they agreed with Jack Cohen, people were watching.

Then he asked if Jack had anything positive to say about the Democratic or Republican politicians in Washington. "Only that 99 percent of them aren't worth the oxygen they breathe," Jack replied. "If I said what I really think of them, they'd lock me up in a FEMA camp when I walked out the studio door."

The host and the guest broke into laughter, then Giordano posed his next question: "Jack, as the son of Jeremiah Cohen, you've no doubt been in the company of some of the foremost economists in the country. What can you say about these men and their economics?"

"Economic 'science' is a pseudo-science, and these men delude themselves and others by pretending to positively conduct the nation's monetary policy," said Jack. "The majority of these economics professors are hubris-filled Ivy League idiots who embrace perverted Keynesian economics, which amounts to rampant money printing, counterfeiting. A typical example is Paul Krackhead, the Princeton Nobel Prize winner who is also a close friend of my father. I've been around Paul quite a bit, and I can tell you that he's a total numbskull, a brain-dead left-wing loony."

Jack continued his attack on elitist higher education: "If the Ivy League schools had a clue academically, they'd jettison their current social science curricula and replace them with courses on Ayn Rand's Objectivism and Murray Rothbard's Rothbardianism. But this isn't going to happen because the federal government controls not only the courses in elementary and secondary public schools, but also the curricula in most universities. They control elementary and secondary education via the national education curriculum known as 'Common Core,' first instituted under Obama; and they control curricula and research at universities via funds and grants — which are really bribes. In short, the unholy marriage of the federal government and education has transformed the bulk of education in America into progressivist brainwashing."

"So I assume you want to abolish the Department of Education?" asked the Judge.

"Yes. Public schools should be done away with. They indoctrinate students, transforming them into politically correct socialists, compliant slaves of the State. America as a constitutional republic means separation of Education and State along with separation of Church and State and Economy and State."

"Jack, you've hit a hot button with your call for separation of Economy and State. Most Americans favor separation of Church and State, but not many would second your call for separation of Economy and State. Most people believe that unregulated free markets would result in all kinds of evils, such as monopolies, exploitation of workers, and unchecked corruption. Therefore, they support strong State intervention in the Economy."

"Judge, these people have been brainwashed by statist propaganda. First, history proves that monopolies are unsustainable over time in a free-market environment. And, in fact, many big monopolies over the past two centuries have been sustained and abetted by government intervention. Second, in a free economy, workers are independent contractors. If they feel exploited by their bosses, they can quit or form unions and strike for improved pay, benefits, and working conditions. Third, a limited constitutional government includes a legal system as well as police and a military. Hence, in a free-market economy, corruption is checked and fraud is outlawed and punished."

Jack concluded by making one last point about the so-called "exploitation of the masses," a common charge levied against big corporations by their socialist critics. "Corporations do not force you to buy their products," he said. "The government, however, does. Big Brother forcefully, fascistically dictates that you participate in their rip-off programs. For example, I have no need of, nor interest in, medical insurance, but I'm forced to buy, or else be taxed for refusing to buy, this product, which is grossly overpriced because of government intervention. In short, it is the government, not 'monopolistic corporations,' that exploits individuals by violating their constitutional rights."

Giordano took another glance at the screen. He thought about working some email questions into the discussion, but as time was running short he decided to return to the subject of the Federal Reserve. "Right now, as we speak, the prices of gold and silver are skyrocketing. Do you think the government will retaliate by aggressively shorting the metals?"

"It's quite possible," said Jack. "The government, in order to prop up the U.S. dollar, is already involved in manipulation of the metals markets — The Fed uses J.B. Morganstern and the Treasury Department works with Goldberg Saks. They can easily ramp up their shorting efforts.

"I never said this would be easy. I hardly expect the government to take my attack on the Federal Reserve System lying down."

Giordano looked at the clock; he had one minute left. He allowed Jack to make one last pitch to his viewers to join the Revolution, then issued a challenge of his own. "I've been told that you have occult powers, including the ability to levitate and dematerialize. Before we say goodbye, would you care to provide our nationwide audience with a demonstration?"

Jack was prepared for that (Mother Mary had told him that Giordano's producer had asked about the possibility of a live display). At first, he was inclined to say no, on the off-chance he might fail. But, because Giordano had been so receptive to his message, and because the vibration in the studio seemed amenable, he decided it was worth the risk. And so, without saying a word, he smiled and elevated five feet above his chair.

All Judge Giordano could do was shake his head. "Folks, seeing is believing. I wouldn't believe it without seeing it with my own two eyes. I can assure you that what we've just witnessed is neither a magic trick nor a studio gag."

With that, Jack descended to his seat and shook Giordano's hand as the program came to an end.

. . .

Jack checked his cell phone as he made his way back to the parking lot. The most pressing message was the one by Mother Mary just a few minutes earlier. He immediately rang her, and she gave him the lowdown. "Both CNN and MSNBC canceled their interviews with you today. They wouldn't give a reason, but my guess is that the government pressured them."

"I'm sure they did," said Jack, unperturbed. "Especially since the ratings would have been through the roof. The news networks wouldn't give up a payday like that unless Mogambo got to them."

"Well, the news isn't all bad," said Mother Mary. "I just heard from Albert Jones. He wants you to do his radio show Wednesday night. Plus the Young Republicons have invited you to be their keynote speaker at their convention tomorrow."

"That's interesting," said Jack. "I thought Kit Kristy was their keynote."

"He was, but they now consider Governor Kristy a RINO sell-out. They want to hear, as they put it, a 'new individualist/capitalist manifesto.'"

Jack told Mother Mary to make the necessary arrangements and that he'd check in with her later.

As he pulled out of the parking lot, he noticed that he was being followed by a black BMW with tinted windows. He hit the accelerator on his Porsche, and the Beemer disappeared in his rearview mirror. Jack felt momentary relief, but the message was clear: Big Brother was watching him, and the surveillance was sure to intensify.

* * *

Tuesday evening, to welcoming applause, Jack took the stage at the Walter E. Washington Convention Center. The Young Republicons, a faction of twentysomethings that many pundits considered to be the political hope of America, resonated with his libertarian message and were eager to hear him speak. Jack began his speech with a statement about moral principles and the legality of gay marriage.

"Moral principles are a subject of great contention within the Republican Party," he said. "On the one hand, we have the conservative Christian fundamentalists, who want to legislate and enforce their vision of morality. On the other hand, we have the social libertarians, who espouse a radically different viewpoint of morality.

"Which vision is correct? For me, it is the latter. The 'wars' on drugs, gambling, and prostitution are wrong on every level. First off, these wars cannot be won because they oppose human nature — they go on forever and cost taxpayers untold billions of dollars. Secondly, these wars are immoral because the government has no constitutional right to police victimless 'crime' (voluntary social behavior that violates no one's constitutional rights). As the renowned political columnist George Will put it: 'Congress exercises police powers never granted by the Constitution. Conservatives who favor federal 'wars' on drugs, gambling and other behaviors should understand the damage they have done to the constitutional underpinnings of limited government.'

"When people ask if I support the legalization of gay marriage, I turn the question around: Why should the government even be involved in the institution of marriage? Marriage should be a *private* contract between *any* two consenting adults. If the government, *immorally*, determines that married heterosexual couples deserve special tax breaks and other benefits (at the expense of singles), who can blame homosexuals for wanting the same?

"Real morality, as the Declaration of Independence and Constitution make clear, is the right to one's own life, liberty, and property. But the

189

immoral State violates these rights, not only when it legislates and polices victimless 'crimes,' but also when, like a Mafia racket, it, in effect, puts a gun to the heads of its citizens and forces them to pay 'protection money' (which the Fed euphemistically calls 'income tax'). The State arbitrarily tiers these rates, enabling them to steal proportionately greater amounts of money from the economically successful. Citizens are brainwashed to believe that they need to pay their 'fair share' (though what this share amounts to is never spelled out). This robbery by the State amounts to the theft of private property, which the Constitution expressly prohibits.

"Democratic and Republican (RINO) liberals carry this robbery to a level that would make Al Capone proud. In fact, the liberals' form of theft mimics Capone's Chicago 'soup kitchen model.' Capone, during the Depression, would use a portion of the protection money he extorted from businesses for soup kitchens for the poor. Capone, a 20th-century Robin Hood, was so popular in his heyday, he probably could have been voted mayor of Chicago. By giving a portion of the money it 'steals' from the 'haves' to the 'have-nots,' the State, via the unconstitutional instruments of welfare and entitlements, buys the votes of the dependent poor and 'leverages' this majority rule (which is really mob rule) to further its own dictatorial power. The goal of the State (the Government Gang) and its partner in crime, the Federal Reserve (the central banksters), is complete socioeconomic control of a brainwashed and subservient populace.

"Individualism (personal liberty) is diametrically opposed to statism (Big Brother fascism), so the latter must be rooted out of the political system. Capitalism (free trade in a free market) is diametrically opposed to socialism (Marxism), so the latter also must be rooted out from the political system. The goal — rooting out the progressivist abominations of statism and socialism is clear — but the question is how to do it.

"The answer is... a revolution! The heart of the American Beast is the Federal Reserve System, and if we can bring it down, we will, in the words of the seventh U.S. President, Andrew Jackson, 'rout the vipers out of the den.'

"Once we clear the den of snakes, we'll put an end to not only the Fed, but also the IRS, the Infernal Rip-off Shit-Fuckers, which has targeted you — the Young Republicons — among other conservative groups."

Blown away by Jack's intensity, the conventioneers rose as one, showering him with applause while invoking his name at the top of their lungs. Jack basked in the moment, allowing their cheers to swell into an overwhelming crescendo before he continued to speak.

"As you know, I've called for a run on the banks and the purchase of gold and silver. Will this plan succeed? It's impossible to say; we're in uncharted territory. But I see no other viable way to end the financial tyranny, the economic dictatorship that is strangling America and the world.

"We cannot achieve our goal through the democratic process, because the Ruling Elite, the white-collar Mobsters, have, via welfare and entitlements, 'bought' the votes of the 'mob,' the masses dependent on them.

"Democracy becomes tyranny when elected officials violate the putatively inviolable constitutional rights of citizens. When demonic democracy destroys constitutional republicanism, the only recourse is... a revolution!"

Again they roared their approval.

"When I was Jesus of Nazareth, I threw the moneychangers out of the temple, but I failed to establish a Teaching that would keep them out," Jack continued. "Hence, as 'punishment,' my Divine Father has returned me to this world to right my wrong, by ending the Fed, the latest, largest, and most egregious version of the 'moneychangers.' It was 'determined' that I would incarnate in the 'heart of the beast,' in D.C., as the son of Jeremiah Cohen, the defacto head of the Fed, and that as Jack Cohen I would confront the 'Money Monster.'

"Think of my battle as David versus Goliath — and with you as my collective 'slingshot,' we can slay Goliath, the evil 'Money Monster' masquerading as the Federal Reserve."

The Young Republicons shook the hall with thunderous applause. They had asked for an individualist/capitalist manifesto — and Jack had delivered, and more. Much more.

• • •

Wednesday morning Jack awoke to the news that Fox News Channel had canceled *Liberty March*. The announcement did not surprise him. Giordano had always been a thorn in the side of the Mogambo administration, and the Judge's ardent support of Jack and his efforts no doubt sealed his fate.

He called Judge Giordano to offer his support. "Somehow I feel responsible."

"It's television, Jack. This happens all the time, so don't give it another thought. My contract with Fox is guaranteed; they still have to pay me for the eighteen months, whether I'm on the air or not. Besides, I have five books on the *New York Times* bestseller list, and I have a deal to write two more. I'm going to be fine."

Later that night, at 9:05 p.m. Eastern Time, Jack appeared live, coast to coast, via telephone on *Media Combat*, the über-popular anti-Big Government radio show with a nightly audience of more than twenty million listeners. Host Albert Jones began the interview by asking a pointed question:

"Since 2013, many investigative journalists who expose government crime have themselves met tragic and untimely deaths. Clearly, the government — Big MoFoBro, as you refer to them — is intent on eliminating anyone who threatens their hegemony. I know I worry for my life. Do you worry for yours?"

"Not in the least," said Jack without any hesitation. "I have no attachment whatsoever to this body-mind called Jack Cohen. I was never born and can never die; I am birthless, deathless Spirit temporarily manifesting as a psycho-physical vehicle in space-time.

"This isn't to say I don't want to stay alive and complete my Divine Mission on planet Earth — I do. But if, for some reason, I fail and get killed, it's not the end of Me or the world.

"This revolution is Divine theatre for me. It's like I'm starring in a galactic Hollywood production, a cosmic drama that pits the good guys, the revolutionaries, versus the bad guys, Big MoFoBro. I love the struggle, and I love the conflict — but in the universal scheme of things, it's just Divine entertainment."

Jones got a kick out of that. As long as they were discussing entertainment, he plugged the upcoming match with Putin before asking Jack to comment on a larger issue: the difficulty in placing bets on events such as the MMA since the U.S. government banned offshore sports betting. Jack prefaced his response by providing Jones' listeners with a capsule history of sports betting:

"In the early part of the century, congressmen opposed to offshore gambling couldn't garner enough votes to outlaw it. But in 2006, a few years after 9/11, Congress passed the SAFE Port Act, to which, at the last moment, the Unlawful Internet Gambling Enforcement Act was added. Through the unconscionable practice of 'logrolling' — tacking on legislation to a bill containing unrelated legislation — the opponents of offshore gambling were deviously able to outlaw it. Moreover, Congress has no constitutional right to prevent American citizens from placing wagers with offshore sports books — but the bastards shut it down anyway.

"The federal government regularly confiscates mega-millions of dollars in cash from players involved in quasi-legal sports betting, and never charges them with a crime. All it wants is their money. The RICO Act enables federal agencies to keep a portion of the booty they confiscate — meaning, steal — from players, so the agencies have incentive to bust anyone they can. And with all the trumped-up charges that the feds can lay on them — such as money laundering, racketeering, and violation of the Federal Wire Act — the players have no recourse but to write off their money."

Jack concluded his homily by further underscoring the corrupt nature of the federal government. "Professional sports bettors can't carry losses forward on their taxes. This discrimination enables the IRS to royally rip them off. But since only a fraction of taxpayers are professional sports bettors, hardly anyone takes notice or cares about this gross injustice."

Jones went to commercial break. When they were back on the air, he asked if Jack had anything good to say about Washington politicians.

"No," said Jack. "Half of them are lawyers, so ours is a government of lawyers, not men. As Fred Rodell, the late esteemed Yale law professor, put it, 'The legal profession is a high class racket.' And these racketeers, these pseudo-intellectuals, make, interpret, and enforce our laws. They are the high priests of our fascist State, and all government power is concentrated in them.

"We don't need more laws, Albert... we need less — *far* less. But these legislators continue to make more to further undermine the Constitution and to further empower and enrich themselves and their Ruling Elite buds. It's their world — or perhaps I should say their New World Order — and we just live in it. My goal, of course, is to end their world."

Jones then addressed the various attacks leveled against Jack from Church leaders, prominent Christians, and the U.S. government itself. "In effect, both Church and State have declared war on you. What can you say about your enemies?"

"We live in a dumbed-down, de-esotericized society, created and perpetuated by both the State (the leviathan government) and the Church (the conventional religious establishment)," Jack responded. "The State, via its army of brain-dead bureaucrats and secular educators, preaches *statism*, servitude to the fascist, neo-Marxist, Mafia government — while the Church, via its collection of depthless pulpiteers masquerading as 'holy men,' preaches 'Churchianity,' blind belief in exoteric Christian dogma. Just as the State, through public schools (including universities), fails to teach *individualism*, the principle of personal and economic liberty espoused in the U.S. Constitution, the Church neglects to teach *spirituality*, the principles of Spirit-baptism and Spirit-communion."

"Sounds like the Matrix," said Jones.

"Exactly," said Jack. "The State, Corporate America, and the Mainstream Media — which obediently pushes the messages of the State and Corporate America — have, in a neo-Orwellian manner, combined to create a Matrix of sorts, a sociocultural zeitgeist that, in effect, puts a ceiling on individual freedom, intellectual inquiry, and spiritual verticality. The Church creates its own form of the Matrix, brainwashing its 'sheep' with an exoteric, anti-mystical, ultra-moralistic version of real Christianity.

"Because there is separation of Church and State in America, people are free to rise above the network of institutional Churchianity," Jack continued. "But because there is *not* separation of Economy and State, people are *not* free to escape the clutches of the Federal Reserve and the IRS. They own and control us financially, and the Police State enforces their dictates, illegally spying on us in the process.

"NSA, the all-invasive, all-seeing Orwellian arm of the Police State, states at their website that their mission is to 'maintain or strengthen privacy and civil liberties protections.' Can there be a bigger joke? Ever since Eric Snowden, a high-level NSA employee, blew the whistle on NSA's all-pervasive *anti-privacy* and *anti-civil liberties* activities way back in 2013, it's been clear what NSA is really about. But nothing has been done about it because the Ruling Elite, the New World Order Globalists, won't allow it."

By the end of the hour, Jack could add Albert Jones to the list of those he'd converted. "I'm a Christian," said Jones, "and I never dreamed that Jesus would return in my lifetime. But I believe Jack Cohen is the reincarnation of the Christ, and that he is here to finish what he started as Jesus of Nazareth. This means the Federal Reserve is toast, and that America will once again be a free country."

He closed the program by exhorting his millions of listeners to support Jack's efforts. "Let's all hit the banks, take out our money, and buy gold — and I don't know about you, but I'm also going to bet some of my money on Jack. I have a hunch he's going to shock the world and bring down Sergei Putin, just as he'll bring down the Fed."

Part 4

The Crossing

THE FOLLOWING MONDAY THE financial markets were in utter turmoil. As people en masse pulled their funds from the banks and bought gold and silver, the Dow Jones fell 800 points. While pundits feared a collapse of the world economy, President Mogambo used his daily White House briefing to assure the American public that the country was "doing just fine" and that there was "no reason to panic."

Behind closed doors, however, the White House knew it would take more than words to stem the tide. Stopping Jack Cohen's revolution became the administration's top priority.

That morning Jack arrived at the Great Grande Institute a few minutes before his scheduled 11:00 a.m. appointment. Conrad McGillicuddy announced his arrival and told him to have a seat. "I hope you're enjoying your fifteen minutes of fame," he said snidely. "I assure you, it will not last."

"You play much poker, McGillicuddy?" asked Jack.

"What difference does that make?"

"You've laid all your cards on the table, without seeing any of mine," said Jack. "You must be awfully sure you've got a winning hand."

"I have all the assurance I need," said McGillicuddy. "Mr. Grande is looking forward, as am I, to exposing you as a fraud. By the end of the day, your followers will abandon you in droves, and your revolution will end."

Jack stared at him coldly. "Conrad, I can see your aura, and I've got to tell you, you're a slime bucket, not worth the oxygen you breathe. If you're as smart as you think you are, by the end of the day you'll accept me as your Savior and repent of your evil ways. Otherwise, I assure you, your fate will be an unpleasant one."

McGillicuddy was about to retort when a statuesque blonde in a form-fitting lab coat emerged from a side door. She introduced herself to Jack. "I'm Camila Edwards, Mr. Grande's assistant. Mr. Grande will see you now."

Jack shook her hand and followed her down the labyrinth of corridors that led to the testing facility. The sight of her ample, undulating ass offered pleasant respite from the vile McGillicuddy.

Grande's lab was about the size of a small auditorium, complete with a stage at the front. There was an assortment of wireless computers and other high-tech gadgetry, some of which Jack recognized from watching videos of Grande's appearances. The device that mattered to him the most, however, was the tripod-mounted camera that was about to record the proceedings.

The Great Grande greeted Jack warmly. "Any luck bending spoons?" he joked.

Jack smiled sheepishly. "Well, with all the talking I did last week, I really haven't had the time. But I'll give it a shot."

With that Camila handed him a spoon. As he laser-beamed his attention on it, the utensil not only bent significantly, but began to melt from the rays of his Mind Power. When the spoon became too hot to touch, Jack let it fall to the floor.

Grande put on a pair of gloves and picked up the spoon. He examined it for a few minutes, then looked at Jack with a smile. "Very impressive, Superman. Now let's see if you can levitate."

Camila led Jack to the stage. There he closed his eyes, assumed a full lotus position and, as he had demonstrated many times before, elevated his body several feet into the air. He hovered above them for several minutes before lowering himself back to the stage.

"Anything else?" he asked.

"I don't think so," smiled Grande. "I'm man enough to admit I was wrong. Your feats have been documented on camera, and Camila will serve as my witness. But because I believe your powers are unprecedented, I would like to perform additional tests to measure the full range of them."

"I would be open to that," said Jack. "But first things first: What about the ten million dollars?"

"You're a man after my own heart," laughed Grande. "I'll need a few days to complete the documentation. You'll have your money by the end of the week."

"Awesome," said Jack as he handed him a card with Mother Mary's contact information. "This is the name of my management team. Once I know that the funds have been wired, we'll discuss additional testing."

With that he shook Grande's hand and left. He had an errand to run at the airport.

Earlier that morning, before he left to meet Grande, Jack received an overnight package from John Mulligan containing a cell phone, a box of Cohiba Esplendido cigars, and a key to a locker at Washington Dulles International. Other than including a note that read "You might need these sometime," John didn't say what the locker contained.

Upon arriving at AID, Jack headed straight for the airport lockers. Inside the locker was a small unmarked box wrapped in plain brown paper. Inside the box were a cell phone and a gold wristwatch.

Jack figured that the cell phone was one of those "off the grid" phones used by intelligence operatives, so that their whereabouts could not be traced. Now that Jack was a government target, as was John, it made perfect sense that any further communications between them remain as covert as possible.

The watch, however, puzzled him. He hadn't asked for a watch, and even if he needed one, he certainly wouldn't have troubled John. But upon further inspection Jack realized that the timepiece had more than one function.

Ah, yes, he thought. *This will come in handy, indeed.*

● ● ●

Tuesday morning began with a ménage a trois with the girls, followed by an erotic massage. Mary was kneading Jack's back when his cell phone rang. It was Timothy Grinder, the U.S. Secretary of the Treasury. He wanted to meet with Jack as soon as possible to discuss what he cryptically described as "a very important matter." "We can have a car pick you up at 10:00 a.m.," he said.

"I'll drive myself, thank you," said Jack. "I may have to move a few things around on my schedule... but, yeah, I'll be there."

Mary McDonald was incredulous. "You're meeting with Tim Grinder? What the fuck is that about?"

"You're a smart girl, Mary. You figure it out."

She stood there glaring at him, her hands on her hips, her breasts heaving from her black leotard. It didn't take long for her to put it together. Now she was even more pissed. "You fucking sellout. You're willing to take a deal, aren't you?"

"Only if the price is right," said Jack as he rose from the table. "If the government can give me the money I want, I'll end my revolution. Simple as that."

She stared at him with hateful eyes and lunged at him. "You piece of shit," she said, pounding him with her fists. "After all I've done for you. After all *everyone* has done for you..."

He clutched her wrists and gently willed her to stop. "In due time you will understand everything," he said. "But for the moment you will have to trust me."

Then he left the room without saying a word and ambled to the shower.

● ● ●

Jack arrived at the Department of Treasury just before 10:30 a.m. He made his way through security, located Grinder's office and found himself seated across from the Secretary of the Treasury by 10:45 a.m. Immediately he made himself at home, extending his legs so that his Nikes rested on Grinder's desk. He pulled out a long, fat Cohiba and promptly lit it without bothering to ask. When Grinder objected, Jack blew smoke in his face without apology and proceeded to laugh out loud.

No doubt Jack was feeling his oats — and as he was only nineteen years old, some might attribute his boorishness to teenage immaturity. But it was more than that. Tibetan Buddhism would say that he was simply exhibiting "crazy wisdom," the sort of unconventional, outrageous, or unexpected behavior that comes from En-Light-ened activity.

"I'll get right to the point," said Grinder. "The President has authorized me to offer you a generous lump sum to end your revolution and the run on the banks. For us, this is the most amenable solution to the problem you are creating for our country and economy. Are you agreeable to this?"

Jack glanced at his new wristwatch before blowing smoke rings into the air. "I think you already know the answer to that, Timmy. Otherwise I wouldn't be here."

"Good." Grinder smiled slightly. Perhaps this might go easier than anticipated.

He told Jack that he was authorized to offer him $50 million. "That is a monstrous sum for anyone, especially a nineteen year-old."

Again Jack roared with laughter. "I'm afraid you missed your calling, dude. You're a regular comedian." Then he sat up, leaned into Grinder's desk and looked him straight in the eye. "I want $50 trillion."

Grinder looked as if all the blood had been drained from his head. "Jack, be reasonable."

"I don't have to be reasonable — I'm not the one with the problem. If you want me to call off the revolution, the price is $50 trillion. Every penny of it will go to paying down the federal debt."

They went back and forth for several minutes. Grinder escalated the offer to $100 million, then $250 million, then finally half a billion dollars. Jack turned him down every time.

Grinder grimaced, excused himself, and then left the room. A few minutes later, the door reopened, only this time it was President Mogambo himself, dressed in his signature black suit and blue necktie. He looked tired, yet considerably younger than his fifty-three years, a remarkable trait considering how the burdens of the Oval Office can age a chief executive.

But what struck Jack the most was the President's attaché case. He couldn't tell for sure, but it looked like it was made of human skin.

"It's a privilege to make your acquaintance," said Mogambo as he shook Jack's hand. "You're a true patriot, and though we have our differences, I believe we can work together to make America a better country. Obviously more money does not mean much to you — I understand that you'll be making millions from the Putin fight — but my guess is that power does. If you join my team, I can practically guarantee that you'll be in my shoes in twenty years. What do you say?"

Jack took another glance at his watch. "Mr. President, to quote Ayn Rand, 'in any compromise between good and evil, it is only evil that can profit.'"

"Are you insinuating that I'm evil?" said Mogambo.

"I'm not insinuating it, I'm *declaring* it," replied Jack nonchalantly. "I can read auras, and yours makes Darth Vader's look benign."

Mogambo's eyes narrowed as he opened his briefcase. He was through playing games. "I want to show you something," he said as he pulled out a half-dozen shrunken human heads and displayed them on the desk. "I'm not *insinuating* anything. I just want you to know my passion."

Jack blew smoke rings into the air. "So you like to shrink heads. Where'd you learn that, in Zimbabwe?"

Mogambo flashed an evil grin. Beyond that he said nothing.

"I assume there's a point to this, Mr. President?"

Mogambo reached inside his pocket and handed Jack a plain white envelope. Inside was a cashier's check for a billion dollars.

"That's cash, Jack, free and clear."

Jack looked at the check, put it back on the desk, and then cupped his palms around the back of his head. As he was seated directly across from the President, the clasp of his wristwatch directly faced Mogambo. "And if I say no?" he asked.

"Then I'm afraid you'll join my friends in that briefcase," said the President. "Certain Christian leaders have been asking me for your head. They want me to crucify you... and I won't hesitate to do it."

Jack rose from his chair, stared down his adversary and tore the check in half. "I'll take my chances, Mr. President."

"And I thought you were a bright young man," said Mogambo. "Turns out you're just another fool."

"Well, you know what they say about fools, Mr. President — sometimes they're wiser than you think." With that Jack Cohen walked out the door without a backward glance.

• • •

Jack was about five minutes from home when he received a phone call from his father. It was the first time they had spoken since that fateful lunch at the

Daily Grill, and Jeremiah sounded desperate. "Son, you've got to accept the deal Grinder offered you. Believe me, you have no choice."

Jack listened impassively. Given how fast news traveled in the Beltway, he wasn't surprised that his dad already knew. But he was in no mood to talk to his father, and it was much too late for reconciliation. "Dad, I have a choice, and I've already made it. The next thing you're going to tell me is that my life is in danger. I'm well aware of that."

"You don't understand," said Jeremiah. "I was told in no uncertain terms that I *have to* convince you to take the deal."

Jack remained unemotional. "Dad, I told you to publicly expose the Fed, and you refused. There is nothing I can do for you now. There is nothing more to say."

Jeremiah pleaded one last time, to no avail. The fear in his voice was palpable. But it was not Jack's life he was worried about — it was his own.

Jack heard gentle sobbing on the end of the line, then the connection cut off.

By then he had pulled in to Mary's driveway. As he entered the front door, the girls were standing there, ready to accost him.

Polly was the first to confront him. "Mary told me where you've been, and I'm as angry as she is. We're going on strike."

"On *strike?*" Jack started to laugh.

"That's right, Jackie Poo," said Mary. "We're not going to massage you, cook for you, have sex with you, or promote ISM. Now that you've sold yourself out, you can buy yourself a staff... either that, or pay us a premium. How do you like that, buster?"

Jack calmly invited the girls to sit down in the living room as he removed his wristwatch. "A gift from John Mulligan," he explained. "Comes with a micro-digital recording device that's straight out of Dick Tracy. Observe."

He proceeded to play the video recording of his meetings with Grinder and Mogambo. "Oh, ye of little faith," he said.

Polly laughed with glee, while Mary was charged with desire. They stripped him of his clothes, removed their own, and wrapped their bodies around him. They hugged and kissed him affectionately before finally jumping his bones.

By the time they awoke it was late in the afternoon, and Jack was famished.

The girls adjourned to the kitchen and prepared him a light snack, followed by a dish of ice cream. As he ate, he told them about Mogambo's attaché case and his penchant for shrunken heads.

Naturally that got Mary's attention. "How do they compare to mine?" she asked. "Do they look as cool as the one of Shitzer?"

"No," said Jack with a Cheshire Cat grin. "You could teach the President a thing or two about head shrinking — who knows? Someday you might."

"Oooh," said Polly. "Does that mean you can predict the future?"

"No, but I do have premonitions," he explained. "My En-Light-ened Vision enables me to foresee karmic currents or flows."

Polly looked at him quizzically. "I don't understand."

"Yes, Jackie Poo," Mary chided him. "Down here on earth we speak English."

He laughed. "If I knew exactly what was going to happen, life wouldn't be fun. But because I have premonitions, I can see karmic waves — you might say I'm a spiritual surfer."

"Now I get it," said Polly. "What are the waves telling you now?"

"That a huge swell will hit Washington, D.C. this week," said Jack. "When it does, the shit will hit the fan."

Mary McDonald reached below and gripped him by the penis. "I'll tell you what my waves are telling me," she grinned mischievously. "Little Jackie needs a second helping." With that the lovers giggled and retreated upstairs.

* * *

Wednesday evening, Jack visited Mother Mary and absorbed himself in some of the rare titles in her spiritual library. He left for home around ten o'clock. The weather was cool yet brisk, perfectly conducive for strolling. He had wandered about a block from the temple when suddenly a massive arm wrapped tightly around his neck. A hooded figure wearing black fatigues and a stocking mask had snuck up from behind.

There wasn't time to panic. At most Jack had but a few seconds to extricate himself from the chokehold. If he didn't, he would be rendered unconscious (and, more than likely, dead).

He kicked his leg straight back with all his might, shattering his assailant's kneecap while causing him to loosen his grip. At once Jack spun around. The man was six inches taller than him, and nearly twice his weight. Ignoring the pain in his knee, the hooded giant drew a switchblade and wielded it menacingly.

Jack kicked the knife from his hand, then smashed his fist into the thug's face, breaking his jaw. Then he hammered his face again with such force, the crushed bones made an eerie grinding sound. The man fell to the ground, dead.

The body had barely fallen when Jack sustained a second attack, also from behind. Another towering figure, also masked, had struck him in the head, causing him to stagger and nearly go unconscious. As blood spurted from the back of his head, Jack instantly identified the assault weapon as a chain.

Fortunately for Jack, the second assailant, though clearly strong, was not as deft as the first. He attempted to wrap the chain around Jack's neck, but Jack was ready and tore it away. Now wielding the chain, Jack turned to face his new opponent, who began to pull out a gun. Once again Jack anticipated the move, using the chain to whip the gun out of the mugger's hand. Desperately the mugger tried to retrieve the weapon — but as he did, Jack pounced on him like a cat and wrapped his arms around his neck. The mugger tried in vain to stand, but as Jack had cut off his air supply, he quickly passed out and fell to the concrete.

Jack unmasked the attacker and laughed loudly; it was Bart Battaglia, the onetime bouncer at Sodom and Gomorrah, whom he had dispatched before.

Jack wasn't surprised that Bart had come after him — after all, he was the one responsible for Bart losing his job. But the first assailant was a mystery. Quickly he checked the man for identification, but found none. That told him the man was probably a professional. But what was his connection to Bart?

He took off his shirt and pressed it against the wound in his head to impede the bleeding. He pulled out his cell and rang Mary and Polly. They would be there in a minute. Given his prior history with Bart, and knowing that Bart would probably lie to the police and accuse him of instigating the attack, he decided to tie up the loose end.

He looked up and quickly surveyed the neighborhood. Everything was quiet and still; no witnesses to be found. He returned to Bart's fallen body and, without hesitating a second, snapped his neck.

"Have a nice long nap," he cracked.

 .   .   .

Mary drove to the hospital, while Polly sat in the backseat, holding Jack tightly. "Honey, I am so glad you're all right. Mary and I are afraid this is just the beginning of attempts on your life. If you're dead, I want to be dead, too."

She rested her head on his shoulder and began to sob. Jack gently caressed her face and tried to comfort her. "Honey, I understand your concern, but you must strive to be like me — unconcerned. You must commune with my Divine Presence and allow my Divine Power to save you. We are all going to die, and our only salvation is in the Holy Spirit."

Then he looked into her eyes and Blessed her with Shakti. Instantly Polly was calm.

They arrived at the emergency room, where Jack was treated with multiple stitches in his head and an ice bag to reduce the swelling. In the meantime, Mary had called the police; by the time Jack was released, thirty minutes later, two uniformed officers had arrived to question him in the waiting room. Jack provided them with his account of the assault — neglecting to mention, of course, that he had broken Bart's neck after incapacitating him. The officers told Jack that the police detective assigned to the case would contact him in a few hours.

 .   .   .

Jack and the girls returned home around 12:30 a.m. They chowed down on leftovers, then Jack went upstairs and called John Mulligan on the off-the-grid cell. By now word of the attack had spread across cable television and Internet news sources, and John had already begun his own investigation. Jack told John that he suspected Mogambo was somehow behind the attempt on his life.

"That's a pretty good guess," said John. "Based on the size of the second guy, I think I know who he is — a freelance assassin with close ties to Mogambo's terrorism czar. The guy works under various pseudonyms, and I'll try to pin down his real name tomorrow. But why Bart was involved, I don't know."

He asked if Jack still planned to go ahead with the Putin fight.

"Absolutely," said Jack. "My head should be OK by then."

"Well, the way things are going, you might have to go underground after the fight," advised John. "Listen, if you're up to it, why don't you fly out to Vegas tomorrow? I want to show you our operation, plus I can give you some more 'special tools,' if you know what I mean."

Jack scanned his calendar. There was nothing on Thursday's schedule that couldn't be rearranged. He asked John to make the arrangements and said that he'd call him in the morning.

• • •

When he returned downstairs, Mary and Polly were being questioned by a police detective named Hartman. He was a large, muscular man, about six foot two, 250 pounds, in a grey suit that looked to be about one size too small.

Jack shook his hand and led him to the dining room table. "Have you been able to identify the assailants?" he asked.

"One of the men has been identified as Bart Battaglia, an unemployed former bouncer at Sodom and Gomorrah. Our sources say you've been there before. Did you know him?"

"Not really," said Jack. "I've only been inside the club once, and on that night I had no problem with the bouncer. You can verify this by checking with the management."

"Any idea why he targeted you?"

"If he was unemployed, like you say, he probably needed money," said Jack. "I'm high profile now. "I'm sure a lot of people would like to see me dead."

Hartman's next question was for Mary McDonald. "You worked at Sodom and Gomorrah when Battaglia was there. What can you tell us about him?"

"The guy was a big bully with a mean streak," said Mary nonchalantly. "He was lazy. I understand he was fired from Sodom and Gomorrah for sleeping on the job. I was glad to see him gone."

Lieutenant Hartman glanced at his notes. "Mr. Cohen, according to your statement, you struck Mr. Battaglia's accomplice in self-defense, killing him by caving his face into his brain with a couple of punches. Is that correct?"

"Yes," said Jack.

"That's what I thought," said Hartman skeptically.

"Is there a problem?" asked Jack.

"Frankly, yes," said Hartman. "The coroner doesn't believe your story — and I'm not sure that I do, either. It is not humanly possible to cause that kind

206

of head trauma without the use of a blunt object."

"Is that an accusation, Detective?"

"No, Mr. Cohen. I'm just having a hell of a time believing your story."

"Then let me help you," said Jack. "Judging from your size, it's apparent that you lift weights. What do you bench?"

"More than you, I'm sure."

"What would you say if I told you that I can do ten reps with your max single without breaking a sweat?"

Hartman eyed Jack carefully. He'd seen a lot of hustlers in his day, but never anything like this. "I'd say that's about as likely as your story being true."

"Fair enough," laughed Jack. "Follow me."

He and Mary led him out to the gym. "What's your max?"

"450 pounds," said Hartman.

"Let's make it interesting," said Jack. To the detective's astonishment, he proceeded to load 550 pounds on the bar.

"Mr. Cohen, if you can bench this even once at your size, you may be the reincarnation of Jesus."

With that Jack lifted the bar off the rack by himself and snapped off ten easy, perfect-form reps.

Hartman didn't think that was possible, and yet he'd seen it with his own eyes. He even had a witness in Mary.

"Well?" smiled Jack.

"I believe it was John Adams who said, 'Facts are stubborn things,'" said Hartman. "And the fact is, Mr. Cohen, you are inhumanly strong. I will let the coroner know it is quite possible that you could have killed Bart's partner with your fists."

He shook Jack's hand and said that he would be in touch if he needed anything else. Mary led him to the front door.

* * *

Thursday morning, Jack flew out to McCarran Airport in Las Vegas, where he was met by an associate of John Mulligan known only as Driver. He was a thick, powerfully built Asian American, about forty years old. Not much of a talker, he was mostly concerned with getting Jack to the designated location without being followed.

He led Jack inside a black Koenigsegg CCX and drove him out several miles into the open desert. Then he stopped the car, seemingly in the middle of nowhere, and entered a code on a remote. To Jack's amazement, the barren desert floor began to move, exposing a tunnel. Driver then led Jack down the tunnel to a large unmarked office where John Mulligan was waiting inside.

John greeted Jack and escorted him to the complex's apartment area and recreational facilities, which included a sizeable gym and small cafeteria. Then he led him inside an immense warehouse that seemed to stretch for miles. The underground building housed tanks, fighter jets, drones, rocket/grenade launchers, laser weapons, and other state-of-the-art armory.

"This is incredible," said Jack. "Where did you get the money for all this stuff?"

"We've had a number of big-money donors behind our cause," said John. "But we need more money — a lot more — if we hope to be ready for the government's inevitable war on us."

Again he advised Jack to relocate to Vegas after the Putin fight. "There's no question Mogambo is after you," he said. "My sources tell me that the other assailant was Bruno Battaglia, a big-time hit man who has done hundreds of jobs for government agencies.

Jack recognized the last name. "Battaglia... must be related to Bart."

"They're cousins," said John. "Bart was there because of his personal vendetta with you, plus the opportunity for a big score. My guess is that Mogambo wanted to take you out via a common mugging so that no one would suspect government involvement. The next time, he'll forego appearances and make sure the job gets done."

John paused to think for a moment. "Listen, I'm going to assign a half-dozen bodyguards to your house. A few of them will also accompany you whenever you leave. In the meantime, I strongly suggest that you relocate the girls and your inner circle to Vegas as soon as possible. I'll see that they're protected."

By now they were back in John's office. Mulligan pulled out a few high-tech tools, including an array of portable explosives, and showed Jack how they worked. "Take these with you," he said. "One or more of them might come in handy this week." He also gave Jack a small burlap pouch that contained special communication devices. "You and your loved ones should only use these until this thing is over. Believe me, Mogambo has NSA monitoring you."

"Thanks," said Jack, now contemplating the possibility he might not see John again in the flesh. Given that reality, he decided they would spend the rest of their time together in Satsang.

"You're my disciple and comrade in arms," said Jack. "This might be my last opportunity to Bless you."

"I can only repeat what Alan Watts once said: 'I have been waiting for an Avatar all my life, and now he has come,'" said John. "You are He, and I will do everything in my power to help you. I now bow down to your Power."

The two men sat in rapt Communion for the next two hours. When it was time for Jack to leave, they hugged as if there would be no tomorrow.

● ● ●

Jack returned home to a double shock. First he learned that his father was found dead in his office, apparently from a self-inflicted gunshot wound. According to news reports, Jeremiah was "increasingly depressed because of the anti-Fed movement spearheaded by his son."

Jack refused to believe that his father committed suicide. For one, Jeremiah abhorred guns; he never owned one, let alone used one. For two, while his father was clearly distraught, that had more to do with Mogambo's bribe than the revolution itself. Indeed, when they last spoke two days earlier, just a few minutes after Jack's meeting at the Department of the Treasury, Jeremiah made it clear to Jack that he was under enormous pressure from the White House to get Jack to accept the offer. When Jeremiah failed to do that, Mogambo had him killed to send Jack a message. There could be no other explanation.

Jack hung his head in silence. While he regretted his father's death, he remained steadfast that he had made the right decision.

He was just beginning to grasp that tragedy when he learned that James Grande and Camila Edwards were found shot to death inside the testing facility of the Great Grande Institute. Though news reports described the killings as "execution style," police officers believed that robbery was a motive, due to the theft of expensive equipment.

Jack didn't buy that, either. Given Mogambo's ties with Conrad McGillicuddy, they had to have conspired to eliminate Grande. It made sense: Grande was about to make public the validity of Jack's siddhis — with him out of the way, Jack would also lose out on the $10 million payoff. The capper was McGillicuddy's statement to the press, which threw suspicion on Jack: "Mr. Grande was about to announce to the world that Mr. Cohen is a fraud. Not to accuse Mr. Cohen of anything, but the timing of his failed testing and the murders certainly does give one pause."

Jack seethed in anger. *That fucking snake. I'll be answering questions about this until the cows come home.*

With Mogambo targeting those who were close to him, Jack knew he had no choice. He had to transport Polly, Mary, Mother Mary, and Brother Bill to John's underground facility as soon as possible. According to John Mulligan, his brother Jim had already left for Vegas.

Polly's eyes filled with tears. "Jack, please cancel the fight and come to Vegas with us," she said as she hugged him tightly. "If you stay here they will kill you. The revolution cannot succeed without you. We need you alive."

"I have to stay and fight Putin, because that is my destiny," said Jack. "Besides, there is no way I'm passing up the billion-plus bucks we'll rake in from the purse and fight wagers." He then assured her that John had arranged for security guards to protect him 24/7.

"Well, in that case, I'm staying with you," said Mary McDonald. "This is my house, and if they kill me here, they kill me here. I'll go down in flames with you, like Bonnie with Clyde."

"If Mary's staying, then I'm staying," Polly insisted.

"No, Polly," said Jack. "You have to go to Vegas. You're the only person alive who knows all about me, all about my history. Should anything happen to me, someone will need to chronicle the story of my life and our revolution. That someone... is you."

Then he drew her body close to his and kissed her like never before. "Please do as I ask," he said. "We'll have one last night together, I promise."

Polly nodded and promised that she would be strong.

"Besides, it's not all bad," he assured her. "Thanks to Conrad, we might get better odds on me against Putin." Polly laughed and went upstairs with Mary.

Meanwhile Jack turned on the television for more details about the killings. He knew it would not be long before he saw McGillicuddy again.

210

* * *

Friday morning Jack awoke to more unsettling news. His voicemail and email were flooded with media requests, asking him to comment on a racy new viral video called "Jack Cohen's True Destiny." Not knowing what this was about, he went online and discovered that someone had posted a video of the night he was drugged inside Sodom and Gomorrah and tattooed by Mary's friend Destiny. The two-minute clip not only included a close-up of the tattoo "Destiny," but footage of Destiny giving Jack a blowjob while he was incapacitated. There were even a few masterfully edited slow-motion replays of Jack's sperm shooting high into the air once he'd climaxed.

Even Jack had to admit that this was funny. Whoever posted the video knew what they were doing.

He was about to ask Mary if she knew anything about this when suddenly he heard her voice booming loud and clear from her bedroom: *That little fucker!* As soon as she saw the video, she knew exactly what had happened.

"When Jud and I were in Destiny's VIP room, he had his camera phone," she said to Jack. "He must have turned it on and recorded you during all the commotion. Had I known he was going to plaster it over the Internet, I would have kicked his fucking ass."

To Mary's surprise, Jack remained perfectly calm. "You were Mary Magdalene when I was Jesus of Nazareth," he said. "Jud must be my Judas."

He called Jud and asked if he had anything to say.

"I asked you for a piece of your Jesus gig pie and you dissed me," Jud said without compunction. "I hate to fuck you like this, Jack, but when the government offered me a million bucks... well, I had to take care of me."

Jack thought about asking Jud how the government came to know about his video, but realized that didn't matter. Instead he reminded his friend of the words of Santayana: "Those who cannot remember the past are condemned to repeat it."

"What's that supposed to mean?" asked Jud.

"Do a little homework, dude," said Jack. "When I was Jesus of Nazareth, you were Judas — and when you betrayed me, you ended up dead. Now I'm Jesus of Washington, and you've betrayed me again... It's not too late to repent and save your soul."

By the time he finished speaking, however, Jud had already hung up.

In the meantime, Jack's land line was ringing off the hook. The networks that had rejected him last week were now clamoring for an exclusive interview.

All Jack could do was laugh. "That's Washington politics for you," he said to himself. "They weren't at my wedding, but they sure want to be at my funeral."

He decided that he would grant only one interview — and that he'd give it to MSNBC. Only it wouldn't be another run-of-the-mill conciliatory interview from a political leader who was speaking to the media only because he'd been caught with his pants down.

No, Jack Cohen was going to blow the minds of the liberal fascists with his politically and spiritually incorrect answers.

• • •

After breakfast, Jack called MSNBC and scheduled his interview for Sunday morning. Then he contacted Mother Mary and Brother Bill, the Mulligan brothers, and Patsy, informing them that he was doing fine and in remarkably good spirits, considering all that had transpired over the past forty-eight hours.

Jack's last call was to the Great Grande Institute — he wanted to make sure that Conrad McGillicuddy was in his office. When he answered, Jack hung up the phone and, without saying a word to the girls, hailed a taxi to the main drag of Washington, D.C., where he was dropped off about a block away from the Institute. He walked the block and entered the building, unannounced.

"What are you doing here?" demanded McGillicuddy.

"I'm about to clean up some karma," said Jack. "You had Grande and Camila killed and falsified my tests, besmirching my reputation and costing me ten million dollars. What do you have to say for yourself?"

"I have nothing to say to you," replied McGillicuddy smugly, "except that you'd better leave. If you don't, I'll have you arrested for trespassing."

With that he reached for the telephone — but never made it that far. Suddenly his right and left temples began throbbing violently, as if his head had been trapped in a vise. When he looked up, he found Jack gazing intently upon him with all his Consciousness-Force. "What... what are you doing?" he mumbled.

"Nothing," said Jack. "I don't have any psychic powers... remember?"

Jack laughed as he continued to laser McGillicuddy with beams of invasive Mind Power. Before long, Conrad crumbled to the floor. As he writhed in pain he threw his hands against the sides of his head and plaintively begged for his life. The attack continued for about another minute until McGillicuddy fell dead.

Quickly Jack felt for a pulse. When he found none, he calmly left the building, walked back to the main drag and hailed a cab back to Mary's.

■ ■ ■

When he returned home, Jack, with Mary along for the ride, drove Polly, Bill, and Mother Mary to the airport. They came back to find six armed security guards stationed around the perimeter of the house and adjoining canyon.

"John Mulligan didn't waste any time," said Jack. "We'll be in good hands."

He took Mary straight to the bedroom, where he ravished her intensely. When they finished they amused themselves by watching the news on MSNBC. The lead story was about the "shocking new video" of the "secret meeting" between Jack and Timothy Grinder. Thanks to selective editing, the only audio on the video was the part where Jack demanded money from Grinder. The footage prior to that (which showed Grinder originally making the offer), as well as the subsequent footage of Mogambo's meeting with Jack, had been conveniently excised.

MSNBC next played interviews with random people in the street. Not surprisingly, the prevalent opinion was that Jack was a traitor for selling out the revolution, not to mention a moral degenerate and a spiritual fraud.

Again Jack could only laugh — if he'd seen the same video, and didn't know any better, he'd probably draw the same conclusion. Besides, he had an ace in the hole in the form of his own recording. He knew it was only a matter of time before he played it.

MSNBC's second story was the death of Conrad McGillicuddy, apparently from a heart attack. "Police found no evidence of foul play," the reporter said, "though homicide remains a possibility, pending the findings of the medical examination."

"Looks pretty suspicious to me," said Mary, arching her eyebrows toward

Jack. "You mysteriously disappear for a couple of hours this afternoon... and McGillicuddy mysteriously turns up dead. That's a hell of a coincidence."

Jack lowered the volume on the remote control and drew her closer to him. "I can't control what other people might think," he said with a mischievous smile. "In the end, the truth will be revealed."

That was all he would tell her for the time being, but in truth he was not concerned. No one had seen him entering or exiting the Great Grande Institute — but even if someone had, it wouldn't have mattered. There was no sign of struggle in the office, nor any evidence of physical violence. No one could have possibly pinned a murder on Jack, because there was no proof. (Indeed, when an autopsy was released a few days later, the coroner ruled that Conrad McGillicuddy had died from natural causes... a massive brain hemorrhage.)

. . .

Jack changed the channel to ESPN, where Stuart B. Smith was interviewing Sergei Putin. "Sergei, how do you see your fight with Jack Cohen playing out? Many claim he has inhuman powers and can levitate. Are you concerned?"

"My only concern is ridding the planet of this man," said Putin with an evil grin. "He is the Antichrist, and must be eliminated. He has no powers — the Grande report proves that. Besides, when I sparred with him, his arm got a little 'ouchie,' and the pansy cried like a baby."

"Honey, why haven't you been interviewed by ESPN?" asked Mary.

"I'm too politically incorrect for them," said Jack. "Guys like Meat Colderman are big Mogambo supporters, so they blackball me to make sure my revolution gets no street cred."

Again he drew her close to him. Disposing of McGillicuddy and hearing his enemies disparage him was enough negative energy for the day; now it was time for some Bliss. He peered intently at Mary and Blessed her with Shakti. They sat in rapt Spirit-full Communion for more than an hour, then made love into the night.

. . .

Sunday morning, Jack appeared via webcam on *The Rochele Maddux Show* on MSNBC. "Jack, both your political and spiritual revolutions are in dire straits, threatened by scandals involving your personal life and behavior," she began.

214

"Surely, this must be a difficult and traumatic time for you."

"Not at all," laughed Jack. "It's actually fun and exciting. I live in this world — but I'm not of it. I'm the Second Coming, and I'm here to finish the work I began two millennia ago."

Maddux found that hard to believe. "Surely you must be upset about the pornographic sex video of you that is now viral on the Internet."

"Not at all," Jack insisted. "That video of me was made before I 'woke up' as Jesus. It was the one and only time I've been in Sodom and Gomorrah. I was drugged by a stripper, and unbeknownst to me, a 'buddy' of mine named Jud — my Judas in this lifetime — caught it on camera and sold it to the Mogambo gang for a million bucks, so they could destroy my reputation."

"You don't expect us to believe that story, do you?"

"You and your viewers can believe whatever you want," Jack smiled. "I say I'm the living Truth."

She turned her attention to the findings of the Great Grande Institute report released by Conrad McGillicuddy. "Prior to his untimely death, McGillicuddy claimed that you were unable to demonstrate any psychic powers under laboratory conditions. Any comment?"

"Yes," said Jack. "The report is bogus, Rochele. James Grande and his assistant, Camila, bore witness to the fact that the laboratory testings substantiated my powers — but they were murdered before they could release the true results. Then Conrad McGillicuddy, the former press secretary for Mogambo, doctored the results to make me look like a phony."

"Those are serious allegations, Jack. Unfortunately Conrad McGillicuddy isn't available to respond to them. Do you suspect foul play in his death?"

"Of course not," he replied wryly. "But as the saying goes, karma's a bitch."

Maddux did her best to suppress her own laughter before moving on to the next question. "What about your father's suicide? Surely, that must weigh heavily on your mind. Not only that, but given the role that you and your movement have played in collapsing the dollar and opposing the Fed, I would imagine that you would feel at least partially responsible for his death.

Again he dismissed her innuendo. "My father's death was not a suicide — he was also murdered. He called me shortly before he was killed, and it was obvious that he was under immense pressure from the Mogambo gang. Secondly, I don't mourn his death. He was a white-collar gangster, the defacto head honcho of the largest counterfeiting racket in the world, the Federal Reserve. I renounced him as my father weeks ago, when he refused to denounce the Fed."

Maddux then brought up the incident outside Mother Mary's temple involving Bart and his cousin. "A question many are asking is how you, Jesus, the Prince of Peace, could violently murder two men?" she asked. "Granted, you were attacked, but as Jesus in the Bible, you taught your followers to 'turn the other cheek.' Here, you seemingly did the opposite... How can you rationalize that?"

"I simply defended myself," he answered impassively. "These men weren't trying to rob me; they were under direct orders by the Mogambo administration to assassinate me. One of the assailants — the man whose identity has not been disclosed up to this point — was, in fact, Bruno Battaglia, a professional hit man who has assassinated dozens of people for government agencies."

"Whoa now, slow down a minute," said Maddux. "I want to make sure I heard you correctly. Are you saying the government hired these men to kill you?"

"That's exactly what I'm saying," said Jack. "Battaglia's body hasn't been identified because, if that news were to be made public, people would put two and two together and figure out who wanted me dead."

"What about Battaglia's accomplice?" asked Maddux. "The two shared the same last name."

"That was his cousin, Bart Battaglia," said Jack. "His identity was disclosed only because it made the mugging look like a personal vendetta and further tied me to Sodom and Gomorrah."

Maddux was flabbergasted. In all of her years covering politics, she thought she'd seen everything — but Jack Cohen was a true original, and she found him difficult to process. She went to commercial break. When they were back on live, she recapped the "startling revelations" he'd made during the first segment of the program. "Before we backtrack and dig more deeply into them, are there any more you want to add?"

"Yes," said Jack, smiling broadly. "MSNBC, almost nonstop, has been playing a clip of me in Grinder's office. This edited clip was provided to the mainstream media by the Mogambo mob with one objective in mind — to savage my reputation. Well, unbeknownst to Mogambo, I had a micro camera hidden on me in my meetings with him and Grinder."

He asked Maddux for permission to play a clip of his own video on the air. Realizing that she had an exclusive on her hands, she instinctively said yes. Jack then moved out of view from his webcam, in order to set up the video feed. Within a matter of seconds, he switched on the video, starting at the point when Grinder first offered him a bribe. The video then showed Mogambo offering Jack a billion dollars, and ended with the President displaying his shrunken heads.

"You can't tell from the video, but the President's briefcase is made of human skin, and those shrunken heads he's displaying are real human heads," Jack said as he reappeared in front of the webcam. "Unfortunately, I don't think it's possible to identify the victims from the video." He concluded by saying that the full, unedited video would become available online later that day on the ISM website.

All Maddux could do was shake her head, as if in denial. "Needless to say, ladies and gentlemen, we will have to wait until we hear from experts on the authenticity of this clip. But, assuming this is true, Jack, we have moved into combustible territory, to say the least."

She paused and cupped her left ear with her hand. From Jack's vantage point, it appeared as though she was receiving instructions from the show's producer. Then she took another commercial break.

"I've just received word from the network to end the interview," Maddux said abruptly. "Good luck in your fight Saturday night."

The webcam screen went blank before Jack had a chance to respond. All things considered, he wasn't at all surprised by the aborted ending. He could only hope that the news of the video would somehow trigger a full-scale congressional investigation and impeachment proceedings.

But with the Senate, the House and the mainstream media all in Mogambo's pocket, Jack knew that would never happen.

* * *

By Sunday afternoon, Jack was the focus of virtually every show on every news channel. When they weren't talking about the unedited Mogambo video or debating its authenticity, they were speculating on the Bruno Battaglia cover-up or connections between Jack and the deaths of his father and Conrad McGillicuddy. Meanwhile, public demonstrations mounted in the streets while the economy remained in chaos.

For their own safety, Jack and Mary remained barricaded inside the house, while Jack desisted from public comments. If they could make it through the week alive, he figured they would be all right.

• • •

In the meantime, that Thursday night, Jud Johnson drove out to the red light district of the city for his weekly poker game. He was feeling mighty good about himself. Now that he was a millionaire, he was ready to look the part. Earlier in the day, after picking up a custom Armani suit from an exclusive downtown tailor, he'd bought himself a classic restored Lincoln Continental — a big car for a big man. He parked a couple blocks off Washington Boulevard and made his way to his destination.

As he walked the Boulevard, he ogled the hookers lining the sidewalk — particularly the taut, light-skinned African-American chick in the platinum wig, zebra-print mini dress, black skin-tight gloves, and six-inch stilettos. He made the same walk every Thursday night and had never seen her before — though in fact they had met on one prior occasion, albeit very briefly, and under much different circumstances. He just didn't remember. If he had, he would have been wise to avoid her.

She smiled seductively at him, reached for his hand, and quickly led him up the stairs to a nearby motel room. She left on her dress (to hide her tattoos), sat him on a chair, and, with her back to him, poured him a beer. She leaned in against the bar, teasing him with her round supple buttocks. Knowing he was distracted, she removed a small vial from her purse and emptied its contents into the drink. Then she turned around, licked her lips suggestively, and handed the beer to her unsuspecting prey.

As he took his first sip, she straddled his lap and slowly, sensuously grinded against his now throbbing cock. He could feel himself about to climax when suddenly he became groggy.

"Come on, baby," she purred as she pulled him to his feet. By the time she laid him on the bed, he was out cold.

She stripped him of his clothes, turned him on his side and hog-tied him, his wrists and ankles bound with his necktie, his belt wrapped around his arms. Then she slipped out of her heels, pulled out a long knife, and laughed sadistically.

By the time the police found him the next morning, his face had been pummeled beyond recognition. His throat was slit, his penis severed. His camera phone lay broken beside him, his wallet picked clean.

She had never killed anyone before, but she planned this night carefully. From the moment she saw Jack Cohen reveal on MSNBC that it was Jud who had posted the video of that night in her VIP room, her only thought was revenge. It was bad enough that she'd lost her job at Sodom and Gomorrah and was reduced to turning street tricks; now that Jud had made her a laughingstock, he needed to pay. When a street contact tipped her off about his Thursday night habit, she put the wheels in motion. She left no fingerprints, wiped the knife, her gloves and the room of any blood, and removed all other evidence, including his clothes.

For a fleeting moment she thought about marking his body with her trademark tattoo, but Destiny reconsidered. The noise of the tattoo machine would attract attention to the room; it wasn't worth the risk.

She dressed herself, slipped out of the room and exited the motel by way of the fire escape. Her blue sedan was parked in a nearby alley, about a block away. She removed her gloves, got in the car, and changed out of the dress and into a spare set of clothes. She stuffed the dress into a trash bag, along with her wig, the gloves, the knife, and Jud's clothes, and drove into the night. Once she left the city limits she pulled off the main road discreetly and tossed the entire bag into the Potomac River.

* * *

Jack's weigh-in took place Friday afternoon. It was the first time he'd left the house since Sunday, and he looked forward to the respite, no matter how brief it would be. After posing for the cameras with Putin, he gave reporters one good sound bite ("When the fight is over tomorrow night, I'm going to hand my opponent two business cards — one for a facial implant specialist, and one for a cremation service"), then left immediately.

He had just returned home when he and Mary heard the report of Jud's murder. "Talk about karma," he laughed. "Jud gets his million from Big

MoFoBro, and lo and behold, he ends up dead."

After channel surfing the various news programs, Jack switched to ESPN, where Meat Colderman was interviewing fight experts Jim Lampshade and Barry Marchant about the match with Putin. All three were unanimous in their opinion that Jack had no chance. "It's an overrated, over-hyped boy against probably the meanest, toughest man who ever set foot in the Octagon," pronounced Lampshade. "This isn't going to be a fight — it's going to be blood sport, a legalized assault on national television, with Jesus 2.0 the victim."

"It will be a virtual crucifixion," added Marchant, "with Jesus once again on the wrong end of the act."

Jack lit a cigar and smiled. He knew they'd be singing a different tune when the dust settled tomorrow night.

He was about to turn off the television when Colderman said something interesting. "There have been rumors that Mogambo, in the interest of the common good, has instructed the MMA to officiate the fight 'lightly,' to let the 'boys be boys' and fight it out between themselves without referee interference. What do you gentlemen make of this?"

"It's the right thing to do," said Marchant — and I've got it on good authority that Mogambo has indeed talked to the MMA. "By allowing Putin to 'fight without a ref,' he is in effect giving him carte blanche to destroy Cohen. Clearly the President perceives Jack Cohen as a threat to national security. The easiest and cleanest way to eliminate this threat is to let Putin 'do his thing.'"

"This fight kills two birds with one stone," chimed in Lampshade. "It eliminates Cohen physically and mentally, exposing him as an all-too-human Avatar. When his fans and acolytes see his crushed physical form, they'll see him broken spiritually as well."

That last remark made Mary McDonald throw the remote at the screen. "How dare he," she said. "Lampshade's talking as if the fight were a *fait accompli*, over before it even begins. Doesn't that upset you, Jack?"

Jack blew a plume of smoke in the air and smiled wryly. "He's just doing his job, honey. After all, he is the 'smartest man in sports,' you know."

The two lovers laughed, then Mary pulled Jack onto the rug, where they rolled around in passion. She undressed the both of them, then put on one of her favorite songs, "Die Young" by Black Sabbath. Then, as they were about to make love, she became very emotional and broke into tears.

"Jack, I don't see the government letting you live," she said softly. "They'll take you out, just like they did Bin Laden. I don't want you to die."

Jack wiped away her tears, caressed her face and Blessed her. "Mary, I was never born, so I can never die; I'm immortal. My body might die, but I will never be apart from you. Your concern is your concession to un-Consciousness... Now turn to me and behold my Brightness."

His comforting words relaxed her, and she contemplated his now palpable Radiance. As the Light-energy penetrated her, she found herself bathing in joy once again, her darkness far behind her. Delighted, Jack drew her on top of him and they made love into the evening hours.

* * *

When they finished, they took a long, hot shower together, then rang their cohorts in Vegas. Polly said she missed them both "like crazy." Mother Mary informed them that she and Bill had tied the knot, then told Jack that, despite all the negative news of the past week, she was still getting some big-money donations to ISM.

"I sold the gold and silver stocks for a healthy profit," she added. "This money, combined with the advance payment from the fight, has enabled us to wager in excess of thirty million dollars on you. We put down as much as we could on the first-round knock-out prop, and the rest on just a win. If you knock out Putin in the first round, you'll pocket over two billion dollars."

Jack chuckled. "Remind me to send Putin a Thank You card for making me a billionaire." Then he put the phone on speaker and led his friends and fellow revolutionaries in a Satsang.

"We'll see you all after the fight," he said as he gave them a final Blessing. "We may have a big surprise for you when we arrive."

Naturally, as soon as they were off the phone, Mary asked him about the big tease. "What's that all about?"

Jack smiled cryptically. "You'll find out in due time," he said as he sent a quick text to his Objectivist friend Paul Goldman.

She tried to press him into revealing more details, but Jack wouldn't budge. Then she changed the subject and asked about the status of Jeremiah

Cohen's will. "Speaking of money, your dad was worth thirty million. Did he leave you anything in his will?"

"Yeah, I'm the sole beneficiary," said Jack. "But that poses another problem. The money has to go through probate. If I'm still alive after it does and try to collect it, that will lead the authorities to me."

"What about taxes?" asked Mary. "Uncle Sam is going to want a big chunk of your two billion."

"Now that's the pot calling the kettle black," laughed Jack. "When you start paying taxes on all the money you've made under the table, I'll start doing the same."

Mary stuck out her tongue. Jack drew her close to him and kissed her deeply.

* * *

On Saturday night, just before nine o'clock at Washington Memorial Sports Arena, Jack sat quietly in his corner of the Octagon while Patsy massaged his shoulders. "Kid, it was a great idea to have the fight here in D.C.," he said. "Now all these piece-of-shit politicians who have come see you 'thrown to the lion,' will watch the lion thrown to you."

Jack looked at him and nodded. "They came for blood sport," said Patsy. "Give it to 'em."

With that Jack strode to the center of the Octagon, where the ref, wisely, didn't ask the fighters to shake. The bell rang, and once it did, Jack hammered a right to Putin's rib cage, staggering him. He followed with a left to Putin's solar plexus that bent him over, and as the Russian attempted to straighten back up, Jack delivered a bone-crushing right to his face that splattered blood all over the ring.

Putin, almost out on his feet, lurched forward and instinctively clinched. Jack ripped off his arms and unleashed a devastating right-left combination that caused the face of his defenseless opponent to cave in. Instantly the champ fell to the canvas in a heap.

Doctors rushed into the ring. A stretcher carted off Putin while Jack watched impassively from his corner. Meanwhile the crowd broke out into a deafening roar of cheers, boos and catcalls. Jack egged them on while raising his hands in victory. He paraded triumphantly around the ring as the new

MMA World Light Heavyweight champion.

He consented to an interview with Stuart B. Smith of ESPN, who had entered the ring. "The power of your blows was almost superhuman," marveled Smith. "Where did it come from?"

"The Holy Spirit, Divine Power, which flows through me without measure," said Jack. "I am the Chosen One, Jesus 2.0, and I am here to restore God's Kingdom on earth."

"Then surely right now your prayers are with your vanquished opponent, Sergei Putin."

"Actually, Stuart, my prayers are with Sergei's victims, the MMA fighters he's maimed, crippled, and paralyzed. I dedicate this victory to them. Even before Putin maliciously injured my elbow in a sparring session, I was intent on taking him out. Tonight is the culmination of that resolve."

Then, to the surprise of Smith and most everyone else, Jack announced his retirement from the MMA. "I've toppled one 'evil empire,' Putin, and now I'll topple another — the Federal Reserve."

Smith paused for a moment. His producer was frantically shouting directions into his earpiece. "Jack, I've just been told we need to cut this interview short. Before we go, do you have any final words for our viewers?"

"Yes," Jack smiled. "Take your money out of the bank and buy gold before it's too late."

With that Jack walked back to his corner and once again hugged Patsy. The two men savored the moment as they slowly made their way to the locker room.

* * *

Thirty minutes later, a Hummer pulled up at the rear entrance of the arena. The driver was one of John Mulligan's bodyguards. Another man, armed, rode shotgun.

Jack and Mary climbed inside. The plan was to have them join the others in Las Vegas early Monday morning. They had packing to do, and one last arrangement to make, but for the moment, all of that could wait. Once they were home, they would celebrate as if there were no tomorrow.

They started kissing passionately when Jack's cell rang. It was Albert Jones of *Media Combat*. The wire services had just reported that Putin had died of severe brain trauma at Washington Memorial Hospital. Jones asked for an impromptu interview to close out the final minutes of that night's program. Jack complied and, before long, he was speaking coast to coast.

"Tonight is a great night for us patriots," Jones told his audience. "We have on the line Jack Cohen, the new MMA World Light Heavyweight champ, the man who obliterated the Establishment's Goliath, Sergei Putin. Congratulations, Jack."

"Thanks, Albert. It's a pleasure to be on your show again."

"By now I'm sure you've heard that Putin died shortly after the fight, as a direct result of your ferocious punches. Do you have any remorse about killing him?"

"None," said Jack. "If he could have killed me, he would have — and without shedding a tear. This was blood sport. He beat up my girlfriend and shredded my elbow when we sparred a few months ago. Moreover, he's permanently damaged a number of fighters. But now, with his demise, his merciless reign as the cruel 'King of MMA' is history."

Jack then addressed the allegation that the President had pressured the MMA into letting the fight proceed with no officiating. "Mogambo wanted Putin to kill me," he crowed. "But his plan backfired. I'm the new 'King of MMA.'"

"That's pretty heavy stuff," replied Jones. "It's clear that Mogambo has it in for those of us who are fomenting the revolution... but he especially has it in for you, because you're the straw that stirs the drink."

"You got that right, Albert — and if I have my way, he'll end up choking on that drink," said Jack. "But in the meantime, I ask that you and your listeners include me in your prayers... and I'll include you in mine."

With that Albert Jones signed off for the evening. He had no idea that he had just concluded his final radio broadcast.

· · ·

Sunday morning began with yet another bombshell. Federal agents had taken Albert Jones into custody, deeming him "a threat to national security." According to news sources, under the National Defense Authorization Act (NDAA), Jones would be detained indefinitely without a trial, and without any right to an attorney.

The news didn't surprise Jack. Mogambo was closing in quickly. Perhaps he and Mary should not wait until Monday to leave for Vegas.

He was about to call John Mulligan for advice when suddenly a fusillade of gunshots rang out from all sides of the house, killing Jack's entire sentinel. Before Jack could react, the front door blew open and a dozen men with assault weapons barged into the kitchen. Six of the men pointed their weapons at Jack and Mary, while the other six searched the premises, including the backyard.

Jack shook his head and sighed. If only he had told Mary to get rid of the Shitzer memorabilia... but now it was too late. Twenty minutes later, the head officer emerged, triumphantly waving the shrunken skull and pickle-jarred penis in front of Jack and Mary's faces.

"Our orders are to bring you in alive," he told them. "No rights will be read to you, because as threats to national security, you have none." He had Jack and Mary handcuffed and led them into the back of an armored vehicle.

Tears filled Mary's eyes as the car pulled out of the driveway. "What do you think they'll do with us?" she asked.

"They'll torture us, then kill us," said Jack. "Our shrunken heads will end up as trophies in Mogambo's collection."

Then he gazed upon her with Love and filled her with Light-energy. "Focus your full attention on me and receive my Grace," he said. "For me this is an inconvenience, an interruption of my eternal Work — but for you it is like a nightmare come to life."

"I'm going to be strong, Jack," she said. "I won't die a whimpering coward. I will set my mind on you and be oblivious to the pain."

With that she swooned and brightened in the Radiance of his Grace, while her tears dried away.

◦ ◦ ◦

The armored vehicle pulled into a small parking lot near a main single-story building. About a hundred feet away, across a stretch of grass, was a smaller structure, which Jack identified as probable housing and dining quarters.

Jack whispered instructions into Mary's ear, and she nodded without saying a word. They were escorted out of the vehicle by eight armed men, who led them into the main building.

Once inside, they were immediately separated. Two of the men dragged the resistant Mary to the smaller building, while Jack was greeted by a man who identified himself as Homer Schmidt, President Mogambo's terrorism czar. Behind Schmidt, at the other end of the room, stood a large wooden cross.

"I was given explicit instructions on how to terminate you," Schmidt began. "Two thousand years ago you were crucified, so this should be deja vu. The only difference is that this time you'll be videotaped — for the viewing pleasure of Baddad Mogambo and who knows who else in the future. For all I know, it could even end up on the Internet, as a message to your fellow revolutionaries."

Before Jack could respond, two of Schmidt's men led him to the cross, removed his handcuffs, and strapped his limbs securely in place. Meanwhile Schmidt pulled out a couple of hammers and a bag of nails from a nearby desk drawer.

"Speaking on behalf of the President, it will bring me great pleasure to drive in the first nail," he said wickedly. "Do you have any last requests?"

"Just one," said Jack, motioning to the pocket inside his jacket. "Do you mind if I smoke one last cigar before I die?"

"Be my guest," said Schmidt. He reached inside the pocket and pulled out the cigar. Upon noticing that it was a Cohiba, he couldn't help but be impressed. "I must say, Cohen, you have impeccably good taste for a man your age."

"Yes," said Jack. "It's one of a kind. I've been keeping it for a special occasion, but this is as good as any."

Schmidt laughed as he stuck the Cohiba in Jack's mouth and lit it. As soon as he did, to the czar's astonishment, Jack Cohen dematerialized, while the cigar fell to the floor in front of his empty clothes and shoes. Before Schmidt could react, the Cohiba detonated, blowing the building and everyone inside to smithereens.

By the time the explosion occurred, Jack had rematerialized in the other building. There he found Mary in the bedroom, along with two uniformed men. They had tied her to the bed and stripped her of her clothes. They were about to rape her when Jack disarmed one of her assailants from behind and used the man's pistol to shoot both men.

"Oh, Jack, I thought I'd never see you alive again," Mary exclaimed.

"Neither did I," said Jack as he freed her from her bonds. "But we're not out of the woods yet. Get dressed quickly and I'll explain along the way."

He removed a set of car keys from the pocket of one of the dead men. He donned the man's uniform while Mary threw on her clothes. Then they raced to the parking lot, where the keys unlocked an empty Toyota Camry. They held their breath as they pulled out of the compound, waiting until it was far in the distance before they whooped and hollered in relief.

"I can't believe we got out of there," said Mary as she planted kisses on Jack's cheek. "But what do we do now? Mogambo will be looking for us."

"That's right, he will be looking for *us*," said Jack. "He won't be looking for anyone else."

Mary scrunched her face. "I don't understand."

"We have one last stop before we leave town," said Jack with a broad grin. "It will make your tattoos and brandings seem minor by comparison."

. . .

Several weeks later, in the early evening, with the sun sinking fast in the west, Dr. Paul Goldman pulled his van out of his garage and watched his house disappear in his rearview mirror. He'd built it himself from the fortune he'd made as a plastic surgeon, and didn't know if he would ever see it again.

In the meantime, in the back of the van, Jack and Mary cuddled on a futon. "Honey, you're more beautiful than ever, if that's possible," he said as he caressed her new, surgically enhanced face. "I can't believe you look like a different person, and yet you're still you."

"Every girl loves a compliment, especially from her lover," Mary smiled appreciatively. "And Dr. Paul did just as good a job on you. Nobody who looks at you will know you were Jack Cohen; they'll just see a hunky young dude with a nasty 'tude."

Paul asked if Jack's siddhis had evolved to the point where he could levitate and dematerialize at will. Jack replied cryptically. "The fact that I was able to dematerialize on the cross was just plain old good luck," he smiled. "After all, as an Objectivist, one certainly can't call it a miracle, can one?"

Again they laughed as they made their way to a private airport at a discreet location. John Mulligan had arranged for one of his operatives to fly the three of them to Las Vegas. As they boarded the plane, Jack imagined what sort of havoc he could wreak upon the gambling industry. While God may not play dice with the universe, as Albert Einstein once asserted, His Son would certainly play dice with the casinos in Sin City.

Mary McDonald playfully punched his arm. "I still don't see how a guy like you can possibly champion a revolution," she said wryly. "You've already lost round one to the Mogambo goons, and now that you're adding gambling to your other sins... I see you going down in smoke."

"Honey, I may have sandbagged in round one, but round two is going to be different," Jack smiled.

As the plane circled the tarmac, he asked her for one of his cigars, making sure that Mary didn't hand him "one of those trick exploding ones." The three of them laughed heartily as the plane flew into the night.